D0051900

*Berkley Sensation titles by Jenna Sutton*

ALL THE RIGHT PLACES
COMING APART AT THE SEAMS

# Coming Apart at the Seams

## JENNA SUTTON

BERKLEY SENSATION, NEW YORK

**BERKLEY**
**SENSATION**

**An imprint of Penguin Random House LLC**
**375 Hudson Street, New York, New York 10014**

COMING APART AT THE SEAMS

A Berkley Sensation Book / published by arrangement with the author

ISBN: 978-0-425-27996-0

PUBLISHING HISTORY
Berkley Sensation mass-market edition / December 2015

PRINTED IN THE UNITED STATES OF AMERICA

10  9  8  7  6  5  4  3  2  1

Cover photos: Pier on the water © Mariusz
Switulski; couple © Diane Diederic / Getty Images
Cover design by Sarah Oberrender.
Interior text design by Kristin del Rosario.

Penguin
Random
House

*To my parents*

*Some people are born with a positive balance
in their life bank.
Thanks to you, I was one of them.
And over the years,
you've continued to make deposits in my life bank,
filling it with love and encouragement.
I am blessed to be your daughter.*

# Acknowledgments

You know those people who can accomplish their goals without any help . . . the people who can do everything by themselves and never falter or fail?

I'm not one of those people.

I need help, especially when it comes to writing a book and getting it published. Fortunately, I received plenty of help with *Coming Apart at the Seams*.

I must give a massive thank you to my mom and my sister for listening patiently as I talked about Nick and Teagan for hours . . . maybe even *days*. You two helped me nail down the finer points of the story. Thank you, Steffanie, for encouraging me to rethink the scene at the ski resort, and by encourage, I really mean *force*. Love you, Sister.

I need to give a shout out to my fabulous critique partners—Jamie, Melinda, and McLean. Your insights made this book so much better. Jamie, you deserve special thanks for your endless patience and encouragement.

I would be remiss if I didn't mention Amy Knupp of Blue Otter Editing for her work on *Coming Apart at the Seams*. You not only made sure my manuscript was in good shape, but you also pointed out a flaw in my pacing that I was too blind to see. Thank you!

I want to thank Beth Phelan of The Bent Agency, along with Leis Pederson and the entire team at Berkley. I feel so lucky to have such a fabulous group of professionals working on my behalf to make me look good.

And finally, I want to give some love to Mike. You don't have to read my books to prove that you're a supportive, loving husband. Doing all the laundry is more than enough.

# Coming Apart at the Seams

# Chapter 1

BLUNDER. GAFFE. MISSTEP. ERROR. SNAFU. ALTHOUGH PLENTY of words described the huge, life-altering mistake Nick Priest had made, none of them quite conveyed his stupidity. He'd had a chance with Teagan O'Brien, but he'd blown it. That was his biggest regret, and he had a lot of them.

As he stared at her across the ballroom, he had to remind himself to breathe. Her long, red dress clung to her curvy body, just tight enough to make every man in the room wish his pants were a little looser behind the zipper.

She reminded him of a starlet from the 1950s with her abundant breasts, narrow waist, and round hips. He'd had the pleasure of shaping those hips with his hands, tonguing her rosy nipples, and sinking into her luscious body, although pleasure didn't really describe what he'd felt when he had been with her.

She laughed, her deep blue eyes glinting in the light from the chandeliers, and her date leaned closer, licking his lips as he got an eyeful of her tits. Nick clenched his hands into fists, barely controlling the urge to ram the fucker's head into the wall.

For more than a year and a half, Nick had been trying to persuade Teagan to give him another chance. But she hated him with all the passion she'd given him during their one and only night together.

He thought about approaching her but discarded the idea. She had become a master at avoiding him, and she would find a reason to excuse herself immediately.

Forcing himself to relax, he settled more comfortably against the wood-paneled wall. He wasn't trying to blend in. He knew that was impossible.

His face and form were highly recognizable from years of playing pro football, and most recently, appearing in commercials for Riley O'Brien & Co., the nation's oldest designer and manufacturer of blue jeans. Since he'd thrown his lot in with the company, he had figured he ought to attend the annual holiday party. Plus, he had known Teagan would be here.

This wasn't the first O'Brien celebration he had attended. He'd known the family for about fifteen years. He had played football with Quinn O'Brien at the University of Southern California, and he had formed friendships with both Quinn and his younger brother, Cal.

The O'Brien brothers were Nick's best friends, two of his favorite people. But his absolute favorite person was their little sister, Teagan. He'd known her almost as long as he had known Quinn and Cal, and before he'd messed things up, he and Teagan had been friends. Best friends, in fact.

He let his gaze wander the ballroom of the Westin St. Francis in downtown San Francisco. With its lavish holiday decorations, it could have been any company party. But the huge photo banners hanging from the ceiling made this one unique.

Every black-and-white image showed a different view of Riley O'Brien & Co.'s signature blue jeans. He was pretty sure the jeans-clad ass in the photos was his own.

He chuckled wryly. The banners proved what he'd always known: he was nothing but a giant ass. He had no doubt Teagan would wholeheartedly agree with that assessment.

Teagan's date touched a curl that had fallen to her shoulder, and Nick growled under his breath when the fucker stroked the smooth skin of her upper chest. He would rather take a direct hit from a 350-pound linebacker than watch that loser put his hands on her. Hell, he'd rather be buried under the entire defensive line than suffer the torture of watching another man paw the woman he wanted for himself.

Moving his gaze from her body, he focused on her face. Her

full lips were painted a deep scarlet that matched her dress, and he took a moment to remember the taste of her mouth, addictive in its sweetness.

Her wavy dark hair was pulled into an elaborate updo, emphasizing her graceful neck and smooth shoulders, which were bared by her strapless dress. Years ago, he'd had his mouth on that supple skin before he had trailed his tongue down into her creamy cleavage.

"Priest."

Jerking his head toward the voice, he was surprised to find Quinn standing next to him. Nick mustered a smile for his old friend, clasping the hand he offered and slapping him on the back.

"It's good to see you," Quinn said. "I'm glad you could make it."

Nick hadn't been sure if he would be able to attend the party. His schedule had depended on whether his team made the playoffs. But they'd lost their last three games, dashing those hopes.

Although it didn't reflect well on him, he hadn't cared much that his team wasn't heading to the playoffs. He was ready to move on, and although he had yet to announce it publicly, he'd decided to retire. He had given enough of his life to the game, and it had given him what he had needed in return. Now he needed something else.

He needed Teagan.

A waiter passed with champagne, and Nick plucked a crystal flute from the tray. "Congrats. Times two," he said, tapping his glass against Quinn's highball.

Only days ago, Quinn had officially taken over as president and CEO of Riley O'Brien & Co. More important, he'd become engaged to Amelia Winger, a sweet little thing with a real talent for fashion design.

"Thanks," Quinn said, a big grin on his face. "I'm a lucky man. A *very* lucky man."

His happiness was almost tangible, and Nick experienced a stab of envy, not because the other man didn't deserve to be happy, but because he wasn't. Far from it.

The two of them slouched side by side with their backs against the wall. The party was in full swing, the band wailing away and the dance floor packed. Hundreds of people milled around the ballroom, the men dressed in dark suits and the women garbed in cocktail dresses. It was one of the few times Riley O'Brien & Co. employees had to dress up. Usually, they all wore Rileys and T-shirts.

Quinn scanned the crowd, visibly relaxing when he spotted his redheaded fiancée. The look on his face was a mix of pride, possession, and adoration. The guy obviously was head over heels in love with his future bride.

Pulling his attention from Amelia, Quinn looked toward Nick. "Listen, Priest, I need to talk with you about something important."

He tensed. As far as he knew, the O'Brien brothers were still unaware that he and Teagan had hooked up.

He nodded, silently directing Quinn to continue. He preferred to say as little as possible so he could hide the severe stutter that had plagued him since childhood.

Quinn was one of the few people who knew about his speech impediment. They'd spent too much time together over the years for the other man not to notice, but he'd never said anything about it. Nick wondered if they were drawn to each other by the simple fact that Quinn talked too much and Nick didn't talk enough.

"I've persuaded Amelia to have a short engagement, and we're in a hurry to nail down the wedding plans."

Nick stifled a grin. He had little doubt how Quinn had persuaded Amelia.

"Cal is my best man, and I'd like you to be my one and only groomsman."

He studied the groom-to-be. He knew it wasn't manly to admit it, but he loved Quinn like a brother. It would be an honor to stand beside him as he made his wedding vows.

Of course, he didn't tell Quinn any of this because it required too many words. It was too much effort to get his brain and his mouth to work together. They were enemies.

"Okay." He focused on shaping the sound that caused him the most problems. "W-w-w-when is the w-w-w-wedding?"

"The first Saturday in March." Quinn sighed. "Ten long weeks away."

Nick chuckled wryly. Compared to the time he'd spent

chasing Teagan, ten weeks was nothing. A hit from the kicker instead of a thumping from a linebacker.

"When are you heading back home?" Quinn asked.

Nick shrugged. He had played for the Tennessee Titans for the past two years, and he currently lived in an upscale suburb outside of Nashville. But now that the season was over, nothing prevented him from staying in San Francisco as long as he wanted. As long as it took.

Quinn narrowed his eyes. "Where are you spending Christmas?"

"Not sure."

"With your dad?"

He laughed, the sound shaded with bitterness he didn't bother to hide. "No."

"Why don't you stay and celebrate Christmas with us? You know Mom and Dad would love to have you." When he didn't reply, Quinn punched him on the shoulder. "And Amelia and I are having a New Year's Eve-slash-engagement party. You can't miss that."

Quinn had unknowingly given Nick the perfect opportunity to spend more time with Teagan. It was more than he could ever have hoped for.

TEAGAN'S FEET HURT, HER HEAD POUNDED, AND HER FACE ACHED from the fake smile she'd pasted on hours ago. She grabbed another glass of champagne from a passing waiter and downed it in one swallow, hoping the alcohol would dull the pain.

It had been a huge mistake to bring Evan to the company's holiday party. In the span of three hours, he'd transformed from a man into an octopus. What else could explain the sliminess she felt when he touched her?

Evan had seemed like a decent guy when she'd met him at an ugly Christmas sweater party. He and his sweater, a truly hideous garment that illustrated the twelve days of Christmas, had caught her eye.

When he'd asked for her number, she'd given it to him without a thought, and she had forgotten about him until he had called a few days ago. He'd asked her out, and she'd suggested they attend the party together.

She hadn't wanted his company, not really. But she had been afraid Nick would be here, and she'd thought a date would be a good buffer.

Teagan didn't trust herself to be within one hundred miles of Nick. No matter how hard she tried to force her body and mind to work together, they just didn't agree. Her mind knew best. It wanted to stay far away from him. But her body . . . oh, it wanted him so badly.

His hard kisses, his hot caresses, his deep thrusts.

It had been years since they'd been together, but she remembered it like it was yesterday. She remembered everything—his taste, his scent, his size.

Warmth trickled between her legs, and she scowled. She *hated* Nick Priest. She hated him for breaking her heart. She hated him for not being there when she had needed him most.

She hated the way her body came alive when he was near. She hated the way her mind always found its way to him when it was left to wander. And most of all, she hated herself for letting him get to her after all this time.

She shifted on her heels, using the pain to force her thoughts from Nick. She looked around the room. Where was Evan?

She wanted to leave, and she needed to let him know she intended to take a cab back to her place. She planned to go home and enjoy a long soak in the tub, and she wasn't up to fending off octopus man.

Teagan rubbed her forehead with the tips of her fingers but stilled when someone came up behind her. She knew without looking that it was Nick. She instinctively recognized his scent and the heat of his body.

Stiffening slightly, she tried to move away from him. But he moved closer, placing his hand on her waist to stop her. He leaned down close to her ear, and his breath made her shiver.

"Stay," he ordered quietly.

"I'm not a dog," she snapped.

He chuckled softly. "Stay," he repeated, dropping his hand to her hip and squeezing lightly to emphasize his command.

A flash of energy traveled from his fingers to all the nerve-rich places on her body—her nipples, her clit, her lips. Desperate to get away from him, she jerked sharply and stumbled into Amelia.

"Whoa!" Quinn exclaimed as he caught his fiancée against him.

Teagan blinked in surprise. She hadn't even noticed her older brother was nearby. He glared at her, his protective instincts on high alert.

"Be careful, T. You almost knocked over Amelia."

She managed to squeeze out an apology, and Nick, damn him, resumed his place behind her. He loomed over her by several inches even though she wore five-inch heels. His height made him one of the best wide receivers in the NFL.

Amelia stared over Teagan's head, her brown eyes speculative. "Nick, I thought I'd see you here," she said, a faint Texas twang in her voice. "How have you been?"

"Fine," he answered, drawing out the word, his baritone rumbling through Teagan's body.

"I was sorry to see you guys didn't make the playoffs," Amelia said. "But there's always next year."

Teagan felt Nick shrug. "Not for me."

At his announcement, Teagan, Amelia, and Quinn all chorused "What?" in varying volumes. Teagan's definitely had been the loudest.

She jerked away from Nick, and this time, he let her go. She spun to face him, and even though she struggled to digest the bomb he'd dropped on them, she noticed how his expensive black suit outlined his broad shoulders. The dark color made his blond hair look even lighter, and his French blue dress shirt showed off his tan.

"What are you talking about?" she asked, staring into the face she dreamed about almost every night.

He was gorgeous—beyond gorgeous.

He knew it, of course he did. But unlike a lot of extraordinarily handsome men, he didn't seem to care much about his looks.

"I've decided to . . . umm . . . retire," he said.

She gasped. "Why?"

"It's time."

"What are you going to do?" Quinn asked.

"Not sure," Nick replied, running a hand through his short hair.

Her hands itched to touch the silky strands. He'd cut his hair since she had seen him a few weeks ago, and the color seemed to change depending on the length. Right now, his hair was a mix of honey and caramel, and as it grew out, it would turn lighter, almost the shade of morning sunshine.

Quinn cocked his head, staring at Nick with a calculating look. He turned toward Amelia.

"Juice," he said, using his nickname for his bride-to-be, "did you know Priest has a degree in American history from USC?"

Amelia smiled, showing the sizable gap between her front teeth. "No, I didn't know that."

"Priest, you didn't know my Grandma Violet, but she was an interesting woman. Kind of eccentric. She was ten times richer than my Grandpa Patrick, maybe even a hundred times richer. The O'Briens made their money by clothing prospectors, but her family actually found gold."

Teagan stared at Quinn. Why was he talking about Grandma Vi? Was he drunk?

Nick narrowed his eyes. "And?"

"Well, you see, Grandma Violet set up an endowment to create a museum that celebrates the history of Riley O'Brien & Co. and the role it played during the California Gold Rush. And that endowment money has to be used by 2017."

Teagan sucked in an appalled breath. *He wouldn't! Would he?*

"What would you think about heading up that project? Laying the groundwork for the museum?" Quinn asked Nick. "It would be part of the company's charitable foundation, which falls under Teagan's purview. She'd be your boss."

Nick slanted a cunning look toward Teagan, his light green eyes glowing like peridots. He smiled slowly.

"I'm in."

# Chapter 2

THE ONLY WAY NICK'S NIGHT COULD GET ANY BETTER WAS IF it ended with his hands and mouth on Teagan's body and his cock buried deep inside her. In the span of an hour, his best friend had asked him to participate in his wedding, issued him an invitation to spend the holidays with the O'Briens, and offered him a new job with their family company.

Quinn had just given Nick every excuse he needed to be around Teagan almost twenty-four/seven. He was so elated he wanted to hug the other man, but he gave him a fist bump instead.

While he struggled to hold back a grin, horror filled Teagan's face. He had no doubt she was hastily evaluating ways to get out of working with him, but there was no way in hell he'd let that happen. He was going to occupy all her time until she allowed him to occupy her heart again.

Quinn leaned close to Amelia and grabbed her hand. "Let's dance," he suggested, leading her to the dance floor and leaving Nick and Teagan alone.

Teagan looked up at Nick, her blue eyes shadowed and her face pale. "Please don't accept the job," she requested huskily.

He didn't respond. He knew she was upset, and it made his conscience twinge. But he reminded himself that he didn't want to hurt her ever again. He was trying to make things right.

He truly believed neither one of them would ever be happy unless they fixed what had gone wrong between them.

He'd written letters to her—he'd lost track of how many—trying to explain . . . asking for another chance. He'd bared his soul in those letters, but she had sent them back, unopened. She had ignored his texts and emails, too. No surprise there.

"I don't understand what you're trying to accomplish," she continued, shaking her head in frustration. "Why are you doing this? Why won't you leave me alone?"

He sighed. There were a lot of things he'd like to say to her, but he knew that even if he could get his mouth to work, she wouldn't listen. He couldn't even blame her.

"I can't."

She narrowed her eyes. "You can't what?"

His heart pounded in a hard, fast rhythm, and he knew the more anxious he became, the harder it would be to speak. He rushed to squeeze out a sentence.

"I can't leave you alone."

She laughed bitterly. "Yes, you can. You have before."

He winced. She was right. He had behaved badly in the past.

Teagan stared into his eyes for several moments, and he tried to let her see how sorry he was and how much he loved her. She squeezed her eyes shut, and when she opened them, the pain in her gaze made his stomach cramp.

He couldn't stop himself from reaching for her. He drew her close, pulling in a lungful of her perfume, the light floral scent at odds with her bold personality. For a moment, she stood within his arms, his hands on the upper swells of her ass and her head against his shoulder. He savored the feel of her soft, warm body, imagining what it would be like to hold her like this whenever he wanted.

Abruptly, she stiffened and pushed against his chest, forcing him to release her. "I don't know what you want from me." Her voice rose. "What do you want?"

*I want you. I always have.*

"You."

Her eyes widened. "No."

"Yes," he countered firmly. He didn't want there to be any doubt in her mind about his intentions.

She backed away from him before turning on her heel and

rushing out of the ballroom. Shoving his hands in the pockets of his suit pants, he stared up at the glass ornaments hanging from the ceiling, debating whether he should go after her.

He was tired of this bullshit. He was tired of chasing Teagan and tired of her running away. They weren't playing tag. This wasn't a game to him.

*She* wasn't a game to him, and she needed to know that. He was miserable without her, and he had a feeling she was just as miserable without him.

He rushed to the door, and once he was through it, he looked up and down the wide corridor. It was empty except for a waiter, and he stopped the guy as he walked by.

"Red dress?"

The guy stared at him for a second before pointing to his right. "Down the hall, turn left. Good luck, man."

Nick jogged down the corridor, following the waiter's direction. There was a fine line between persistence and stalking, and he knew he was close to crossing that line. Hell, he might have already crossed it. The thought made him sick to his stomach, but the thought of his life without Teagan made him even sicker.

Hooking a left, he saw her leaning against the wall about thirty feet away. She turned her head as he approached, her eyes widening in alarm. Straightening, she put her hand out like a traffic cop when he was close enough to touch her.

"Teagan—"

"I'm not interested in hearing anything you have to say," she interrupted fiercely.

He growled. Even when he wanted to, he couldn't get a fucking word in edgewise. She was just like her brother: she talked too much. He wished she'd shut the hell up for just one goddamn minute. He had been trying to explain his shitty behavior for eighteen miserable months.

"We're not friends. We're not lovers. We're nothing. *Nothing!*" she continued loudly.

He didn't want to have this conversation in the hall. Encircling her wrist with his fingers, he tugged her down the corridor. He jiggled the knob on the first door he came to, but it was locked.

*Shit.*

"Let go, Nick. Right now!"

Teagan tried to slow their progress by pulling against his grip, but he continued down the hall. He didn't want to hurt her, but he couldn't—wouldn't—let her go.

*Never again.*

"Nick! You asshole! Let go of me!"

He tried the next door, and thankfully, it swung open. The light from the hallway permeated the darkness of the room enough for him to see it was a linen closet.

*Perfect.*

Pulling Teagan inside the room, he slammed the door behind them. He turned her until her back pressed against the door, and he faced her.

Darkness cloaked them, but he didn't need to see. He could feel her, smell her, and hear her all around him. She panted lightly, and those little gusts of breath made him think about the sounds she made when she came. Blood rushed to his cock, and he shook his head in an effort to focus.

He wanted to talk to her, and he needed every bit of brainpower he had to force the words out of his mouth. He pressed his tongue against the back of his front teeth, an exercise that sometimes helped when he had a hard time speaking.

"I—"

"I hate you." Tears made her voice thick. "I hate you."

A crater of sorrow formed in his chest. There was no way she hated him as much as he hated himself.

He moved closer until her full breasts flattened against his chest. Finding her face in the dark, he brushed her tears away with his thumbs. She gulped, and he dropped his hands to her waist before leaning down to nuzzle her hair.

He pressed his lips against her ear. "Shh," he murmured over and over.

This wasn't the first time he'd soothed her tears, and he wished he wasn't the cause of them now. Finally, her breathing calmed, and she stopped crying. He started to move back, but she turned her head, and her lips grazed his. She gasped, and the feel of her soft lips sent a jolt through his whole body.

Clenching his fingers in the silky material of her dress, he opened his mouth against hers, tracing her lips with his tongue before easing it inside her mouth. He moaned as her tongue slid wetly against his.

The first time he'd kissed her, so many years ago, he'd nearly eaten her alive. He'd been so hungry for her, and his hunger hadn't abated since then. If anything, it was worse.

He sucked on her tongue, and she brought her hands up to his shoulders, pushing at his suit coat. He let go of her to shrug it off and dropped it to the floor.

Her hands were at his waist, pulling his dress shirt loose from his pants before reaching beneath his cotton undershirt to run across his stomach. He groaned against her mouth, so relieved to feel her touch once again.

Bringing his hands to her face, he tilted her head so he could kiss her more deeply before pulling back to trail his mouth across her cheek and down her smooth neck. He sucked lightly on the fragrant skin before turning his attention to her pulse, pressing his tongue against where it beat in her throat.

His heartbeat thundered in his ears, the blood racing through his body to pulse in his cock. He was hard—harder than he'd ever imagined he could be—because of her. She'd always had this effect on him, even when he hadn't wanted her to.

He didn't know if she had any idea what she did to him, but she could very easily bring him to his knees. In fact, he was ready to beg.

Gripping the material of her dress, he slowly pulled it up until he could feel the smooth flesh of her thighs against his fingers. He knew it was only a matter of time before she came to her senses and pulled away from him, and he needed a taste of her before she did.

Since their one magical, horrible night, he'd dreamed about putting his mouth on the sweet spot between her legs again. The taste of her had tormented him for years.

He knelt in front of her, wishing the light were on so he could see the dark hair covering her mound and the pink folds of her pussy. He ran his hands up her inner thighs until he reached the edges of her panties.

The fabric felt flimsy, insubstantial, and he used both hands to pull on it, hoping he could tear it from her body. Much to his displeasure, the material held. Frustrated, he gave her panties a hard yank, using the same strength he employed to grab an uncatchable football out of the air.

Teagan gasped as the fabric ripped but didn't say anything. For once, she was silent, and he felt like roaring in victory.

Moving closer, he raised her leg so it rested on his shoulder. He nuzzled her springy curls and pulled in a deep breath, trying to memorize the smell of her arousal.

Using both hands, he pushed back her plump folds with the tips of his fingers. He found the place where wetness flowed from her body, and he lapped it eagerly with his tongue. She tasted like all his favorite flavors, sweet and spicy, tart and tangy. He couldn't get enough, and he had to force himself to calm down, to take his time with her.

She held his head against her, panting loudly. "Oh, God, I forgot how good your mouth feels," she breathed.

He replaced his tongue with two fingers, sliding them in and out of her body, and focused his attention on her clit. He sucked lightly on the hard little nub until Teagan clenched her hands in his hair and began to rock against his mouth.

As he continued to plunge his fingers inside her, he swirled his tongue around her clit, back and forth, until she chanted his name. He bit down lightly on her nub, and she cried out, her internal muscles pulsing around his fingers.

He stayed with her until the very end before removing his fingers and mouth. Dropping her leg to the floor, he rose to his feet.

Would an orgasm make her more willing to listen? That hadn't been his intent, but he could always hope.

"Please let . . ." he said, but she cupped her hand around his erection, and the rest of his words died in his throat.

*Please let me explain.*

She fumbled with his belt, somehow managing to unbuckle it in the dark. Popping open the button on his pants, she unzipped his fly and pushed her hand inside his boxer briefs.

"I want this," she demanded, wrapping her hand around his cock.

His heartbeat thundered in his ears. He wanted to be inside her, but he hesitated because she had said "this" rather than "you."

She squeezed him lightly. "Now."

Grabbing his wallet from his pants, he pulled out a condom. He ripped open the packet, the sound loud in the small linen closet, and sheathed his cock. Stepping between her legs, he hooked his arms under her ass and lifted her against the door.

She wrapped her legs around his waist, and he found her mouth in the dark as he eased inside her. She was swollen from her orgasm, and he groaned as her hot flesh enveloped him. Even though she was wet, she was extremely tight.

"Nick," she panted against his lips. "Too much."

He sucked on her tongue as he nudged into her with tiny pumps of his hips, making sure he didn't hurt her. By the time he was completely inside her, he dripped with sweat, his dress shirt and undershirt clinging to him.

Gripping her ass in both hands, he pulled out completely to thrust into her. They both moaned at the friction, the wet slide of his cock against her folds as it entered her pussy.

He'd never felt this kind of pleasure, not even the first time they had been together. Back then, he hadn't realized how he felt about her, but now he did, and that made everything better—and worse.

She pulled back from his kiss with a gasp. "More," she demanded.

Squeezing his eyes shut, he tried to hold back his orgasm. He shifted her higher to get a better grip on her ass and plunged into her, using all the muscles he'd honed from years of being a professional athlete. He set a fast, deep rhythm that rubbed his cock across her clit with every thrust.

She whimpered. "Oh, I'm coming again," she whispered, surprise coloring her voice. She let out a low moan as her pussy vibrated with deep clenches.

He gasped as a trail of fire spread from his spine into his balls before erupting from his cock. His knees buckled as he came, pleasure crashing over him in waves, and he barely managed to hold on to her. After several moments, he pulled out of her snug body, letting her feet drop to the floor.

He rested his face in her hair, trembling in the aftermath of the most intense sexual experience of his life. His eyes stung with emotion, and he was pathetically grateful for the darkness.

He wished he could stop time. He wanted to stay here in this moment, cocooned in this small space, her taste in his mouth, her scent in his nose, and her cries of pleasure echoing in his ears.

She pushed against his chest, forcing him backward, and he tripped on his underwear and pants, which were pooled around his ankles. Catching himself against one of the shelves, he groped around until he found a towel and removed the condom.

He quickly pulled up his underwear and pants. He didn't want to have this conversation bare-assed. He was forced to leave his trousers unbuttoned and belt unbuckled, though, because his hands shook—the same hands that had been steady and sure enough to catch more touchdown passes than any other wide receiver in the NFL, regardless of the pressure he'd been under.

He felt Teagan move and heard her searching for something in the darkness. Seconds later, the overhead light flickered on. He blinked against the brightness, and when his eyes finally adjusted, he sought out her face. Her eyes were red and smudged with mascara, and lipstick was smeared around her mouth and chin.

She looked horrible—and beautiful. The only thing he wanted in this world or the next.

They stared into each other's eyes, and as she opened her mouth to speak, he wanted to fold his hand over it. He wanted to beg her not to ruin this moment. Instead, he clenched his jaw and waited. He could tell by the look in her eyes her words would eviscerate him.

"This was a mistake," she said flatly.

And with that short, simple statement, she threw them into the past.

## Chapter 3

Boston—Four Years Ago

"HE THINKS HE'S GOD'S GIFT TO WOMEN," BEBE BANERJEE COM-plained before raising her wineglass and taking a big gulp of the California merlot.

Teagan snorted. "I know," she said, agreeing with her best friend's assessment of their boss, Jasper Benjamin Donaldson the Fifth.

She and Bebe were in Teagan's condo for their weekly "wine down." The night of whining and wine drinking was a tradition they'd begun shortly after they met nearly three years ago.

Teagan and Bebe were one year away from finishing a four-year program at Harvard University that would allow them to obtain both a law degree and an MBA. They were spending the summer interning at one of the most prestigious law firms in Boston.

It was a decision Teagan was beginning to regret because working for Donaldson was awful. It was worse than getting a Brazilian bikini wax while having a root canal while wearing too-tight stilettos.

Pure undiluted torture.

"He's such a douche," Teagan added, using her brothers' favorite insult. She usually winced when she heard it, but the description was so vividly appropriate she had to use it.

She deepened her voice to ape Donaldson. "Call me JD, girls. It's not just my initials, you know. It stands for *Juris Doctor*."

Bebe broke into peals of laughter, a bright, melodic sound that made Teagan smile. She'd been beyond lucky to meet the other woman on the first day of orientation at Harvard.

Bebe had quickly become Teagan's best friend, not just a convenient friend in a strange new city. She trusted her like she had never trusted another person outside of her family.

At first glance, the two of them had little in common. Bebe was Indian, and she had lovely olive skin and golden eyes, quite a contrast from Teagan's almost ghostly white complexion and blue eyes.

Her friend's almost-black hair was shiny and lustrous, and she always wore it in a low bun. She literally never let her hair down.

Unlike Teagan, who edged toward plump, Bebe was slender. And even though Teagan was only average height, just a few inches over five feet, the other woman was much shorter, almost diminutive in stature.

Bebe was the first in her family to be born in the United States. Her parents had emigrated from their native India to further their medical careers. Her father was one of the foremost infectious disease experts in the world, while her mother was a well-known heart surgeon practicing at Johns Hopkins Hospital in Baltimore.

Once you got past their drastically different appearances and backgrounds, though, Teagan and Bebe had a lot in common. Like Teagan, Bebe came from a family of overachievers.

Bebe had two older brothers who were the source of considerable parental pride. Both of her brothers were physicians who not only boasted medical degrees but PhDs in their respective fields, and they had already made their mark on the medical community.

Bebe, meanwhile, was a huge disappointment to her parents because she favored law and business over medicine. As a result, Bebe was driven to prove her worth. She constantly strived to achieve more academic and professional success so she could get her family's attention, if not their approval.

It was something Bebe and Teagan had in common. While Teagan definitely was not a disappointment to her parents, it was hard to shine in Quinn's and Cal's shadows.

It was maddening how easily everything came to them. Her older brothers had achieved athletic and academic success with minimal effort. And it didn't hurt that they were both blessed with good looks. Teagan had heard her friends sigh over Quinn's smile and Cal's eyes for most of her life.

In fact, she had little doubt her modest popularity in high school with other girls had more to do with her hot brothers than her own sparkling personality. Whenever her brothers were around, Teagan felt invisible. They sucked all the air out of the room with their big personalities.

Bebe's laughter trailed off, and her expression turned serious. Teagan raised her eyebrows at the abrupt shift in her best friend's mood.

"I'm worried about you, Teagan."

"Worried?" she echoed with surprise. "Why?"

"JD isn't harmless. His family is more than wealthy. They remind me of the Kennedys. They're powerful and influential."

Teagan tilted her head, digesting Bebe's words. In San Francisco, the O'Brien family was well known, wielding considerable political and social influence because of their wealth and roots in the community. But this was Boston, and Bebe was right about JD and his family.

Bebe met Teagan's gaze over the rim of her wineglass, her eyes serious. "You're a challenge to him. In fact, I doubt anyone has ever said no to him." She paused, making sure Teagan was paying attention. "I don't like the way he looks at you. It's rapacious."

Teagan laughed. Bebe had an impressive vocabulary, and she routinely threw around words that would win triple points at Scrabble.

Bebe frowned. "Please don't laugh this off. You need to be careful."

Realizing Bebe was truly upset, Teagan sobered. "Beebs, I think you're worrying for no reason. I'm pretty sure he's like this with all the interns. Don't you remember that third-year, Lydia, saying she had trouble with him?"

Bebe nodded. "I remember. But you still need to be careful."

Despite Bebe's warning, Teagan wasn't worried about JD. He was a snake with no fangs—slippery but ultimately harmless.

"JD can't hurt my career," she reminded Bebe.

Unlike a lot of interns, Teagan wasn't worried about what she was going to do after graduation. Once she had her degrees in hand, she had every intention of taking her place in the family company. Her dad had promised there would be a place for her when she came home.

Quinn and Cal already worked for Riley O'Brien & Co. Quinn would probably end up taking over the company once their father retired, but Teagan didn't expect that to happen anytime soon.

Her father loved Riley O'Brien & Co., and he enjoyed working. More than likely, he wouldn't retire for another twenty years, and even then, he'd probably still come into the office just to make sure his kids kept things on track.

"I'm not talking about your career, Teagan. I'm talking about you . . . your person." Bebe took another sip of her wine before continuing. "I think you should wear different clothes to work."

*"What?"*

She always dressed professionally, and she couldn't believe Bebe would find fault with her work clothes. Bebe continued as if Teagan hadn't spoken.

"Pantsuits with jackets that button all the way to the neck maybe."

"Seriously, Bebe?"

"Yes, seriously."

"What was wrong with what I wore today?"

The navy cropped Michael Kors jacket with big white buttons and a matching sheath dress was one of Teagan's favorite outfits. The length of the skirt was modest, falling just above her knees, and the rounded neckline of the dress showed no cleavage.

She'd finished the outfit with red sling-back pumps and a red beaded choker. She had thought it was a perfect mix of professional and stylish.

"It wasn't ugly enough. Or loose enough. And it showed your legs."

Teagan was mortified Bebe thought her clothes were too tight and that she showed too much skin. No matter what she wore, it was hard to minimize her DDs unless she hid them under a baggy T-shirt, and she didn't think that would cut it at Price, Latham & Donaldson.

"So you think my clothes are too tight? Too revealing?"

She was vain enough not to want to go up a size. She already was in the double-digits. Unfortunately, she had Grandma Vi's body shape, voluptuous on a good day, chunky on a bad day.

Teagan supposed she should count herself lucky she didn't take after her great-great-grandfather, who'd been nearly seven feet tall with a fifty-inch waist. His mountainous physique had probably come in handy back in the rough-and-tumble days of the Gold Rush.

"No! You're missing the point!" Bebe exclaimed. "I think JD is a predator, Teagan, and he's fixated on you. That's why you need to do everything you can to make him shift his attention *away* from you." She pointed at Teagan. "And it would also help if you would keep your mouth shut."

Teagan sighed. She'd never been very good at that.

THE VIEW OF THE CHARLES RIVER FROM NICK'S NEW CONDO was nice enough, especially on this sunny summer day, but he wished he could still see the Rocky Mountains from his windows. Unfortunately, Denver was no longer his home, and the Denver Broncos were no longer his team.

He'd spent seven years playing for the Broncos after they made him a first-round draft pick right out of college. He had hoped he could spend his entire career there, even though he'd known it was unlikely.

When it came right down to it, players were commodities. They weren't people—they were just arms and legs, hands and feet, to be sold to the highest bidder—and the Boston Colonials had made Denver an offer for Nick it just couldn't refuse.

He shook off thoughts of the trade. It was done, and there was no reason to think about it anymore. He needed to accept that he was back on the East Coast, only a few hours from where he'd grown up.

Only a few hours from his father.

Thoughts of Simon Priest filled Nick with a bitter mix of anger and disappointment. His father wore many hats: academic, economist, author, and speaker.

Officially, Simon taught economics at Syracuse University, but when Nick had been in high school, his father had authored a book on global economic drivers that had caught the attention of the mainstream media. Almost overnight, he'd become one of the most-sought-after interviews on cable TV networks like CNN and MSNBC.

Over the past decade, Simon's renown had grown, and he spent the majority of his time presenting at global economic conferences. He excelled at the very thing Nick didn't: talking.

From the moment Nick had been diagnosed with a speech disorder in kindergarten, his father had treated him as a body without a brain. In fact, most people treated Nick that way. Because he didn't say much, they assumed he was a dumb jock. Most of the time, he agreed with them.

His stomach growled, and he headed into the kitchen and grabbed an apple off the counter. He hadn't eaten lunch, and he was starving. He wished the food fairy had stopped by and filled the refrigerator with delicious, healthy meals. Unfortunately, he didn't have a food fairy, although he was scheduled to interview four personal chefs this afternoon.

The first candidate was supposed to arrive—he checked the time on his mobile phone—right now. His phone buzzed to let him know he'd received a text, and he popped open the screen to read the message from his agent, Elijah Farris.

"Don't forget interviews. One p.m. Paulette Andrews."

Elijah was awesome. He went above and beyond to help his clients. Along with Quinn, he was one of the few people who knew about Nick's stutter, and he was very protective of Nick's privacy.

Without question, the lack of privacy was the thing Nick hated most about being a professional athlete. He didn't mind the pressure to win, the fickle fans who cussed you one moment and loved you the next, or the aches and pains from having a 300-pound man throw you to the ground.

But he definitely didn't like living in a fishbowl. It was hard enough for him to speak without worrying that millions of people were going to hear him sound like an idiot.

That was why he turned down interviews and said no to endorsement deals that would require him to speak, regardless of the millions of dollars he would make. And he had to be careful the people he hired wouldn't turn around and sell some

salacious story to the media. He could see the headline now:
P-P-P-POOR PRIEST CAN'T SPEAK.

He wasn't the only NFL player who had a speech impediment. Darren Sproles, a running back with the Philadelphia Eagles, served as a spokesperson for the Stuttering Foundation, a national nonprofit. But his stutter wasn't nearly as bad as Nick's.

Just then, the doorbell rang, and Nick made his way across the shiny hardwood floors to the door. As he opened it, he automatically shifted his gaze downward, expecting the personal chef to be shorter than he was.

Surprisingly, he was almost eye to eye with the older woman in front of him. Her stick-thin body was clad in baggy black-and-white-checked pants and a red smock with "Chef Letty" embroidered on it.

He looked down, half expecting to see heels, although that would have looked pretty weird with her chef outfit. But no, her big feet were covered in those ugly clog shoes that doctors and nurses favored, so that meant she was probably a couple of inches over six feet.

Smiling, she held out her hand. She had big teeth to go with her big feet. Her blue eyes were bright, and her silver hair was styled in a modified crew cut

"Letty Andrews," she said with a heavy Boston accent.

Nick shook her hand, and as usual, he didn't bother to introduce himself. Letty's gray eyebrows rose at his silence, probably in disapproval. He knew people thought he was rude, but if he didn't have to talk, he wasn't going to.

He gestured for her to come in, and she reached into the hallway to grab the handle of a rolling suitcase. He eyed it with trepidation.

*Is she planning to move in? I haven't even hired her yet.*

Letty sailed through the door ahead of him, and he got a whiff of something spicy. Saliva burst in his mouth, and he swore his teeth elongated at the thought of eating whatever smelled so good. He laughed under his breath, imagining himself as a vampire scenting fresh blood, and Letty turned to look at him, a curious expression on her face.

Ignoring her unspoken question, he led her to the kitchen

and pointed to one of the chairs surrounding the rectangular wood table. "Ha . . ." He stopped and cleared his throat, a trick he used to hide his stutter. "Have a seat."

Tilting her head toward him, she gave him an assessing glance before pulling the suitcase toward the table. As she leaned down and grabbed the tab of the zipper, he noticed it opened from the top.

"It's a rolling insulated bag, not a suitcase," she explained, clearly reading his mind.

The moment she flipped open the top, the spicy smell he'd noticed earlier poured from the bag. He dropped into the chair closest to it, almost drooling.

Letty pulled a red cloth placemat from the bag along with a white china plate and a set of silverware wrapped in a white cloth napkin before arranging everything in front of him. As she removed a small bud vase with a white daisy from the bag and placed it on the table, she slanted an amused glance toward him.

"You can't enjoy a meal without a nice table setting."

Nick barely heard her because his eyes were fixed on the bag, eager to see what delights she'd brought. Taking several aluminum containers from the bag, she deposited them on the table in front of him. She popped the tops off the containers, and pointing to each dish, she described the food within.

"Roasted chicken with asiago polenta. Crab cakes with spicy rémoulade. Pan-seared flank steak with mushroom sauce. Sautéed shrimp with wasabi cream. Poblano mac and cheese. And chocolate mint bars and peanut butter pie for dessert."

Nick knew he probably resembled a cartoon character with his eyes bugged out of his head and his tongue rolled out of his mouth. He licked his lips, unsure where to start.

Letty chuckled. "Allergies?"

He shook his head.

"Anything here you don't want?"

He shook his head again, and she dished up spoonfuls from every container, filling his plate to the brim. She unwrapped his silverware before handing him the fork and placing the napkin in his lap.

"Eat," she ordered as she sat down.

Spearing a shrimp on the tines of his fork, he brought it to his mouth. A world of flavors and textures hit his tongue: the slight sweetness of shrimp, the hot bite of wasabi, and the smooth silk of cream.

"Umm," he moaned. "Good."

She frowned. "Don't talk with your mouth full." She made a *tsk*ing noise. "It's rude."

Nick narrowed his eyes at her bossiness. They'd known each other for less than ten minutes, and she thought she could tell him what to do? He swallowed and wiped his mouth with his napkin.

"You're hired."

## Chapter 4

THE OVEN TIMER SOUNDED AT THE SAME TIME TEAGAN'S PHONE rang, and she sprinted across the room to grab the phone.

"Hello," she said as she rushed back to the oven. She didn't want her double-fudge brownies to burn.

"Hey there, baby girl."

Her father's strong baritone rumbled across the line, and her heart expanded. She was a daddy's girl through and through, and she loved it when he called her out of the blue.

"Hi, Daddy," she replied, holding the phone against her shoulder so she could don an oven mitt. "What's up?"

"Oh, I'm just driving home from work, and I thought I'd call my favorite daughter."

She laughed. "Funny. As far as I know, I'm your only daughter," she said as she pulled the brownies out of the oven.

He chuckled. "As far as I know, too. How was your day?"

"Pretty good."

She was lying, just a little bit. Despite her efforts to keep her head down and wear ugly clothes over the past several days, JD continued to pursue her. She'd had the misfortune to be alone with him in the elevator today, and he'd backed her against the wall and tried to kiss her. She was going to have to be very careful not to be alone with him.

Grabbing a knife, she stuck it in the brownies to see if they were done. It came out clean, so she turned off the oven and put the brownies on the stove to cool.

"Learn anything new?" her father asked. "Do anything fun?"

They were the same questions her dad had asked her every single day of her life since she was a little girl. When she'd been a teenager and sullenly answered *no* to his queries, he had speared her with his blue-gray gaze.

"That's your fault, baby girl," he'd said.

Not a day went by that she didn't think about his response. It was a reminder that she was responsible for her own happiness.

"I did learn something new, and I'm about to do something fun."

"Oh, yeah? What do you have planned? A boy?"

She laughed. "Daddy, I'm twenty-six years old. I don't date boys anymore. I date men."

And then she laughed when she realized that she didn't sound very mature, since she still called her father "Daddy." But if all daughters had fathers as fabulous as hers, they'd call them "Daddy," too, no matter how old they were.

"Well, now, that's good to know. But you still haven't told me about your daily dose of fun."

"Brownies. Fresh out of the oven."

He laughed. "Teagan, honey, if you think brownies are fun, maybe you need to go out with a boy. A bad boy."

A hard knock on her door distracted her. She frowned. It was seven o'clock on a Thursday night, and she wasn't expecting anyone.

"Daddy, I need to go. Someone's at the door."

"Make sure to check the peephole. I love you."

"Love you, too," she replied before disconnecting the call.

She reached the front door and, heeding her father's advice, leaned up to peer out the peephole. She blinked a couple of times, certain she was seeing things because it looked like Nick Priest stood on the other side of the threshold.

He raised his fist and banged on the door again, and she jerked in surprise. *Why is Nick here?* She hadn't seen him for a couple of years.

Her first thought was something was wrong with Quinn,

but then she discarded that idea because she'd just been on the phone with her dad. If something had happened to her older brother, he would have told her immediately.

After unchaining the lock, she disengaged the deadbolt and pulled open the door. "Nick, what are you doing here?" she exclaimed, reaching up to give him a hug. "I'm so happy to see you!"

He hugged her back, a light squeeze like he always gave her, and she leaned back to look at him. God, he was gorgeous. He must have sold his soul to the devil, because no one could be so handsome just by the luck of the draw.

He smiled down at her, his even, white teeth flashing against his bronzed skin. Golden stubble covered his lower face, and his light green eyes sparkled. His hair was almost down to his shoulders, so blond it was the color of corn silk.

"I can't believe your hair." She tugged on a strand. "You look like you should be on the cover of a romance novel or in a pirate movie. Arrgh."

Laughing softly, he cocked his head toward the interior of her condo. "Inside."

She stepped back and waved him in, enjoying the view as he walked ahead of her. Yes, Nick was Quinn's best friend, and no, he'd never once shown any interest in her as anything other than his best friend's little sister.

But that didn't mean she was blind. The man was physically perfect, at least in her opinion. And his choice in jeans was perfect, too. She got a weird thrill as she saw her last name sewn on the fabric hugging his butt.

She pulled her gaze from his tight behind and ogled his broad shoulders, which were covered in a plain black T-shirt. Too bad it wasn't tighter. She wouldn't mind seeing some hard muscles outlined in soft cotton.

He stopped near the kitchen, his nose twitching like a rabbit's. Crossing her arms over her chest, she raised her eyebrows.

"Let me guess . . . you want me to share my brownies?"

His only response was a smile. She'd known this man for more than a decade, since Quinn had brought him home from college the summer between their freshman and sophomore years. Over time, Teagan and Nick had figured out a way to communicate even though he barely talked.

At first, she'd thought Nick was shy. She had been sure he'd warm up once he got to know her and her family. But eventually she realized he wasn't shy at all. He just didn't like to talk.

His silence didn't bother her. She'd grown up with two brothers who talked too much, and it was kind of nice to be around someone who listened more than he talked.

Beckoning him into the kitchen, she headed over to the stove, where the brownies were cooling. She grabbed the knife, and as she cut two big pieces, Nick came up behind her and leaned over her shoulder.

He was focused completely on the brownies, and she would bet her last dollar he didn't even realize he was pressed so tightly against her she could feel the heat from his chest and his breath against her hair. He might be oblivious, but she noticed.

Teagan wasn't ashamed to admit she found Nick attractive. Heck, every female who had gone through puberty felt a little quiver of longing when faced with his hotness. But there was nothing between them. There never had been, and there never would be.

From the first moment she'd met Nick, Teagan had known he was way out of her league. That knowledge had prevented her from crushing on her brother's best friend. It also had made it possible for them to become friends—buddies who hung out when the opportunity arose.

She elbowed Nick in the ribs to get him to step back, and he grunted a little before moving away from her. Grabbing a couple of napkins, she wrapped his brownie and handed it to him.

"Milk?" he asked, his expression hopeful.

She shook her head in amusement. They'd fallen back into their old habits pretty quickly.

"You're like a five-year-old," she teased as she poured him a glass of milk.

Nick shrugged, clearly not offended by her assessment. He took the milk and brownie and waited on her to lead the way to the living area.

She sat down on one end of her navy velvet sofa and tucked her legs under her. He plopped down next to her, taking up way too much space. With a sigh, he propped his tennis shoe–clad feet on her coffee table. After placing his napkin-wrapped brownie on his flat stomach, he broke off a piece of it and popped it into his mouth.

"What are you doing here?" she asked again.

He turned his head, and their eyes met. He swallowed before answering, "Traded."

Quinn had told her Nick had been traded to the Colonials, but for some reason, it hadn't really dawned on her that they'd be living in the same city. "Right. I forgot. How long have you been in town?"

He made a humming noise. "Seven days."

She cocked her head. "Are you counting the days or something? Why not just say a week?"

He took a big gulp of his milk and waved his hand around the room. "Like your place."

"Me, too. Although I probably paid way too much for it."

"You can afford it," he noted with a shrug.

He was right. Thanks to Grandma Violet, Teagan was an heiress. Her grandmother had divided her estate equally among her grandchildren, and they all had trust funds in the millions.

"When I got the news I had been accepted to my program, I planned to rent an apartment near campus. But the rental housing in Cambridge is horrible."

"Spoiled," Nick noted, giving her a big wink.

She laughed. "You think I'm spoiled?"

He nodded emphatically as he took another bite of brownie. The teasing glint in his eye took the sting out of his words, though.

"If you had seen some of the apartments . . . they were worse than a frat house." She shuddered dramatically. "They were *disgusting*."

He chuckled. "Spoiled."

Her condo was one of two penthouse units in a six-story building that had been built in the early 1900s. It had been a hotel prior to being redeveloped into housing, and every single unit had a different floor plan.

Her particular condo featured a large living area that flowed into the kitchen and dining space. It had two bedrooms, one of which she used for an office, and two full bathrooms. By Cambridge standards, it was luxurious.

"You're right," she admitted. "You know, this is the first time I've ever lived by myself. I think I'm officially an adult," she added.

He stared at her for several moments, his eyes assessing. She was a little unnerved by his scrutiny, so she nabbed his glass of milk and took a drink. He pointed to her mouth.

"What?" she asked, running her fingers across her lips.

"Milk."

"I have a milk mustache?" He nodded, and she laughed softly. "So much for being an adult."

NICK COULDN'T TAKE HIS EYES OFF TEAGAN–WHO WAS DEFInitely an adult, despite her milk mustache. He didn't recall the last time he'd seen her, but something was different. He frowned, trying to figure out what it was.

He had known her since she was a teenager, and he still remembered the first time he'd met her. He had expected a female version of Quinn and Cal: tall, lean, and blessed with good looks.

As a horny twenty-year-old, he'd thought he might have the opportunity to break the best friend commandment that said, "Thou shalt not mess around with younger sisters." But he'd quickly discarded that notion as soon as he received his first glimpse of Teagan.

He and the O'Brien brothers had been tossing around a football in their expansive backyard when a short, round, young girl ran out of the house to greet them. She'd worn a Catholic school uniform complete with white button down shirt, navy plaid skirt, and knee socks.

A lot of guys fantasized about girls in school uniforms, and maybe, just maybe, Nick had been one of them . . . at least until he'd seen Teagan in hers. She definitely had *not* been sexy.

To say she'd been an awkward teenager was being generous. Truthfully, she had been downright unattractive with her frizzy hair, splotchy skin, and mouthful of braces.

Teagan placed the remains of her uneaten brownie on the coffee table. She leaned back and pushed up her glasses before flipping her long ponytail over her shoulder.

*Glasses!* That's what was different. She wore glasses with

thick tortoiseshell frames that turned up at the ends like cat's eyes.

He gestured toward her face. "Glasses?"

She touched her glasses, almost as if she'd forgotten them. She shrugged.

"Too much time reading law books and looking at a computer screen."

He studied her. Her eyes were a deep, pure blue, and the glasses made them look bigger. They glinted behind the lenses, and when she blinked, he noticed her dark eyelashes. They were long and kind of feathery.

"Cute," he said.

She cocked her head. "What's cute?"

"You. Your glasses."

Her eyes widened, and her cheeks turned pink. He stared at Teagan, realizing he hadn't really looked at her in a long, long time.

*On purpose.*

Her skin wasn't splotchy anymore. It was smooth and unblemished and reminded him of the whipped cream Letty had put on his mixed berry parfait this morning. And now that he thought about it, Teagan's mouth was almost the same color as the raspberries that had been in the parfait, and her eyes were a similar shade to the blueberries.

He licked his lips, remembering how delicious the parfait had been. Then he shook his head a little, trying to dislodge the sexual thoughts about Teagan that had no business being in his mind.

"School?" he asked.

"I'm seventy-five percent finished with my program. I like to say it that way so it sounds like I'm almost done. Otherwise, I'd have to say that I have a year left."

She smiled, showing her straight white teeth. Those braces she had worn had done their job. Her teeth were perfectly aligned, no gaps to be seen. The essence of her smile was still the same, though. It was just as sweet and engaging as he remembered.

When they'd met, it had been easy to overlook Teagan's awkwardness because she had been so friendly and funny. They had established a weird conversational rhythm he'd never experienced with anyone else. He could say one word, and she'd fill in the blanks, making it easy for him to communicate with her.

Sometimes he wondered if she even heard his stutter . . . if it even registered in her consciousness. While most people got a pained look on their faces when he spoke, Teagan's expression never changed.

Moreover, she'd never mentioned his speech impediment, not even in passing. And that was strange because she wasn't the kind of person to ignore the elephant in the room—especially when the elephant was as gigantic as his stutter.

His inability to speak without sounding like an idiot prevented him from making friends easily, yet Teagan had become his friend. And they'd stayed friends even though they only saw each other rarely. That was why he'd been so happy when Quinn had reminded him that Teagan was in Boston, too.

Nick had been bored out of his mind earlier this evening, and he had considered changing into some nicer clothes and going out to a bar. He knew he would have no trouble finding sex because women liked the way he looked, and ninety-nine percent of them didn't seem to care if he said anything or not.

They were content to use his body and ignore his mind, and he felt the same way about them. As long as his partner had a wet, welcoming pussy, he was satisfied. He didn't want her to open her mouth unless it was to suck his dick, and he didn't care about her life goals, only that they didn't interfere with his.

Just as he'd headed into his bedroom to shower, his phone had buzzed to alert him that he had a text. The message had been from Quinn: Teagan's in Boston. Go visit her.

Once he'd known Teagan was in town, he couldn't stop thinking about seeing her. If he wasn't able to hang with Quinn and Cal, their little sister was the next best thing. And once he'd seen her, all the nervous energy he had felt earlier drained away.

He placed his glass on the cocktail table, and she leaned forward to grab a coaster for it. As she did, her pink T-shirt rose a little in the back, exposing a sliver of smooth, white skin and the top of her lacy, red panties.

His cock twinged, and he jerked his eyes away from the sight. *Jesus, what's wrong with me?*

She was his best friend's little sister, and now that he was older, he respected what that meant: hands off. More important, Teagan was *his* friend, which meant the same thing.

He might be a dumb jock, but he was smart enough to know he could get sex anywhere. Friendship was harder to come by. Teagan was one of the few people he genuinely cared about, and he wasn't going to mess that up by thinking about her naked.

"What have you been doing?"

He tensed, worried for a second she had noticed he'd been checking her out. But he relaxed when he realized she'd been asking about what he had been doing since he'd moved to Boston.

"Nothing."

"There's a lot to do here. Lots of history. The Red Sox."

He nodded. He knew Boston could be a fun place, but he didn't want to explore the area by himself.

She looked at him for a moment, tapping her fingers against her lips. The action highlighted how full they were—plump and luscious.

His cock twitched, and he shifted uncomfortably as he tried to remember how long it had been since he'd had sex. Not that long. And *definitely* not long enough for him to be getting hard over Teagan, for fuck's sake. Maybe he *should* have gone to a bar instead of coming to see her.

"Want to hang out this weekend?" she asked.

## Chapter 5

SATURDAY WAS LAUNDRY DAY, AND TEAGAN WAS HONEST enough to admit she hated spending one of her free days washing, folding, and putting away clothes. Fortunately, she had a washer and dryer in her condo, so she didn't have to make the trek to a dark and dank laundry room or a busy laundromat.

She was spoiled in a lot of ways, but at least she did her own laundry. Many of her fellow Harvard students used laundry services. But she had a thing about strangers touching her unmentionables.

If you excluded her immediate family, only one person had laid a hand on her underwear: her ex-boyfriend, Jason. He'd also had his hands (and other body parts) on the flesh inside her underwear. But he was the only one.

Quinn and Cal had tapped so much Catholic school ass that Teagan had been appalled at how easily girls gave it up. They'd made an impression on her—a bad impression—and she'd held on to her virginity until college.

She had wanted her first time to mean something. Actually, she wanted every time to mean something, which was why she hadn't been with anyone since she and Jason had broken up three years ago.

Teagan frowned. To say they'd broken up made it sound like

it had been a mutual decision, and there had been nothing mutual about it. *Jason* had broken up with *her*.

She and Jason had started dating her sophomore year in college. She'd liked him a lot, and eventually she had fallen in love with him. But how much did a nineteen-year-old really know about love?

They definitely hadn't known much about sex. Jason had been a virgin, too, and they'd fumbled their way through foreplay, oral sex, and finally intercourse. He was a smart guy, but it had taken him a year to figure out how to give her an orgasm without her help. She'd done her best to tell him what she liked.

She hoped her next lover had a lot of experience and could give her mind-blowing orgasms just by looking at her. She scoffed at the thought. Who could do that?

An image of Nick Priest popped into her head, and she laughed mirthlessly. She had no doubt he had plenty of experience. She'd seen pictures of him surrounded by beautiful women who looked like sex on stilettos, and if he was anything like her brothers, he had no trouble finding willing bed partners.

Nick was probably a horrible lover, though. Since he was so good-looking, he probably didn't even try to please his partner. Most likely, he just lounged on the bed in all his muscular, bronzed glory and let someone else do all the work.

She slammed the door of the dryer shut with more force than necessary, annoyed at the direction of her thoughts. It wasn't as if she were ever going to get the chance to find out if Nick was a pathetic lover or a four-orgasms-in-one-night kind of guy.

She scowled. She hadn't heard from him in over a week, not since he'd rebuffed her offer to hang out. She knew it was hard to adjust to a new place, and she'd been trying to be nice when she had issued the invitation.

He'd stared at her for a long time before looking away and muttering "no." Actually, she was pretty sure he had said "hell no," but she couldn't figure out why he'd been so rude.

Nick had never once been cruel to her in all the years she had known him. He'd always had a smile for her, even when her brothers had told her to stop bugging them.

She had managed to hide how much he'd hurt her feelings, and he had left her condo after a few more minutes of one-sided conversation. She didn't expect to see him for another couple of years.

Hefting the laundry basket in both hands, she made her way through the kitchen. As she turned toward her bedroom, she heard a knock on her door.

She propped the basket overflowing with clean clothes on her hip to free her hand. Bebe had mentioned she might come by for dinner and a movie, so Teagan opened the door without checking the peephole.

"Hey, you're here early . . ."

Her visitor was not Bebe. It was Nick.

Surprise made her silent, and he moved his hand over her head and pushed open the door. As he walked into her condo, she stumbled backward out of his way, bobbling the laundry basket.

She watched in dismay as a pair of plain white cotton underwear floated from the top of the laundry pile to land on his foot. He followed her gaze, and before she could drop the basket and scoop them from the floor, he bent down to pick them up.

She groaned under her breath. Why, oh why, couldn't they have been one of her pretty pairs instead of the old granny panties she favored when she felt especially fat or had her period?

Before she could jerk them out of his hand, he held them up and waved them as if he were surrendering a battle. He smiled, the skin around his eyes crinkling.

"Sexy," he said with a wicked glint in his green gaze.

She growled. "Shut up, Nick Priest. You jerk!"

He burst out laughing when she grabbed them from his big hand. She tucked the panties into the basket and held it in front of her, wishing it would make her invisible.

"Why are you here?" she asked rudely.

"Red Sox."

She cocked her head. "You want to go to the game?"

He nodded, taking two tickets out of his back pocket. The motion pulled his T-shirt tight across his chest, and she couldn't help but stare as his pectoral muscles flexed.

She considered his invitation. He must be really desperate for company if he was asking her to go to a baseball game with him. She thought about declining his offer as rudely as he'd declined hers. But she wasn't sure Bebe was going to come by, and she didn't want to spend Saturday night alone.

And she really loved baseball. Plus, the Red Sox were playing well after an early-season slump. It might be a really good game.

"I'll go on one condition . . ."

He raised his eyebrows, a silent question.

"You're buying the beer and hotdogs."

He smiled slowly. "Deal."

NICK WANDERED AROUND TEAGAN'S CONDO WHILE HE WAITED for her to change. Photos filled her big bookcase, and he spied one that looked familiar. He picked it up to give it a closer study and realized he'd snapped it the day he and Quinn had graduated from USC.

Quinn was in the middle, and his parents, James and Kate, flanked him. Cal stood next to their mother, and Teagan was hugged up against her dad.

Everyone had huge smiles on their faces, but Teagan's smile was the brightest. When this picture had been taken, she'd just finished her freshman year at Stanford.

Her adolescent awkwardness had disappeared, leaving a young woman with bright blue eyes and wavy dark hair that shined almost blue-black in the sunlight. Her roundness had transformed into an hourglass shape, and except for her height, or lack thereof, this was the girl he had expected to meet when he'd heard Quinn and Cal had a sister.

No doubt about it, the O'Briens were extraordinarily good-looking. But what really made them extraordinary was the love they had for one another.

Nick had never known another family that loved like the O'Briens. From what he could tell, James and Kate had a strong, loving marriage. They adored their kids, a sentiment their kids returned. Nick had been lucky they'd been willing to welcome him into their circle and eventually make him an honorary member of their family.

In a lot of ways, the O'Briens were more his family than the Priests. Of course, Nick only had his father, since his mother had died when he was a toddler.

Nick hadn't seen his father in more than a year. Simon never suggested that they get together, and Nick didn't, either.

They weren't estranged; they were just strangers, which was even sadder because that meant there were no feelings there at all. Nick couldn't claim the fault was entirely his father's. When he had stopped trying to prove to Simon that his speech disorder didn't impact his ability to learn, only his ability to communicate, their relationship had died a slow death.

He heard Teagan's footsteps and returned the picture to the bookcase, taking care not to dislodge any of the other framed shots. She came to a stop slightly behind him, and the sweet scent of strawberries drifted to him. The smell reminded him of her lips, which reminded him of the dream he'd had about her a few nights ago.

*Shit.*

After he'd left Teagan's condo last week, he had decided he wouldn't contact her again—no texts and no visits. But just a few days later, here he was, in the same place, thinking the same thoughts. And now he had to spend hours with her, smelling strawberries and thinking about her lips.

*I'm an idiot.*

And his mouth had nothing to do with it. It was his dick.

Teagan moved closer to see what had caught his attention. She bumped him with her hip.

"That was a good day. Do you remember it?"

"Yeah."

James and Kate had thrown a graduation party for Quinn at a new restaurant in downtown Los Angeles, just a few miles from the USC campus. While everyone else had been enjoying good food and good friends, he'd been enjoying a good fuck with one of the waitresses in the alley. He was pretty sure no one had missed him while he'd been gone. He had been quick, but they'd both gotten off, if his memory served.

"I remember you disappeared for twenty minutes or so," she said dryly. "About the same time one of the waitresses went missing."

*Huh. Someone had noticed.*

Shoving his hands in his pockets, he turned to face her. She wore a red T-shirt with "Red Sox Baseball" written across the chest, and even though it wasn't tight, his eyes were drawn to her breasts. They were larger than average, and he wondered if her nipples were dark like cherries.

*Damn! I have to stop thinking about her breasts. And her nipples.*

She'd paired the T-shirt with dark-washed jeans and red canvas sneakers, and he wondered if she had chosen lacy panties like she'd had on the last time he visited or the plain ones he'd touched earlier. Then he wondered if she had a bush or if she was bare.

*Damn! I have to stop thinking about her panties. And what those panties cover.*

She'd pulled her hair into a ponytail, and the end of it hung out the back of the Red Sox baseball cap she wore. He was pretty sure she had put on some makeup, too, since her eyelashes looked even longer, and her skin seemed to shimmer.

She smiled, and he noticed her lips were shiny with gloss. Then he thought about what his cock would look like sliding in and out of her mouth.

*Damn! I have to stop . . .*

"Ready?" she asked.

He nodded, and she turned to walk to the door. Naturally, his gaze fell to her ass, and he gasped in disbelief. Her jeans were not Rileys. They were the *competition*. He was appalled.

"No Rileys?"

Stopping midstride, she looked over her shoulder at him, her gaze both incredulous and accusing. "Were you checking out my butt?"

"Habit," hc admitted sheepishly.

"You're not allowed to do that." She frowned. "We're friends."

"Friend, yes. Dead, no."

# Chapter 6

THE LINE TO THE NEWEST ROMANTIC COMEDY WAS LONG AND composed entirely of women. Apparently, there were a lot of single gals in Cambridge looking for something to do on a Saturday night.

"Ugh, do we have to wait?" Bebe groaned.

"Patience is a virtue," Teagan replied.

Bebe scowled. "I have enough virtue, as you well know," she replied bitchily, hefting her hot pink bag over her shoulder.

Teagan snickered at the other woman's comment. At twenty-five, Bebe was still a virgin, partly by choice, partly because of a lack of opportunity, at least according to her.

Bebe's eyes narrowed. "You're not exactly experienced."

Teagan shrugged, unable to dispute Bebe's assessment. She was a cliché: the quintessential good girl.

Her thoughts, meanwhile, were a heck of a lot less pure than her body. In her imagination, she got down and dirty with Nick Priest almost every night. Her vibrator had received quite a workout over the past several weeks.

She always felt a little guilty whenever she fantasized about Nick. The poor guy had no idea thoughts of his six-pack abs and tight backside got her off night after night. He would probably be horrified she moaned his name when she came.

Even though they'd spent so much time with each other over the past seven weeks, he still treated her the same way he always had: she was a good buddy, one of the guys, his best friend's little sister.

If they were dating, they probably would have passed the point where they were exclusive and having sex. She saw him two to three times a week. He'd stop by and they'd go out to dinner or he'd show up at her door with takeout. They'd spend the rest of the evening talking, maybe watch a little TV, and then he'd leave.

They usually spent Saturdays together, too. Nick would show up midmorning, and they would spend the rest of the day doing something fun or touristy or both.

They'd attended two Red Sox games, gone on a walking tour of Boston's historic neighborhoods, visited Paul Revere's house, and explored the New England Aquarium. In addition, they'd celebrated the Fourth of July on the banks of the Charles River, drinking beer and enjoying the Boston Pops Fireworks Spectacular.

He never called or texted, and they never made plans in advance. He just showed up.

Teagan was ashamed to admit she looked forward to his visits so much she'd started to decline other invitations because she didn't want to miss him, if and when he knocked on her door.

Today she'd waited until early evening for him to show, and when he hadn't, she'd felt a bewildering mix of emotions. Mostly, she'd been disgusted by herself for being too available. She had turned into the pathetic girl who sat by the phone, only she sat near the front door.

She'd spent more time with Nick over the past several weeks than she and Jason had spent together during the final year of their relationship. He'd always found a reason not to see her. She shook off memories of her ex-boyfriend. She didn't want to ruin her night out with Bebe.

"We should have bought tickets for the movie in advance, because it will probably be sold out by the time we get to the front of the line," Teagan noted.

Bebe's shrug clearly conveyed her lack of concern. "I'd rather get some ice cream from Tosci's."

"Why didn't you say so? I'd choose ice cream over a movie any day."

Tosci's, or Toscanini's officially, had the best ice cream in the United States, maybe the whole world, and Teagan wasn't the only one who thought so. She made a mental note to take Nick there soon.

Bebe and Teagan abandoned the line at the movie theater and headed off toward Central Square, where Tosci's was located. As they strolled along the busy sidewalk, Bebe returned to their previous conversation.

"Speaking of sexual experience, have you heard from Jason in a while?"

"I got an email from him a few days ago."

When Jason had broken up with her, she'd accepted his decision gracefully. She hadn't cried or begged, and she hadn't tried to change his mind. No guy was worth humbling herself like that, especially if he didn't want her in the first place.

"Do you think he wants to start something with you again?"

"No, I don't think so. His emails are friendly, but we don't talk about anything important when he calls. I think he just wants to stay in touch."

"Would you get back together with him if he wanted to?"

She considered Bebe's question. At one time, she'd thought she and Jason would get married and have a family.

Even though they hadn't enjoyed the kind of passionate relationship her parents had, she had been content with him. She had never expected to experience an all-consuming kind of love like her parents had found. It was rare.

"I'm not sure how I would react if Jason told me that he wanted to get back together. I'm not in love with him anymore, but we do have history together."

"You also have history with Nick Priest," Bebe said archly.

Teagan sighed in exasperation. "Bindu Banerjee, I've already told you that Nick and I are just friends."

"That's what you say, but you sure do spend a lot of time with him. Don't you wonder why he seems to prefer your company over anyone else's?"

"Not really. He doesn't know anyone else in Boston."

Bebe snorted. "He's hotter than hot. He's a conflagration, and I'm sure he could find company if he wanted to."

"Conflagration? Do you have to show off your Ivy League vocabulary all the time?"

Bebe ignored her teasing. "Maybe he's secretly in love with you and afraid to say anything."

Teagan laughed. "Oh, Bebe, you are *so* wrong."

She couldn't imagine Nick being in love with anyone. In all the time she'd known him, he'd never had a steady girlfriend or anything remotely recognizable as a relationship.

She'd never even seen him with the same woman twice. More than likely, he had a stable of women he called whenever he wanted sex, and they dropped everything when he got in touch, eager to get their hands on his hot body.

"If you met him, if you saw us together, you'd know how wrong you are," Teagan continued. "He's bored, and I'm convenient. I'm his platonic booty call."

Bebe choked. "There is no such thing! In fact, that's an oxymoron."

"You know what I mean," she replied, waving her hand.

"So you're telling me you feel nothing for him but friendship?"

"That's right. Nothing but friendship."

*And lust. I can't forget that.*


JUDGING BY THE FROWN ON TEAGAN'S FACE, TEN O'CLOCK ON a Sunday morning was too early for Nick to show up at her condo. It had taken several minutes of intermittent knocking for her to come to the door, but finally she'd answered.

As he took in her wild hair and slumberous eyes, he was blindsided by the thought she might have company. A sour taste flooded his mouth, and he swallowed to get rid of it. He must be hungry.

He had wanted to visit the John F. Kennedy Presidential Library and Museum today, and he'd thought Teagan might be interested in going with him. But maybe she was busy.

Maybe someone had kept her up late last night, kissing her pink mouth and caressing her curvy body. He scowled, uncertain if he was annoyed because he was thinking about her naked *again* or because he was thinking about her naked with someone else.

She stared at him for a moment before opening the door wider and gesturing for him to come in. He breathed a sigh of relief. She was alone.

"Do you want some coffee?" she asked, her voice husky from sleep. "I definitely need some."

She turned toward the kitchen, and he trailed after her. She wore a fuzzy robe that was the exact color of the pistachio mousse Letty had made last week, and he wondered if it would feel as soft as it looked.

Settling himself on one of the metal stools situated around the granite bar, he hooked his feet in the rungs and focused his gaze on Teagan. As she stretched up to reach into the cabinet, the tie of her robe loosened.

He sucked in a breath. Was she naked under that robe?

*God, I hope so.*

*What? No, you don't!*

Her robe fell open as she measured coffee into the coffee-maker, and he exhaled, in relief, not disappointment, damn it, that she wore something underneath it. But then she turned to fill the coffeepot with water, and he got a good look at her pajamas. A scrap of black material barely covered her tits, and a tiny pair of matching shorts barely hid her crotch.

The color made her skin look like fresh powder at his favorite ski resort, and he could see the hard points of her nipples against her top and the enticing indention of her belly button above the waistband of her bottoms.

He tore his eyes away, but it was too late. The hard-on he'd woken up with had returned, and he cursed under his breath.

Her head jerked toward him at the sound, her eyebrows winging up her forehead. "What?"

"Nothing," he mumbled.

He enjoyed Teagan's company, but if his body kept acting this way whenever he was around her, he was going to have to stop hanging out with her. It was impossible to avoid touching her altogether, and walking around half hard wasn't comfortable.

He'd always had complete control over his body, unlike his mouth, and he didn't know why it got excited around Teagan. She was his *friend* and his best friend's little *sister*.

He'd been having sex four times a week, sometimes five, with a couple of women he'd met at the gym, so it wasn't as if he were sex-deprived. He might need to add another woman to the rotation, maybe someone dark-haired and blue-eyed.

Teagan pulled her robe closed and cinched the tie around her waist before leaning against the counter. She yawned, not one of those delicate ones that women give behind their hands, but a jaw-popping one.

"Late night?" he asked.

He told himself he was way too interested in what she'd been doing, but that didn't stop him from leaning forward to hear her response. She nodded, but surprisingly she didn't elaborate. He narrowed his eyes. Was she purposely not telling him what she'd done last night?

"Doing?" he persisted.

The coffeemaker beeped, and Teagan pushed away from the counter without answering. She opened the cabinet, pulled out two mugs, and filled them with coffee.

Grabbing some half-and-half from the fridge, she splashed a generous amount in his mug, just as he liked it. She dumped a huge amount of sugar into her coffee, and he shuddered at the thought of how sweet it would be.

She placed his mug in front of him before picking up hers. She gazed at him over the rim of it as she blew on her coffee.

"So, you're bored," she stated flatly. "You're desperate for company, and you want to do something touristy today."

She took a small sip of her coffee, waiting for his reply.

"Right," he answered, although he wasn't being entirely truthful.

He wasn't desperate for company. He knew other people in the city now. In fact, he knew more than a few in the biblical sense. And he definitely wasn't bored. How could he be when he spent so much time with Teagan?

"What do you have in mind?" she asked, pushing her tangled hair away from her face.

"Brunch. JFK Library."

She stared at him, an unreadable expression on her pretty face. When she didn't respond, his stomach cramped a little at the thought that she might not want to go with him. The outing wouldn't be any fun without her.

After a long moment, Teagan nodded and left him in the kitchen, presumably to get ready. As he raised his mug and took a drink, he realized two things: he didn't like her coffee, and he didn't want to spend his free time with anyone but her.

## Chapter 7

"I HAD NO IDEA MY FAMILY HAD SO MUCH IN COMMON WITH JFK's family," Teagan said as she stood in front of a large exhibit in the John F. Kennedy Presidential Library and Museum.

Nick looked over the plaque next to the exhibit, which traced the thirty-fifth president's ancestry all the way back to Ireland, where the Fitzgerald and the Kennedy families hailed from.

"Most Irish immigrants came to America because of the potato famine, you know, but my great-great-grandfather got here several years before that happened. We don't know for sure why he left Ireland, but we think he got into some trouble with the British."

Nick cocked his head, interested to hear more about the man who built Riley O'Brien & Co. He loved history, and that was why he'd decided to major in American history at USC.

A lot of people assumed he had chosen history because it was an easy major. There were certain undemanding majors that jocks picked so they could maintain their academic eligibility, and history was one of them.

But he'd settled on history because he'd always been interested in the past and how it impacted the present. People would be surprised to find out he watched the History Channel a lot more than he watched ESPN.

"How d-d-d-did he get to the Bay Area?" he asked.

"We're not sure. My Grandma Vi was interested in genealogy, and she found out he came here on a coffin ship from Dublin. He arrived in Boston in 1839, and then he showed up in San Francisco in 1843."

"Go on," he prompted Teagan, using one of his many verbal tricks that encouraged other people to keep talking.

She stared at him. "Are you really that interested?"

He nodded emphatically, and she smiled. He stared at her rosy lips, watching them shape words he had trouble pronouncing.

"Well, once Riley O'Brien arrived in San Francisco, he opened a dry goods store. His store was known for having the largest selection and the best price—basically the Walmart of the 1800s."

Her description made him laugh. She certainly had a way of painting a picture with a few words. It was just one of the many reasons he had so much fun when he was with her.

"One of the biggest mysteries about Riley O'Brien is where he got his money to open the store," she continued.

He raised his eyebrows. By and large, Irish immigrants had been poor, and the ones who'd had money were usually involved in all sorts of illegal activities.

"Criminal?" he guessed.

"Maybe. But there might be another explanation. Grandma Vi found a book with a bunch of posters advertising fights across the U.S. in the early 1840s, and some of them referred to a brawler called the Irish Mountain. I think the Irish Mountain was Riley O'Brien."

"Makes sense," he agreed. He couldn't imagine many men who would have been larger than Riley O'Brien. "And the jeans?"

Teagan nodded, understanding his question. Sometimes he felt as if she could read his mind.

"It's kind of a long story," she warned him.

"Continue," he directed, using yet another verbal prompt. He had a lot of them.

"We're not sure how Rileys came to be, exactly. It's urban legend, for the most part. Apparently, quite a few of Riley O'Brien's customers were angry the pants he'd sold them weren't very durable."

"Prospectors?"

"No, the Gold Rush hadn't started yet. These were just regular working guys. Somehow he got the idea to make pants out of the same canvas material that tents were made out of. Of course, the material was a light color, and it showed dirt, so he sent a swatch of tent material to fabric manufacturers in France looking for a similar material in a darker color. They sent him a fabric called *serge de nimes,* which is basically serge fabric from the town of Nimes. That's why it's known as denim."

"France?"

"Yes. Back then, the French were a lot more advanced than other countries in producing textiles. Riley O'Brien had to ship the denim in bulk from France to San Francisco, where he had a team of seamstresses to sew the pants."

"Cool."

He found the entire history of the O'Brien family fascinating. In fact, he knew more about Teagan's ancestry than his own. He didn't know the origin of his last name, and he didn't know where his ancestors were from.

Teagan shifted next to him, drawing his gaze. Her sundress was the color of watermelon, and a cardigan sweater of the same color draped over her arm. And just like watermelon, she looked cool and sweet and reminded him of summer.

She had twisted her dark hair on top of her head, leaving her shoulders bare except for the skinny straps of her sundress. It dipped a little in the front, revealing her abundant cleavage, and Nick wished for the hundredth time she'd worn something else—something that didn't make him think about running his tongue down the valley between those plump mounds.

They'd reached the end of the permanent exhibits, and Teagan turned to face him. "Do you want to see the special exhibit, too?"

He nodded. He was really excited about the exhibit, which was called *Moon Shot: JFK and Space Exploration.*

"I'm so glad." She smiled brightly. "I saw it advertised on the side of a bus, and I've been dying to see it since then."

She shifted her brown leather bag from one shoulder to the other, and he noticed deep red grooves where its straps had dug into her creamy skin. It must be heavy.

For some reason, it bothered him that the bag had marred her smooth skin. He didn't want her to have to lug it around any longer, so he reached over and gently pulled it from her shoulder.

Holding the bag loosely in his grip, Nick was surprised by how much it weighed. *What the hell does she have in it? A set of encyclopedias?*

He transferred her bag to his shoulder, where it settled comfortably. He couldn't care less if someone saw him carrying a purse. There weren't many people who doubted his masculinity, at least not to his face.

Teagan smiled in appreciation. "Thanks. My shoulder was starting to hurt."

Before he thought about it, Nick stroked the marks on her shoulders, running his fingers over them. Her skin was so warm and smooth, and he couldn't stop himself from tracing her delicate collarbone before touching the silky skin of her throat.

She swallowed, and he felt the movement against his fingers. She looked up into his face, her eyes a dreamy dark blue behind her glasses.

"Nick," she said huskily, "are you only spending time with me because you're bored? Because you don't know anyone else in Boston?"

"No."

"Then why?" she asked, her voice barely above a whisper.

Frowning, he dropped his hand from her throat. He didn't know why he kept coming back to her door, time after time. He didn't know why he craved the sound of her voice, the sight of her smile, the music of her laughter.

He didn't know why he thought about her when they weren't together, even when he fucked other women. He didn't know why he was surly and bad-tempered on the days when he didn't see her.

He didn't know why . . .

TEAGAN DIDN'T KNOW WHY SHE'D ASKED SUCH A STUPID QUES-tion when she already knew the answer: Nick spent time with her because they were *friends*.

She needed to keep reminding herself of that fact before she made a fool of herself over him. He already had enough women doing that.

She turned away from his golden good looks and headed

into the special exhibit, determined to focus on how President Kennedy had managed to get America to the moon before Russia.

As she studied a model of the Friendship 7 Project Mercury space capsule, Nick joined her. She gave him a sideways glance, noting that he managed to look manly even though he carried a purse.

His big hand pressed against the leather, holding it close to his body, and not for the first time, she noticed his fingers. They were long, tapered, and tipped with short nails. She really loved his hands, and when they were together, she stared at them a lot, imagining them on her breasts and between her legs.

He had really nice forearms, too—tan and sinewy with muscle. She especially liked it when he wore a long-sleeved, button-down shirt and rolled up the cuffs in front of her. It was so erotic, and it always made her panties damp.

Right now, though, a short-sleeved USC T-shirt showed his forearms. It was ancient, maybe even one of the shirts he'd had since college, and the faded red cotton was soft and clung tightly to his torso, almost like he'd outgrown it a bit.

He'd paired the tee with khaki cargo shorts that had definitely seen better days. They were frayed at the bottom, and one of the pockets was missing.

She wondered if his shorts were loose enough to slip her hand in the waistband and run her fingers across his abs. Saliva pooled in her mouth at the thought of what might be under his shorts. She wanted a peek, just so her fantasies would have some basis in reality.

Pulling her gaze from his drool-worthy body, she found him staring at a picture of the moon with a rapt expression. She imagined he'd sported the same look when he was a little boy.

"You wanted to be an astronaut when you grew up. Am I right?"

"Yeah," he answered without taking his eyes off the picture.

"Why did you want to be one?"

He met her eyes. "Because the moon"—he cleared his throat—"is far away."

"And you wanted to be far away?"

He nodded, his eyes shadowed. He moved to stand in front of a glass display case that held a Project Mercury spacesuit, helmet, and boots.

Teagan digested his answer. She knew his mother had died when he was young, too young to remember her. She couldn't imagine growing up without a mother. She was a daddy's girl, but she and her mom had a special relationship, too.

"When did you stop wanting to be an astronaut?"

"I didn't."

She frowned, wondering why he played football if he wanted to be something else. She strongly believed people should follow their dreams.

"Did you ever think of pursuing it?" she asked, moving to the next part of the exhibit, a lunar sample that was brought back to Earth by the Apollo 15 mission.

"No."

"Why not?"

"Too tall."

She'd never considered Nick's height might be an issue. How strange that one of the things that made him a great wide receiver also prevented him from being an astronaut.

"You?" he asked.

She cocked her head. "What?"

"Your little-girl dreams."

"Oh, I wanted to be a ballerina, just like thousands of other little girls. But I changed my mind when I was twelve or thirteen."

"Because?"

When she didn't answer, he turned to spear her with his light green gaze. He raised his eyebrows, a silent question.

"Obviously, I don't have the body of a ballet dancer," she replied, laughing self-consciously.

Nick's eyes narrowed before dropping to her chest, and she resisted the urge to shield her breasts with her sweater. She wasn't ashamed of her body, not exactly, but it was certainly more *robust* than she would have liked.

"No," he said slowly. "You don't."

Teagan wished she had lied and told him that she had wanted to be a lawyer when she grew up. Desperate to change the subject, she asked, "When do you leave for training camp?"

"Tomorrow."

"Oh! I didn't know it was so soon."

Nodding, he clasped her elbow to move her out of the way

as a large mass of people walked by. He dropped his hand to her waist, and the heat of it burned through her thin sundress.

They'd reached the end of the special exhibit, and he ushered her out the door with a hand on her lower back. He touched her a lot, casual contact that didn't matter to him but made her heart beat faster.

Once they were back in the museum's main area, she turned to him. Although she rarely bought anything at museum gift shops, she had a hard time bypassing them.

"I want to stop by the gift shop before we leave."

He groaned, and she shook her head in exasperation. "Give me twenty minutes, and I'll meet you out front," she promised.

He nodded and walked off, but she called him back after only a few steps. "I need my purse."

Grinning, he handed it over before heading outside. She turned toward the gift shop, and she'd barely stepped over the threshold before she spotted something she just had to have. She quickly completed her purchase and walked outside with ten minutes to spare.

She looked around the grounds, enjoying the view. Located at the tip of the Columbia Point Peninsula, the museum overlooked the entrance to Boston Harbor and the islands to the east of Dorchester Bay. Pine trees, shrubs, and wild roses dotted the land around it.

Teagan spotted Nick about fifty yards away, sitting on a bench. His blond hair glinted in the sunlight, beckoning her toward him. When she sat down next to him, he shot her a surprised glance.

"It didn't take me long to find what I was looking for," she said, placing her purse on the ground between their feet.

He nodded as a strong breeze blew a strand of his hair into her face. Waving it away, she tucked it behind his ear.

"Are you going to cut your hair anytime soon? It's almost as long as mine."

She was exaggerating, but she'd never seen it so long. It was thick and shiny, and she knew women who paid thousands of dollars a year to reproduce the shade he came by naturally.

He nodded. "Before I leave."

"Is this some kind of silly superstition?" she asked, cocking her head.

He laughed softly. "Silly? No."

"So you let your hair grow out during the off-season, and then cut it right before training camp?"

"Yeah."

"Do you cut it throughout the season?"

He nodded.

"How long have you had this *tradition*?"

He smiled at her word choice. "Since my first season in Denver."

"Are you nervous about playing with a new team?"

Turning his head, he met her eyes. Something flicked in their depths before he looked away.

"Yeah."

"What's making you the most nervous?"

He rolled his shoulders, and she waited patiently for him to answer her question. When he didn't, she nudged his shoulder with hers.

"Tell me."

"New teammates, new plays, new coaches."

"I'd be petrified."

He jerked his head toward her, a look of astonishment on his face. She didn't know why he was so surprised, though.

"Change is hard for everyone," she pointed out. "I definitely don't handle it well. I had a really hard time adjusting to Boston. Being so far away from home really sucked. And I don't know what I was thinking, getting an MBA and a law degree at the same time. If not for Bebe, I probably would have flunked out."

"No," he said doubtfully.

"Yes," she countered. "Undergrad was way too easy, and I wasn't prepared for Harvard. The pressure. The expectations." She pushed a loose strand of hair from her face. "The Colonials wanted you because they need a star wide receiver to get to the Super Bowl, right?"

He nodded. "They've been losers in the playoffs."

"Are you worried about not being able to perform?"

His lips quirked, drawing her attention to his mouth. After a moment, he let loose with a deep chuckle.

"No," he answered with a smirk.

When she realized her question had an obvious sexual

overtone, although unintentional, she blushed, and his chuckles turned into full-fledged laughter. Obviously, he enjoyed her embarrassment.

She leaned over and punched him in the upper arm. "Nick Priest, I am trying to have a serious conversation with you!"

He caught her hand with his, wrapping his other arm around her shoulders and pulling her close to his side. They sat there silently for several minutes with her hand nestled in his and his arm curved around her.

Teagan fought the urge to lean her head against his chest. She was very much afraid the crush she'd managed to avoid as a teenager had caught up with her. That knowledge compelled her to release his hand and shake off his arm.

She leaned down to grab her purse and heard a muffled noise from Nick's vicinity. Glancing up, she found him staring at the water.

"Did you say something?"

"No," he muttered without looking in her direction.

Pulling her purse onto her lap, she rummaged around in it until she found the bag containing her gift shop purchase, a metal moon keychain. She fished it from the bag and turned to him.

"I bought you something."

He brought his attention to her, and she pressed the keychain into his palm. His long fingers curled around it, and he brought it close to his face to study it.

"It's the moon—for those times when you want to be far away. Maybe it can be your good luck charm for training camp."

Closing his hand over the moon keychain, he dropped it to his lap. "Thanks."

A few more words slipped past her lips without thought. "I'm going to miss you while you're gone."

Silence hung between them as they gazed toward the water. Then he leaned his head against hers. "Ditto," he said, his voice barely a whisper of sound.

# Chapter 8

NICK CIRCLED THE BLOCK NEAR TEAGAN'S CONDO FOR THE fourth time, trying to find a parking space big enough for his Escalade. Cambridge had to be the absolute *worst* place on the planet for parking, and he barely resisted the urge to bang his fist against the steering wheel.

He hadn't seen Teagan in almost a month, and this was the first opportunity he'd had to visit her since he'd left for training camp. He'd gotten stuck in traffic, and now it was almost seven o'clock.

Like most NFL teams, the Colonials conducted their training camp away from their home base. He'd spent more than three weeks in Arizona with his new team along with a handful of days in San Diego for their preseason game.

Although he'd been exhausted from the stress of camp and the pressure of his first game as a Colonial, he'd had trouble falling asleep. After lying in bed for two hours without nodding off, he'd taken matters into his own hands. Literally.

He'd started off fantasizing about one of the blondes he had been fucking before he left. She was tall with a decent-sized rack and narrow hips. He couldn't remember what color her eyes were, and he was a little hazy on her name, too.

Sometime between the first stroke and his climax, her hair

had turned dark and shiny and her eyes had become smoky blue. And those weren't the only changes, either. Her tits had grown larger, her hips had become fleshier, and she'd shrunk about five inches in height.

She had transformed into Teagan, and he'd come so violently he worried he had ruptured something. Afterward, he was horrified. He never, *ever* thought of Teagan when he masturbated.

But then he'd given himself a free pass. Training camp was so intense there was no time for any extracurricular activities, which meant Nick had gone without sex for thirty long days. Surely he could be forgiven for one lapse in judgment.

When he had woken up this morning, he'd felt happier than he had in weeks. He'd texted Monday—that wasn't her name, that was just the day of the week when they had sex—and they'd met in a hotel room downtown where he'd done her against the wall, on the bed, and in the shower.

He would have preferred to spend that time with Teagan, maybe take her to lunch so they could catch up. But he didn't know where she was interning because she'd never mentioned the name of the law firm.

Noticing a car pulling out just a few steps from Teagan's building, he rushed to nab the spot. Since he'd moved to Boston, he had become a pro at parallel parking. Once he had eased his SUV into the space, he jumped out and headed toward the building. He ran his fingers over the moon keychain Teagan had given him before pocketing his keys.

Although he usually took the stairs to the sixth floor, he decided to use the elevator because it would get him to her sooner. In less than a minute, he knocked on her front door, running a hand over his hair while he waited for her to answer. It had grown out a bit from the buzz cut he'd had before he left for training camp, but it was still really short.

The door opened, and he smiled, expecting to see Teagan. Instead, a tiny Indian woman stood in the doorway.

"Hi, Nick," she said softly.

She acted like they'd already met, but he'd never seen her before. Nonetheless, he knew exactly who she was because Teagan talked about her all time.

"Bebe," he returned.

She looked over her shoulder before stepping out of the

condo and pulling the door shut behind her. He moved back to give her some room, wondering what was going on.

"Before you come in, you need to know that something happened today," she said, looking up at him with solemn eyes.

His heart rate picked up. Adrenaline surged through his body, making it hard for him to speak.

"T-t-t-tell me," he finally squeezed out.

"Our boss cornered Teagan in the law library and assaulted her."

He stared at Bebe, sure he had misunderstood what she'd just said. "Assaulted h-h-h-her?" he asked, his voice hoarse. "W-w-w-what do you m-m-mean?"

She cocked her head, and he knew she wondered why he sounded like an idiot. But he didn't care. He just wanted answers.

"He didn't rape her. He just kissed her and grabbed her . . ." She gestured toward her chest.

Nick's panic morphed into rage, and his vision blurred in a haze of red. *I'm going to kill the motherfucker who dared to lay hands on Teagan when she didn't want them there. I'm going to use every bit of my strength to beat her boss to death, and when I'm finished, I'm going to piss on the corpse.*

"Nick." Bebe touched his arm to get his attention, and he flinched. "She's fine. Earlier she was ranting about castrating JD and making sure he never bothered another woman again. She's in the shower right now." She eyed him thoughtfully. "I just thought you should know."

He squeezed her shoulder, trying to show his thanks. She smiled.

"It's nice to meet you finally," she said. "But you're not as good-looking as I'd thought you'd be."

Her comment shocked a croaky laugh out of him, and he knew she was trying to defuse his murderous rage. He tilted his head toward the door.

"Inside," he demanded.

He needed to see Teagan. He needed to hear her, touch her, and make sure she really was okay.

Bebe opened the door, and he followed her inside to the living area. He was too upset to sit down, but she settled on the sofa and pulled her legs under her.

"Teagan tells me you guys have known each other for a long time."

He nodded, his gaze fixed on the hallway. He took a step that direction, but Bebe stopped him by saying, "Give her a few minutes, okay?"

He turned toward her, exhaling roughly and running his hands over his face. They shook a little bit, and he silently recited the first few lines of the Gettysburg Address to calm down. It was an old trick that usually worked to relax him, but right now it had very little impact.

"You played really well yesterday."

Dropping his hands, he stared at Bebe. Was she fucking kidding him? He couldn't think about football right now.

"Nick?"

He heard Teagan's voice from behind him, and he spun around, taking in her appearance in one quick glance. Her hair hung in wet tendrils around her face, and she wore a baggy Harvard sweatshirt over a pair of bright pink pajama pants.

They stared at each other for a heartbeat before she rushed toward him. He moved forward and caught her, pulling her tightly against him as she burst into tears.

Out of the corner of his eye, he saw Bebe jump up from the sofa. He caught her gaze, giving her a look that said, *I've got this.* She nodded her understanding.

"I'm going to run to my place and grab some clothes and stuff so I can spend the night," Bebe said as she left the room.

He rubbed Teagan's back, trying to soothe her. She cried softly, little hiccupping sobs that had him clenching his fists against her back. He *hated* that she was hurting, and he hated feeling so damn powerless to help her. In that moment, he would have done anything to make her feel better.

Walking backward to the sofa, he brought her with him. He dropped down onto the cushions and grabbed her around the waist to pull her onto his lap, tucking her head against his shoulder and draping her legs sideways across his.

"Shh," he crooned over and over while her sobs ripped out his guts.

They sat like that for a long time. Eventually, she stopped crying and swiped her eyes. The cuff of her sweatshirt fell back, revealing dark bruises around her wrist, and he tensed, instinctively knowing her asshole boss had put them there. He ran the tip of his finger over the bruises and the delicate bones of her wrist, and she sighed.

"I tried to avoid him," she said, her voice wobbly. "I made sure not to come in early or stay late. I went out of my way not to talk to him directly or call any attention to myself. I even wore ugly clothes so he wouldn't notice me."

Rage bubbled inside him. She shouldn't have had to do those things. She should have been able to go where she wanted, say what she wanted, and wear what she wanted without worrying about some fucker assaulting her.

Nick knew he wasn't a nice guy. He was a selfish, self-absorbed bastard, and he cared more about himself than anyone else.

He screwed too many women, thinking of them as pussy rather than people. But he never fucked anyone who thought of him as anything more than a convenient lay, and he didn't break their hearts or scar their souls.

He didn't hurt women, physically or emotionally. He loathed men who did.

"It's not your f-f-f-fault."

"Bebe warned me." She started to cry again. "She told me he was rapacious. That was her exact word. *Rapacious*." She sobbed harder. "And he would have raped me, Nick."

He pressed Teagan closer, nausea rising in the back of his throat at the thought of her being hurt like that. He swallowed hard, trying not to be sick.

"He would have raped me," she repeated thickly before laughing, a sound edged with hysteria. "But I was wearing too many clothes. Bebe told me to wear pantsuits. That saved me. If I had been wearing a dress, he would have raped me."

He squeezed his eyes shut, the word "rape" echoing in his head. He didn't believe in God. He didn't believe in anything, really. But just then, he sent up a silent prayer.

*Thank You for keeping her safe.*

BEFORE SHE'D SEEN NICK STANDING IN HER LIVING ROOM, TEA-gan had thought she was fine. She'd pushed the incident with JD to the back of her mind, telling herself that nothing—*nothing*—had happened.

Yes, he'd pushed her against a bookcase. Yes, he'd forced her hands over her head, gripping her wrists until she cried out. Yes, he'd kissed her, forcing his tongue into her mouth. Yes, he'd squeezed her breasts roughly. Yes, he'd shoved his hand between her legs.

But he had stopped before he'd raped her. And that was the most important thing, at least in her mind.

She had no doubt JD wouldn't have stopped if a third-year associate hadn't come into the library. He'd heard footsteps and pushed her away from him as if she were the one who had attacked him.

Nick exhaled loudly, and she nuzzled closer to him. He was so warm, and she had been so cold when she'd arrived home. Even a scalding-hot shower hadn't helped. But now she was pretty toasty.

She was slightly embarrassed she'd cried all over him, but she hadn't been able to help herself. Something had broken open when she had seen him, and all she'd wanted was his arms around her.

She had missed him so much while he'd been away at training camp. She had missed seeing him when she came home from work, and she had missed playing tourist with him on the weekends.

Teagan couldn't pretend any longer that all she felt for him was friendship. But she was smart enough to know friendship was all she was going to get from him, and that was better than nothing. It was more than most women received from him.

"You're going to be okay," he said quietly.

She nodded. The incident with JD had scared her, and she knew it wasn't something she was going to forget easily, but she *was* going to be okay. Thanks to Nick, she already felt better.

She needed to figure out what to do about JD's assault. She couldn't let him do this to another intern, but it was her word against his. And there was no DNA evidence, thank God.

She decided to postpone that decision for a while so she could enjoy Nick's embrace. It wasn't likely that she would ever have the opportunity to be so close to him again.

She closed her eyes and let his warmth soak into her, loving the feel of his strong arms around her and his hard chest against her cheek. The last thought she had before sleep claimed her was a prayer.

*Thank You for letting Nick be here to comfort me.*

## Chapter 9

"CAN I HAVE YOUR AUTOGRAPH?"

Nick looked up from his salmon to see an attractive thirty-something woman standing next to the table with pen and paper in hand. Resting his fork on his plate, he took them from her and scrawled his name.

"What about your number?" she asked with a come-hither smile—the same smile he'd seen on thousands of faces over the years.

He printed his jersey number below his name and tried to give the paper and pen back to her. Her smile widened.

"What about your phone number?"

He laughed, shaking his head. Even after all these years, he was still surprised by how shameless female fans could be. Actually, male fans could be pretty shameless, too.

"No?" she asked, eyebrows arched. She held out another scrap of paper, this one with ink already on it. "Here's mine," she offered.

When he didn't take it, she tucked it under his plate. "Just in case you want some company," she said before grabbing the pen and paper with his autograph and sauntering off.

Nick picked up his fork, ready to get back to his meal. Letty's food was better, but this salmon was still pretty good.

He looked up from his plate to find his agent staring at him from across the table, his brown eyes assessing. Elijah had scheduled the meeting weeks ago, and he'd suggested Nick meet him for dinner at his hotel.

Elijah liked to check in with him on a regular basis, and the two of them always had plenty to discuss. His agent handled almost every aspect of Nick's professional life, including contracts, endorsement deals, and even media relations. He wasn't sure how Elijah juggled it all, since he was always on the go and rarely in his office in Los Angeles.

"It looks like the women of Boston have welcomed you with open arms and legs," Elijah noted, waggling his bushy gray eyebrows.

Nick grunted. Groupies were part of pro sports. It was one of the reasons why athletes had such a high divorce rate.

He'd heard his married teammates talk about how difficult it was to be faithful to one person when faced with the constant temptation of easy women. He had no idea if they were exaggerating or not. He had never committed to one woman for more than a few hours. He'd never wanted to, and he doubted he ever would.

Elijah leaned back in his chair, slouching slightly and resting his hands on his small paunch. Nick had hired the older man just days after he'd announced his plans to participate in the NFL draft when he had been a senior at USC, and except for the O'Briens, there was no one he trusted more.

"I got a call from *People* magazine a couple of days ago. They want to feature you in their 'Sexiest Man Alive' issue. You won't be *the* Sexiest Man Alive, though, just one of them."

Nick barely stopped himself from rolling his eyes. He'd rather be articulate than sexy, though he would settle for coherent.

"They want to do an interview," Elijah continued.

Nick grimaced. He would rather have his fingernails ripped out with pliers than do a magazine interview—or any kind of interview, for that matter.

"I hope you told them n-n-n-no."

He couldn't imagine many people would find him sexy after he stuttered his way through an interview. Just the thought of it made his stomach churn.

"I told the editor that I'd ask you. Do you want to do it?"

*"Fuck, no."* He shook his head in disbelief. "W-w-w-why did you even need to ask?"

"Because a good agent doesn't assume anything about his clients, even if he's known a particular client for so long that he considers him family."

Nick smiled at Elijah's explanation. "No interviews, old man."

Elijah picked up his whiskey sour and took a few sips, allowing Nick to finish his dinner. When the server came by to remove their plates, Elijah asked to see the dessert menu.

Nick's most recent dessert craving was blueberry pie, and he blamed Letty. She had made one for him last week, and it had been so delicious he'd eaten it all in one day. Every time he had walked by the damn thing, he'd been compelled to shovel some into his mouth. It was a good thing he had worked his ass off on the field the next day.

Pulling his phone from his pocket, he sent a quick text to his talented chef: More blueberry pie please.

Elijah cleared his throat. "You like Boston?"

"Yeah." He returned his phone to his pocket. "It's okay."

When he'd been hanging out with Teagan on a regular basis, it had been better than okay. But now it kind of sucked.

Players didn't have a lot of free time during the regular football season, which meant their personal lives suffered. Nick had never really minded the time he had to commit during the season. But the grind had started to get to him because it prevented him from spending time with Teagan.

It was almost October, and he hadn't had a chance to see her more than a couple of times since the season had kicked off. She was busy with school during the day and study groups at night, and his schedule was equally demanding.

A lot of people thought being a pro athlete was easy. After all, players only had to work a few months out of the year, work was actually a game, and they got paid millions of dollars.

The average Joe didn't understand that athletes packed an entire year's worth of work into a four-month season, five if you made it to the playoffs. During the week, they spent at least ten hours a day practicing on the field, reviewing game-day video, studying playbooks, and attending team meetings.

Throughout the season, football players also worked on the

weekends. If they had an away game, they usually traveled on Friday, sometimes Saturday, and played on Sunday. If they had a home game, they were expected to rest on Saturday so they would be fresh for the game.

Nick missed talking to Teagan, and if he could speak like a normal person, he would pick up the phone and call her. But he couldn't, so he didn't.

He didn't talk on the phone unless there was no other option. He considered texting the greatest invention of all time, and he could count on both hands the number of phone calls he'd made this year.

The server dropped off the dessert menus, and Nick gave his a quick review. No blueberry pie.

"I'm hearing good things from the Colonials," Elijah said as he looked over his dessert menu. "They're thrilled with your performance on the field. They really believe you're going to take them to the Super Bowl."

"Maybe. It's too soon to tell. The d-d-d-defensive line is playing better, but it collapses w-w-w-without warning."

"They're inconsistent, that's for damn sure," Elijah said, nodding in agreement. "Do you like the coaches? Your team-mates?"

"They're okay," Nick replied, placing the menu on the table.

"Nick," Elijah sighed. "Talk to me. This is the last year you have left on your contract, and I think the Colonials are going to want to extend it. Do you want to stay here?"

Nick considered Elijah's question. There was no reason to stay in Boston. By this time next year, Teagan would be back in San Francisco. As the thought crossed his mind, he shook his head in annoyance. Where Teagan lived had absolutely nothing to do with his football career.

"I don't care w-w-w-where I play. I just w-w-w-want to play."

All he really cared about was squeezing every bit of value out of his body before it gave out on him. He figured he had two years, maybe three years left, and he needed to make all the money he could because his prospects after football weren't that great.

Most retired pro football players either became coaches or TV commentators. Neither one of those careers was an option for him.

Some players started businesses, but he didn't think that was a viable option, either. What did he know about running a business? He had a degree in history, which was pretty much useless.

Teagan, on the other hand, could run a *Fortune 500* company in her sleep. She was that smart—so much smarter than he was. And she was beautiful, too. Every time he saw her, she looked even better than the last time.

Elijah continued to talk, and Nick forcefully redirected his thoughts from Teagan. He shouldn't notice how her eyes sparkled when she was happy or the color of her lips.

"You're the best wide receiver in the NFL. Period. You don't have to play for the Colonials if you don't want to. You have options. Whatever you want, I'll make it happen."

There was nothing tying him down, keeping him in one place or beckoning him to another. There was *no one* tying him down, and Nick told himself that he was happy about that.

When he didn't reply, Elijah sighed gustily. "Fine. We can table this discussion for now. We need to talk about a couple of endorsement offers that look good."

Nick got paid a lot of money to catch footballs. But he got paid even more for allowing companies to use his face and form, along with his name, of course. Last year, his endorsement income had eclipsed thirty-three million dollars. He had deals to advertise a number of products, including deodorant, razors, socks, and sport drinks.

He wondered what else he could possibly endorse. He liked to use the products he supported, a little truth in advertising, if you will.

"Tell me about the offers," he requested.

"Trojan wants you to be the face of their new marketing campaign."

"Condoms?"

"Exactly," Elijah answered, smirking slightly.

Nick laughed. He definitely used those.

TEMPTATION CAME IN MANY FORMS, AND TEAGAN HAD A HARD time withstanding it, even when she knew better. She tried, she really did, but she and self-control were frenemies apparently.

If they were bosom buddies, she'd be twenty pounds lighter, she wouldn't have a crush on Nick Priest, and she wouldn't be standing in an antique store in Beacon Hill about to purchase a piece of expensive jewelry she'd probably only wear a couple of times.

Teagan and Bebe had made the trip from Cambridge to Beacon Hill to spend their Saturday browsing through the swanky shops and boutiques on Charles Street. Known for its ornate row houses and decorative iron work, Beacon Hill was one of Boston's smallest and most historic neighborhoods. It was dotted with perpetually burning gaslights, large trees, and flowering window boxes.

It was a perfect day to stroll along the brick sidewalks that traversed the neighborhood. The sun was shining, not a single cloud dotted the bright blue sky, and the light breeze was neither too chilly nor too warm.

Teagan loved fall in New England. Since she'd grown up in Northern California, she had never experienced a real seasonal turn until she'd moved to Boston, where the leaves glinted gold and red and the air was scented with burning wood from fireplaces.

"Which necklace do you like best?" Bebe asked.

Teagan gazed longingly at the two necklaces. They both would be a lovely addition to her vintage jewelry collection.

Grandma Vi had bequeathed her sizable jewelry collection to Teagan when she had died. They'd had a unique relationship, far closer than most grandmothers and granddaughters, and it hadn't surprised anyone when she'd gifted the collection to her.

Grandma Vi had specified her only granddaughter would receive the collection when she finished college or on her thirtieth birthday. On the day Teagan graduated from Stanford, her parents had given her the key to the safe-deposit box where the collection was stored.

When she'd first seen the jewelry, she had been stunned, and not just because it was worth millions of dollars. The real value was the history it held.

The collection included pieces from Grandma Vi's mother and grandmother. Some of them were one hundred years old, and many had been made from gold that Grandma Vi's grandfather found during the Gold Rush.

Teagan believed they belonged in a museum instead of locked away in a bank vault. Over the past several years, she'd added to the collection, although she rarely wore the pieces except for very, very special occasions.

She had been a freshman in high school when Grandma Vi had passed away, and her death had devastated Teagan. She'd spent a lot of time with her grandmother. She had loved her stories, especially those recounting how Grandma Vi and Grandpa Patrick had met and fallen in love.

Patrick O'Brien had been a real ladies' man in his day. With his dark hair and blue eyes, he could have had his pick of women. He'd passed down his good looks to his son and grandsons.

Grandma Vi, on the other hand, had been plain and unremarkable except for her big boobs (according to Grandma Vi). But she must have been more remarkable than she'd thought, because Grandpa Patrick's tomcatting ways ended the moment he clapped eyes on Grandma Vi (according to Grandpa Patrick).

Grandpa Patrick had died just a few months after Grandma Vi. He'd told Teagan that her grandmother had kept his heart warm, and that it was going to freeze up without her. To this day, Teagan believed her grandfather had died of a broken heart.

Bebe tapped the display case, drawing Teagan's attention. She tucked her memories of her grandmother and grandfather away for another time and place.

"I like this one better," her best friend said, pointing to a necklace that featured delicate silver filigree studded with amethysts of varying sizes.

Bebe's favorite wasn't too surprising, since she was partial to purple. The other necklace was a spectacular example of 1920s Art Deco design with large emerald pendants set in gold.

Teagan ran her finger across one of the round lavender-colored stones, before tracing the emeralds. She loved both necklaces, and she was having a hard time deciding which one she preferred. Maybe she should employ some self-control and walk away without whipping out her Amex.

"I don't need any more jewelry," she said, trying to talk herself out of buying anything.

"No one *needs* jewelry," Bebe replied, laughing lightly. "It's a treat."

Teagan disagreed. A treat would be spending the day with Nick, taking a leisurely drive through the countryside and stopping at a historic inn for dinner. A better treat would be ending the day with him in her bed, her hands gripping his tight behind as he moved inside her.

She shook her head in exasperation, fighting the urge to fan herself. She had it bad for Nick Priest.

*Really bad.*

Teagan was almost glad they were both too busy to see each other as much as they had during the summer. The more time she spent with him, the more she wanted him, even though she knew there was no chance of getting what she wanted.

And that was a good thing because she knew she wouldn't be able to handle Nick or his lifestyle. No matter where he went or what he did, he attracted women.

They stared at him with covetous, avaricious eyes. They propositioned him when Teagan stood right next to him. Usually he didn't notice the attention, and when he did, he ignored it . . . for the most part.

Teagan knew Nick's status as a pro athlete was part of his appeal. But even if he were an IRS agent or a trash collector, women would ogle him and try to get him into their beds.

If and when Nick decided to have a relationship, the woman he chose would have to be completely sure of her appeal so she didn't feel threatened. Of course, she'd probably be a famous model, so that wouldn't be a problem.

Teagan, meanwhile, did not possess the amount of confidence necessary to combat jealously and insecurity. Growing up, she'd been an ugly duckling in a family full of swans. Her mother was a cool blond beauty, while her father was a strikingly handsome man.

And if she evaluated Quinn and Cal objectively instead of through the lens of a little sister, she had to admit both of them were gorgeous—tall, dark, and handsome. Like Nick, they were head turners, and women were eager to drop their panties for them.

Teagan knew she'd outgrown her ugly duckling stage. But

it had lasted for so long that it still influenced the way she viewed herself.

She'd been in middle school when she had first realized she lacked the good looks the rest of her family had in abundance. When she'd lamented the fact to Grandma Vi, the older woman had reassured Teagan.

"Honey, you've got the O'Brien genes, don't you worry," she'd said. "You just need to grow into them. One day, men are going to walk into walls when they get a look at you."

So far, no man had been so intent on eyeballing Teagan that he'd crashed and burned, and she doubted that day would ever come. But Grandma Vi hadn't been completely wrong. Teagan *had* grown into her looks.

She'd learned to tame her thick, wavy hair, her skin had cleared up, and her braces were a long-ago memory. The extra weight she'd carried around her middle had shifted to her breasts and her hips, although her stomach was never going to be flat, and her thighs were never going to be trim.

Teagan knew she was reasonably attractive, but she wasn't stunning, not like the rest of her family. And she definitely wasn't on the same level as Nick and the women he dated casually—the women he touched intimately with those big, strong hands.

She was ashamed to admit she'd Googled Nick when she should have been studying. She'd spent hours reviewing photos of him online, paying particular attention to those that showed him with women. Unlike her brothers, who apparently liked variety, Nick had an obvious type: very tall, very blond, and very skinny.

*The exact opposite of me.*

Teagan sighed, disgusted with herself for wanting to be Nick's type. She needed therapy. *Retail* therapy.

"I'll take both necklaces."

## Chapter 10

"ARE YOU ALMOST FINISHED?" NICK GROWLED, PACING AROUND the kitchen in his condo.

"Yes, master—I mean, Nick," Letty replied.

He glared at her, and she shot him a saucy grin before picking up a stack of aluminum food containers. She took her time arranging them in the large wicker picnic basket sitting on the granite island, and he fought the urge to demand that she hurry up.

He double-checked the time on his phone. He didn't want to be late picking up Teagan. He had a bye week, which meant no game, and they were going sailing.

Although he never made plans with Teagan in advance, he hadn't wanted to miss the opportunity to spend his one free Saturday with her, so he'd texted her earlier in the week to make sure she was available. The last couple of times he'd stopped by her condo, she hadn't been there, and he hadn't seen her in almost a month.

Crossing his arms over his chest, he tapped his foot impatiently as Letty grabbed a couple of cold packs from the freezer. She placed them carefully around the food before adding some cloth napkins, melamine plates, and utensils.

"Teagan must be really special," Letty said.

*Yes, she's special. She's unlike any other woman I know. She's smart and funny and interesting. And I love her laugh.*

"Sailing is the perfect date," Letty continued. "It's fun and romantic. And I made a feast for you two, lots of finger foods so you can feed each other tidbits. Hubba hubba."

He stared at her. This wasn't a date. Where the *hell* had she gotten that idea?

Letty opened the fridge and pulled out two bottles. After wrapping them both in dishtowels, she placed them in the basket before closing the lid and fastening the latch.

"I thought chardonnay would be best for the meal, but I also packed a bottle of champagne if you really want to get in the mood," she added with a big smile. "I included a corkscrew, too."

He slapped his palms on the island in front of Letty, glowering at her. Her eyebrows shot up at his aggressive stance.

"I'm going sailing w-w-w-with Teagan."

"I know," she replied, her brow wrinkling in confusion.

"You know she's just a friend," he said, his voice hard. "This isn't a d-d-d-date."

Letty cocked her head and pursed her lips. "I think it's time for you to admit that you feel more than friendship for Teagan."

He immediately wanted to refute her claim, but he had to wait for his mouth to catch up. "N-n-n-no, I don't."

Teagan was his friend—nothing more. He was a guy, and it was perfectly natural for him to notice she was attractive. As long as he didn't act on it, it was not a problem.

*Not. A. Problem.*

"Nick, you're forgetting that I was here, working late, the night you found out her boss had attacked her. When you got home, you were a *mess*. You wouldn't have been that upset if you didn't care about her."

Nick made a sound of frustration. He hated to think about that night . . . hated to think about anyone hurting Teagan.

"Of course I w-w-w-was upset. She's like f-f-f-family."

Letty leaned against the island. She stared at him for several moments before patting the top of his hand.

"You're going to be late for your nondate. Get going."

He nodded, relieved to put an end to the pointless and stupid conversation. Hefting the picnic basket, he rushed out of his condo and made the haul to Cambridge in record time.

He was busy looking for a parking space when he saw Teagan exit the building. She hurried toward his SUV, and he put it in park so he could get out and open the door for her. Before he could unbuckle his seatbelt, she opened the passenger door and jumped in.

He turned toward her, intending to say hello, and she leaned over at the same time. Her lips grazed his—soft, smooth, and luscious—before she gasped and jerked away.

Clenching his fists on the steering wheel, he fought the desire to cup his hand around her head and pull her mouth back to his. His lips tingled, and he tasted peppermint when he licked them.

She touched her fingers to her mouth briefly before dropping her hand to her lap. Her eyes were wide, and the look on her face could only be described as horrified.

If he'd ever wondered how Teagan would react if he pushed the boundaries of their friendship, he now had his answer. He told himself he didn't care because there were thousands of women who wanted to kiss him.

*That's right—thousands.*

"I'm sorry! I was aiming for your cheek!" she exclaimed, talking so fast her words almost tripped over each other. "I was t-t-t-trying to ki-ki-kiss your cheek like I always d-d-do!"

He stared at her, feeling as if he'd been thrust into a weird alternate reality. For a moment, she had sounded just like him.

He could tell that Teagan was appalled by their almost kiss, but he didn't want the whole day to be ruined. He needed this time with her. It was hard not to see her for weeks and weeks, and this outing was going to have to sustain him for a while.

"Go ahead." He turned his head and pointed to his cheek. "P-p-p-plant one on me."

Laughing softly, she leaned over and dropped a quick peck on his cheek. She drew back, grabbing the seat belt and clicking it in place.

"Let's go. I love to sail. I've been looking forward to it all week."

He'd been looking forward to something all week, too: seeing her. He didn't give a flying fuck about sailing. Still, he was glad they were doing something she would enjoy.

Shifting the Escalade into drive, he headed toward the marina at a moderate speed. Now that Teagan was here with him, there was no need to rush.

After several minutes of silence, he glanced toward her as she stared out the window, tapping her lips with the tips of her fingers. He wondered why she wasn't talking. Whenever they drove somewhere, she usually chattered the whole way.

"T," he said, just to get her attention.

He'd fallen into the habit of calling her by her first initial, just like her brothers.

*But you're not her brother,* a little voice inside him whispered.

He sure as hell didn't need the reminder. He and his cock were well aware of that fact.

Dropping her hand, she shifted in the seat so she could look at him. "I talked to my mom last night. I told her we were going sailing, and she told me to say hi and give you a hug for her."

Nick smiled. Kate was a hugger. In fact, all the O'Briens were huggers. It was how they said hello, good-bye, and almost everything in between.

Teagan continued, "She's renovating the kitchen, and I swear she spent forty-five minutes telling me about her new cabinets. She's decided to go with a color called 'fresh sage,' which is basically light green. I asked if she was sure that green cabinets were a good idea, and she told me that I'm not adventurous enough."

He chuckled. "Go on," he prompted.

"I told her that I'm adventurous where it matters: the bedroom."

He jerked his head toward her, certain she hadn't said what he thought he'd heard. Her blue eyes held a wicked little glint, and her glossy lips tipped up at the corners.

"You did not."

He couldn't tell if she was joking, but it didn't really matter. Her words had already sunk into his head and settled into his groin.

"I did, too," she replied, nodding emphatically.

"And?"

"After a few moments, during which I envisioned her mouth opening and closing like a pet goldfish, she said, 'Good. I'm glad to hear it.'"

He guffawed. Teagan's laughter joined his, and the sound of it filled his chest until he felt weightless. Just like an astronaut floating in space.

"I THINK I'M IN LOVE," TEAGAN SAID.

Nick choked, spewing a mouthful of chardonnay across the table. He hastily deposited his wineglass beside his plate and grabbed his napkin, pressing it to his mouth. As he fell into a coughing fit, Teagan reached over to pat his back.

Had he choked because of what she'd said? If so, she was definitely offended. Was it really so hard for him to imagine her in a romantic relationship? Just because she hadn't been on a date in a while didn't mean she was a loser in the romance department.

*Did it?*

She promised herself then and there she would start dating again, even if it meant she had to be the pursuer. The men in Cambridge better watch out.

After a few moments, Nick stopped coughing and dropped back against the striped seat cushions that ran along the sides of the boat. He cleared his throat loudly and inhaled.

"W-w-w . . ." He stopped and cleared his throat again. "With?"

"Letty, of course."

"Letty," he echoed.

Teagan nodded. "I've never had such delicious food. Not even at the best five-star restaurants. If she were here, I'd have to kiss her."

Nick stared at her. There was a glint in his eyes she'd never seen before, one that made her stomach feel shaky, although she didn't know why exactly.

She turned her head to gaze around the boat. When Nick had mentioned sailing, she had envisioned a smaller vessel. Apparently, he didn't do small, because the boat was at least one hundred feet in length and so luxurious it deserved the description "yacht." In addition to the open deck, it had a saloon, a covered dining area, and a private sleeping compartment.

For a moment, Teagan let her imagination run wild. If she and Nick were lovers, they would have devoured Letty's delicious food and then retreated to the bedroom to devour each other.

They would have popped open the champagne Letty had included, and Teagan would have poured it on Nick's chest, letting it pool in his navel. She would have sipped the liquid from his well-defined pecs and sucked the remaining droplets from his flat brown nipples before licking her way down his chest to nibble his hard abs . . .

"More wine, miss?"

She looked up, her fantasy dissolving as the steward came into focus. *Boo. I hadn't reached the best part yet.*

"Yes, thank you."

She and Nick sat in the deck's open dining area, which was shaded by the yacht's second level. The bench seats were designed in an L-shape, and a table was bolted to the floor in front of them. He had claimed the short side of the L while she sat on the other. They were close enough that their legs and feet touched under the table.

She could barely withstand the temptation to drop her hand under the table and place it on his upper thigh. If they had been lovers, she would have bypassed his leg and gone right for his crotch, maybe even sliding down his zipper and easing her hand inside to stroke his penis.

The thought made her antsy, and she accidentally bumped his knee for the tenth time. When she shifted to give him more room, she knocked over his wineglass. He wasn't able to slide from the banquet seat fast enough to avoid it, and the golden liquid splashed into his lap.

With a gasp, she grabbed her napkin. "I'm sorry!" she exclaimed, dabbing wine from his crotch. His flat-front khaki pants were soaked, like he hadn't made it to the restroom in time.

"I'm so clumsy," she babbled as she continued to rub vigorously at the wet spot. "I have been my whole life. You've probably noticed. I think Quinn and Cal got all the hand-eye coordination."

His hand shot out and gripped her wrist. She looked up into his green eyes, which seemed to glow against his bronzed skin. Very slowly, very deliberately, he removed her hand from his lap and placed it on the table. Holding his napkin against his crotch, he scooted out from behind the table and stood up.

"Maybe there's a hair dryer around here, and you can use it to dry your pants . . ."

He stalked into the saloon, presumably to track down the steward, and she collapsed against the cushions, covering her face with her hands.

Why did she always humiliate herself around Nick Priest? Was it some kind of cosmic law that she had to look and act like an idiot in front of him?

Wasn't this morning's accidental kiss enough embarrassment for one day? She cringed at the memory of how stupid she'd acted in the SUV. Their lips had barely touched, and she had totally overreacted. She'd been so worried that Nick would think she had done it on purpose, that he would somehow figure out that friendship was only a small part of what she felt for him.

She *never* wanted him to know. He'd feel sorry for her, maybe even pat her on the head like a lovesick puppy, and never want to hang out with her again.

*Gah!* She had regressed into a teenage girl.

Teagan grabbed her wineglass and took a huge gulp before tilting her head back and draining it. Then she rose, put on her sunglasses and floppy hat, and headed toward the bow of the boat.

Leaning against the rail, she tried to lose herself in the beauty of the open water. It was a lovely day for a sail. The sky was clear, and it had warmed up enough for her to remove her lightweight jacket.

She had been so excited when Nick had asked her to go sailing. She knew he had limited free time during the season, and she'd been flattered that he wanted to spend one of his days off with her.

She'd told him that she had been looking forward to it all week, but she had purposely made it sound as if she had been excited about sailing. The truth was she'd been looking forward to spending time with him. She didn't care what they did as long as they were together.

Being with Nick always made her feel good, but it also was

a little unsatisfying. It was like having a gourmet meal but being denied dessert.

Teagan got most of Nick, but not all of him. She knew the minute he dropped her off at her condo, he'd be on his phone with one of his harem to schedule a time and a place to meet for some hot sex.

She tried not to think about it, and most of the time, she was successful. But sometimes, when she felt especially wistful, she let herself think about what it would be like if she got to have her dessert and eat it, too.

Footsteps sounded behind her, and a moment later, Nick joined her at the rail. She peeked at his crotch to see if he'd been able to dry his pants, but he had untucked his shirt, and she couldn't tell without being obvious that she was looking.

She glanced up, hoping he hadn't caught her staring. Mirrored aviator sunglasses covered his eyes, and he held two huge chocolate sugar cookies. He passed one to her along with a paper napkin, and she studied the large sugar crystals sprinkled on top of it.

Most people preferred plain sugar cookies or chocolate chip, if given the choice, but they didn't know what they were missing. Homemade chocolate sugar cookies were similar to Oreos, without the cream filling, and they were soft and delicious.

"Did you ask Letty to make my favorite cookie?"

He nodded, leaning his hip against the rail so he could face her. The sun shone on his blond hair, and it looked as if he had a halo around his head.

*Behold the angel Nick Priest.*

"How did you know they're my favorite?"

Shrugging, he took a big bite of his cookie. She did the same, moaning a little when the rich cocoa flavor hit her tongue. She wished broccoli tasted that good.

As she chewed, she wondered when she had mentioned that chocolate sugar cookies were her favorite. Because Nick was so quiet, she had way too much opportunity to prattle on and on about stupid subjects. At one time or another, she'd probably blurted out her favorite brand of tampons, and he had likely committed that fact to memory as well.

Nick was so different from most guys she knew. He paid attention.

"You're not a normal guy."

"Excuse me?" he replied, his dark gold eyebrows arching above his sunglasses.

"Except for you, I truly believe all men have attention deficit disorder, even my dad."

He barked out a laugh. "Oh, yeah?"

She frowned. He thought she was joking, but she wasn't. Unlike other men, Nick listened to her with complete and total focus. He never seemed to tune her out the way Jason always had.

Her ex-boyfriend had liked to talk about the things that were important to him, but he'd never shown much interest in the things she cared about. She hadn't realized how self-absorbed he was until they'd broken up. Spending time with Nick reinforced the fact that Jason had been an ass.

"I'm serious," she insisted. "Men don't listen when women talk. Jason didn't listen to me. He didn't care about what I had to say or what I thought."

Nick's laughter abruptly stopped. Moving closer, he swiped his thumb across the corner of her mouth, brushing cookie crumbs away. The touch of his finger against her lips sent a tingle down her spine.

"He's an idiot."

"For not listening to me?" She laughed mirthlessly. "Or for not wanting to be with me?"

"Both."

# Chapter 11

NICK'S PHONE BUZZED WITH A TEXT MESSAGE. AFTER PULLING on his T-shirt, he grabbed the phone from his open locker before sitting down on one of the wooden benches in the Colonials' training room.

He'd run routes for five exhausting hours, and he was eager to head home. He was starving, and Letty had promised lasagna.

The text was from Teagan: Free for some Friday night fun?

It was the first time he had heard from her since he'd dropped her off at her condo after they had gone sailing nearly a month ago. The Colonials were playing at home on Sunday, so he was free to hang out with her if he wanted to.

"Hey, Priest, what's up?"

He looked up, seeking the source of the question. He zeroed in on Andy Duncan, a rookie running back who could tear through 300-pound linebackers as if they were made of paper.

"Did you get some good news?" Duncan asked, pointing to Nick's phone. "You got a goofy smile on your face, dude."

He shook his head, and the other man gave him an assessing glance before sitting down next to him on the bench. With his bright red hair and freckles, Duncan was a grown-up version of the kid on the cover of *MAD magazine*. He was cocky, and he liked to run his mouth, but damned if Nick didn't like him anyway.

"Then why are you smiling?"

*Because Teagan wants to spend time with me.*

"It's a chick, right?" Duncan asked, slugging him on the shoulder with his meaty fist. "Is she hot?"

*Hell, yes, Teagan is hot. So hot I nearly combust when I'm near her.*

"Does she have big tits or tiny, bite-sized ones?" Duncan continued, bringing his hands toward his chest to outline a woman's figure. "What about her ass? I love a woman with a soft, pillowy ass."

Nick squeezed his eyes shut, trying not to think about Teagan's luscious breasts and her round ass. Wasn't it bad enough he dreamed about them?

"Have you fucked her yet? Is she a screamer?"

He stood abruptly and shoved his phone in the front pocket of his Rileys. He couldn't listen to this anymore.

Grabbing his gym bag, he said good-bye to Duncan by slapping him on the back of the head and made the trek to his Escalade. Nick popped the locks, threw his bag in the back, and jumped in the driver's seat. But instead of starting the SUV right away, he leaned his head back against the headrest and closed his eyes.

He wasn't sure it was a good idea to hang out with Teagan anymore. They always had a good time when they were together, but it was getting harder and harder for him to keep his hands to himself.

He'd told Letty all he felt for Teagan was friendship. But that was a lie. A huge, giant whopper.

He wanted Teagan—wanted her more than he'd ever wanted a woman. Part of it had to be the fact that she was forbidden fruit.

If she weren't his best friend's sister and his friend, too, he would have done anything and everything he could to get inside her pants. If she were anyone else, he would have fucked her nine ways to Sunday by now.

He had been fighting his desire for Teagan for months. At first, he'd tried to deny it, and when he couldn't do that any longer, he'd tried to ignore it.

But ignoring it only worked for so long, and at that point, he'd pushed the desire down deep, determined never to act on it. That didn't stop his subconscious from dreaming about her almost every night, though. He regularly woke up with an erection so hard it could cut diamonds, and she was the one he thought about when he pleasured himself.

*I'm teetering on the edge of fucking disaster.*

He groaned, recalling their sailing trip. She hadn't even noticed what her touch had done to him—more proof she saw him as a friend and nothing more. And even if Teagan *were* interested in getting naked with him, it would be a huge mistake for them to get involved. She had "relationship" written all over her. Hell, it was practically tattooed on her forehead.

She was made for marriage, babies, white picket fences, and minivans, and he wasn't cut out for that kind of life. Other men might want those things, but he didn't.

All the experts said communication was the key to long, satisfying relationships, and he could barely speak. He couldn't imagine any woman who would be willing to put up with a guy who was minimally coherent under the best circumstances and completely mute under the worst circumstances.

His stuttering doomed his chances for normal relationships. It had ruined the most important relationship in his life—the one with his father—and it would ruin any romantic relationships, too.

He'd spent twenty years and hundreds of thousands of dollars on speech therapy, and his stutter was still classified as severe. He had learned techniques to work around it, and more important, he'd learned tricks to hide it from even the most observant person.

Normal people had no idea how horrible it was to stutter. They just opened their mouths and words came out. They didn't know what it was like to want to speak but not be able to do so.

Stuttering was emotionally and socially debilitating. It obliterated self-esteem and corroded self-value because no one liked to talk to a stutterer. It was painful to hear and painful to see. People became impatient waiting on words to come out, so they just interrupted or talked over you. Some even walked away, regretting that they'd engaged you in conversation in the first place.

But that wasn't the worst of it. The worst was that people

associated the ability to speak with intelligence, and more often than not, they treated stutterers like idiots.

Nick had been the object of pity and ridicule for most of his childhood. When he'd turned fourteen, though, three things had happened to change his life.

The first thing was a blank slate. His father accepted a tenured position at Syracuse, and they moved away from the place where everyone knew Nick and his stuttering. He was able to start fresh as a no one from nowhere.

The second thing was a trick. By the time they moved, Nick had learned to hide his stutter, so the other kids never noticed his speech impediment. The teachers, meanwhile, were happy to have a quiet student who didn't cause trouble.

The third thing was football. When he enrolled in high school in Syracuse, his dad forced him to try out for every sport. He excelled at football, and his dad made it clear that football was Nick's only chance for a decent life.

Football had given him purpose. It had given him a way to make a living without having to talk. And it had given him more money than he'd ever dreamed of.

But it hadn't solved everything. Nick still stuttered—and he still tried to hide it.

Frankly, it was a miracle he had any friends. If he put his hands on Teagan, eventually he would mess up the friendship he had with her, and in doing so, he would risk his friendship with the rest of her family. The O'Briens were pretty much the only people who cared about him, and the thought of losing them made him break out in a cold sweat.

He pulled his phone from his pocket and typed a reply to Teagan: Sorry. Busy. He placed his finger on the Send button but pulled back before pressing it.

Shouldn't he at least find out what kind of fun she had in mind?


"SORRY IT TOOK ME SO LONG," BEBE SAID AS SHE ENTERED TEAgan's condo. "The food wasn't ready when I got there."

Teagan grabbed the brown paper bag from Bebe's arms so her best friend could remove her jacket. "Thanks for picking it up."

Taking a deep breath, she pulled in the spicy scent of Indian food. Her stomach rumbled loudly.

"No problem, *kanya*," Bebe replied as they headed to the kitchen.

Although she'd grown up in the United States, Bebe spoke several languages that were native to India, and she often called Teagan *kanya*, which meant "girl" in Hindi. It was the way she showed affection.

Teagan pulled two plates from the cabinet while Bebe gathered silverware from the drawer. She opened the bag, removed the takeout containers, and began to dish up the food.

"I'm starving," Bebe announced. "Don't be selfish with the tandoori chicken."

"You said you didn't want any."

"I changed my mind," Bebe replied, narrowing her eyes. "Don't make me hurt you."

Teagan laughed. Despite her small stature, Bebe *could* hurt someone. She was a master at Muay Thai kickboxing.

"Wine or something else?"

Bebe gave her a look that said, *Do you even need to ask?* Smiling, Teagan pulled a bottle of Riesling from the fridge. It would complement the spicy food better than one of the red wines she had on hand.

The two of them had to make a couple of trips to the living room to transfer food and wine, but eventually they got settled on puffy pillows on either side of the coffee table. Bebe raised her wineglass.

"To the end of yet another round of exams."

"Hear, hear," Teagan said, clicking her glass against Bebe's and taking a sip of wine.

"How do you think you did?"

"I'm sure I'll get A's on every exam because I had a really smart study partner," she answered, winking at Bebe.

"My study partner is smarter than your study partner."

Teagan laughed, raising her glass to the other woman. Bebe would deny it, but she had a cheerleader personality. Her "You can do it, I know you can" attitude was the reason why Teagan hadn't dropped out their first semester.

She owed a lot to Bebe, and she was going to miss her when they graduated. Her best friend had her heart set on working for one of the big biotechnology companies, so she'd probably stay in the Boston area.

Teagan's phone dinged, and she vaulted to her feet to get it. She was anxious to see if Nick would accept her invitation. She thought she'd left her phone in the kitchen, but it wasn't there, so she hurried to her home office, the only other place it could be. It was on her desk, and she lunged for it.

She exhaled noisily when she saw the message was from Marshall Brants. He wanted to confirm their date on Saturday night, and she quickly responded before heading back to the living room. She plopped down on her pillow, and Bebe shot her an inquiring glance.

"It was Marshall," she said, answering Bebe's unspoken question.

Marshall was in the same joint program she and Bebe were in, but this was his first year at Harvard. They'd met in the common area in the business building.

Since she had promised herself that she would start dating again, she'd said yes when he had asked if she wanted to meet him for coffee. Their mini-date had gone well, and later that day, he had called to ask her out to dinner. Since then, they'd gone out a few times.

"He seems nice," Bebe noted. "And he's really good-looking."

Teagan nodded. "He *is* nice."

Marshall was from Houston, and he was friendly and outgoing. He was thirty years old and had undergraduate degrees in chemistry and geology.

"And you're right, he is good-looking."

Marshall was a couple of inches over six feet with a fit physique from all the cycling he did in his free time. His dark brown hair was thick, and his brown eyes reminded her of bittersweet chocolate.

"He's not as good-looking as Nick Priest," Bebe pointed out.

Teagan snorted. "No one is as good-looking as Nick Priest."

Bebe gave her an appraising glance. "Tell me again why you're going out with Marshall."

She sighed. They'd had this conversation before, but Bebe was like a dog with a bone.

"Because I'm a single female looking for male companionship."

"That sounds like an ad for a gigolo."

"That's not a bad idea." She snickered. "Maybe I should post something online."

"Seriously, Teagan, why are you going out with Marshall when you really want Nick?"

"To quote the Rolling Stones, 'You can't always get what you want.'"

Bebe cocked her head. "Why not?"

Teagan blew out her breath in frustration. "Bebe! I don't want to talk about this again."

"I'm just trying to understand why you would waste your time with another guy when you could be with the one you really want."

"A starving man doesn't bypass a ham sandwich just because he would prefer prime rib."

Bebe's eyebrows shot up. "So you're the starving man, Marshall is the ham sandwich, and Nick is the prime rib. Do I have that right?"

"Yes."

"So what you're really saying is you're just going to take what you can get instead of going after what you really want."

Teagan huffed in exasperation. "It's not about what I want. It's about Nick, and what he wants and doesn't want. He wants to be friends. He doesn't want me *like that*, and I'd rather be his friend than nothing at all. Why is that so hard to understand?"

Bebe took a big swallow of her wine before carefully returning the glass to the coffee table. She pressed her lips together, and Teagan feared her best friend was about to let loose with a lecture.

"Because you're making an assumption. You don't know for sure."

Teagan snorted. "We've been hanging out for months, *months*, and he's never once indicated he's interested."

"I think Nick is more than interested, Teagan. I think he has feelings for you."

"*What?* Why would you say that? You've only met him one time."

"Because of the way he reacted when he found out that JD assaulted you."

Teagan frowned. *JD. What an asshole.*

Teagan had reported JD's assault to the Boston police. She also had notified Harvard and encouraged the university to sever all ties with Price, Latham & Donaldson. And finally, she had filed a formal complaint with the law firm's HR department. She'd done all she could to prevent JD from ever hurting another woman again.

Bebe continued, "When I told Nick what happened, the look on his face was scary. If JD had been within touching distance, I think he would have killed him."

Teagan nodded. "He's very protective of me," she agreed. "I think he sees himself as a big brother, since Quinn and Cal aren't here."

Bebe shook her head stubbornly. "He cares about you."

"I have no doubt that he cares about me. He's an honorary member of the O'Brien family, and he cares about all of us."

Bebe threw up her hands. "Fine! Have it your way. Nick Priest considers you a friend and nothing more. In fact, he thinks of you as an annoying little sister and not a woman at all. Does that make you happy?"

Teagan stared at Bebe. "No," she admitted. "It doesn't."

Bebe nodded. "Of course it doesn't." Her lips curled in a small smile. "You know, there's a very simple way to find out if I'm right. You can say: 'I want to put my hands all over your body. Take off your clothes.' And if Nick rips off his shirt, you'll have your answer."

"Oh, my God!" Teagan exclaimed, laughing incredulously. "You know you would never in a million years have the guts to say that to a guy, and you're suggesting that I do it? You are crazy, Bindu Banerjee."

Bebe grinned. "Go for the prime rib, *kanya*."

# Chapter 12

NICK SIPPED HIS HOT CIDER, ENJOYING THE CRISP SWEETNESS of apples and the warm bite of cinnamon against his tongue. Next to him, Teagan stumbled a bit on the uneven sidewalk, and he grabbed her arm with his free hand.

"Hold on to me," he ordered.

"I should have worn tennis shoes," she said as she linked her arm though his and wrapped her hand around his forearm. "I don't know what I was thinking. Stupid."

They were strolling through the streets of historic Salem, Massachusetts, site of the infamous witch trials. Teagan had arranged for them to participate in a candlelit walking tour of haunted houses and locations, and tennis shoes definitely would have been more practical.

But he wasn't going to complain about her tight jeans and her high-heeled knee boots, not when she looked so damn good in them. She'd paired them with a cropped brown leather jacket, and he was grateful it hid the shape of her breasts, or he'd be fighting the urge to ogle those, too.

"It's much colder than I thought it would be," Teagan said, shivering a little. "I should have worn a heavier jacket."

They had been walking for a while, and they'd already visited several buildings, including the Old Salem Prison. Now they were heading toward the Old Salem Burying Point, America's second oldest cemetery. Nick was interested to hear about the cemetery's inhabitants, particularly Colonel John Hathorne, the notorious Hanging Judge of the witch trials.

"Brrr." She shivered again and burrowed closer to him. "You need to share some of your body heat."

He bit back a groan as he thought about how he'd like to share his body heat, his bare skin sliding against hers, his cock moving deep inside her. She might be cold, but he was burning up.

He *never* should have accepted her invitation. He'd been an idiot to think he had enough self-control to withstand the temptation of Teagan.

He was so angry with Teagan, with himself, with the world. Why couldn't she be ugly and unattractive? Why couldn't he find her repulsive? Why couldn't she be a stranger whom he could fuck without worrying how it would mess up his life?

*Why? Why? Why?*

He didn't want to stop spending time with Teagan. He had more fun with her than he'd ever had with anyone else, and that included her brothers. In fact, she'd edged out Quinn for the title of best friend.

Despite the sharp edge of lust he felt when he was with Teagan, he was more relaxed and comfortable with her than he was with anyone else. He didn't feel pressure to talk, which helped his stuttering, and when he did speak, she understood him like no one else ever had.

She made him laugh. She made him think. She made him hard.

*And that's the problem.*

He took a deep breath, the smell of burning leaves and smoking chimneys filling his lungs. Maybe he was overreacting.

He doubted he'd be able to spend any time with Teagan over the next couple of months, since the Colonials were playing well and the pressure was on to make the playoffs. Plus, she'd be heading home for Thanksgiving in less than two weeks and then gone again for winter break, which lasted from mid-December to mid-January.

By then, he probably would have moved past this unfortunate attraction he had for her. He would probably laugh when he thought about how worked up he'd been over a girl he had known for more than a decade.

"If I had lived here in the 1690s, I think I would have been hanged as a witch," Teagan said.

Startled, Nick turned his head to look at her. The streets were lit with old-fashioned lanterns, but he couldn't see her expression.

"Because?"

"Because I'm trouble, you know that," she joked, nudging her hip against him.

*And truer words have never been spoken.*

"Seriously, I have no doubt I would have done something to draw attention to myself, not on purpose, of course. Maybe I would have laughed too loudly or I would have bent the rules a little. And that would have been it."

Nick pondered her statement. If anything, her looks would have drawn attention. He'd read that some of the women who'd been accused of witchcraft had been singled out because they had filled men around them with evil, impure thoughts. In other words, they'd incited lust.

Since Teagan incited lust in him, Nick could imagine she would have done the same thing to men in the seventeenth century. They wouldn't have been able to resist the lure of her smoky eyes and luscious lips.

"You, on the other hand, probably would have been seen as an angel. People would have thought God himself had sent you from Heaven."

Her words shocked a laugh out of him. "Angel?" he repeated.

"They would have been blinded by your handsomeness," she teased. "They never would have guessed your angelic looks hide a sinner."

Teagan's voice had turned husky when she'd said "sinner," making the fine hairs on the back of his neck stand up. *Is she flirting with me?*

He stared at her, wishing he could see her face. She joked and teased, but she never flirted.

*Am I imagining things? Is it just wishful thinking?*

She was right, though: he *was* a sinner. And he wanted to sin with her—on top of her, behind her, and inside her.

They reached the cemetery, and the guide spent a few minutes telling the group about Colonel John Hathorne. During the trials, Hathorne had taken on the role of a prosecutor rather than an impartial judge. His questioning had always begun with a presumption of guilt rather than innocence, and he had appeared to be on the side of the accusers.

"What a jerk," Teagan muttered. "Guess he never heard of judicial bias."

Nick laughed softly. She was adorable.

"I'll never understand how people can just stand by and let bad things happen," she added.

Unfortunately, Nick had personal experience with "bystander syndrome." He'd been bullied because of his stuttering, and the other kids had stood by and watched because they didn't want to draw the attention of the bullies.

It was a sad fact of life that bullying occurred everywhere from school yards to corporate America. And obviously, it wasn't new. The Salem witch trials were proof of that.

The guide finished his spiel and encouraged them to explore the cemetery on their own for a few minutes before meeting back at the entrance. He handed out tapered candles and passed around a lighter.

Nick set his cider on one of the headstones and lit his candle before taking care of Teagan's. The candle bathed her face in light, making her creamy skin glow and her blue eyes shine.

"Ready to explore?" she asked.

Oh, yeah, he was ready to explore. But not a moldy old cemetery . . .

"Let's go this way," she suggested, pointing to a path on their right.

With a nod, he grabbed his cider. He didn't want to be accused of littering a graveyard, for God's sake.

"I'm going to break my ankle," Teagan predicted direly, curling her arm tightly around his. "I'm too klutzy to be poking around a cemetery in the dark."

They stuck to the path and eventually came upon a headstone that was easily four times larger than the others. Teagan dropped his arm and stepped forward to run her fingers over the dates engraved on the stone.

"Twins," she murmured. "They were only two years old when they died. How sad. I wonder what happened."

She turned to face him. As she stepped forward, her heel

got caught on a loose piece of stone. She stumbled, dropping her candle as she tried to keep herself from falling.

He threw down his candle and cider to catch her. Grabbing her by the waist, he hauled her against his chest to steady her. She laughed breathlessly, and the sound rasped over his senses to settle in his groin.

Needing to put some space between them, he stepped away from her. His foot sank into a depression in the ground, and he stumbled backward, pulling her with him as he fell.

He landed with a thud on his back with Teagan sprawled on top of him. He lay there for a moment, his arms wrapped tightly around her waist and her hair covering his face. He got a whiff of vanilla and mint from the silky strands before blowing them away from his lips.

She squirmed, and he loosened his arms. Pressing her hands against his chest, she tried to push herself up, but she couldn't get purchase. She shifted, digging her knee into his thigh only an inch or so from his balls.

"Stop," he growled, swatting her hard on the ass.

Teagan jerked against him but stilled. After a moment, she scooted down his body like a caterpillar until her legs straddled his waist. She sat up, her ass nestled against his cock. He'd already been revved up before she had fallen on him, and now he was fully erect.

She was trembling, and he settled his hands on her hips, digging his fingers into her jeans. Could she feel his hard-on?

It was completely dark without the candles, so he couldn't see her face. But he could hear her, and after a couple of seconds, he realized she was laughing softly.

He stared up at the stars. Maybe it was his imagination, but they seemed to be winking at him.

"I warned you this would happen," she choked out between giggles.

*I wish someone had warned me about you.*

TEAGAN SHIFTED ON TOP OF NICK'S STRONG BODY, AND HIS erection pressed against her. Even through their jeans, he was long and hard, and she widened her legs to settle more fully against him.

She thought about the conversation she'd had with Bebe. She would never get a better opportunity to find out if Nick was interested in her as more than a friend. His erection suggested that might be the case.

The thought made her breathless. She sucked in a lungful of cold air, providing some much-needed oxygen to her brain.

"Nick, do you have an erection?"

He tensed but didn't answer her. She wiggled backward so his erection was situated more toward her center than her butt, and he groaned.

"Do you?" she persisted.

"Yes," he answered, his voice hoarse.

"Is it for me?"

She could hear his breathing in the dark, but she couldn't see his face. She wiggled again, a little shimmy, and he hissed something inaudible.

His hands clenched her hips hard before sliding toward her behind. He pressed her more firmly to him, and she rocked against his hardness. It felt so good she did it again, and he raised his hips to meet her.

"Is it for me?" she repeated when he didn't answer.

He cleared his throat. "No," he replied finally. "It's just"—he hummed a little—"biology."

Disappointment flooded her, along with a hefty dose of embarrassment. Of course his erection wasn't for *her*. Any normal man would get hard when a female body was plastered against his crotch.

She swung her leg over his body to kneel beside him. He sat up, and she could feel his breath against her face, scented with apple cider.

Teagan wanted to lean over and press her mouth against his. She wanted to lick his lips and suck on his tongue. But she knew he didn't want that. If he did, he would have rolled her beneath him and put his hands and mouth all over her.

Nick stood up, grabbed her hands, and pulled her to her feet. They were so close the front of her jacket touched his, and she battled the urge to lean against him.

"I'm sorry," she said.

She was always apologizing to him for doing or saying

something stupid. But this was it. She wasn't going to spend any more time with him. She was only torturing herself.

"Are you okay?" she asked. "Fans would put a hit out on me if you were hurt and unable to play."

"Not hurt," he muttered, dropping her hands.

She looked around, trying to spot the candles. The moon provided a little bit of illumination, but only enough to discern large shapes.

"Do you know where we are? How to get back to the entrance?"

She gave him a moment to answer. When he didn't, she continued.

"Do you have a secret superhero ability that allows you to see in the dark? I wish I had one that would make me disappear."

He laughed softly, his breath stirring her hair. Her knitted cap had gone missing in the kerfuffle.

He found her elbow in the dark and turned her in the opposite direction. He clasped her hand, linking his fingers through hers, and tugged her along with him as he moved forward. Apparently, he wasn't lost and blind like she was.

She sighed, quite disheartened by the way the evening had disintegrated. She'd put a lot of thought into planning something fun, and she had been thrilled when Nick had accepted her invitation.

She wished now that she'd never come up with the idea to visit Salem or, at the very least, that she had been smart enough to wear sensible shoes. But she had wanted to look good for Nick. She had wanted to look sexy, and sensible shoes were the opposite of sexy.

When they'd first started hanging out, she hadn't put a lot of thought into what she wore when she was with him. Now she spent hours agonizing over her clothes and shoes, her hair, even her scented body lotion.

After a few minutes of wandering the cemetery, they met up with another couple from the group who still had their candles, and the four of them made their way to the entrance. The guide clapped his hands.

"Fabulous! Our stragglers made it back safe and sound.

Let's get going. Our last stop is the tercentennial memorial for the witch trial victims."

The group made its way to the memorial, which was located next to the cemetery. She and Nick walked side by side, their hands entwined as if they were a couple.

The memorial and the surrounding area were flooded with light, and the two of them read over the names of the people who'd been hanged. Nick pointed out several names on the memorial, and Teagan stepped closer to read them.

"I didn't know men were accused of witchcraft and hanged. I thought it was only women. The townspeople clearly believed in gender equality," she noted dryly. "They were equal-opportunity fanatics."

Nick chuckled, and she wondered if he laughed with any of the women he had sex with. She wondered if he even *liked* them.

The thought made her sad and angry, and she wanted nothing more than to go back to her condo so she could cry and throw things, maybe at the same time. She let go of his hand and turned to face him.

"Ready to go?" she asked.

He stared at her for a moment before smoothing his hand over her hair. Easing his fingers into the strands, he lightly stroked the back of her head.

"Lost your hat."

She shrugged. "I have others."

He found a tight muscle at the base of her skull and pressed his thumb against it, rubbing gently. Moaning a little, she dropped her head against his chest.

"That feels so good," she mumbled into the front of his bomber jacket, letting her mind wander as he continued his massage. "I'm too tense. Maybe I should have sex with Marshall. He could probably get me off at least a couple of times if I helped."

Nick stopped abruptly, and she moaned in protest. He slipped his other hand into her hair until he cupped her head in both palms. He tilted her face until she stared into his eyes.

"Who's Marshall?"

For a few seconds, his question didn't register. When it did, she gasped and jerked away from him. He didn't have time to untangle her hair from his fingers, and he tore several strands from her scalp.

"Oww," she yelped, tears springing to her eyes.

His eyes widened, and he hastily unwound his fingers from her hair. They stared at each other for several moments before she found her voice.

"How do you know about Marshall?" she asked tremulously.

She was very afraid she already knew the answer. He cocked his head, his dark blond eyebrows arched over his green eyes.

"Please tell me I didn't say that stuff out loud." She cleared her throat. "Did I?"

He nodded. She groaned and covered her face with her hands.

*I must have a virus, a horrible virus that causes my brain to misfire. And it's fatal. It kills by humiliation.*

"I want to go home now," she said, dropping her hands.

He shook his head. "Tell me about Marshall."

Turning on her heel, she started toward the sidewalk as fast as her high-heeled boots would take her. Nick caught up with her in two strides, grabbing her arm and pulling her around to face him.

"Tell me."

"It's none of your business," she snapped, shaking off his hand.

His eyes narrowed. He moved closer, sliding his fingers into one of the belt loops on her jeans to tug her toward him.

"Now," he demanded, his voice hard.

She huffed in frustration. Why was he so interested? She knew he wasn't jealous. Did he feel obligated to vet her dates since her brothers weren't around to protect her?

"He's just a guy I've been dating."

He frowned. "How long?"

"A few weeks."

He clenched his jaw, and she wondered what he was thinking. She placed her hand on his chest and looked up at him.

"Nick, I know you think you have to play big brother, since Quinn and Cal aren't here, but you don't need to worry." She patted his chest. "Marshall's a nice guy. You'd like him. He's from Texas, and he loves football. He's a big fan of yours."

He jerked his fingers from her belt loop and stepped away from her. Propping his hands on his hips, he looked up. She followed his gaze, wondering why they were staring into the night sky. After a long moment, he sighed and dropped his hands to his sides.

Meeting her gaze, he tilted his head toward the sidewalk. "Let's go."

He started toward the lot where they'd parked the Escalade, and she trailed after him. The sidewalk wasn't well lit, and she stumbled, cursing under her breath.

*I'm going to burn these boots when I get home.*

Nick turned and hurried back to her side. Taking her hand, he curled it over his arm.

"Can't let you fall," he said, looking down at her.

It was too late. She'd already fallen.

*Hard.*

## Chapter 13

CHIPS AND GUACAMOLE. *CHECK*. CHICKEN WINGS. *CHECK*. VEG-
etables for the ridiculous people who came to a Super Bowl
party and expected to eat healthy. *Check*.

Teagan shifted the football-shaped plates and napkins
closer to the end of the dining room table to make room for the
brownies and cupcakes she'd made this morning. She had
been too excited to sleep, and she'd jumped out of bed at six
and started to bake.

She'd used a football-shaped cookie cutter on the brownies
and piped white icing on them in the outline of football laces. She
had decorated the cupcakes with green icing and green coconut
to mimic grass before topping them with little plastic footballs.
The treats were super cute, and she was quite proud of herself.

Bebe came to stand beside Teagan, holding trays in both
hands. She handed Teagan the tray with the cheese and fruit
and held up one covered with meatballs.

"Where do you want these?" Bebe asked.

"Anywhere you can find room," Teagan answered as she
deposited her tray on the table.

Bebe nodded, squeezing the meatball tray next to the salsa.
Teagan stepped back from the table to give it one final look and
tweaked the banner that read "Super Bowl: The Big Game."

"You went to a lot of trouble to make this party perfect," Bebe mused. "At the very least Nick should have agreed to stop by. Oh, wait, he can't. He's busy . . . in Miami."

Teagan scowled at Bebe. "Very funny."

Nick was in Miami because he'd taken the Boston Colonials all the way to the Super Bowl. In less than thirty minutes, he would be playing for the Lombardi Trophy.

Bostonians were in a frenzy because it was the first time their football team had made it to the Super Bowl in several years. Nick was their hero, for today at least. Tomorrow he might be the most despised man in the city.

"You need to relax, *kanya*."

"I can't. I'm too excited."

"I know. You've been excited since Nick showed up on your doorstep last summer."

"Shut up."

Bebe laughed. "You have no sense of humor where Nick is concerned."

"A sense of humor?" Teagan repeated. "What is there to laugh about?"

"Oh, I thought it was pretty funny that you accidentally kissed him, spilled wine on his lap, and tripped him in a graveyard. Not to mention closing your scarf in the door of his SUV and almost hanging yourself when he dropped you off." She arched a dark eyebrow. "Were you trying to reenact a scene from the Salem witch trials since you'd just been there?"

"Bebe," Teagan groaned. "Please, please, don't remind me."

Her best friend, the wretch, giggled. "Tell me again what he said."

"No."

"Come on," Bebe cajoled. "I love it when you say it out loud."

"No."

"I'll help you with your org behavior project if you say it."

Teagan eyed the other woman. Her organizational behavior project was going to be a *bitch* to complete, and she'd love to have Bebe's help.

"He said: 'Hanging is too good for you.'"

Bebe convulsed into laughter. "He's right," she said between giggles.

The expression on Nick's face had been a combination of

incredulity, exasperation, and laughter. Teagan wished that, just once, he would be the one who was embarrassed in front of her.

"Why are we still talking about this when it happened months ago?"

"Because it's hilarious. *Hilarious*."

"A true friend wouldn't find such joy in my misfortune."

"Then I'm definitely not your true friend because I do find joy in your misfortune," Bebe quipped. "And speaking of misfortune, I wish I had been there to see Nick's face when you had your mental lapse."

"Mental lapse? It was like my brain imploded."

She placed her palms against her hot cheeks. She was still embarrassed she'd blurted out such private thoughts about Marshall, and it was even worse that Nick had been the one to hear them.

Bebe leaned her hip against the table and crossed her arms. Thin gold rings covered her slender fingers, kind of like a fortune teller. Teagan didn't know why her best friend wore them, but she knew they had some kind of special meaning to her.

"Why do you think you're such a hot mess around Nick? Does he make you nervous?"

Teagan considered Bebe's question. She felt a mix of emotions when she was with Nick, but nervous usually was not one of them.

"Actually, I think it's the opposite. I'm too comfortable around him, so I don't watch what I'm doing or where I'm going or what I'm saying. It's like I forget everything, and I'm just there, in the moment, with Nick."

"Have you heard from him today?"

She nodded. She'd sent Nick a text earlier this morning: Good luck. I'm cheering for you. A few minutes later, she had received his reply: Are you wearing my jersey?

Nick had sent her an official Boston Colonials jersey with his name and number on it for Christmas. It had been waiting for it under the tree at her parents' house when she'd flown home to San Francisco.

The jersey had been a surprise, but it wasn't the first time Nick had bought something for her. After their trip to Salem, he had sent her a knitted cap to replace the one she'd lost.

That one had been light pink, but he'd sent her a cap that was a deep bluish-purple, similar to the color of delphiniums. He had included a note: *Matches your eyes.* After she'd read it, she had hugged it and the cap to her chest, just like a love-struck teen.

*I'm pathetic.*

She hadn't seen Nick since their trip to Salem, which had been in mid-November. She'd texted him a couple of times to wish him a Happy Thanksgiving and to thank him for the jersey.

She had also texted him to wish him luck for all his playoff games. He'd responded every time but with short answers—exactly the way he talked.

Earlier today, she'd asked Bebe to take a picture of her wearing the jersey, and she had sent it to Nick. In reply, he'd texted: Looks good.

He was lying. It was too long and baggy, but she loved it because he'd given it to her. Sometimes she even slept in it.

*I'm pathetic.*

A knock sounded on her front door. Her guests had arrived.

"Party time," Teagan announced, heading toward the door.

"How many people are you expecting?" Bebe asked, trailing after her.

"Thirty or so."

"I'm going to run to the bathroom before everyone gets here," Bebe said.

Teagan nodded and went to welcome her first guest. It was Marshall, and when he saw that no one else was around, he backed her against the wall in the foyer and kissed her until they were both breathless.

He pulled back and met her eyes. "Hi."

She smiled. "Hi."

She and Marshall had been dating for nearly four months. They weren't exclusive, although she wasn't dating anyone else, and neither was he. He'd dropped hints that he wanted them to be, but she had ignored them.

They weren't having sex, either. They kissed, and she allowed him to cop a feel every now and then, but he hadn't put his mouth anywhere other than her lips nor had his hands strayed below her waist.

It wasn't because she was a good girl. It was because she refused to have sex with one man while she was in love with another.

She was in love with Nick Priest. A man who would never love her back. A man who'd never had a relationship with a woman based on anything other than sex.

She'd downplayed her feelings for him as a crush because that had made it easier to pretend they would go away. But they hadn't gone away.

What had started out as friendship and a little bit of lust had turned into something deep and intense. When she was with him, she felt like she mattered—like her thoughts and her feelings were important. She had never felt that way before.

But she knew loving Nick would bring her nothing but heartache, and that was why she continued to date Marshall. She wanted to give herself a chance to fall in love with someone who would love her back. Someone who could commit.

She wasn't in any hurry to get married and start a family, but she wanted those things eventually. Marshall was a good man, and she could tell he'd be a good husband and father.

Marshall bent down to kiss her again. He was a good kisser with firm lips and nice technique, and it was no hardship to spend a few minutes with his mouth on hers. He curled his hands around her hips and pulled her closer until his erection pressed against her stomach. She drew back, and he groaned.

"What am I doing wrong, honey?"

"Nothing." She stared into his dark brown eyes. "You're not doing anything wrong."

*You're just the wrong man.*

"Then why did you pull away?" he asked, his voice filled with concern and confusion.

"We're not alone. Bebe's in the bathroom."

It was the truth, but it also was an excuse. For some reason, she had no problem kissing Marshall, but the moment she noticed he had an erection, she felt like she was cheating on Nick.

It was ridiculous because she and Nick weren't a couple. They were friends. And she had no doubt that Nick had an active sex life. He wasn't thinking about her when he was with other women.

Another knock sounded, and she moved to open the door. Marshall stopped her and pointed to his crotch, where an erection tented his khakis.

"I need a place to hide out for a few minutes."

She smiled. It might make her feel guilty, but it also was nice to know at least one man got an erection because of *her* and not just simple *biology*.

"Down the hall. My bedroom's on the left, study on the right."

He gave her a quick kiss before jogging toward the hallway. Bebe peeked her head around the bathroom door.

"All clear?"

Teagan laughed and waved her into the room before opening the door to let in a group of people she and Bebe knew from school. Within minutes, her condo was packed with people wearing Colonials gear. The big-screen TV was on but muted until the game started so people could chat while they filled their plates with party food.

Marshall made sure everyone had drinks, and when she caught his eye from across the room, she mouthed, "Thank you." He winked at her, and in return she gave him a big smile.

"You're leading him on, *kanya*."

The smile slipped from her face. She turned to face Bebe.

"I'm not," she protested. "I really like him."

"I know you do. But as long as Nick is in your life, there's no room for anyone else."

Teagan worried that Bebe was right. Nick filled her mind, whether she was awake or asleep, and her heart overflowed with love for him.

"You think I need to cut Nick completely out of my life?"

The thought of it made her chest tight. But then she reminded herself it was inevitable. She was moving back to San Francisco when she graduated in four months, and his life was wherever football took him.

Bebe hesitated, but before she could answer Teagan's question, someone yelled out the game was starting. Teagan rushed to the living area to turn on the volume.

Four hours later, the party had quieted down. Everyone was focused on the television because the Colonials were down by three points with only thirty-five seconds left in the game.

The Colonials quarterback tried to run the ball on the first down, but the opposing team stopped the running back from gaining any yards. The quarterback was sacked on the second down.

It wasn't looking good for the Colonials, and Teagan wondered what Nick felt in that exact moment. Even though she knew it was foolish, she closed her eyes and sent him a message with her heart: *I'm with you no matter if you win or lose.*

The teams lined up for the third down, and the center snapped the football to the quarterback. The quarterback let loose with a long spiral intended for Nick, but it was obvious that he'd overshot it. The ball was too high.

Teagan held her breath as Nick jumped, his arm reaching toward the sky, his right hand outstretched. The ball ricocheted off his fingers, and it hurtled toward the ground until he scooped it from the air with his left hand. He pulled it down toward his side and landed with a slight stumble right in the middle of the end zone.

Touchdown Colonials!

Teagan pressed her fingers against her mouth, tears springing to her eyes. The man she loved had just won his first Super Bowl.

She wished she was there so she could . . . do what exactly? Hug him and pretend that all she felt was friendship? Watch him celebrate by drinking too much and then stand by and smile as he took a strange woman back to his hotel room to screw her?

She'd fallen in love with Nick Priest, and it was the stupidest thing she had ever done.

# Chapter 14

"PRIEST, YOU ARE A FUCKING *GOD*," QUINN PROCLAIMED, SLAPping Nick on the back and giving him a one-armed hug.

"Agreed," Cal said and duplicated Quinn's actions when his brother stepped away.

Nick laughed at their exuberance. He'd invited Quinn and Cal to Miami to attend the Super Bowl and, depending on the outcome of the game, help him celebrate a win or mourn a loss.

He hadn't seen the brothers since he'd moved to Boston, and he was excited to hang out with them. The three of them planned to have a few drinks in the hotel bar before stopping by a couple of parties. Tomorrow morning, they'd probably wake up with pain in their heads and strange women in their beds.

The bar was closed to the public for exclusive team use, and the three of them settled into one of the circular booths in the corner. The server came by a minute later to take their order, and once she'd left, Nick slouched against the booth.

He was still hyped up from the game, but he also was exhausted. The season was over. His team had won it all, and he'd caught the winning touchdown. He couldn't believe it. It was something every pro football player dreamed of . . . the pinnacle of success.

For a heartbeat, when the ball had bounced off his fingers,

he'd been sure it was over. He still didn't know how he had caught it as it had plummeted toward the turf. It had been a once-in-a-lifetime kind of catch.

The server delivered their beers, and he took a swallow of his Blue Moon. He'd had a few beers in his suite, and he already had a nice buzz going on.

He usually avoided over-imbibing because a few of his Denver teammates had told him he talked a lot when he was drunk. No one mentioned his stutter, and he figured that was because they expected a drunk to trip over his words. But tonight he was with friends, and he didn't have to be so careful.

A group of women walked by, all hotter than hell. They wore short dresses and stilettos, and he enjoyed the view along with Quinn and Cal.

"The women in Miami are so . . ." Cal hesitated, clearly trying to find the right word. "Fuckable," he concluded.

Nick laughed. They were indeed.

"Did you see that tall redhead?" Cal asked, nudging Quinn's arm.

"I'm not a fan of redheads," Quinn responded, his lip curling with distaste. "They're pale and freckly."

"You don't know what you're missing," Cal said, waggling his eyebrows. "They've got freckles in some very interesting places."

"I'll take your word for it," Quinn replied dryly before turning to Nick and holding up his beer bottle. "To an incredible catch."

Cal raised his bottle. "To an incredible catch," he repeated.

The three of them tapped their bottles. Nick laughed and shook his head.

"I still can't believe I caught that goddamn ball."

"Neither can I," Quinn stated emphatically. "It's going to go down in the history books as the most amazing catch ever made in a Super Bowl game. I guarantee it."

"How do you feel now that you've won your first Super Bowl?" Cal asked, sounding remarkably like a sports reporter.

"Might be the only one."

"Bullshit," Quinn countered. "You're at the top of your game."

Nick smiled. He felt pretty amazing. The only thing that would make him happier was if Teagan were there to celebrate with him.

The smile slid from his face. *Teagan.*

He was supposed to be over her by now. He hadn't seen her in months, but apparently the phrase "out of sight, out of mind" didn't apply to her.

Today, the thought of Teagan had prevented his humiliation in front of the whole world. He had tried to make his way off the field as soon as the game ended, knowing he'd be swarmed with people, but a cute little blond reporter from ESPN had caught him right before he'd reached the tunnel.

Shoving a mic in his face, she'd asked: "How do you feel about winning the Super Bowl your first season with the Colonials?"

As he had stared into the unblinking black eye of the camera, he'd thought about Teagan. He'd imagined they were eating take-out in her condo, and she'd asked him how his day had been. He pretended that he was talking to her, and by some miracle, he managed to squeeze out "Good" without stuttering.

After that, he'd practically sprinted back to the locker room. He had skipped the post-game press conference, and he knew everyone would have plenty to say about that. The media would probably blast him, and fans would think he was an asshole.

He had already been fined by the NFL commissioner for not attending the pre-Super Bowl media events. All team members were required to attend at least one pregame press conference or pay a hefty fine. But Nick was more than happy to pay it as long as he didn't have to open his mouth in public.

"Did your dad come to the game?" Quinn asked.

"He said he w-w-w-was going to. Haven't seen him, though."

Nick shrugged, trying not to show how much it hurt that his only living parent couldn't bother to show up for the single most important game of his pro career. He hadn't received a text or a phone call from his dad to congratulate him on the win, either.

He'd called Simon after the Colonials had won the division playoffs. The conversation had been awkward even though he used all of his speech techniques to avoid stuttering as much as possible.

He had offered to send his dad a ticket to the Super Bowl, and Simon had agreed to attend. But he'd warned Nick that he couldn't stay in Miami to visit, since he had to catch a plane to

Abu Dhabi for an economic summit. Apparently, he'd decided to bypass the game and go directly to the conference.

Nick didn't want to talk about his dad anymore, so he directed his attention back to Quinn and Cal. He was eager to catch up on their lives.

"Anything new?" he asked.

"I bought a house," Quinn replied. "It's a big Victorian in Laurel Heights."

"W-w-w-with your trust fund?" Nick queried, smirking a little.

He loved to rag the O'Brien boys about their cushy, trust-fund lifestyle. But it *was* a joke because they were two of the hardest-working men he knew.

"Priest, you don't have any room to talk. Your bank account has more zeroes than mine," Quinn said. "But my dick is still bigger."

Nick chuckled, ignoring the slur. He didn't have any insecurities about the size of his penis or what he could do with it.

"I w-w-w-work for my money," he reminded them.

"You call strutting around with no shirt for a deodorant commercial 'work'?" Quinn sneered. Cal laughed and fist-bumped his brother.

"Are you living in the house?" Nick asked Cal. The brothers had lived together in a condo in San Francisco's Cow Hollow neighborhood for the past several years.

"*Hell, no.* You know Quinn is a slob. I couldn't handle his mess anymore."

They had finished their beers and ordered another round. Nick spotted several of his teammates in the bar, and all of them were just as buzzed as he was. Some were already plastered.

"What are you going to do now that you've won the big game?" Quinn asked.

"Relax."

"So you're going to have sex," Cal quipped. "That's how I relax."

Cal's comment made him think about Teagan and her claim that she was too tense. He ground his teeth, wondering if she had gone ahead with her plans to have sex with Marshall, the nice guy from Texas who loved football.

When she had told him she'd been dating Marshall, a wave

of jealously unlike any he'd ever felt had crashed over him, and he had acted like a caveman. It was irrational, but he hated to think of her with another man.

He hated to think of someone else finding pleasure inside her luscious body. He knew he couldn't touch her, but he didn't want anyone else to, either.

"What's the matter, Priest?" Cal asked. "You have a weird look on your face."

Nick stared at him, wondering what Cal would do if Nick admitted he wanted to have sex with Teagan. He imagined Cal would smash his beer bottle over Nick's head before trying to gut him with the broken glass.

And when Cal was done with him, Quinn would step in. Nick winced at the thought because the older O'Brien brother had an upper cut to rival Mike Tyson.

"He's probably thinking about a woman he'd like to have sex with," Quinn said. "Am I right?"

Nick jerked toward Quinn, who had a speculative glint in his blue eyes. They looked so much like Teagan's he had a hard time tearing his gaze from them.

"No," he answered, lying straight to their faces.

There was a woman: their little sister. Their beautiful, brainy, fuckable little sister.

"There's always a woman, Priest," Cal scoffed. "You're a dog."

Yeah, he was a dog. But he had managed to keep his hands off Teagan, even when she'd sat right on top of his dick. True, he hadn't been able to resist a tiny bump and grind, but ultimately he had held on to his self-control.

Obviously, he'd lied when he had told her that his erection wasn't for her. But he couldn't risk losing her friendship and the friendship of the rest of her family.

Nick had considered the situation from every angle, and he'd had a breakthrough while eating a piece of Letty's chocolate cake. She had told him that she'd had to make two cakes because she had messed up the icing for the first one. Apparently, the bad icing had soaked the cake, making the entire dessert inedible.

As he'd sat there enjoying devil's food cake with cherry vanilla icing, he had realized the situation with Teagan was just like Letty's ruined dessert. The cake was his friendship with Teagan and her family, and the icing was sex with Teagan.

Cake was better with icing, but there was always a chance the icing would turn rancid, ruining the cake, too. And Nick would rather eat cake with no icing than not have any dessert at all.

His phone buzzed in his pocket, and he fished it out to read the text. It was from Teagan. I'm so proud of you!! Come see me when you get home.

He closed the screen and placed his phone facedown on the table. He wanted nothing more than to see her. He'd been tempted to send her a ticket so she could be there with him, but ultimately decided not to because she was too much of a distraction. And he didn't want to explain to her brothers why he wanted her there.

He didn't understand it himself. He didn't *want* to want Teagan, and he knew they couldn't be together, yet he couldn't stay away from her. And it drove him crazy that she saw him as a surrogate big brother.

"One of your women?" Cal asked, arching an eyebrow toward Nick's phone.

Nick shook his head. "Your sister."

*Who definitely is* not *one of my "women."*

Quinn took a long pull on his beer before placing it between his palms. Rolling it back and forth, he stared at Nick.

"Do you see Teagan very often?" Quinn asked.

"No."

It wasn't a lie, not exactly. The word "very" was subjective.

Nick didn't want Quinn and Cal to know just how much time he spent with their sister, although he had no reason to feel guilty. Not really.

But they were smart guys, and they would find it strange that Nick chose to hang out with Teagan when he could be with other women—women he could fuck and forget.

"Have you met this guy Marshall?" Cal asked.

Nick shook his head. He was afraid of what he'd do if he ever came face-to-face with the man Teagan was dating.

"Maybe you should check him out," Quinn suggested. "That's what we'd do if we lived in Boston."

Somehow Nick resisted the urge to bang his head against the

table. Apparently, Teagan wasn't the only person in the O'Brien family who thought he should play the role of big brother.

"She's *not* my sister," he growled.

Cal's eyes narrowed. "That's true. But you can watch out for her . . . make sure he's a decent guy. Although I personally think she's way too smart to get involved with an asshole."

Nick's phone buzzed again, and he grabbed it before Quinn or Cal could. They were nosy bastards.

It was another text from Teagan. You're going to have to sign my jersey when you get back. It will be a collector's item!

He laughed quietly. It was nice to think he'd be remembered in history books even if it was just for catching a football.

Another text popped up, also from Teagan. It will be so valuable I won't be able to sleep in it anymore!

*She sleeps in my jersey?*

He groaned under his breath. He knew what he was going to dream about tonight.

# Chapter 15

NICK CHECKED HIS PHONE AGAIN, WONDERING WHY TEAGAN hadn't texted him back. He'd sent her messages for a couple of days with no reply. He didn't think he'd done anything to make her angry, so why was she ignoring him? He didn't know if he should be pissed or worried.

He pulled open the door to Teagan's building, relieved to escape the bitter cold. Boston was in the throes of a winter storm, which wasn't unusual for mid-February. It was so frigid ice crystals had formed in the corners of his eyes as he'd made the short walk from his Escalade to her building.

Joe, the part-time concierge, came around his reception desk to greet Nick. A huge smile covered his face, and his bald head gleamed under the overhead lights.

"Mr. Priest," he exclaimed, grabbing Nick's right hand and pumping it enthusiastically. "Congratulations on winning the Super Bowl. You've made us proud!"

He smiled, returning the man's handshake. Joe had always been very accommodating, letting him come in and out of the building without checking in even though visitors were supposed to be monitored.

"I haven't seen Miss O'Brien for a couple of days," Joe said. "I'm not sure she's home."

Nick frowned, wondering where Teagan could be. It was the middle of the semester, and she had classes to attend.

Nodding his thanks to Joe, he headed toward the elevators. He'd returned from Miami a little more than a week ago. The city of Boston had thrown a big parade to celebrate the Colonials' win, and since then, he'd tried to lie low.

It was always awkward when fans approached him. He was happy to sign autographs and pose for pictures, but all too often they wanted to talk with him. He knew they thought he was rude when he didn't respond to their questions, and it was better to avoid those situations altogether.

He had wanted to see Teagan as soon as he had arrived in Boston, and he'd been patient as long as he could. He had waited and waited for her to respond to his texts, and finally he'd decided to just drop in on her. He'd made up his mind to wait if she wasn't home because it had been way too damn long since he had seen her.

Once he reached the sixth floor, he made his way to her condo and knocked loudly on the door. He pressed his ear to it, trying to determine if anyone moved around inside the unit.

He heard nothing but silence, so he banged on the door with the end of his fist instead of his knuckles. He kept at it for a minute or so, but dropped his hand when the door stayed stubbornly closed. Resting his hands on his hips, he looked up at the ceiling, trying to control the desire to pound on the door with both fists.

*Where the hell is Teagan?*

Grabbing his phone from the pocket of his jeans, he opened the text screen. He furiously typed a message to Quinn. Maybe her older brother knew where she was.

Just as he finished the message and hit the Send button, Teagan's door swung open. Looking up, he saw her leaning against the door frame. Her fuzzy green robe hung open over a pair of cream-colored flannel pajamas printed with tiny pink flowers, and thick gray socks covered her feet.

Her hair was pulled back haphazardly, and it was dull instead of shiny like usual. Her face was flushed, her eyes were red-rimmed and watery, and her nose was pink and raw-looking.

She clutched a box of tissues in the crook of her arm, and except for a cough syrup commercial on TV, he'd never seen anyone look so sick and pathetic. He stepped forward, and she held out her hand like a traffic cop.

"Nick," she croaked. "You need to stay away. I don't want to make you sick."

"Flu?"

"I think so. Everyone at school seems to have it."

Raising her arm, she coughed into her elbow, a hoarse, hacking noise that made him wince. She sounded horrible.

"You should go. I'm a human petri dish." She pulled a tissue from the box and wiped her nose. "I'll text you when I'm better, and we can go to a hockey game or something."

He studied her as she swayed a little on her feet. He didn't want to leave her like this. What if she needed something? She was too sick to go out in this kind of weather.

"Do you have medicine? Food?"

She pressed her lips together, and he noticed they were chapped. She was a mess.

"I'm okay," she replied, which didn't answer his question.

He suspected she was lying just so he'd leave. She clearly didn't want company.

She sneezed into her tissue before letting out a tired sigh. "See you later," she said and then closed the door in his face.

He stood there for a moment, staring at the door, before sending a text to Quinn to let him know he'd located Teagan. Next he scrolled through his contacts, found Letty's name, and fired off a text to her asking what kind of supplies he should buy for Teagan.

Ten minutes later, he stood in the cold and flu aisle of the closest grocery store. Apparently the whole damn city was sick, because it was almost cleaned out.

He checked Letty's list and grabbed some ibuprofen and acetaminophen from the shelf, along with some cough syrup and a decongestant she had recommended. He added some Vicks VapoRub, cough drops, lip balm, and a heating pad before heading to the grocery section.

He didn't know what Teagan had stocked in the condo, so he filled the cart with all kinds of food, including ready-made soup, crackers, and juice. He grabbed a six-pack of beer for himself and headed to the checkout.

On the way there, he passed by the floral department and

saw a sign that read "Don't forget Valentine's Day" and a countdown board that showed there was only one day left. He stopped and looked around, surprised he hadn't noticed all the roses and balloons when he'd walked in.

He wondered if Teagan had made plans with Marshall to celebrate the most romantic day of the year, and he was ashamed when he realized he was glad she was too sick to go out with the other man.

*I'm a selfish bastard.*

Pushing his cart closer to one of the displays, he picked up a fluffy white teddy bear. The stuffed animal held a red velvet heart with "Adore Me" embroidered on it, and its fur was really soft.

He tossed the bear into his cart and evaluated the roses. He reached for a bouquet of red roses before jerking his hand back. Even he knew red roses meant passion. He looked around, trying to find a bouquet of yellow roses for friendship but didn't see any. Guess no one bought yellow roses for Valentine's Day.

Standing with his hands on his hips, he considered his other color choices: pink or lavender. The pink roses were pretty. They reminded him of Teagan's lips. But he really liked the lavender roses better.

He picked up a bouquet and read the label, which told him that lavender roses meant enchantment. He laughed softly, shaking his head.

*Who comes up with this bullshit?*

TEAGAN ROLLED OVER, MOANING AS PAIN SHOT THROUGH HER head. She could barely think it hurt so badly. And she was cold, so cold her bones ached. She felt so awful she wanted to cry, but she didn't have the energy. She coughed and was startled by how awful it sounded.

She heard a rustle and froze. *Is someone in my bedroom?* The lamp on the bedside table flared to life, and she gasped when she saw Nick standing next to her bed.

"What are you doing here?" she asked, her voice so hoarse it was barely audible.

She struggled to sit up, and he bent down to help her, holding her up with one hand while he arranged her pillows behind her with the other. As he removed his hand, she fell back against the pillows.

Reaching out, he pressed four tablets of varying colors and sizes into her hand. She stared at the drugs, her mind foggy.

"Take them, T," he directed, plucking a glass of water from the nightstand.

She tossed the pills into her mouth, and he held the glass to her lips, tipping it to give her the water she needed to wash them down. Her throat was so sore she had a hard time swallowing.

Returning the glass to the nightstand, he picked up a bottle of cough syrup and a spoon she hadn't even noticed. He poured some of the dark liquid into the spoon, bringing it to her lips. Like a child, she opened her mouth wide, and he poured in the medicine.

She shuddered at the taste, smacking her lips, and his mouth quirked. He deposited the bottle and spoon on the table and sat down on the edge of the bed. He stared at her, his green eyes roaming over her face, and she was so miserable she didn't even care he was seeing her at her absolute worst. She cleared her throat, wincing at how scratchy it was.

His eyes narrowed, and he pulled a cough drop from his shirt pocket and handed it to her. She unwrapped it and popped it into her mouth, letting it soothe the dry achiness.

"How did you get in?" she asked when her throat could handle words.

"Joe."

Joe could have lost his job for letting Nick into her condo. She imagined he must have been pretty persuasive to get the concierge to break the rules.

"What did you bribe him with?"

Nick smiled. "Season tickets. Fifty-yard line."

She shivered, feeling like she might throw up at any moment. He frowned and stood up.

"Blankets?"

She pointed to her closet before scooting down against the pillows. She had never been so sick, not even when she was a little girl. She didn't know why Nick had decided to come back, but she was grateful because she really needed someone to take care of her. Closing her eyes, she drifted away.

The room was dark when she woke up, the red numbers of her alarm clock reading 4:23 a.m. She was lying on her side with blankets piled over her. A heating pad was on top of them, taking the chill away. She desperately needed to go to the bathroom, but she didn't want to get out of bed. Finally, she pushed back the covers and sat up.

"Oh," she exclaimed as the cold air seeped through her pajamas.

"Okay?" Nick asked, his voice coming out of the dark.

She jumped, startled because she had thought he'd left hours ago. She reached over and turned on the lamp.

Nick slouched in the overstuffed chair situated in the far corner of her bedroom. A blue blanket draped across his muscular torso and long legs, and his blond hair stuck up. His eyes were sleepy, and gold stubble shadowed his lower jaw.

She sighed, feeling more pathetic than ever. She'd fantasized about Nick being in her bedroom, and he was actually there . . . when she had the flu.

"T," he said, a question in his voice.

"Bathroom," she croaked.

He sat up, pushing aside the blanket, and started to rise. He obviously intended to help her to the bathroom.

"No!" she exclaimed as loudly as her broken voice would allow. "I don't need help."

He eyed her before standing and leaving the room. She exhaled in relief, grateful he'd realized she needed some privacy. She trudged to the bathroom, which was attached to her bedroom. By the time she'd finished her business, she was so exhausted and dizzy she could barely move.

She stumbled into her bedroom to find Nick standing by the bed. He propped the pillows against the headboard and pulled the covers back so she could climb in. Once she was settled, he handed her a steaming mug.

"What is this?"

"Tea. Lemon. Honey."

Bending down, he stuck a thermometer in her mouth and placed his hand against her forehead before moving his arm until the inside of his wrist rested against it. When the thermometer beeped, he snatched it from her mouth, and she caught a glimpse of the digital display: 103.9.

He stared at the thermometer, his eyes widening with alarm. "*Shit*," he swore fiercely, grabbing a bottle from the nightstand and shaking a couple of pills into his hand.

He held them out to her, and she took them with the tea, hoping the hot liquid would not only soothe her throat but also stay in her stomach. The heat hurt her lips, which were cracked from fever and dehydration, and she ran her tongue over them.

He sat down next to her, pushing her hair away from her face before cupping his palm around her cheek. She turned into it, relishing the feel of his cool fingers against her hot skin.

"You are *really* sick. Should w-w-w-we go t-t-t-to the ER?"

She cocked her head. Why was he talking like that? He sounded weird. He looked weird, too, like a wavy image in a fun house.

Her head felt funny, and she pushed the mug toward him, splashing tea over his fingers and hers. Closing her eyes, she let the darkness claim her.

When she finally rejoined the land of the living, her pajamas were soaked with sweat, which told her that her fever was finally gone. The pain in her head was barely noticeable, and her body wasn't aching like it had been for the past four days.

Grayish-white light flooded her bedroom, and the clock on her nightstand read 11:07 a.m. She'd slept almost sixteen hours. No wonder she felt better.

She sat up, swung her legs to the side of the bed, and stood. So far, so good. She made her way to the bathroom with no trouble, and once she was inside the small space, she gathered her courage and looked in the mirror above the sink.

*Sweet Mother of God!*

## Chapter 16

THE WEATHERMAN WAS A LIAR. HE'D PROMISED NO PRECIPITA-
tion, but the entire Northeast was snowed in.

Nick muted the weather report on Teagan's big-screen TV
and made his way to the kitchen. He'd heard the shower running a while ago, so he assumed she felt better.

Opening the fridge, he pulled out some butter and the cheese
he'd bought last night. Teagan needed to eat something, and veg
etable soup and grilled cheese sandwiches were on the lunch
menu.

After rummaging around in the cabinets, he found a skillet
and put it on to preheat before opening the soup and dumping
it in a pot. While the soup heated, he slathered the sourdough
bread with butter and lightly grilled it before adding slices of
cheddar, Monterey jack, and Swiss cheese.

Letty called them grown-up grilled cheese sandwiches,
and he loved them. They'd be even better with bacon. Everything was better with bacon.

Teagan's bedroom door opened, and he heard her light tread
on the hardwood floors as she came down the hall. He flipped
the sandwiches before turning to face her. She stopped abruptly
when she saw him. They stared at each other across the room,

and he ran his gaze from the top of her head to the tips of her toes and up again.

Her long, dark hair waved loosely around her face, shiny from its recent wash. Her cheeks were tinted pink, but thankfully no longer red from fever, and her eyes were much brighter. Her nose and lips still looked a little raw, but overall, she looked a thousand times better.

A light blue flannel nightgown with a long line of buttons enveloped her from neck to knees. Her legs and feet were covered in fuzzy black socks that started right where her nightgown ended. They looked a little like leg warmers, but they were tight and clingy.

It was a decidedly unattractive look, nothing sexy about it, yet all he could think about was unbuttoning those tiny little buttons, one by one, until he bared her plump breasts to his gaze. He'd been fantasizing about the color and taste of her nipples for months.

Or maybe he could take the easy route, pulling that old lady nightie up and over her head so he could lay his hands on her bare ass. He was desperate to shape its round curves and touch her smooth white skin.

Teagan joined him in the kitchen, and before he could say anything, she wrapped her arms around his waist and rested her head against his chest. He squeezed her to him, rubbing big circles on her back.

She had scared him last night. *A lot.*

She'd been burning up, totally out of it, and none of the drugs he had poured into her mouth had seemed to help. He'd been so worried he had called Letty in the wee hours of the morning to get her opinion on whether he should take Teagan to the hospital.

He relied on Letty more than he'd ever let himself depend on anyone. She had become an important part of his life, and he trusted her to give him good advice, especially since she'd raised three children.

Letty had told him to keep a close watch on Teagan, so he'd slept in her room, checking on her every hour. When her fever had finally broken this morning, he had been so relieved he'd felt light-headed.

The smell of burning bread drifted to his nose, and Nick

reached behind him to turn off the stove. The movement pushed his chest against Teagan's, and he tried not to notice her breasts.

He was pretty sure she wasn't wearing a bra because he could feel how full and firm they were. His heart rate increased, pumping blood straight to his cock, and he stepped back to put some room between them before he had to explain why he had an erection . . . *again*.

She looked up, and he smoothed her hair away from her face. It smelled fruity, like tangerines maybe, and his taste buds quivered. He pushed down the urge to nuzzle his nose into her hair before licking his way down her neck.

"Thank you for taking care of me."

He smiled. Her voice sounded like the offspring between a bullfrog and a goose.

"You're such a good friend," she continued.

*Friend.*

The smile slid from his face. He was starting to hate that fucking word, especially when Teagan's kissable lips said it.

"You're going to get sick, you know," she warned. "I already gave this to Bebe."

He shrugged. He didn't get sick a lot, and when he did, he rode it out alone. He remembered having strep throat in high school and being so sick he could barely move. His dad had been in New York City for a book tour, and he'd been irritated when Nick had called him. He had told him to "use his head and find a doctor."

Nick shook off the memory, focusing on Teagan's face. She wasn't wearing any makeup, and her skin looked dewy from the shower.

"You won't be so blasé about it when you're suffering with this plague," she predicted. "You'll blame me for giving it to you."

He stared into her eyes. He already suffered from something she had given him: a bad case of lust.

She sniffed the air before peeking around him. Her eyes widened.

"Did you cook?" she asked incredulously.

He nodded, a little insulted by her shock. He was a grown man, and he knew how to make a simple meal. He laughed under his breath when he realized he might be just a tad too offended. Grilled cheese sandwiches weren't exactly adult fare.

She stepped around him, and he turned to see what she was doing. Bending down, she opened the lower cabinet and reached inside. He watched as the hem of her nightgown inched up and continued to rise until he could see the top of her creamy thighs.

Saliva pooled in his mouth as he thought about the moist pink flesh barely covered by the flannel. He had to clench his hands into fists to stop himself from reaching out and easing his fingers between her legs.

She stood up, her hands filled with two oval plates and two matching bowls. "These are my special soup and sandwich platters," she said as she placed them on the granite counter. "They have a built-in place for the soup bowl."

He touched her elbow, and she lifted her face to look at him. She smiled, a tiny curve of her chapped lips, and he tilted his head toward the dining room.

"Sit."

Surprisingly, she did exactly as she was told, and he couldn't stop himself from watching the sway of her ass as she left the kitchen. He rubbed his hand over the back of his neck, massaging the tight muscles.

Although he'd expected his desire for Teagan to fade, it hadn't. In fact, it had grown exponentially. Even when her hair had been stringy and her nose had been runny, he'd wanted to be close to her.

He ran his hands roughly over his face. He didn't know what to do, but he knew he couldn't go on like this.

He moved to the stove and plated their lunches, giving himself the burned sandwich. Carrying the plates into the dining room, he found Teagan standing beside the table. She turned to face him, and he noticed she held the bear he'd bought her.

"Is this guy for me?" she asked, holding up the bear.

He nodded, depositing the plates on the table.

"And the roses? Are they for me, too?"

He nodded again. He had tossed the lavender roses on the table when he'd returned from the grocery store. He had been in such a rush to get some medicine into her, he'd forgotten to put them in water, and they'd wilted a little bit.

Teagan looked down, rubbing one of the bear's ears between her thumb and her forefinger. He wondered if maybe he'd made a mistake. After all, she wasn't *his* Valentine.

"Why did you get them for me?"

"You're sick," he answered, but he didn't know if that was the truth.

He didn't know why he'd bought the bear and the roses. They had been an impulse purchase, one he regretted now. She nodded and returned the bear to the table before sitting down.

"Apple juice or tea?"

She shrugged lethargically, and he could tell she felt bad again. She needed to get some food in her stomach before she went back to bed, though.

"Eat. Then b-b-b-back to bed."

"I'm not hungry," she said, her chapped lower lip pushed out in a small pout.

*Poor baby.*

"Just a few bites," he negotiated, dropping a kiss on top of her head as he walked back to the kitchen to grab some juice.

"*GROUNDHOG DAY* IS THE BEST MOVIE OF ALL TIME," TEAGAN said, reclining against her velvet sofa.

"*Terminator*," Nick countered as he draped a blanket over her.

After lunch, he had tucked her into bed like she was a little girl, and she'd slept for four hours. When she had woken up and stumbled from her bedroom, she'd been surprised to find him on her sofa watching the History Channel and drinking a beer.

While Teagan had been napping, Letty had dropped off a change of clothes for Nick and homemade dinner for two. He'd showered and changed into a navy blue thermal pullover that outlined his chest and arms in mouthwatering detail and a pair of sand-colored cargo pants that made his butt look like a work of art.

Right now, his crotch was level with her face, and she wished she had the right to reach out, unzip his pants, and slide her hand inside. She wished she had the courage to take him into her mouth and damn the consequences.

Thinking of the treasure to be found inside his pants, she

licked her lips, and Nick's eyes fell to her mouth. He frowned before pulling a tube of lip balm from his hip pocket and handing it to her.

She'd been thinking about giving him a blow job, and he'd been thinking she needed lip balm for her chapped lips. *Stupid man.*

"Drink?" he asked as she slathered ointment on her lips and handed the tube back to him.

Nick was determined to keep her well hydrated, but she wasn't sure she could swallow much more tea or juice without floating away. She declined his offer, and he grabbed the TV remote from the coffee table and handed it to her. He pointed to her legs, and she pulled her knees to her chest so he could sit down.

Settling himself against the cushions, he reached for her feet and draped them across his lap. He delved under the blanket and tweaked one of her big toes before starting to massage her foot. His hands were so warm she could feel the heat through her knee socks. She shivered, and he turned his head to look into her eyes.

"Okay?" he asked.

She nodded. He could touch her anywhere and anytime, and she wouldn't say no. In fact, she'd probably say more.

It was almost impossible to hide her feelings for Nick. When she'd seen the bear and flowers he'd bought her, she had almost burst into tears. Didn't he realize he was torturing her with his friendship? How could he expect them to spend so much time together without her falling in love with him?

Who wouldn't love a man who took such good care of her when she was sick? Who could resist the lure of a man who not only looked like a Greek god but also laughed at her stupid jokes?

Teagan stared at the TV remote, rubbing her finger over the Pause button. Although she'd tried to move forward, her life was on pause. She was waiting for Nick to miraculously wake up one day and decide he wanted to be with her.

Maybe she should grow a pair and just tell him she felt more than friendship for him. She didn't have to show all her cards by telling him she was in love with him. She could play it cool.

What was the worst that could happen?

Closing her eyes, she imagined telling Nick she wanted to be more than friends. And then she imagined the horror on his gorgeous face, the pity in his eyes when he told her he didn't want her "that way."

And what if he found her attractive? To use a cliché, he wasn't relationship material. She knew sex was the most she could expect from him. And the worst part about it? She wouldn't even be the only woman in his life.

She groaned softly. She couldn't imagine anything worse than being just another member of his harem.

"Feeling bad again?"

Teagan opened her eyes to find Nick staring at her, a look of concern on his face. It was obvious he cared about her—he wouldn't be here otherwise. But she knew she couldn't read anything into it.

He cared about her whole family, and she knew he'd do the same for her brothers. In fact, she'd bet he *had* taken care of her brothers when they'd overindulged in liquor and loose women.

"I'm feeling better. You can relax, Nurse Nightingale."

He laughed, moving his hands to massage her lower leg. His hands were strong, and she imagined him shifting them higher until he could slip his long fingers inside her.

Wetness trickled from her body, and she resisted the urge to squirm against the sofa. She wondered what he'd do if she unzipped his pants, climbed on his lap, and rode him until they both were mindless with pleasure.

"You're flushed," Nick noted. "Sure your fever isn't back?"

Teagan exhaled loudly. She had a fever all right, but it was because of him, not the flu.

She pressed the button to play the DVD and waited for the opening credits to fill the screen. They had debated which movie to watch, going back and forth between her favorites and his, until he'd taken it upon himself to make the decision alone.

She had no doubt they'd end up watching *Terminator* . . . again. The man seriously loved his cybernetic organisms. She, on the other hand, seriously loved Nick Priest.

"What are we watching?"

Nick slanted an amused glance toward her. "*Groundhog Day.*"

*Groundhog Day* was her favorite movie, but Nick wasn't a

fan. Apparently he didn't like watching a womanizing jerk relive the same day over and over until he finally—*finally*—got a clue. Maybe *Groundhog Day* hit too close to home for Nick.

*And now I'm just being bitchy.*

"Are you going to make rude noises throughout the whole movie like you did last time?" she asked.

He narrowed his eyes. "Maybe."

Nick switched his attention from her leg to her other foot, pressing his thumbs deep into the arch. *Bliss!*

A low moan escaped her. Maybe she didn't need to have sex with Nick to have an orgasm. He might be able to make her come just by rubbing her feet.

He shifted deeper into the sofa, shaking his head slightly. Teagan cocked her head.

"Why don't you like *Groundhog Day*? I love the idea of being able to relive the same day."

He didn't answer, just continued to massage her foot, and she pressed her toes into his stomach. His entire body jerked, his eyes shooting to her face.

"Don't you have any days you want to relive?"

"No," he replied slowly, his eyes bright in the shadows of the living room.

"What about the day of the Super Bowl? You could relive how great it was to win."

"No," he said again, laughing softly.

"Why not?"

He stared at her for a moment. "I could never catch that ball again. *Never.*"

She nodded. No one could believe he'd caught it. It had been uncatchable.

"You should relive bad days. Not good ones," he added.

"What do you mean?"

"Leave good days alone. Fix bad ones."

She considered what Nick had said. She'd always imagined how great it would be to relive the good days, to enjoy them over and over again. But having the opportunity to relive a day that went sideways, to go back and fix something that went wrong, would be beyond awesome.

"Do you have a lot of bad days you'd like to relive?"

"Some," he replied, looking down at his lap as he continued to rub her foot.

Even though people assumed Nick's life was perfect, she had no doubt he'd had his fair share of bad days. Yes, he was talented, good-looking, and wealthy. But he'd grown up without a mother, raised by a father who was, by all accounts, a cold, unfeeling asshole.

He had lived his entire life without love, while Teagan had been blessed with an abundance of it. Her life was filled with people who loved her: parents who would do anything for her; brothers who adored her; and friends who cherished her.

But she was greedy. She wanted Nick to love her.

## Chapter 17

IT WASN'T A DATE. IT *WASN'T*.

That's what Nick told himself as he walked down the hall-way to Teagan's door. It was her birthday, and the two of them were going out to dinner before heading to a new club to listen to some music.

Friends dressed up and went out together all the time. It wasn't a big deal.

When he had told Letty about their plans, she'd grinned. "I wondered why you bought a new suit when you have a closet full of them . . . and a new shirt and tie . . . and new shoes."

As he'd left his condo to pick up Teagan, Letty had smoothed his Dolce & Gabanna suit jacket and adjusted his tie before patting him on the cheek. It was something a mother would do for her son on prom night.

"Enjoy your nondate," she'd said, an amused twinkle in her eyes, as if she knew the truth.

And maybe she did. Maybe she knew how badly Nick wanted this to be a date—how much he wished the night would end with him and Teagan naked.

Reaching Teagan's door, he smoothed his hand over his hair to make sure it wasn't sticking up and adjusted his tie for the fifth time. He shot his cuffs, the gift bag in his left hand shaking with the motion.

As he stared at the smooth wooden door in front of him, he took a deep breath and then another. He couldn't ever remember being nervous over a woman, not even when he'd been a teenager. Even back then, he had been in control of his emotions.

But he was nervous now—nervous about a nondate with a friend. He knocked on the door, and a few seconds later, he heard Teagan's muffled voice.

"Just a minute," she called.

He took another deep breath, readying himself for his first look at her in three weeks. As she had predicted, she'd given him the flu. It had lasted for more than a week, and he had been sicker than he'd ever been.

Letty, bless her soul, had been there to take care of him. And he'd needed all the TLC she had provided. Teagan had texted to check in, but he hadn't told her he'd been sick because he hadn't wanted her to feel guilty.

He adjusted his tie again and inspected his new shoes while he waited for Teagan to open the door. The door swung open, and he jerked his eyes from his Salvatore Ferragamos to Teagan. He sucked in a breath when he saw her, astounded by the vision in front of him. He couldn't remember ever seeing her dressed up like this.

*Holy shit, she's stunning. Absolutely stunning.*

Her dark hair was arranged loosely on top of her head, drawing attention to her neck and shoulders. Her emerald green dress left most of her upper chest bare except for wide straps, and her breasts plumped above the low-cut square neckline. The gold and emerald necklace encircling her neck drew attention to the creamy mounds, and he struggled against the impulse to bury his face in her cleavage.

Her dress flared from her waist in floating folds, hitting well above her knees. Sheer stockings encased her shapely legs, and nude-colored heels covered her feet. They were so high he wondered how she could walk in them.

As he brought his eyes to her face, he noticed the green dress made her eyes look even bluer, so vibrant they were almost indigo. Gold eye shadow shimmered on her lids, and her long lashes framed her eyes.

"Hi," she said, her glossy lips turning up in a bright smile. "I'm sorry I made you wait."

He didn't respond because he was even more tongue-tied than usual. She opened the door, waving him in, and he trailed after her.

"I need to grab my coat. It's way too cold for me to go out without it. I'll be right back," she said over her shoulder as she headed down the hall to her bedroom.

Placing the gift bag on the tall granite bar that separated the kitchen from the living area, he shoved his hands in his pockets to make some extra room near his crotch. He exhaled loudly, wondering how he was going to hide an erection in his new suit pants. They were a tad more formfitting than his others, and he should have thought about that when he'd had the pants fitted, damn it.

"Is that my birthday present?" Teagan asked as she came back into the living room, a cream-colored wool coat hanging over her arm. "Can I open it right now or do you want me to wait?"

He nodded, tilting his head toward the brightly colored gift bag. She smiled and threw her coat over the back of the barstool before eagerly reaching for her present.

Digging through the pink tissue paper, she pulled out a square leather jewelry case. She placed it on the bar and opened the lid, gasping when she saw the necklace inside.

He knew she collected vintage jewelry, and he'd wanted to give her something she would like. He had contacted a local jeweler and told him what he was looking for, and the jeweler had found several pieces for Nick to review.

Before he had begun the search for her birthday present, he hadn't known diamonds could be almost any color. He'd seen white diamonds, of course, as well as yellow, brown, and pink, but he hadn't been aware there were blue, green, and orange diamonds, too.

He had debated over which piece to buy her, but he hadn't been able to resist this necklace once he'd seen it. It was a collar of white and colored diamonds set in platinum and cut in the shape of various flowers that were interwoven together with smaller diamond clusters.

He moved to stand beside her as she gazed down at the necklace. He'd never bought a piece of jewelry for anyone, and he hoped he'd done a good job picking something Teagan would like.

"Nick, this is beautiful," she said huskily before looking up at him. "You know, most women would say something like 'It's too much. I can't accept it.'"

He shook his head. He wanted her to have it. He wanted to give her something special, something that would remind her of him.

"But I'm not most women," she continued, a glint in her eyes he didn't recognize. "I'm going to put it on and twirl around the room."

He laughed. She was right. She wasn't most women. She was one-of-a-kind.

Removing the necklace from the case, she turned so her back was to him. She bent her head forward until he could see the fine dark hairs at the nape of her neck. He wondered what those tendrils would feel like against his lips, and his mouth tingled.

"Would you take off my necklace so I can put this one on?"

He unclasped the emerald necklace, laying it on the bar. She handed him the one he'd bought her, and he draped it around her neck before closing the clasp.

He ran his finger lightly across the precious metal, and although he told himself he needed to stop, he stroked it along the slope of her shoulder, relishing the feel of her soft skin. She slowly turned to face him, and he dropped his hand.

Placing her palm over the necklace, she traced the gems with her fingers. "How does it look?" she asked, gazing up into his eyes.

He stepped back so he could get the full effect of the necklace. Ever since he'd seen it, he had thought about what it would look like around her neck, resting above the enticing swells of her breasts.

It looked even better than he'd imagined, and when he was alone in his bed late at night, he would think of her wearing nothing but this necklace. He would think of her on top of him, the diamonds glinting against her chest as she rode him, and her name would be on his lips when he came.

"Nick, how does it look?" she repeated.

Clearing his throat, he pressed his tongue against his front teeth to get his mouth to work. "Perfect."

She smiled and twirled around, her arms outstretched and her head tilted back. Her dress belled outward at the motion, and he saw a flash of a garter belt and the tops of her stockings under it.

*Seriously?*

What woman wore a garter belt and stockings nowadays? Didn't they all wear pantyhose, the least sexy undergarment in existence?

Nick squeezed his eyes shut, knowing his late-night fantasy now included a garter belt and stockings. And maybe the shoes. They were pretty hot, too.

Opening his eyes, he saw her stumble to a stop. She laughed as she teetered a little on her heels before making her way toward him. When she got close enough, she grasped his biceps, leaned up, and kissed his cheek. It was so close to his lips he felt as if she had kissed the corner of his mouth.

"Thank you so much," she said as she drew back. "I will cherish this necklace. *Always.*"

She looked at him, and her lips quirked a bit. Reaching up, she swiped her thumb across the outer curve of his lips.

"Lipstick," she explained before pointing to her own lips. "It's a new color called 'Inevitable.' Do you like it?"

He imagined her on her knees in front of him with her "Inevitable"-shaded lips wrapped around his cock. Yeah, he liked it just fine.


NICK SILENTLY CURSED LETTY. IT WAS HER FAULT HE AND TEA-gan were having dinner in a restaurant better suited for lovers than friends. He should have known she'd been up to something when she had convinced him to change the reservation at the last minute from the restaurant he'd chosen to one her chef friend had recently opened.

Located in a trendy area of Boston, the restaurant was dubbed Plum, and now that he was there, he knew why. The entire décor was done in shades of plum, from the dark brownish-plum wood floors to the light lavender color on the walls.

It should have been ugly, but somehow it worked. In fact, the whole space was amazing.

He and Teagan were ensconced in a high-backed booth upholstered in dark purple velvet. It was encircled by floor-to-ceiling plum-colored curtains, and the filmy drapes created a sense of intimacy, along with the dim sconce lighting on the wall and the votive candles on the table.

The restaurant was beyond romantic. It gave off a sensual, sexy vibe, and if he and Teagan were more than friends, this was exactly the kind of place he would have taken her right before he took her back to his condo and stripped her out of that green dress.

Nick fought the urge to loosen his tie and pop the top button on his dress shirt. He was overheated and on edge, and he wasn't sure how he was going to get through the rest of the evening without jumping on Teagan like a rabid dog.

He wondered if there was a way he could graciously get out of taking her to the club after dinner. Maybe he could fake a stomachache.

Every time he saw her, he promised himself it would be the last time. And yet he always broke his promise because he didn't have the willpower to stay away from her. Somewhere—somehow—he was going to have to find some. Otherwise, he was going to ruin the best thing in his life.

"I'm so glad I'm spending my birthday with you. And I'm so excited about this club we're going to later."

Her eyes shone in the glow of the candles, and her luscious lips turned up in a small smile. She was happy, and he didn't have the heart to disappoint her by cutting their night short just because he couldn't stop thinking about her naked.

"This is such a unique restaurant," she added. "It's so . . ."

She pressed her lips together, clearly trying to come up with the right word to describe it. She gave a little shrug, which made her necklace—the one he'd given her—sparkle in the light.

"It's so *lush*," she said finally, nodding a little bit, as if she were agreeing with herself.

He stared at her, trying to keep his eyes on her face. *She* was lush, from her thick hair and plump lips to her ample breasts and curvy hips.

She took a sip of merlot, and he watched as her pink tongue darted out to swipe a rogue droplet of wine. His cock twinged, and he knew a full-fledged erection was only moments away if he continued to look at her lips. He pulled his gaze from her and fiddled with his silverware, just to keep his eyes off her.

"This is probably the last time I'll get to have any fun for the next couple of weeks because midterms are coming up."

He nodded. Teagan was a very dedicated student, and he knew she studied a lot. She claimed she had to hit the books hard to get good grades, but he doubted that was the truth. Without question, she was the smartest person he'd ever met. If brains were cars, Teagan's was a Ferrari, while everyone else's was a Ford.

"But after midterms, I am going to *relax* with a capital R. Bebe and I are going to Bora Bora for spring break, and we're going to lie on the beach and drink margaritas."

Nick imagined Teagan in a skimpy bikini, her breasts overflowing from two tiny triangles and her pussy barely covered by a strip of stretchy material. He cleared his throat to push back the moan that had built there.

Thank God she was going with Bebe. If she'd told him she was going with Marshall, he might have tracked down the other man and caused him bodily harm to prevent him from vacationing with Teagan.

"Marshall invited me to go skiing with him in Whistler, but I wanted to go somewhere warm," she added.

He clenched his fingers around his knife. The relationship between Teagan and Marshall must be serious if the man had asked her to spend spring break with him. But if it was that serious, wouldn't she have celebrated her birthday with Marshall instead of Nick? Wouldn't she prefer to spend this special occasion with the other man?

Maybe they weren't serious. Maybe they weren't having sex.

Nick shook his head. There was no way a normal, redblooded man could spend so much time with Teagan and not want to fuck her. God knew he wanted to, over and over again.

Teagan placed her hand over his, lightly squeezing his fingers. He looked up as she leaned forward, and his eyes dropped to her cleavage. The pale skin between her breasts seemed to shimmer, enticing him to taste it.

"Nick, are you okay? You're even quieter than usual." She grimaced. "I talked the whole way here, and now I'm talking some more. You're probably bored to death."

He shook his head. She *never* bored him. He found her fascinating, the way her mind worked and the way it led her from one thought to another. He loved to hear her voice, loved to learn her opinions on any subject, from potatoes to politics.

"Not bored," he said emphatically.

She smiled and stroked the top of his hand. Her touch shot through him like an electric current, and he casually moved his hand away from her.

"So what did you do today?"

"Visited the kids."

The first year he'd played for Denver, the team had partnered with the local children's hospital for a charity dinner. All the players were required to attend the event, as well as a party at the hospital.

Being around the kids, even though they were sick, made him feel good. It was so easy to make them happy. They didn't care if he could talk or not. They were just glad to see him.

From that moment on, he'd made a point to stop by at least once a week during off-season to hang out. When he'd moved to Boston, he had continued with his routine. He never scheduled the visits. He kept it low key because he didn't want the media to make a big deal out of it.

He always brought a bag full of team gear to distribute and stayed to toss around a football or play videogames. Occasionally, he painted fingernails and toenails for the girly girls, and when his hair was long enough, he let them play beautician. More than once, he'd ended up looking like a Rastafarian.

"You have a hard candy shell and a gooey marshmallow center," Teagan teased, a big grin on her face.

He frowned, disliking her description of him. Hanging out with sick kids didn't make him a nice guy. He got more out of the visits than they did. He was too selfish to do something truly altruistic. He always had been, and he always would be.

## Chapter 18

WHY DO THESE THINGS ALWAYS HAPPEN TO ME? AND WHY DO
*they have to happen when I'm with Nick?*

Teagan stared down at the tall patent leather heel that had
been attached to her shoe just seconds ago. Now it was stuck
in a crack in the sidewalk.

She, meanwhile, had to suffer the freezing concrete in her
stockinged feet because it was impossible to wear one five-
inch heel and one flat shoe. Nick stood beside her, his hands
on his hips and a bemused expression on his face.

"How the hell did that happen?" he asked, shaking his head.

She bent down to try to pull the heel from the sidewalk, and
Nick jerked her upright, muttering a curse under his breath. He
was a little rough with her, and she frowned. He'd been acting
weird all night, and she didn't have any idea why. It wasn't as
if she'd forced him to take her out for her birthday.

Squatting down, he wrenched the heel from the crack. As he
rose, he handed it to her, and she wrapped her fingers around it,
barely controlling the urge to impale herself with the sharp end.

Once again, her clumsiness had ruined an outing with Nick.
One moment, they'd been talking as they waited for the valet
attendant to bring his Escalade, and the next moment she had
been hanging on to him for dear life as her heel snapped off.

Thanks to her faulty footwear, they wouldn't be able to go to the club. She wouldn't be able to sit close to Nick and listen to bluesy music. She wouldn't be able to slow dance with him, their bodies pressed together so tightly she could feel his heat all around her.

She was so disappointed tears prickled the backs of her eyes. She pressed her tongue to the roof of her mouth to push them back because she didn't want Nick to see her cry, especially since he'd probably think she was sobbing over her stupid broken shoe.

The maroon SUV came to a stop in front of them, and Nick pulled open the door for her. She angrily tossed her shoes and purse in, and he raised a dark blond eyebrow before offering his hand and helping her into the vehicle.

Clicking her seat belt in place, she turned to look out the window. She wished she were someone else and somewhere else— maybe a tall, skinny blonde lounging in Nick's bed.

Nick stepped into the SUV, and the valet attendant shut the door, cocooning them in silence. She shivered a little, and he turned on the heat full blast toward their feet.

"T, it's not a big deal," he said, his voice soothing. "Let's grab another pair of shoes and then go to the club."

"No," she muttered, crossing her arms over her chest.

He laughed softly at her pique, and she ground her teeth together in an effort to stop herself from yelling at him. Even though she knew it was irrational, she was burning mad at Nick. Why, she didn't know.

She was so . . . so . . . so . . . *hot* for him. She was angry because she was sexually frustrated. She was a keg of dynamite just waiting to be lit, and Nick didn't have a match.

She growled under her breath at that inaccurate statement. Nick had a match. He just didn't have one for *her* keg. Marshall, on the other hand, definitely had one.

She'd been stupid to hope Nick would get a clue. He was never going to see her as anything but a friend, so she was going to go home, call Marshall, and let him do what he'd wanted to do for months.

"Stop," she demanded. "I want to take a cab home."

Nick slanted an amused glance toward her, which made her even angrier. She'd never thought she had a bad temper, but clearly, she had deluded herself. She felt all kinds of new emotions with Nick, and right now, aggression flooded her veins.

"No," he said, his voice mild.

"Yes," she shouted, her voice echoing throughout the SUV.

Turning his head, he speared her with his brilliant green gaze. His expression was no longer amused.

"No," he repeated, and this time his voice wasn't nearly so mild.

Knowing she had no choice, she pressed her lips together and turned away from him. They made the trip to her condo in silence, tension heavy in the SUV.

The moment Nick pulled up in front of her building, she grabbed her shoes and purse and jumped from his Escalade. She slammed the door shut without thanking him for a nice evening or even saying good-bye.

The sidewalk was freezing, and she hurried into the building. Stepping into the elevator, she hit the button for her floor before pulling her phone from her beaded clutch. As it ascended, she typed a text message to Marshall: Are you busy?

The elevator chimed, letting her know she'd arrived. The doors opened, and suddenly Marshall stood in front of her.

"Oh! I just texted you." She stepped out of the elevator. "What are you doing here?"

She didn't give him a chance to answer before stalking toward her condo. The moment she got him alone, she was going to rip off her clothes and his. She hoped he was ready because she was going to use his body all night long. And she wasn't going to pretend she was with Nick, either.

Marshall fell into step beside her, gesturing toward her shoeless feet. "What happened there?"

"Nothing," she answered curtly.

She unlocked her door, and Marshall followed her inside, closing the door behind them. She threw down her shoes beside the door and tossed her purse and coat on the bar once she reached the kitchen.

Marshall gave her an appraising glance, starting at her feet and ending with her eyes. "You look gorgeous, Teagan. Absolutely stunning."

She frowned. She'd spent four hours getting ready, and Nick hadn't said one word about her appearance. Not *one freaking word* about her gorgeous new dress or her sexy new shoes, which were clearly defective.

She'd paid $427 for those damn patent leather heels, and she was going to demand her money back. But not until she'd spent all night having sex with Marshall.

"I stopped by to say hello, but it looks like you were out on a date." He shook his head slightly. "This might not be the right time to talk about it, but I don't want you to date other guys. I want us to be exclusive."

Teagan closed her eyes. She didn't want to have this conversation, not now, not when she was so emotional. She wasn't sure she had the finesse to say no without hurting his feelings.

"Marshall, it wasn't a date," she said, a placating note in her voice. "I was out with Nick for my birthday. We're just friends, you know that."

Even as she said it, she knew she lied. Nick was the reason why her relationship with Marshall had stalled.

He shook his head before gesturing toward her dress. "A woman doesn't dress like that to go out with a friend. You don't even dress like that to go out with *me*."

She looked away, unable to dispute Marshall's claim. He was right. She only dressed this way for one man. She only bought sexy lingerie and new clothes for Nick. She only bought do-me heels for Nick.

*Nick. Only Nick.*

Marshall looked toward the gift bag and the jewelry box on the bar before eyeing her. "Did *Nick* give you that necklace?"

She touched the cool gems encircling her neck. "Yes."

She had been surprised Nick had bought her a birthday present, although she didn't know why exactly. He had bought her gifts before—the jersey, the knitted cap, the cuddly bear.

But she had been more than surprised when she'd opened the box. She had been nearly speechless. Except for himself, he couldn't have given her a gift she would have liked more.

She'd never seen a more exquisite piece of vintage jewelry in her whole life, and she had seen a lot. She had no doubt he'd spent a lot of money on the gift, probably more than most people's annual salaries.

At first she had wondered if she should accept such an expensive present, but ultimately she'd decided to say "thank you" instead of "no thank you." She didn't know whether he bought jewelry for anyone else, but she figured she probably deserved it more than those other women, who cared only about the size of his penis or his bank account.

At least she loved Nick.

"*Jesus*, Teagan," Marshall said, laughing incredulously and shaking his head. "That necklace is easily worth seventy grand, probably more. It's not something a man gives to a *friend*. It's something he gives to his girlfriend or his wife. Or his *lover*."

She blinked at his vehemence. He was almost frothing at the mouth he was so upset.

"You're either lying to me or you're lying to yourself when you say that you and Nick are *just friends*," he continued fiercely. "Which is it?"

She stared into his dark eyes, uncertain how to answer him. She was in love with Nick, but as far as Nick was concerned, they *were* "just friends."

A sharp knock sounded at the front door, and both of them looked toward the sound. Scowling, Marshall stalked toward it, and she hurried after him. He flung open the door, his tall body filling the opening. Teagan peeked around him to see who was on the other side, gasping when she saw Nick.

Nick's eyes narrowed on Marshall, and his lips thinned when he saw her behind him. Edging Marshall out of the way, she moved in front of him.

She didn't know what to do. Should she step out in the hall to talk to Nick? Invite him in? Ask Marshall to leave?

Before she could make a decision, Nick stepped forward, almost steamrolling over her and Marshall. They were forced to shuffle backward into the foyer until they reached the living area.

She stood between Nick and Marshall, who glared at each other over her head. She felt like peanut butter between two slices of bread, so she stepped back and gestured toward Marshall.

"Marshall, this is Nick Priest. Nick, this is Marshall Brants. I've mentioned you to each other."

Nick must have left his suit jacket and tie in his SUV because he was dressed only in his light gray dress shirt, charcoal suit pants, and leather dress shoes. The expensive cotton shirt clung to his arms and chest, outlining his musculature, and the dark trousers emphasized his height.

Marshall, meanwhile, was dressed casually in a pair of jeans and a long-sleeved plaid shirt. He was a good-sized guy, but Nick seemed so much larger and far more physically imposing.

Marshall slowly extended his right hand to Nick, but instead of accepting it, Nick put his hands on his hips and stared down at Marshall's hand as if it were covered in oozing sores. He met Marshall's gaze, tilting his head toward the door.

"Leave," Nick demanded, his voice low and menacing. "*Now.*"

Marshall dropped his hand with a sound of disgust. "That's what I thought," he said before beckoning Teagan toward him. "Walk me out."

She hurried to comply, trailing after him as he strode down the hall. He pulled open the door and turned to face her. He hesitated for a moment, looking over her head. Glancing over her shoulder, she saw Nick at the end of the hall, watching them with his arms crossed over his chest.

Marshall leaned closer and put his lips against her ear. "If Nick is just your friend, I'm the fucking Easter Bunny. He wants you. The only question is whether you want him. Do you?"

Teagan hesitated. She hadn't been fair to Marshall by dating him while she was in love with Nick, and she knew she'd behaved badly. He shook his head when she didn't answer him.

"*Goddamn it,*" he said, running his hand through his dark hair. "Let me know when you figure it out." He turned to walk down the hall, but he only took a few steps before looking over his shoulder. "I don't want to wait, but I will. You're worth it," he muttered before striding off.

She slowly closed the door, leaning her forehead against the smooth wood. This was all Nick's fault. If not for him, she'd be in love with Marshall and one step closer to happily ever after.

Making her way back to the living room, she stopped in front of Nick. His hands were in his front pockets, his gaze focused on her face.

"Why are you here?" she asked, crossing her arms over her chest.

He didn't answer, nor did he move a muscle or change his facial expression.

"I'm pretty sure we said good night," she added. "Or at least it was implied when I slammed the car door."

His eyes narrowed, and it took her a moment to realize he was angry. *Really angry.*

Nick was a fairly easygoing guy, and she'd never seen him anything more than slightly annoyed. She wondered if he was angry because he was jealous.

Was Marshall right? Was it possible Nick actually felt more than friendship for her? And if he did, what was she going to do about it?

"Why were you so rude to Marshall? I can't believe you refused to even shake his hand. What's your problem?"

Clenching his jaw, he pulled his hands from his pockets and planted them on his hips. He rolled his lips inward as if he was trying to prevent himself from letting loose with a bunch of curse words.

"I told you he's a nice guy. You just lost a big fan."

He snorted rudely, and she stepped closer, poking him in the chest with her forefinger. He didn't move an inch, so she pushed him with the palm of her hand.

"There was no reason to be a jerk!" She pushed him again, a little harder. "You're such an *ass*!"

He sucked in a deep breath and grabbed her wrist, pulling her up against his chest. She searched his eyes, but she couldn't tell what he was thinking.

"Are you jealous, Nick?"

"No," he answered immediately, letting go of her wrist and stepping away from her.

"I think you are."

He laughed, but she thought it sounded forced. He backed up a couple more steps, and she followed. She was done being his friend.

*Done.*

"You know what Marshall told me?"

Nick's eyebrows shot up, and she placed her fingers on her necklace, stroking the diamonds. "He told me a man doesn't buy a necklace like this for a friend. He buys it for a *lover*." She paused to provide some emphasis to her next statement. "Or someone he *wants* to be his lover."

His eyes widened before his gaze fell to her hand. She trailed her fingers from the necklace to her cleavage, closely watching his face for any reaction. He swallowed before jerking his eyes away from her chest. She wasn't sure if that response was enough to justify throwing herself at him.

"Is Marshall right? Do you want to be my lover?"

Nick stared at her, his face unreadable. She took a deep breath, and his delicious scent flooded her senses. She wanted him so badly, enough to risk everything.

His rejection. Her pride.

Their friendship.

"Do you want to be my lover?" she repeated as she stepped close enough to feel the heat of his body against hers.

Reaching out, she hooked her fingers in the waistband of his pants right above his belt buckle and pulled him to her. He resisted for a second before shuddering and closing his eyes. He inched forward, and she knew.

She *knew*.

"Do you want to be my lover?" she repeated huskily, noting the erection visible behind his zipper.

While he stood unmoving, she unbuckled his belt and popped the button on his pants before pulling the tails of his dress shirt from them. He was breathing in deep gusts, and she slowly undid the buttons on his dress shirt until it fell open to show his snowy white undershirt.

She stroked her hands over his cotton-covered stomach before pulling his undershirt from his pants. Delving under it, she lightly ran her fingernails through the silky hair sprinkled across his abs, and he quivered under her touch.

He opened his eyes to meet her gaze, and finally—*finally*—she recognized the glint she'd seen there for months now: desire.

Grasping his right hand, she pressed it against her breasts. His long fingers clenched in the silky material of her dress as if he wanted to tear it from her body.

"Do you want to be my lover?" she asked one last time.

She waited for him to answer, squeezing her thighs together to ease the ache of arousal that had been building for far too long. Before the night was over, Nick was going to soothe that ache, hopefully more than once.

"You do," she said, answering her own question when he remained stubbornly silent. "Now kiss me and put us both out of our misery."

## Chapter 19

*KISS ME.*

Teagan's demand echoed in his ears. He'd been fantasizing about kissing her for months, but he wasn't going to put his mouth on her. Any part of her.

He wasn't going to ruin their friendship. He *wasn't*.

Nick stared at his fingers. They were clenched in the green fabric covering her breasts, just inches away from her cleavage. He forced himself to let go of her dress, dropping his hand and lifting his eyes to her face.

She tilted her head as she met his gaze, placing her hands on his chest and rubbing lightly. The warmth of her palms heated him through his undershirt, and he trembled with the desire to feel her hands all over him.

Shaking his head, he stepped away from her. He had to leave. *Immediately.*

Her hand shot out to grab his waistband, stopping his progress. She sighed, clearly exasperated with him. Before he could take a breath, she unzipped his pants just enough to ease her hand inside his boxer briefs. She gripped his cock, and he moaned at the pressure from her smooth fingers, his vision blurring from the pleasure.

"You lied to me. This," she said, squeezing his cock, "*is* for me. It's not just biology."

*Of course it's for you. I get hard anytime you're near.*

"It's mine," she continued, stroking his shaft, "and I want it."

Her hand was relentless, stroking and squeezing, and he felt a twinge deep in his balls. Placing his hand over hers, he stilled her torturous touch.

"I want you," she said huskily. "I have for a long time."

Her words stunned him. He'd truly had no idea she wanted him, and that knowledge sent desire surging through his body, eroding his good sense like a tsunami obliterating everything in its path.

"Are you going to give me what I want, Nick?" she asked, licking her rosy lips.

He was so turned on he couldn't form a single word. And even if he'd been able to, he didn't know if that word would be yes or no.

She rubbed her thumb over the tip of his cock, and he gasped. Blood roared in his ears, but he could still hear her.

"I want you on top of me, around me, inside me."

Closing his eyes, he groaned at the images her words created in his mind. She laughed softly, and he raised his lids when she took his hand in hers. She led him down the hallway to her bedroom, and he followed docilely, like a dog on a leash.

She'd left the two bedside lamps on, and they bathed the entire room in a golden glow. Lavender linens and puffy pillows covered her queen-sized bed, and she backed him against it, lightly pushing his chest until he sat heavily on the side.

She nudged his knee, and he widened his legs so she could step between his thighs. The position put her face almost even with his, and she leaned forward, placing her mouth against his. He clenched his hands in the silky material covering the down comforter to keep from reaching for her.

"Give me what I want," she whispered, her soft, full lips caressing his. She opened her mouth, slowly running the tip of her tongue across his bottom lip before sucking lightly on it. And that was all it took.

He lost it.

Gripping her waist, he pulled her against him, toppling

them backward onto the bed. He rolled her under him, settling his lower body between her legs before shoving his fingers into her hair and slanting his mouth over hers.

She opened to let him in, and he moaned in relief. He felt like a man who'd just had his first sip of water after wandering through the desert for days.

He'd wondered how she would taste for months and months, and now he knew. She was deliciously sweet, better than any dessert he'd ever had, and he licked deeply into her mouth. Her tongue slid against his, and he sucked on it before feeding her several deep kisses.

He needed to come up for air, but he didn't want to give up her mouth. She gasped, and he pulled back to stare into her eyes. They were so dark they were almost navy, and he traced one of her dark eyebrows with his thumb.

"That was a pretty amazing first kiss." Her luscious lips turned up at the corners. "But I sure had to wait a long time to get it."

Because he couldn't help himself, he lowered his head and covered her mouth again. He couldn't get enough of her, and he nipped her lower lip before running his tongue over the small bite. He sucked her tongue into his mouth, savoring the glide of it against his lips, and played with her mouth for several minutes.

She pulled back from his kiss, gasping for air, and he followed her lips until she giggled against his mouth. Moving her hands to his shoulders, she pushed his dress shirt down his arms.

"Off," she demanded.

He knew this was a mistake . . . that he should stop now before he made things even worse. But instead, he levered himself into a kneeling position to shrug off his dress shirt. He threw it on the floor before pulling his undershirt over his head and tossing it behind him.

She looked up at him, her cheeks pink and her eyes hazy. Running her gaze from his face to his chest, she let out a breathy little sigh that raised the fine hairs on his body. She trailed her fingers lightly across his stomach before making a second trip with her fingernails, causing him to break out in goose bumps.

"Oh, you're *so* much better than my fantasies," she said, her voice almost reverent. "And my fantasies were pretty incredible."

She exhaled loudly as she traced his lower abdominal muscles, and the movement drew his attention to her breasts. Since she was on her back, they were barely contained by her dress, and his mouth tingled at the thought of being able to touch and taste them.

Inside his head, the voice of reason had grown fainter. It was barely a whisper now: *You can still salvage the situation,* it told him. *But you have to stop now. You can't go any further.*

She brought her cobalt-blue gaze to his face. "Do you know what I wished for tonight when the chef brought out my slice of birthday cake? When I blew out the candle, I wished the night would end with us in bed together and you deep inside me."

He sucked in a breath. He'd wished for the same thing, hundreds of times, if not thousands.

Grasping the waistband of his underwear, she pulled him down to cover her. Her breasts flattened under his bare chest, the silky fabric of her dress cool against his hot skin. She licked her lips, her mouth just inches from his, and he stopped thinking about what he shouldn't do and started thinking about all the things he was going to do once she was naked.

"I bought this dress for you, Nick. I wanted to look good. I wanted you to notice me. To want me."

He noticed everything about her: the way she scrunched her nose when she tried not to laugh, the way she rubbed her right eyebrow when she was tired, and the way she tapped her lips when she was nervous.

She had no idea how much he wanted her. And it wasn't because of her damn dress, either. But it definitely looked good. And it would look even better on the floor.

Accepting the inevitable, he slipped his hand inside the bodice of her dress and delved inside her bra, cupping her breast in his hand. It was warm and firm, and her hard, velvety nipple poked his palm. He shaped her breast gently, and she sighed softly.

While he continued to caress her breast, he nuzzled the tender skin behind her ear, pulling in a deep breath scented with her perfume and her own unique fragrance. He sucked lightly on her skin before trailing his tongue down the side of her neck. She arched it to give him access, and he nipped her smooth white skin.

Suddenly, she pushed against his chest. "Stop."

He closed his eyes briefly, torn between crushing disappointment and overwhelming relief. Thank God one of them had enough sense to stop this runaway train before it derailed and plunged into a ravine. He rolled off her, falling to his side, and she launched herself off the bed as if it were on fire.

Teagan spun to face him, but to his surprise, she reached toward her side and pulled down a zipper he hadn't even noticed. He propped himself up on his elbow, his eyes locked on her luscious body.

She shimmied out of that gorgeous green dress, bending down to step out of it. The movement pushed her breasts together, creating some magnificent cleavage, and he promised himself that before the night was over, he was going to run his tongue up and down that valley.

She rose, and he took in her va-va-voom body with its big breasts, small waist, and ample hips. Saliva pooled in his mouth, and he had to wipe his lips to keep from drooling. She was everything he'd imagined, but more. *So much more.*

He could see her creamy skin peeking through her black lace bra, and her tiny matching panties and a black garter belt highlighted her pussy. The thigh-high stockings he'd seen earlier covered her shapely legs, and he wondered if she was going to give him a show and remove them or if he'd get to pull them off.

She turned to drape her dress over the chair in the corner, and he couldn't hold back a moan when he saw the globes of her ass and the tiny strip of black lace between them. He'd love to slide his cock down that sweet crevice before pushing into her pussy from behind.

He wondered if she liked that position or if she preferred another. He was willing to do it whatever way she wanted as long as she let him inside her.

Climbing back on the bed, she knelt next to him. Her stomach wasn't even close to flat, but that wasn't a problem for him. In fact, he liked the fact that she was softer than he was.

He circled her bellybutton with his forefinger, the action bringing a blush to her cheeks. He reached up to smooth her pink skin, tracing her cheekbone with the tips of his fingers.

She looked down, her dark eyelashes fanning her cheeks. They were so long they looked fake, but he knew they were real because they had been exactly the same length when she'd been burning up with a fever.

She was so beautiful, and if he'd been able to form any words, he would have told her so. Instead, he reached up and pulled a sparkly pin from her hair. He wanted to run his fingers through the dark strands.

She raised her arms to remove the rest of the pins, pushing her breasts into his face, and he couldn't stop himself from sticking his face in her cleavage and giving it a long lick. He growled when he felt the smooth skin of her breasts, and she laughed, obviously thinking he was playing. She had no idea how close he was to throwing her down, ripping off her panties, and taking what he needed.

He pulled her down toward him until he could roll her onto her back. He leaned over her, and she smoothed her hand over his hair before dropping it to his face. Turning his cheek into her palm, he savored the feel of her skin against his.

He was a little worried about how turned on he was. Blood pulsed in his cock like he was only seconds from coming, and he still had his pants on. He'd never felt this kind of overwhelming arousal before, and he was afraid it was because he was with Teagan.

She took a deep breath, and her lace-covered breasts pressed against his chest, reminding him that he had two pretty presents to unwrap. Reaching between them, he unhooked her bra clasp and pushed the lacy cups away. He moaned under his breath when he saw the creamy mounds.

Breasts had never been his favorite body part, but Teagan's were fucking spectacular. They were even bigger than he'd imagined, definitely the largest *real* breasts he'd ever seen. They were firm and round and tipped with nipples the color of raspberries, and he couldn't wait to get his mouth on them.

Dropping his head, he pulled one of her pebbled nipples into his mouth. She tasted so good against his tongue he forgot to be gentle, and he sucked strongly. She gasped, clenching her fingers in his hair, and pulled his head back a little.

His control was shredded, and he knew he had lost his finesse. It had never been a problem before, but he'd never been this worked up, either. He wanted to make this good for Teagan, but he was so on edge he wasn't sure he would be able to give her an orgasm before he shot off.

"Nick, I don't need any more foreplay. I've wanted this for months. Every time you brushed up against me, it was foreplay.

Every time you touched my arm or my back or my hand, it was foreplay." She smiled, her eyes shining brightly. "You need to take off your pants, put on a condom, and get down to business."

Her words shocked him so much his eyes widened and his mouth dropped open. *Is she serious?*

She laughed softly, and she was still laughing when she leaned up to kiss him. She twirled her tongue around his before smacking his ass.

"Take these off," she directed, tugging on his trousers. "Condoms are in the top drawer of the nightstand."

He debated whether to do as she'd asked. He definitely didn't need any more stimulation, but he wanted to touch her. He wanted to learn what she liked, what made her moan, what made her cry out. He wanted to give her so much pleasure she forgot every other man she'd ever been with before him.

He wanted her to remember him. And he sure as hell didn't want her to remember him as her worst lover.

Swinging his legs over the side of the bed, he sat up. He took his time untying his shoes before removing them and his socks. He used the activity to bring his body and his mind under control.

He stood and removed his boxer briefs and suit pants, allowing his erection to spring free. Pulling open the top drawer on the nightstand, he removed a box of unopened condoms.

He stared at the box, wondering if it had been a while since she'd needed condoms or if she went through so many she had extra boxes on hand. He clenched his jaw at the thought of her with another man but pushed it out of his mind.

*He* was the one who was here now. *He* was the one who was going to spend the entire night inside her.

*Me. No one else.*

Opening the box, he removed three condoms and placed them on the nightstand. Teagan laughed softly.

"Three? Isn't that a bit optimistic?"

He shook his head. The way he felt right now, the whole box wouldn't be enough.

He crawled over her, kneeling between her legs. He eyed her garter belt and stockings, trying to decide if he wanted to take them off. They were every man's fantasy—his included—and he opted to leave them on.

Hooking his fingers in her lacy panties, he pulled them from her body. She was nearly bare except for a thin strip of dark hair running down the middle of her pussy, and he traced it with the tip of his forefinger.

She widened her legs, and he dipped his finger between the pink folds, groaning when he felt how wet and hot she was. He eased a finger inside her, his vision narrowing when she let out a low moan and rocked against his hand.

Slipping a second finger inside her, he placed his thumb against her clit and stroked lightly. He circled the hard little nub before pressing on it. As more wetness flowed from her body, he pushed his fingers deeper.

"Maybe I wasn't clear enough when I told you I didn't need any foreplay," she gasped.

He ignored her, flicking her clit with his thumbnail. He thrust his fingers inside her again, pressing deep and pumping in and out.

"I need more than your fingers. I've never been able to come this way."

*Hmm.* That sounded like a challenge, one he couldn't ignore in good conscience.

Withdrawing his fingers, he squeezed her clit between his thumb and forefinger and rubbed up and down, a little trick he'd read about in *Maxim* magazine. She moaned, and he did it again, making her jerk against him.

She was panting, little gusts of breath that let him know he was doing something right. He squeezed her clit harder before pressing his thumb against the bundle of nerves and plunging his fingers deep inside her.

"Oh!" she cried, stiffening. "Oh, my *God.*"

Her pussy clenched on his fingers, the tight ring of muscles vibrating with an intense orgasm. He smiled, immensely pleased he had accomplished something she'd claimed was impossible.

He pushed deeper inside her, flicking his thumbnail over her clit at the same time. She let out a little squeal, and her pussy pulsed against his fingers again.

*And that might be number two.*

As she whimpered softly, he pulled his fingers from her body to grab a condom. His hands weren't steady, so it took him a little longer than normal to sheath his cock in latex.

When he finally got it on, he quickly settled himself on top of her, hooked her leg over his hip, and thrust deeply inside her.

He moaned as her hot flesh enclosed him. She was unbelievably tight, almost virginal. She cried out, and he froze.

*Fuck! Did I hurt her?*

He pulled out a little, worried he'd been too rough. He was larger than average, and she had him so revved up, he'd forgotten to be careful with her. He'd forgotten everything but the overwhelming need to be inside her.

She wrapped her arms and legs around him and palmed his ass. Digging her nails into his cheeks, she pressed him deeper as she raised her hips.

"Oh, you feel so good," she breathed. "You're so big. I can feel you everywhere."

Squeezing his eyes shut, he tried to ignore her voice. He was almost senseless with pleasure, and every word out of her mouth pushed him closer and closer to the edge.

He pulled out to sink into her again, and she tightened her legs around his hips. He tried to find a rhythm, but he was too far gone to do anything but plunge erratically into her.

He'd never felt like this before. His body was completely out of his control, driven solely by instinct rather than intellect. He dropped his head to kiss her, pushing his tongue into her mouth as he nudged deeply inside her body.

She moaned his name against his lips. "I'm coming again," she gasped.

Her words sent him over the edge. Cupping her hips in his hands, he thrust hard against her. He climaxed in a blinding rush, the pleasure edging to pain as his cock jerked inside her again and again.

Shuddering, he collapsed on top of her. He'd never come so hard. His ears rang and his vision was dark and blurry.

He buried his face in her fragrant hair, breathing heavily as she stroked her hands over his back and sucked his earlobe. He shivered from the heat of her mouth, his cock twinging. He groaned in disbelief. It wasn't possible for him to want her again. He was barely conscious.

"That *definitely* was worth waiting for," she whispered into his ear.

# Chapter 20

TEAGAN'S FLIGHT FROM BOSTON TO SAN FRANCISCO WAS ON time, and she had to be at the airport in less than an hour. But first she was going to stop by Nick's condo. She hadn't seen him or talked to him in more than a month, not since the night of her birthday dinner. But she really needed a shoulder to cry on, and his shoulder was the one she wanted most of all.

Quinn had called her last night to drop the bomb that their dad had colon cancer, and she was flying home so she could be with her family when they met with his oncologist. Her misguided parents had planned to wait to tell her until after they'd met with the doctor because they hadn't wanted to disrupt her final weeks of school. But Quinn had shared the bad news, not only because he was a good brother but also because he knew she would have torn him apart if he'd kept it from her.

The town car glided to a stop in front of a three-story brownstone, and her gaze settled on the black numbers next to the bright red door. She'd never been to Nick's home, but Quinn had texted the address to her.

The driver jumped out and ran around to open her door. As she exited the car, she warned him she wasn't sure how long she would be.

She reached the top of the stairs and pulled in a deep

breath, trying to calm her stomach. Ever since she'd received Quinn's call, she had fought nausea. Sometimes when she was really stressed, her stomach freaked out, and she was more upset than she'd ever been in her life from the combined worry about her dad and the situation with Nick.

Their night together had been intense and intimate, and she'd been emotionally raw and physically exhausted the next day. He'd left her condo while she'd been sleeping, and she knew him well enough to understand he was having a hard time dealing with the shift in their relationship. He hadn't called, and he hadn't texted, and she hadn't tried to contact him, either, because she'd convinced herself that he needed time to adjust.

She'd made it through midterms, and she had tried to enjoy spring break in Bora Bora with Bebe. But she'd checked her phone fifty times a day, hoping she would hear from Nick.

As the days had gone by with no word from him, she'd wondered if she was fooling herself.

Maybe he didn't need time to adjust. Maybe she was just another forgettable lay in a long line of one-night stands. She really didn't believe he would treat her like that, though.

She used the brass knocker hanging on the door, and moments later, the door swung open. A tall, gorgeous blonde filled the doorway, and Teagan double-checked the numbers beside the door.

"I'm sorry. I must have the wrong address. I'm looking for Nick Priest."

The young woman tilted her head, her long, honey-colored hair falling over her shoulders. She was dressed casually in black yoga pants, a formfitting red T-shirt, and ballet flats.

"You have the right address. How do you know Nick?"

Teagan frowned as the sick feeling in her stomach crawled up her throat. She swallowed, trying to push down the nausea.

"We're fr . . . is he here?"

"I'm Vanessa. And you are?"

"Teagan O'Brien."

Vanessa eyed Teagan, her silvery-gray gaze assessing. She opened the door wider and stood to the side.

"Come in," she invited, waving Teagan inside.

Teagan stepped into the foyer, and Vanessa closed the front

door with a sharp click before turning toward her. "Can I take your jacket?"

She shook her head, pulling the jacket closer to her body. Suddenly, she was freezing, almost as if she had the flu again. She brushed her hand over her forehead, which was beaded with sweat. Her body didn't seem to know if it was hot or cold.

Vanessa shrugged and turned to head down the hall. When Teagan hesitated, she stopped, her eyebrows raised.

"Coming?" she asked.

Teagan trailed after Vanessa, wondering who the hell she was, why she acted like she belonged in Nick's condo, and why she was there so early in the morning.

The blonde led her into a large, high-ceilinged living area. A set of brown leather furniture filled the space, and she gestured to a chair.

"Have a seat. Nick's in the shower, but I'll let him know you're here so he can hurry. He takes the longest showers."

How did Vanessa know such a personal detail? Teagan didn't know that about him. Her stomach lurched at the evidence she and Vanessa were both members of Nick's harem.

"Bathroom?"

Vanessa pointed toward a hallway on the other side of the room, and Teagan dashed toward it. She barely made it before she threw up her breakfast in painful heaves. She huddled on the floor against the toilet, her eyes stinging and her ears ringing.

Finally, her stomach settled, and she rose to clean up. She rinsed her mouth and wiped away the mascara that rimmed her eyes before running the sleeve of her jacket under the water because there was vomit on it.

She checked her hair before pulling it into a ponytail and did a final review in the full-length mirror. Her face was ghost white, and her eyes were red-rimmed. Even worse, they also had dark circles under them because she hadn't slept last night after Quinn's phone call.

*Isn't it just fabulous I'm going to see Nick when I look like shit?*

Of course she'd get sick at his house instead of in the comfort of her own condo. She had never felt such a horrible lack of control over her emotions. She was coming apart at the seams.

It had been a terrible idea for her to show up at Nick's condo unannounced, even though he did it to her all the time. She had never imagined one of his women would be here. She'd been almost sure he never brought women home.

Although she had known it was unlikely, she'd nurtured the hope that Nick wanted to have a relationship with her. Vanessa's presence in his condo certainly nipped those hopes in the bud.

So many emotions swirled though her, but the strongest one was despair. She'd taken a risk, hoping Nick wanted her for more than one night, and it hadn't paid off.

She was tempted to stay in the bathroom, but eventually she took a deep breath and made her way back down the hall toward the living area. She stopped abruptly when she saw Nick. He stood in the middle of the room, his arms crossed over his chest.

He wore a Colonials T-shirt and ratty black athletic pants. His feet were bare, and his hair was wet from his shower. He radiated health, which made her feel even more wretched.

Her stomach lurched again when she saw his face. His lips were compressed, and his eyes were distant. She continued into the room, stopping a couple of feet away from him.

They stared at each other for several heartbeats, and she wished he would wrap his arms around her and give her the comfort she so desperately craved. She was scared, and she needed him.

"Hi," she said, her voice raspy from anxiety and her earlier bout of vomiting.

He didn't respond to her greeting, and she nervously wiped her sweaty hands on the front of her jacket, her heart thudding heavily. "I'd hoped that you would be glad to see me, but obviously you're not."

His facial expression didn't change, and he didn't respond. He'd never been cold and unfriendly with her, and his lack of warmth made her heart ache. She told herself to leave before she made the situation worse. But her damn mouth opened anyway.

"I thought you just needed time to accept what happened between us, but you clearly regret our night together."

He nodded, humming a little before he spoke. "Mistake."

She sucked in a breath, feeling as if he'd punched her in the stomach. She didn't know what she'd expected, but it wasn't this.

"Why?"

He pressed his lips together but didn't answer her question. Panic built in her chest, making it difficult to pull in a deep breath.

"Talk to me, damn it," she demanded, her voice thick.

He looked up at the ceiling, obviously wishing he were anywhere but here with her. Tears welled in her eyes, and she tried to blink them back.

"It wasn't a mistake," she said, hating the desperation in her voice. "We're good together."

He shook his head slowly. Tears trickled down her cheeks, and she wiped them away with the sleeve of her jacket, the one she hadn't vomited all over.

He cleared his throat. "Forget."

"Forget?" she repeated incredulously. "You want me to forget that you touched every inch of my body? You want me to forget what you feel like inside me? Is that what you want me to forget, Nick?"

Her voice had risen with each question, yet his expression hadn't changed. He nodded.

"I don't want to forget it. It was the best night of my life."

She wasn't exaggerating. And it wasn't an exaggeration to say the past twenty four hours had been the worst day of her life.

"It meant something," she added.

He shook his head slowly, and a wave of anger washed over her. He had to be lying.

"Yes, it did," she countered. "It meant something to me. And it meant something to you, too. I know you care about me."

He shook his head again, and she swallowed thickly. Did he know he was destroying her?

"It wasn't just sex for me," she whispered. "I'm in love with you."

His eyes widened, a mix of incredulity and disgust on his handsome face, and he dropped his hands to his sides. He backed away from her, and she closed the space between them.

Placing her hands on his chest, she looked up at him. "I don't want to lose you."

She hated herself for begging, but words broke free from her heart and spilled out of her mouth. "It's okay if you don't want to be with me—if you don't feel the same. We can still be friends. I promise it can be like it used to be."

She meant every word she said. She would take whatever he was willing to give her.

Shaking his head, he gripped her wrists and gently pulled her hands off his chest. "No."

"What?" she gasped. "You don't even want to be friends anymore?"

"No," he repeated, releasing her hands.

She shook her head in disbelief, unwilling to accept what he had said. "But why?"

He stared into her eyes for a long moment before turning on his heel and striding from the room. Seconds later, Vanessa joined Teagan, a bottle of water in her slender hands. She handed it to her before gesturing toward the front of the condo.

"Nick asked me to show you out. He wanted me to say good-bye for him."

"IT'S GOING TO BE OKAY, *KANYA*."

Teagan looked at Bebe, who perched on the edge of the bathtub. Her vision wavered a little bit, and her best friend patted her knee.

"Breathe, Teagan."

Teagan nodded, shifting on top of the hard lid of the toilet. She took a deep breath, trying to breathe through her mouth rather than her nose so she wouldn't throw up again.

She placed the pregnancy test on the bathroom counter, lining it up with the other three tests that were already there. All four had big plus signs on them.

*Congratulations! You're pregnant!*

She'd had no idea she was pregnant even though she had been fighting nausea off and on for weeks, along with exhaustion. She had thought it was stress-related. Her emotions had been all over the place, something she'd also attributed to stress. She'd been bitchy one moment and teary-eyed the next.

Bebe must have noticed Teagan's moodiness because this evening after class, she'd shown up at her condo with a bottle of wine and a plastic bag printed with the name of the local drugstore. Teagan had reached for the wine, intending to open it, but Bebe handed her the bag instead, saying, "This first, and then we'll see about the wine."

Teagan had peeked inside the bag, expecting chocolate. She laughed incredulously when she saw the pregnancy tests inside it.

"There's no way I'm pregnant," she had said, supremely confident.

Bebe had raised her eyebrows at Teagan's claim. "Go pee on a stick, *kanya*, and then we'll talk," she'd said, pointing toward the bathroom.

Turned out that Teagan wouldn't be drinking any wine that night, or for the next nine months.

"You have to tell Nick."

"I know," she replied before starting to cry again.

Bebe leaned forward, wrapping her arm around Teagan and pulling her close. She rubbed her hand up and down Teagan's arm.

"You've always said you wanted kids," Bebe reminded her. "In fact, you said you wanted a lot of kids."

"I know. But I never envisioned being a single mother. I wanted a husband, and I wanted my kids to have a father."

"Your baby has a father."

Yes, her baby had a father. A man who used women and threw away friends like garbage. A man whom she loved more than anything or anyone.

She hiccupped, and Bebe handed her a tissue so she could wipe her eyes. She dabbed them and looked up to meet Bebe's golden gaze.

"You're only seven weeks pregnant. It's not too late to have an abortion."

Teagan shuddered, pressing her hand against her lower stomach. She'd barely had time to wrap her mind around the fact that she was pregnant, but she already knew she wasn't getting rid of this baby. Somehow she already loved it as much as she loved its father.

"No," she said fiercely.

Bebe nodded, clearly unsurprised by her vehemence. She resumed her perch on the tub, tilting her head.

"You're going to be a great mother, *kanya*. This baby won the mommy lotto."

Teagan laughed huskily. *What would I do without Bebe?*

Her best friend had been waiting at the airport when she'd

returned from San Francisco, shell-shocked and heartbroken. Teagan's dad was *sick*, and her whole family was struggling to come to terms with his illness. His colon cancer was advanced, stage IIIB. The oncologist had recommended surgery to remove part of her dad's colon, along with radiation and chemo.

Teagan couldn't wait for school to be over so she could move back to San Francisco permanently. She was so eager to get home she wasn't even going to go through the pomp and circumstance of graduation.

Her dad's type of cancer had a five-year survival rate of less than fifty percent. He was fighting for his life, and she needed to be there with him.

And now she had to think about a baby—Nick's baby.

"How did this happen?" Teagan asked, shaking her head in disbelief.

"I assume that's a rhetorical question, since you know how babies are made," Bebe replied, laughing lightly.

"I'm serious! We used condoms every single time. And they were brand new. And I got my period."

"Condoms are one of the least effective forms of birth control. They have a twenty percent failure rate, which means one out of five women will get pregnant, even with proper usage."

"Seriously?" Teagan glared at Bebe. "You're giving me a lecture on birth control now?"

Bebe continued, ignoring her snarky comment. "You said your period was early and really light. So it was probably spotting from the implantation of the embryo in the uterine wall."

She stood and scooped the pregnancy tests from the bathroom counter, dropping them in the wastebasket. She beckoned Bebe from the small room with a crook of her finger, and they headed toward the living area, where she collapsed on the sofa.

As Bebe curled up in an armchair, she asked, "Are you still planning to move back to San Francisco as soon as finals are over?"

Teagan looked at Bebe in surprise. "Of course. Why wouldn't I?"

"Because the father of your child is here."

She considered Bebe's point. She didn't know what to expect from Nick when she told him she was pregnant. She dreaded the conversation, especially after what had happened the last time they'd talked.

She wished she could erase that horrible morning in his condo from her memory. She had humiliated herself, first by telling him she was in love with him and then by begging him to be her friend.

Nick had disappeared from her life as if he'd never existed. It was eerily familiar to when Jason had broken up with her, and she wondered why it was so easy for the men she loved to forget her.

Nick had made it clear he didn't want to have anything to do with her. He didn't even want to be friends with her any longer, and that hurt more than him saying their night together didn't matter.

And now he was never going to be free of her because she was going to be the mother of his firstborn child. Or maybe not. Maybe he had a whole passel of illegitimate children. How would she know?

"I'm scared to tell Nick about the baby."

"I would be, too. But you still have to do it. You have to give him a chance to do the right thing."

"And what is the right thing exactly?" Teagan asked sarcastically. "I don't need his money. I have plenty of my own."

"You know it's not just about money," Bebe countered softly. "You need to give him the opportunity to be a father. It's up to him whether he takes it."

## Chapter 21

THE CONCRETE STAIRS WERE COLD AGAINST THE BACKS OF Nick's knees, and he shifted to find a more comfortable position. He'd been sitting in the stairwell of Teagan's building for more than an hour, trying to work up the courage to knock on her door.

It had been three weeks since she'd stopped by his condo, and he'd had plenty of time to think about how badly he'd fucked things up. He didn't know what to do to make them right, but he had to do something because he was a miserable bastard without Teagan. And he finally knew why: he was in love with her.

Letty was the one who'd finally made him see the truth about his feelings for Teagan. He was ashamed he hadn't figured it out on his own, but he was grateful the older woman had opened his eyes.

The night he had spent with Teagan had scared the shit out of him. It had been unlike anything he'd ever experienced, and when he had woken up in her bed just before dawn, he'd had a meltdown to rival Chernobyl.

There was no other way to describe it. His chest had felt tight, and he'd been overwhelmed by a sense of doom. He'd been convinced he had destroyed their friendship—convinced he had destroyed everything.

On some level, he had realized the difference between sex and sex with someone you loved. And instead of trying to work through things, he'd run away.

He had needed time to adjust, just like Teagan had said. She knew him better than he knew himself, and that was one of the reasons he'd gone bat shit crazy in the first place.

In the weeks following their night together, he tried to forget the taste of her lips, the smoothness of her skin, and the look in her eyes when he was deep inside her. He tried to forget the way he felt when he was with her.

He had called Tuesday, a woman he'd been screwing on and off for months, and met her in a hotel room just like always. But her eyes hadn't been blue enough, her hair hadn't been dark enough, and her smile hadn't been sweet enough, so he'd left her in the room without unzipping his pants.

He had wanted Teagan and only Teagan. But even then he hadn't realized why. He was *such* a fool.

He ran a hand over his hair, wondering how he was going to explain his feelings to Teagan when he could barely squeeze out a word. The conversation they'd had at his condo was proof he turned nearly mute when he was upset. He still couldn't believe what he'd said to her that morning. Or better yet, what he hadn't said.

He had been so shocked to see her, and he'd been torn between wanting to kiss her and wanting to kick her out of his condo. He should have fallen to his knees and begged her to forgive him for leaving her bed without a word, and then he should have taken her to his bedroom and worshipped her body.

At the time, he hadn't understood his feelings for her, and when she had asked him if he regretted their night together, he'd answered honestly. He had regretted it, and he had thought it had been a mistake.

But he hadn't been honest when he had let her think it hadn't meant anything. The opposite was true.

And he had no idea what he'd been thinking when he rejected her after she told him she loved him. He wondered how she could love him when he'd never done anything to earn her love. He had been convinced she had confused love with great sex. And holy shit, it had been more than great. It had been mind-blowing.

But he had really fucked the duck when he'd told her he didn't want to be friends anymore. After having sex with her, he'd known he couldn't go back to the ways things used to be. He would have been all over her every time they were together.

But he hadn't been able to articulate that. She'd misunderstood, and he hadn't done anything to set her straight because he figured it was for the best.

Vanessa had obviously told her mother about Teagan's visit because Letty gave him an ear-blistering unlike he'd ever received. She'd arrived at the condo just minutes after Teagan had left, and she'd ranted at him for nearly an hour.

She ended her lecture with a bomb. "You're in love with Teagan!" she'd screeched.

Her words had hit him with the force of a 350-pound linebacker, and he'd immediately denied it. In response, Letty had slapped him on the side of the head as if he were a five-year-old who'd just stolen a cookie from the cookie jar.

"You're an idiot!" she'd bellowed directly into his ear, damn near deafening him.

And she had been right. He was an idiot for not realizing long ago that he was in love with Teagan, and he *hated* himself for it. He knew Teagan must hate him, too—with good reason.

After Teagan's unexpected visit to his condo and Letty's eye-opening lecture, he had needed some time alone. He had packed a duffle bag and booked a flight to Denver, and when he arrived in Colorado, he holed up in an isolated cabin high in the Rocky Mountains with his phone turned off.

When he finally turned it back on, fifty messages were waiting for him. Most of them were from Quinn, Letty, and Elijah, but a few were from Teagan. She hadn't said much, only asking him to call her. As soon as he'd heard her messages, he'd jumped on a flight back to Boston.

Quinn's messages had passed along the bad news about James, and Nick knew Teagan would be devastated by her dad's diagnosis. He'd come directly from the airport to see her, but chickened out when he reached her floor.

He shifted again. If he didn't get up soon, his knees were going to ache like a bitch tomorrow.

The door to the sixth floor opened behind him, and he

lurched to his feet. He turned and stepped up to the landing, hoping it wasn't Teagan. He wasn't ready to face her yet.

*Shit.*

It was Marshall Brants.

Marshall froze when he saw Nick, his eyes narrowed in dislike. After a tense moment, he stepped closer, and Nick realized the other man was much larger than he'd remembered. In fact, he reminded him a little bit of Quinn, except for the brown eyes.

"What are you doing here?" Marshall asked, planting his hands on his hips. "Teagan told me less than an hour ago that things were over between the two of you."

Nick worked to keep his face impassive, but he obviously failed because Marshall smiled mockingly. "Yeah, she's done with you. I don't know what you did, but man, she hates your guts. You had your chance, and you fucked up. *Big-time.*"

Nick tried to step around Marshall. He had to see Teagan. *Right now.*

Marshall blocked him, and Nick battled the impulse to smash his fist into the other man's face. He didn't think Teagan would be very happy if he got into a fistfight in the stairwell of her building.

"Why can't you leave her alone?"

When Nick didn't answer, Marshall's eyebrows rose. "You're a real asshole, you know that? Teagan kept telling me you were a nice guy who wasn't interested in her, but I knew something was up."

Marshall shook his head. "We're just friends," he said in a high falsetto, obviously mimicking Teagan. "Really good friends, but just friends." He made a rude noise. "I knew you wouldn't waste your time with her unless you wanted to fuck her."

Marshall held up his hands, palms out. "I don't blame you, man. I've been trying to get in her pants for months. I wondered why she wouldn't let me in, but now I know. You were cock blocking me."

Nick clenched his fists. He was fucking ecstatic Teagan hadn't slept with Marshall, but he was *this close* to ramming the man's head into the wall.

"You can get a piece of ass anywhere," Marshall said,

pushing Nick's chest with both hands and forcing him into the wall. "Why do you have to mess with Teagan?"

As Nick stared at Marshall, he suddenly realized the other man wasn't just jealous. He was trying to protect Teagan. That fact alone prevented Nick from taking Marshall apart with his bare hands.

"She's too good for you. Hell, she's too good for me." Marshall sighed. "She's amazing." He poked Nick's chest with his forefinger. "And she deserves more than a dickhead like you."

Nick swallowed thickly. Marshall was right. Teagan was amazing, and she definitely deserved more than a dickhead like him.

"What do you have to offer other than money?" Marshall continued. "She doesn't need that. What she really wants is a husband and kids. Are you willing to give her that?"

Nick pushed Marshall away from him, and the other man stepped back. He pointed at Nick.

"Do you really think you can make Teagan happy? I don't. In fact, I doubt you could even be faithful to her." He shook his head. "I don't know why I'm wasting my breath," he muttered, starting down the stairs. "You're just another rich, entitled athlete who treats women like shit. You're worse than Tiger Woods. *Asshole*."

Nick watched Marshall's broad back disappear down the stairs before sinking down onto the top step. Bracing his elbows on his knees, he dropped his head into his hands and considered Marshall's question.

What could he offer Teagan? He loved her, but he didn't know if he'd be good at *loving* her.

He had never been in love before. He was an emotional virgin. And before Teagan, he didn't think anyone had ever loved him. Maybe his mother had loved him, but there was no way for him to know.

He didn't know how to be a boyfriend, let alone a husband, and he definitely didn't know how to be a father. In fact, his stuttering guaranteed he would fail in all those roles. It was a death knell for relationships.

When he'd come here today, he had only been thinking about himself. He hadn't thought about what was best for Teagan. Was it better for her to go back to San Francisco and move on with her life with another man—one who could communicate clearly, one who had more to offer than Nick?

The thought made him sick. He didn't want to let her go. He didn't know if he *could* let her go.

Rising to his feet, he pulled open the door to the sixth floor. The hallway stretched in front of him, dull and empty—just like his life without Teagan. He hesitated on the threshold for several heartbeats before closing the door and starting the walk back down the stairs.

Yes, he was a selfish bastard. But he loved Teagan, and for once—*for once*—he was going to put someone else's happiness above his own.


TEAGAN PLACED A STACK OF SHIRTS IN ONE OF THE SUITCASES on top of her bed and turned toward her closet to pull several pairs of pants from the hangers. She threw them on the bed and began folding them.

"Are you sure you feel well enough to pack?" Bebe asked. "Maybe you should lie down and let me do it."

"I'm fine."

Bebe's soft sigh carried from the corner of Teagan's bedroom, where she sat in the overstuffed chair. Teagan glanced toward her best friend, who watched her with concern.

"Okay, I'm not fine," she admitted. "But I have a million things to do before I go back home to San Francisco."

"I know," Bebe said sympathetically. "Are you still having cramps?"

"No."

The physical pain from her miscarriage was gone, but the emotional pain was still there. She worried it might never go away.

The cramps had started during the final exam for her organizational behavior class. She'd felt slightly off all day, but she and Bebe had stayed up late the night before studying for the exam, so she'd blamed it on a lack of sleep.

The first twinge in her lower abdomen had been a painful shock, but when it disappeared after a few heartbeats, she'd relaxed and continued with the exam. A few minutes later, she'd felt as if a huge fist had gripped her lower half and squeezed.

She had known immediately something was wrong, but she hadn't been able to move. She'd been paralyzed by pain and fear. Fortunately, Bebe had been right next to her. Her best friend was fabulous in a crisis, and she had Teagan in the ER in less than fifteen minutes.

But it had been too late. Teagan had lost her baby.

*Nick's baby.*

The on-call ob-gyn told her these things just happen sometimes—it just wasn't meant to be. And the doctor assured her there was no reason she couldn't have other children.

But Teagan knew this was her one and only chance to have Nick's baby. She'd been pathetic enough to think if she couldn't have him, at least she would have his child. But she couldn't even have that.

She had wanted the baby like she'd wanted nothing else in her life, even its father. She'd wanted to see what she and Nick had created, maybe a dark-haired, green-eyed little boy or a blond-haired, blue-eyed little girl.

"Still no word from Nick?"

Teagan shook her head, trying to push back the wave of rage that threatened to pull her under. Nick had never even known about the baby because he hadn't bothered to return any of her phone calls or texts.

She hadn't wanted to break the news about her pregnancy in a voicemail or text, so all of her messages were short and to the point. "Call me. I need to talk to you." But he'd never responded.

Bebe made a sound of disgust. "What a *jerk*. I wish he were here so I could take him down."

Teagan smiled sadly. Bebe had been one of Nick's biggest fans—not a football fan, but a fan of the man himself. She'd been convinced Nick and Teagan would end up together. But now he was on Bebe's black list.

He was on Teagan's black list, too. Her love for him was slowly turning into something ugly—something shaded with anger, disappointment, and disgust. It was transforming into hate.

He had abandoned her when she'd needed him the most. She had needed him when she found out about her dad's cancer. She had needed him when she writhed in pain and sobbed from the knowledge their baby was gone.

But he hadn't been there.

The doctor had told Teagan that her miscarriage was no one's fault. In fact, the woman went out of her way to make sure Teagan didn't blame herself. And she didn't, not really.

But she blamed Nick. And she didn't care if she was being irrational or unfair. Maybe she wouldn't have miscarried their baby if Nick hadn't rejected her. Maybe her body wouldn't have been so overwhelmed with stress it couldn't sustain a pregnancy.

She still didn't understand why Nick had acted the way he had. She knew she'd been the aggressor the night they'd finally had sex, but he had wanted her, too. In fact, it seemed as if he hadn't been able to get enough of her. He'd taken her so many times she lost count.

She had looked into his eyes when he was deep inside her, and she had seen more than desire. And the way he had touched her had felt like love.

But maybe he was just really good in bed. Maybe he was like that with all his lovers.

"Are you going to tell him you were pregnant and miscarried?"

"No. I hope I never talk to him again. I hope I never see him again."

Teagan didn't know how she'd react if and when she saw Nick again. She had known loving him would bring her nothing but heartache, but she hadn't been able to stop herself.

She had imagined what it would be like to have sex with him, but she'd never really thought it would happen. And she'd never considered the possibility of having a child with him.

"You're not going to be able to avoid him entirely," Bebe warned. "He's an honorary member of your family, you said."

Teagan shrugged. Since he wanted nothing to do with her, she was sure he'd find a way to avoid any messy encounters.

"Are you going to tell your brothers what happened?"

"No!" Teagan shuddered at the horrific thought. "Of course not."

She never wanted anyone in her family to know what had happened between her and Nick. It was too private.

*Too painful.*

"Why not? They'd beat the shit out of him," Bebe said gleefully.

Teagan suspected Bebe was right. Quinn and Cal were über-protective of her, and she had little doubt that Nick's best-friend status wouldn't protect him. If anything, her brothers would probably consider his behavior even more deplorable because they trusted him.

"How do you know what they'd do? You've never even met them."

"I feel like I know them because you talk about them all the time. Cal would hold Nick down while Quinn beat him to a bloody pulp."

"I don't know about that," Teagan said. "Cal is more laid-back than Quinn, but when he loses control . . . let's just say it's better to be far away from him when it happens."

Teagan passed Bebe a pile of shirts. "Make yourself useful, Ms. Banerjee."

They lapsed into a comfortable silence for several minutes as they focused on folding Teagan's clothes. Bebe sniffled, and Teagan looked up to see her best friend's big golden eyes full of tears.

Dropping the shirt she'd been folding, she rushed to Bebe's side and knelt next to her. "What's wrong?" she asked, placing her hand on Bebe's knee and squeezing.

"I'm going to miss you."

"I'm going to miss you too, Beebs," she replied, tears springing to her eyes.

"Things are going to really suck without you here. I know I sound pathetic, but at least you have your family waiting for you. I don't have anyone."

Teagan nodded. Bebe wasn't being dramatic. She didn't have many friends, and her family only got in touch with her when they wanted to harangue her for disappointing them.

But Bebe's affection wasn't one-sided. Teagan didn't want to go for months without seeing her best friend, either.

"I know you've already accepted the job with BioEdge, but there are a lot of biotech companies in the Bay Area. Why not think about working for one of them? We could see each other as often as we wanted. We could even be roommates."

Bebe shook her head. "I'd love that, but it's not realistic. Those companies are start-ups. They're biotech incubators, and they have to funnel their money into research. The East

Coast biotech companies pay almost double, and I need every penny I can get."

Teagan had wondered how Bebe had paid for Harvard, especially since her parents had cut her off financially. She'd assumed her best friend had taken out student loans, and once Bebe graduated, she would have to start paying them back.

Like many college students, Bebe probably was drowning in debt. Teagan wondered if she would allow Teagan to pay off her student loans as a graduation gift or if she'd be offended. Bebe was unpredictable, so it could go either way.

"What about working for Riley O'Brien? I know a few executives there," Teagan quipped.

"No. I appreciate the offer, but I want to use my degrees."

"I understand."

Bebe had undergraduate degrees in biochemistry and molecular biology. She had gone to medical school when she'd graduated from Northwestern University, and she had obtained her medical degree, but she had declined to go through her residency.

"What are you going to do once you get back to San Francisco?" Bebe asked, clearly wanting to change the subject.

"I'm going to be working in Riley O'Brien's law department. My dad and I talked about it, and he thought I could make the biggest impact there."

"And what about Nick?"

He'd told her to forget their night together. She was going to do one better.

She was going to forget him.

# Chapter 22

Present Day—San Francisco

SHE'D JUST HAD SEX IN A LINEN CLOSET. WITH NICK.

Teagan cringed, ashamed and disgusted by her behavior. *What is wrong with me? Where is my self-respect?*

"This was a mistake," she said, an observation for him and a reminder for her.

Nick sucked in a breath, and she knew he remembered that morning in his condo when she had discarded her pride and made herself an object of pity. It was something she thought about every single day, even though she tried not to.

Her legs shook, and she leaned against the wall to steady herself. Her body had yet to come down from the orgasms he'd given her, and she squeezed her thighs together to stop the internal pulses.

"I'm going to forget this ever happened," she said.

She prayed she could push it from her mind. God knew she hadn't been able to forget their one and only night together.

His eyes narrowed as he realized what she was doing, repeating almost verbatim their conversation from that morning so long ago. A conversation that was burned into her soul.

"It didn't mean anything," she added.

She wouldn't allow it to mean anything. And she ignored

the voice inside her that said it meant *everything*. The voice that said he still had the power to hurt her.

He shook his head, but she didn't know if he disagreed with her statement. He met her gaze, and the look in his eyes made her stomach churn.

"It meant something," he said slowly, as if the words were pulled from him. "Then and now." She tried not to let him see how his words impacted her, but her heart rate picked up. She crossed her arms over her chest.

"No."

"Yes." He cleared his throat. "It . . ." He hummed a little, and she tilted her head, wondering what he would say. "It meant something to me," he continued.

His words made her body flash hot and cold, and she rubbed her hands over her arms. Now he was the one repeating their previous conversation.

"It was just a quick fuck between two strangers," she countered, wincing internally at her bad language.

She rarely cursed and could count on one hand the number of times she'd said "fuck" outside the bedroom. But she needed to remind herself how he had treated her the last time they had been together.

Nick flinched at her words, his eyes shadowed. Clenching his jaw, he looked down.

"I know you're not picky. You'll stick your dick anywhere," she said, unsure whether she was trying to warn herself or insult him. Maybe both.

He jerked his head up, his eyes locked with hers. He paled a little under his tan, and she pushed down the guilt that swamped her. She had never talked to anyone the way she was talking to him, and more than likely, the things she said hurt her a lot more than they hurt him.

"I'm not special," she added. "You made that clear."

He laughed softly, the sound shaded with bitterness, and she frowned, confused by the pain she heard in it. He'd hurt her, not the other way around.

"You're special," he said hoarsely.

"Really, Nick?"

He nodded, and she laughed, a sharp sound completely

devoid of humor. "Wow. I can't imagine how you treat women who aren't special. I didn't feel special when you acted like I was a one-night stand. I didn't feel special when I told you I loved you, and you had Vanessa toss me out of your condo. And I definitely didn't feel special when you ignored my messages that I needed to talk to you."

"I can explain . . ."

He exhaled loudly. Stepping closer, he wrapped his big hand around the back of her neck and stared into her eyes, his gaze searching.

"So sorry," he finally said.

She squeezed her eyes shut, wishing he'd said these things when it could have made a difference—when she'd been pregnant with his baby and wanted nothing more than for them to be a family.

"Sorry," he repeated before leaning forward and kissing her, a gentle brush of his lips.

She turned her face, and he dusted tiny kisses over her cheek. He brought her mouth back to his, and she let herself enjoy the feel of his lips against hers, smooth and firm.

Opening her mouth, she invited him in, and he moaned against her lips. He swept his tongue inside her mouth, and she sucked on it, savoring the taste of him, strong and spicy with a trace of champagne.

She wasn't sure how long they kissed, but it was long enough for him to drop his hands to her hips and pull her against his burgeoning erection. She pulled back from his mouth, and he groaned in objection.

Stepping away from him, she waited until he opened his eyes, and then she slapped him across his face as hard as she could. His head snapped sideways, and he pressed his palm against his cheek. He slowly turned his head back toward her, his eyes wide with surprise and some other emotion she didn't recognize.

"I've been waiting for years to do that, but it never seemed like the right time. But *this*"—she waved her hand around the room—"is definitely the right time."

He dropped his hand, revealing a bright red mark where she had struck him. The sight of it gave her perverse pleasure that she'd hurt him, although it wasn't nearly as much as he'd hurt her.

"I told you to leave me alone. I told you not to touch me. And now I'm going to tell you again: stay away from me, Nick."

He stared at her, and she sucked in a deep breath, a little worried about how he would react. But then he smiled slowly, his green eyes so bright they were almost incandescent. He laughed softly, rubbing his cheek.

"Better than tears, T."

She growled, enraged by his comment. She hated to be reminded of how many times she'd cried in front of him.

He took a step toward her, and she spun away from him, lunging for the doorknob. She twisted it, trying to escape from the small room, but he slammed his hand against the door. She was trapped between his body and the door, his front pressed against her back. She elbowed him in the ribs, and he grunted but didn't move away.

"How many times do you need to slap me before you forgive me?" he rasped into her ear.

Pulling her earlobe between his lips, he sucked lightly. She gasped at the heat of his mouth, goose bumps breaking out all over her body.

He smoothed his hands down her sides before cupping her hips. He pressed into her, his erection huge and hard against the upper swells of her behind. She gritted her teeth, trying to ignore the fact that she was so turned on, wetness trickled down her inner thighs. Jerking her head away from his mouth, she flattened her hands against the smooth wood of the door and slanted a hateful glare over her shoulder.

"I'll never forgive you," she vowed. "I hate you. If you were on fire, I wouldn't toss water on you. If you were drowning, I wouldn't throw you a life preserver. If you were bleeding, I wouldn't tie a tourniquet. If you were—"

Nick curled his hand over her mouth to silence her, laughing huskily against her ear. He squeezed her hip gently with the other hand.

"I get the picture," he said as he fisted her dress in his hand, raising it to her waist and baring her entire lower half.

He slid his hand across her hip toward her stomach and cupped her mound. Tracing her labia, he eased his fingers between the folds. He gathered moisture from her body, drawing it upward toward her clit and circling it lightly with his long fingers.

"Do you hate this?"

Dropping her forehead against the door, she bit her lip in an effort to hold back a moan. He squeezed her clit between his thumb and forefinger, rubbing gently, and a zing went through her body.

He knew exactly how to touch her to make her fall apart, and she knew it would only take a few more strokes before she came again. She locked her knees and tried to wiggle free, but he just moved closer until she could feel him all around her—until she couldn't smell anything but him and her own arousal.

Nick worked his fingers inside her, those long fingers she still fantasized about. He twirled them around, pressing against a particularly sensitive spot inside her, and a moan escaped her. Chuckling darkly against her ear, he repeated the motion.

Her vision blurred as he slid his fingers in and out, occasionally brushing over her clit with light strokes. Curving her hand over his, she pressed his fingers deeper and held him against her as she climaxed silently. Her body clamped down on his fingers, the pleasure so intense she was almost numb in the aftermath.

He'd given her three orgasms in less than an hour. It was a miracle she wasn't comatose.

Withdrawing his fingers, he smoothed her dress down her body before turning her to face him. He placed his palm against her cheek, forcing her eyes to meet his.

The expression on his face scared her. He looked at her as if she was special—like this meant something. But she'd been down that road before, and she didn't like where it took her.

His eyes narrowed, and he dropped his head to kiss her, a kiss that felt as if he passed his soul to her. She pulled back, gasping for breath.

"Why won't you leave me alone? There have to be other women out there you want to . . . fuck."

He rubbed his thumb over her lower lip, and his eyes turned predatory. Leaning forward, he kissed her again, tracing her lips with his tongue before gliding it into her mouth.

*God, I love the way he kisses.*

He ended the kiss with a sharp little nip on her lip. Sliding his hand into her hair, he leaned his forehead against hers.

"Only you."

"Only me," Teagan echoed in disbelief, jerking away from him.

"Yes."

"You don't really expect me to believe that, do you?"

"Truth."

NICK DIDN'T BLAME TEAGAN FOR NOT BELIEVING HIM. BUT HE *was* telling the truth: she was the only woman he wanted to fuck. More important, she was the only woman he'd ever loved, and the only woman he wanted to spend his life with.

She was also the only woman—the only person—whom he would allow to say the things she'd said without retaliating. He deserved her harsh words, and he wanted her enough to accept any verbal abuse she threw his way.

Teagan took a deep breath, her luscious breasts rising under her red dress. He was still semi-erect from playing with her pussy, and his cock twitched. Pulling his eyes from her breasts, he focused on her face.

Her lips were turned down in a frown, and her eyes were shadowed. His heart pinched at the unhappiness he saw on her face.

Before he'd messed things up, she had been a truly happy person, fun-loving and funny. Quinn had told him that when she'd come back from Boston, she'd been drastically different, solemn and sarcastic.

Her older brother had attributed the shift to maturity and their father's illness, but Nick knew the real reason: he'd broken her heart. He thought he had a pretty good idea how she'd felt because he had broken his own heart when he'd walked away from her.

He had truly believed it was the best thing for her. But it had nearly destroyed him to do it. Eventually he'd realized the kind of love he felt for Teagan wasn't something you walked away from. It was something you couldn't escape.

He had realized something else, too: Teagan wasn't the kind of woman you walked away from. She was the kind of woman who haunted you, no matter how much you tried to move on with your life.

After she had moved back to San Francisco, Nick had tried to return to the life he'd had before he had fallen in love with her. He'd picked up women, fucked them in hotel rooms, and forgotten them.

But he hadn't been able to forget Teagan. And every time he had touched another woman, he pretended she was Teagan.

He'd told himself it was for the best. He'd told himself he had no other options because Teagan was better off without him. But the meaningless sex he had enjoyed before Teagan had left him feeling empty instead of satisfied.

With his personal life a mess, Nick had tried to focus on his job. But his performance on the field suffered, and his coaches demanded to know why his mind wasn't on the game anymore. The fans were even angrier, wondering why he'd gone from Super Bowl winner to regular season loser.

Despite his poor performance, the Colonials had wanted to extend his contract. But Nick had asked Elijah to get him out of Boston. Everywhere he had looked, he was reminded of Teagan.

When the Tennessee Titans had expressed interest in signing him, he'd told Elijah to make a deal. He'd been desperate for a change, hoping a new city would help him get over Teagan.

He was smarter now, though, and he knew he'd never get over her.

As Teagan leaned back against the door, she looked up at the ceiling. The position exposed her white throat, and his lips tingled with the desire to worship that smooth skin.

"It doesn't matter what you want, Nick, because I don't want you."

Squeezing his eyes shut, he tried to block out her words. He didn't believe she meant what she'd said, but it still felt as if she had kicked him in the balls. He reminded himself that he'd just been inside her luscious body, and she had come three times. She wanted him.

And she sure as hell hadn't said *no*. In any language.

"Liar," he muttered.

She jerked upright, spearing him with her dark blue gaze. "What did you say?" she asked, her eyes narrowed with menace.

"Liar," he repeated loudly.

She gasped and stalked toward him. "I'm not lying," she claimed, poking him in the chest with the tip of her red-polished nail.

Wrapping his fingers around her wrist, he pulled her against him. He leaned down until his nose almost touched hers.

"Liar."

Her eyes widened, and she jerked her wrist against his hold. Loosening his fingers, he let her go.

"We had sex, yes, but that doesn't mean I want *you*." She stared into his eyes. "You should know that better than anyone. When we had sex before, you made it clear you didn't want me, not even as a friend."

Panic built in his chest, and he tried to push it down. He had to stay calm so he could keep talking. This was the first time he'd even come close to getting her to listen.

"You misunderstood."

She laughed incredulously. "I misunderstood?"

He nodded.

"How did I misunderstand? I told you things didn't have to change. I told you that we could go back to the way things used to be. Just friends. And you said no."

"Couldn't go back," he squeezed out. "T-t-t-too hungry for you."

Teagan's mouth fell open. "What?"

Words backed up inside him, and he cleared his throat. She crossed her arms over her chest, clearly waiting for him to provide an answer. Too bad he didn't have a whiteboard. If he did, he could draw a fucking picture for her.

"Needed time to adjust," he said slowly. "Like you said."

"Time to adjust?" She shook her head. "When I said you needed time to adjust, I didn't think it would take years."

It hadn't taken years. But it had still taken too long.

*Way too long.*

"Maybe you did need time to adjust. But I needed something, too. I needed *you*. My dad was sick, and I was . . ."

She swallowed, turning her head away from him. He studied her profile—her dark, feathery eyelashes, the plump curve of her lips, the delicate shape of her nose.

He wanted to see her face every day for the rest of his life, and that was what he was fighting for. He wasn't going to be content until his ring was on her finger and her last name was Priest. Or O'Brien-Priest. He was willing to compromise on some things.

Teagan met his gaze, her face expressionless and her eyes cold. She spun toward the door, grabbing the handle.

"I don't need you anymore, for any reason," she said without turning around. "And I don't want you, either."

And he stood there, silent, as she left the linen closet, closing the door behind her with a soft click.

# Chapter 23

LETTY MET NICK AT THE FRONT DOOR WHEN HE ARRIVED AT HIS big house in Nashville. He had been tempted to stay in San Francisco, since Christmas was only a few days away, but ultimately he'd decided to fly back home.

He wanted to talk with Letty about Quinn's job offer and discuss what had happened with Teagan. He also needed to pack enough clothes to get him through the next few weeks until his stuff could be shipped to San Francisco.

"Hi, cutie," she said, leaning up to kiss his cheek. "How was your trip?"

When Nick had signed the deal with the Tennessee Titans a little more than two years ago, he'd asked Letty to come to Nashville with him. Her extended family lived in Boston, but her husband had died only a couple of years before she'd come to work for Nick. He had been a cop, and he'd died in the line of duty.

Boston held painful memories for Letty, which was why she'd agreed to move—that and the fact that Nick had bribed her. He'd offered to pay for college for all three of her kids, under-grad for Kyla and Ben and graduate school for Vanessa. He had plenty of money, and Letty was worth the investment, since she handled so many responsibilities, including personal assistant, housekeeper, and chef.

Propping his black suitcase against the textured wall in the high-ceilinged foyer, he hugged Letty to his side. She patted his back, gesturing toward the kitchen with her other hand.

"Are you hungry? I made chicken pot pie."

He nodded, and they made their way down the slate hallway to the big kitchen. With its exposed brick, glass-front oak cabinets, and granite countertops, it was his favorite room in the house.

Located in one of Nashville's most exclusive neighborhoods, the house was nearly ten thousand square feet with a four-car garage. It also had separate guest quarters, which was where Letty lived, and a huge outdoor entertaining area with a pool.

He had gotten the house for a steal. The owner had lost his shirt in a bunch of bankrupt commercial real estate deals, and he'd been desperate to off-load the mansion. The guy had liked luxury, and he'd designed the house with high-end finishes and high-tech touches.

More than any other place Nick had ever lived, the house felt like home. But he was sure it wasn't because of the bricks and mortar. It was because of Letty. She had brought heart to the house in the form of home-cooked meals, fresh flowers, and unique knickknacks.

While she bustled around the kitchen, he washed his hands in the farmhouse sink and grabbed a Shiner Bock from the fridge. He sat down on one of the wooden barstools situated around the bar and took a long swallow.

Letty leaned against the counter in front of him. She'd stopped wearing her chef uniform long before they had moved to Nashville, and she was dressed casually in a pair of khaki pants and a blue sweater that matched her eyes.

"Well? Did you see Teagan?"

He nodded.

"Did you have a chance to talk to her?"

He nodded again.

"What happened?"

When he didn't answer, Letty sighed in exasperation. She was used to his silence, but she didn't like it.

"Use your words, Nick."

More often than not, Letty treated him like a five-year-old. And for some strange reason, it didn't bother him. In fact, he kind of liked it.

"I apologized, and she slapped my f-f-f-face. *Hard*."

"Good for her," Letty chortled. "You deserved it."

"I know."

In fact, Nick knew he deserved more than a slap, and he would gladly take whatever punishment Teagan doled out as long as it gave him what he ultimately wanted: her.

Although he was sure other men wouldn't think a slap in the face was progress, he was convinced it was a huge step forward. Teagan's anger was so much better than her tears. And it was a hell of a lot better than ignoring him or just walking away, which was what she usually did.

"Is that it?"

"No."

The oven timer buzzed, and Letty grabbed a pot holder to pull the pot pie from the oven. She placed it on the stove, and the delicious smell of flaky pastry wafted to him. His stomach growled, reminding him that he hadn't eaten anything except an egg white and spinach omelet at the hotel restaurant this morning.

"The pot pie needs to cool for fifteen minutes or so. While we're waiting, you're going to tell me everything, and I'm going to make a salad."

He frowned. There was no way in hell he was going to tell Letty *everything* that had happened in that linen closet.

"So . . . you apologized, she slapped you, and then what?" she asked as she pulled vegetables from the stainless steel fridge.

Nick shifted on the barstool. He didn't want to think about what had happened next, at least not in front of Letty. But later tonight when he was in bed, he'd definitely think about it.

"She left."

Letty frowned, her hands full of carrots and tomatoes. She dumped them on the counter before turning to him.

"Did this happen at the party? Did she slap you in front of everyone?"

He shook his head, and Letty gave him an appraising glance. Heat filled his face, and he looked down, picking at the label on his beer bottle.

"Where?"

"Linen closet."

Letty silently absorbed his answer before snickering. "That explains why your face is so red."

He growled, and she laughed at his embarrassment. Trying to ignore her, he took another swig of his Shiner.

"Linen closets are so perfect for quickies."

He choked a little on the mouthful of beer, swallowing noisily. She knew him too well.

"Shut up," he muttered.

Letty guffawed as she grabbed a colander from one of the lower cabinets. Her shoulders shook while she rinsed the vegetables and placed them on a large cutting board.

Her mirth was infectious, and after a moment, Nick started to laugh. Letty had become the mother he'd never had, and he adored her. She had helped him get through the terrible months after he'd walked away from Teagan. More important, she had been by his side in the hospital after he'd been in a car accident only a couple of months after they'd moved to Nashville.

A truck driver had fallen asleep at the wheel of his tractor trailer, and the big rig had crossed the highway's grassy median and smashed into the side of Nick's Escalade. The accident had totaled his SUV, and the paramedics had said it was a miracle Nick had walked away from it with only a few broken ribs, some scrapes and bruises, and a concussion.

It should have killed him.

When Nick had woken up in the hospital, and Letty had told him what happened, he'd realized the God he had never believed in had given him a second chance. He'd vowed he wouldn't waste it.

While he'd been lying in a hospital bed under the influence of narcotics, he had spilled his guts to Letty about why he'd walked away from Teagan. He'd told her about the conversation with Marshall, sharing his fears about his stuttering and its harmful effect on relationships, along with his doubts about his ability to be a good husband and father.

He and Letty had talked a lot about Teagan—the way he felt when he was around her, their unique way of communicating, and how much he missed being with her. He had also explained the fear he'd had of ruining his friendship with Teagan and her family.

Nick had even told Letty about his childhood, what it had

been like to grow up without a mother. He'd revealed his broken relationship with his father, describing how Simon had viewed Nick's lack of verbal skills as proof that he lacked intelligence.

Letty had listened intently, and when he'd finished, she had sighed loudly and smoothed his hair just like a loving mother. Then she'd thumped him on his bruised forehead and told him he was a jackass.

Without a doubt, Nick owed Letty. She had saved him from himself. After all, she was the one who'd finally clued him in to his real feelings about Teagan when they were in Boston. Later on, she helped him realize his stuttering wasn't an insurmountable problem. His unwillingness to try to overcome it was the real problem.

He loved Teagan enough to try to be the man she deserved. And he loved her enough to give her the marriage and children she wanted. If he were honest with himself, he wanted those things, too, but only with her.

After the accident, he had become single-minded in his efforts to win Teagan back, even though he hadn't seen her in more than a year. He'd needed a couple of months to recover, and during that time, he'd written dozens of letters to her. And when his body had healed, he'd gathered his courage and flown to San Francisco to see her.

He and Letty had discussed the best way for him to approach Teagan, and he'd rehearsed what he had planned to say to her. But when he'd shown up at her condo in downtown San Francisco, he'd taken one look at her and was unable to squeeze out a single fucking word.

While she'd stood there shocked and silent, he'd done the only thing he could do: he'd kissed her. And that meeting had set the tone for every single interaction since. Every time he saw Teagan, he ended up kissing her instead of talking to her. It was his default setting—using his body to communicate his feelings.

He always intended to explain why he had walked away from her and why he had come back. But she would ignore him, or she would say things he didn't want to hear, and the only way he could shut her up was by filling her mouth with his tongue.

Letty grabbed a knife from the butcher-block holder on the island and started chopping carrots, the blade moving so fast it was a silver blur. Nick watched, torn between awe and apprehension. He didn't want to have to race her to the ER with her severed finger in a cooler.

"What's the next step in our plan to get Teagan back? Do we need to come up with a better one?"

He already had a new plan, and it involved moving to San Francisco and taking on the role of Teagan's subordinate before he assumed a more permanent and enjoyable role. When he didn't answer, Letty looked up. She cocked her head, her gray bob swinging against her ears.

"Nick?"

He decided to broach the subject of his relocation gently. He didn't know how she would react to the news.

"Quinn's getting married, and he asked m-m-m-me to be a groomsman."

Letty smiled. "That's a big honor. When's the wedding?"

He told her, and she raised her brows. "That's fast. Is Amelia pregnant?"

Nick laughed, shaking his head. "I d-d-don't think so. I think he's afraid she'll get away." He shifted on the stool. "Quinn offered me a job, too."

Letty tossed the carrots into a yellow Fiesta bowl. Grabbing a tomato, she began slicing it into quarters.

"What kind of job?"

He told her about the endowment and the museum, and her blue eyes lit up. "What a great opportunity for you!"

Nick smiled. Letty had such a loving, generous heart, and he was lucky she'd made room for him in it.

"It's in San Francisco."

She nodded. "I assumed so."

"Come with me?" He waited a beat before hitting her with the big guns. "It's closer to Vanessa."

Letty's oldest daughter was working on her master's degree in architecture at the University of California-Berkeley. Kyla, meanwhile, was in Ohio at Miami University, and Ben was in Nick's hometown attending Syracuse.

Letty smiled. "Do you think Teagan will want a live-in housekeeper?"

# Chapter 24

TEAGAN EYED AMELIA'S PINK-AND-WHITE-STRIPED APRON. IT had two rows of ruffles around the hem, and "Domestic Goddess" was embroidered across the chest in dark brown thread.

It was cute, but it wasn't something Teagan would have expected Amelia to wear. Her thoughts must have been evident on her face because Amelia smiled and gestured to the apron.

"Quinn bought it for me," she explained, leaning against the kitchen island. "It's an inside joke."

Teagan nodded, settling herself on one of the barstools grouped around the soapstone bar. She had stopped by Quinn's house, or rather Quinn and Amelia's house, to discuss the job offer he'd made to Nick.

She had to convince her older brother to either rescind it or transfer responsibility of the museum project to Cal. Although she had little hope Quinn would agree to withdraw the offer, she didn't see why he'd balk at letting Cal take the lead on the project. After all, Cal was in charge of global marketing and communications, and the museum project made just as much sense for his department as it did for hers.

When Teagan had arrived at the Victorian, Amelia had let her know Quinn was playing basketball with Cal at their gym.

The other woman had invited her in, and Teagan had reluctantly agreed to wait for her older brother.

Teagan liked Amelia, and she hoped the two of them would eventually become friends. At one time, they'd been friendly and heading that direction, but right now, their relationship was more than a little strained.

If Teagan were honest with herself, she would admit the strain was all her fault. In fact, she'd almost destroyed Amelia and Quinn's relationship, and neither her brother nor his future wife was very happy with her right now.

Without Quinn's knowledge or support, Teagan had hired Amelia to revamp Riley O'Brien's women's division. She'd never expected her brother and Amelia to fall in love.

From a physical perspective, Amelia was relatively unremarkable if you didn't take into account her long, curly red hair. She was short and had a somewhat pear-shaped body. Her brown eyes were ordinary, and her face was covered in freckles like the typical redhead.

Most people would agree Amelia was cute but certainly not pretty. And she definitely wasn't stunning like the other women Quinn had dated in the past.

But when Teagan had introduced Quinn to Amelia, her older brother had almost gone into a trance. He'd been completely and totally enthralled with the petite redhead. Amelia, for her part, had been equally fascinated with Quinn, although she'd tried to hide it.

When Teagan had realized Quinn and Amelia were attracted to each other, she had made the most of it. She'd thrown them together every chance she could, hoping to soften Quinn enough to accept the redesign.

She'd manipulated both of them, never imagining their attraction would move beyond sex to love. And it was definitely love—deep, soul-sucking O'Brien love—the same kind of love Teagan had felt for Nick.

Amelia straightened, clearing her throat and pressing her lips together. Teagan tilted her head, wondering why the other woman looked so distressed.

"Teagan, I know things have been . . . tense between you and me." She swallowed deeply. "I love your brother. I love him more than I've ever loved anyone, and I don't want to start my life with him with a cloud hanging over us." She drew in a deep breath. "Can we try to be friends? Or at least pretend, for his sake?"

Like most little sisters who adored their brothers, Teagan had doubted any woman would be good enough for Quinn. But as she stared into Amelia's brown eyes, she considered the possibility that she might have been wrong.

Amelia loved Quinn as much as Teagan did, maybe more. And the other woman might be average in the looks department, but she definitely was special.

"We don't have to pretend, Amelia. I want us to be friends, too."

Amelia's mouth fell open, and Teagan frowned. Had she really expected Teagan to rebuff her?

"I owe you an apology," Teagan admitted. "I'm sorry I put you in such a difficult position."

Amelia snickered a little, and Teagan cocked her head. The other woman clapped her hands over her mouth, her eyes wide.

"Why are you laughing?"

"I'm sorry," Amelia replied, her cheeks cherry red. "Your brother is a terrible influence on me. When you said 'position' . . . well, never mind."

Teagan grinned, more than convinced Amelia and Quinn were going to be very happy together. A second later, she sobered, realizing she owed the other woman more than an apology. She owed her an explanation.

"Amelia, I need to explain why I did what I did."

"You already explained. I understand what you were trying to do."

Teagan sighed. She hadn't been entirely honest with Amelia about the reasons for the redesign.

"I *was* worried about the company's future, and I *did* want to be able to wear Rileys and look good in them. But the redesign was about Nick."

Amelia knew something was going on between Teagan and Nick because she'd seen them kissing several weeks ago. The Titans had been playing the San Francisco 49ers, and since Nick had been suspended for helmet-to-helmet contact, he'd been watching the game from Riley O'Brien & Co.'s suite in the new stadium.

If Teagan had known Nick would be there, she never would have attended the game. But she'd arrived late, and he had already been there.

Teagan hadn't wanted to attract the notice of her parents or her brothers, so she'd bided her time until she could slip out. She should have headed directly for her car, but she'd needed to use the restroom, so she made the trek to the ladies' room.

Nick had been waiting for her in the hall when she emerged. She had ignored him, or at least she'd tried to, but he backed her up against the wall, pressing his hard body against hers.

He'd stared into her eyes, and she waited for him to say something—anything—but just like always, he had been silent. She'd tried to duck under his arms, but he shoved his big hands into her hair and settled his mouth on hers, tracing her lips with his tongue until she let him in.

She had wanted him so badly, but somehow she came to her senses and told him to stop. And just as he had lowered his head again, Amelia interrupted them. Teagan had begged Amelia not to mention what she had seen to anyone, and Amelia had promised to keep quiet.

"I'm confused," Amelia admitted. "What does Nick have to do with your plan to revamp the women's division?"

"When I came home from Boston, I was not in a good place emotionally. I was having a hard time forgetting . . ."

No matter how hard Teagan had tried to move forward with her life, she had thought about Nick and their baby all the time. She'd marked the months that passed by how far along in her pregnancy she would have been or how old their baby would have been.

Even her dad's cancer hadn't been enough to take her mind off Nick and everything she'd lost. She had been a mess until the day she picked up a fashion magazine and read an article about the best and worst women's jeans.

Rileys had ranked as the absolute worst, and Teagan had been embarrassed and dismayed. But for the first time in months, her thoughts and emotions hadn't been focused on Nick.

She had purposefully shifted her focus—her *obsession* with Nick—to the women's division. And when Quinn had ignored her ideas to revamp it, she'd become fixated on figuring out a way to make it happen. She had transferred her anger and disappointment from Nick to Quinn, and in doing so, she had damaged her relationship with her brother and almost wrecked his relationship with Amelia, too.

Tears dripped down her face, and she brushed them away, embarrassed and angry she still was so emotional about something that had happened years ago. Amelia rounded the bar and wrapped her arm around Teagan.

"It's obvious something bad happened between you and Nick. I'm here if you want to talk about it, but you don't have to explain."

She squeezed Teagan lightly. After a moment, the shorter woman pulled away and met her eyes.

"Will you be my bridesmaid?"

Teagan sucked in a surprised breath. Her brother's fiancée had a much more forgiving nature than she did.

"Are you sure? Aren't you still mad at me, just a little?"

"How can I be mad at you, Teagan? You're the reason why I'm here today, wearing an obscenely large diamond ring and only weeks away from marrying a man with a good heart and a great butt."

Teagan laughed soggily. Amelia was going to be a fabulous sister-in-law.

"Your engagement ring *is* gaudy," she agreed. "And Quinn does have a good heart. But I have no comment on his butt."

"I'm a lucky girl," Amelia said, laughing softly.

"Is Ava Grace your maid of honor?"

Ava Grace Landy was Amelia's best friend. The country music star also had introduced Teagan to Amelia.

"Yes. She's flying in later tonight to spend Christmas and New Year's with us, and then she'll be back in late February to help with the final wedding plans." Amelia glanced at the clock on the microwave. "Quinn's going to be home soon." She patted Teagan's back. "Go wash your face, you look like a raccoon."

Teagan hopped off the stool and did as Amelia instructed. When she returned to the kitchen, she found Quinn and Amelia kissing as if they hadn't seen each other for months.

She cleared her throat, and Quinn held up his forefinger as he continued to kiss his fiancée, indicating he needed a moment. Teagan sighed loudly in exasperation, and Amelia jerked away from him, her face flushed.

"I'm sorry! I didn't hear you come back into the kitchen."

"You were busy," Teagan said, waggling her eyebrows.

Quinn stepped behind Amelia and wrapped his arms around her. He looked over her curly head to meet Teagan's eyes.

"What's up, T?"

"I wanted to talk to you about asking Nick to head up the museum project."

Amelia squeezed Quinn's forearms to get his attention. She winked at Teagan.

"I need to get the guest room ready for Ava Grace. Teagan, I'll see you tomorrow."

Quinn patted Amelia on the butt, watching her as she left the room. He turned back to Teagan, eyebrows raised.

"So what's on your mind?"

Teagan took a deep breath. This conversation was critically important to her sanity, and she couldn't afford to mess it up.

"I'm not sure Nick is the best choice. And I'm sure he'd understand if you told him that you had reconsidered your offer."

"I disagree. I think Priest is perfect for the job."

"Why?" she asked, trying to keep the desperation from her voice. "He doesn't have any experience. He doesn't have a background in museum planning or museum studies."

Quinn frowned. "Priest is a smart guy. I'm sure he'll be able to figure it out." He shrugged. "We were planning on hiring experts to help us anyway. He can manage them."

Teagan nodded. She wasn't going to argue about Nick's intelligence because she agreed with Quinn. She just didn't want to work with him.

Quinn cocked his head, his blue eyes narrowed. "Do you have a problem working with Priest?"

Teagan widened her eyes, pretending confusion. She shook her head. "No, of course not." She hoped Quinn would be fooled by her acting. "I just want to make sure we honor Grandma Vi's wishes and create the very best possible museum. That's all."

Quinn smiled, his eyes glinting under the recessed lighting. "You're going to be involved in every aspect, T. You're going to supervise him, remember? You can be as hands on as you want."

Teagan pushed back images of being hands on with Nick. She couldn't handle seeing him every day, closed in a small office with just the two of them. It would kill her.

"Well, actually, I wanted to talk with you about that, too. My group is really busy right now, and my plate is overflowing. I was thinking it might be better for Cal to take on the museum project."

Quinn shook his head, crossing his arms over his chest. He leaned his behind against the kitchen counter.

"Cal's busy, too, T. He has as much on his plate as you have on yours."

"You're right," she said, trying to be agreeable. "Cal is really busy. Maybe it would be better to postpone the project until one of us has more time."

He huffed out a laugh. "There's never going to be a good time for this project. And you know things are only going to get busier."

She nodded, trying to think of what else she could say to change Quinn's mind. Maybe she could provoke his possessive nature.

"Are you sure you want Nick hanging around the Riley O'Brien offices? You know how women act around him. He'll probably be a huge distraction." She paused meaningfully. "I know Amelia thinks he's good-looking."

"I'm not worried," Quinn replied, his lips quirking in a small smile. "She likes me better."

He gazed at her, his eyes speculative. She worked to keep her face impassive, afraid of what her big brother might see.

"You're a woman. Is Priest a distraction for you?"

*You could say that.*

# Chapter 25

THE O'BRIEN FAMILY CHRISTMAS TREE SURELY RIVALED THE ONE in the White House. Teagan stared up at the Douglas fir, which had to be at least twelve feet tall. It dominated the formal living room in her parents' house, where everyone had gathered to open presents.

Hundreds of ornaments covered the lush evergreen. Some were homemade, some outrageously expensive. But each one had a special meaning to someone in the O'Brien family.

Christmas was an all-day affair in the O'Brien household. It started with Christmas breakfast, followed by a frenzy of gift giving and then a huge dinner. After stuffing themselves, the family spent the evening either watching holiday movies or playing games. More often than not, they all fell asleep on the sofas in the family room.

Teagan's father walked up beside her and wrapped his arm around her shoulder. He pulled her to his side, squeezing tightly.

"Merry Christmas, baby girl."

"Merry Christmas, Daddy," she replied, easing her arm around his waist and leaning her head against him.

Teagan was relieved she couldn't feel his ribs beneath his oatmeal-colored sweater. He'd lost a lot of weight while he battled colon cancer and was just now starting to put back on some of the pounds he'd lost.

"Are you ready to open presents?" he asked, his eyes bright instead of dull like they'd been for the past couple of years.

"Of course. I was ready to open all of them last night."

Her dad laughed. "Weren't you satisfied with the one you opened?"

When Teagan was seven years old, she'd begged her parents to let her open just one present after they'd returned from Christmas Eve Mass. They'd refused, telling her that she had to wait for Santa Claus.

She hadn't liked their answer, and she'd snuck downstairs in the middle of the night and opened all her presents. To add icing to the Christmas cookie, she'd hidden all her parents' presents so they couldn't enjoy them.

She had been a little brat. But instead of punishing her, Teagan's parents had created a new tradition, and now everybody got to open one present of their choosing on Christmas Eve.

*Is it any wonder I'm so spoiled?*

Teagan's dad gave a contented little sigh, drawing her attention from the tree. She pulled back to look up at him, since he was nearly a foot taller than she was.

After surgery, several months of radiation, and three rounds of chemo, her dad's cancer was finally in remission. It had been a long, ugly road, and he'd suffered tremendously, along with everyone who loved him.

Teagan had done her best to be supportive during his treatment. She'd attended doctor's appointments with him, driven him to his radiation appointments, and kept him company while he received his chemo. Cal and Quinn had done the same thing.

Quinn had taken their dad's illness much harder than Teagan had expected, probably because he'd been forced to take on James's responsibilities at Riley O'Brien & Co. Even though her actions regarding the women's division suggested otherwise, Teagan thought her oldest brother had done a great job leading the company.

"Our family is growing," her dad said, a note of satisfaction in his voice. "Amelia, Ava Grace . . . two more sweethearts to join my favorite girls."

Teagan smiled, amused that her father referred to his wife of nearly thirty-six years as a girl. Her mother loved it, though, and every time he called her *my girl* she giggled like a teenager with a crush.

To the outside world, James was a hard-ass. He was almost as quiet as Nick, and he was the perfect example of the strong, silent type. But when it came to his family, he was the proverbial pussycat.

"And Nick's here, too," her dad continued, a huge grin on his face. "He hasn't been able to spend Christmas with us since he and the boys were at USC."

Teagan tried not to scowl. Yes, Nick was here, ruining her Christmas. But everyone else was over the moon that he was spending the holiday with them, especially James. He adored the younger man, considering him another son.

Before Nick had broken her heart, Teagan had thought the connection between her dad and Nick was sweet. Now it made her want to puke.

But Teagan had to hide her real feelings because she didn't want her parents or her brothers to find out about what had happened between her and Nick. And Nick, damn him, was completely taking advantage of that fact. He knew she wasn't able to ignore him or slap him in front of her family, and everywhere she turned, he was there.

He had squeezed in next to her in the car as the family headed to the church for Christmas Eve services. He had stood beside her at Mass, his arm brushing against her breast at least ten times. He had crowded her in the kitchen as she made coffee, pressing his hard body against her back as he leaned over her shoulder.

The absolute worst had occurred this morning when he'd sat next to her at the breakfast table. He'd sneaked his warm hand under her skirt to caress her thigh, and when she'd stood up, she had been afraid there would be a huge wet spot on the chair.

And now he was just steps away, leaning against the fireplace mantle and watching her intently with those gorgeous green eyes.

"Okay, everyone, find a seat," her mother ordered, clapping her hands. "It's time for presents."

Teagan made a dash for one of the damask armchairs, determined to avoid sitting near Nick for the next hour. She exhaled loudly in relief once she sat down, tucking a leg underneath her.

She slanted a furtive glance toward Nick. He had noticed her haste, and his kissable lips quirked in amusement. He waited until everyone else had taken a seat before sauntering over to where Teagan sat. Perching on the wide arm of her chair, he leaned back slightly and edged toward her.

She got a whiff of his cologne, a delicious woodsy scent, and growled under her breath when he shifted even closer. The jerk laughed softly before settling his big hand on the back of her neck. It was hot against her skin, and she shivered.

He stroked his thumb against the side of her throat, and her nipples hardened. She casually moved her head away from him but then snapped it back when she realized her face was almost in his crotch.

"I'm so excited," her mother exclaimed, standing next to the tree. "Look at all these presents I get to distribute! I feel like Santa Claus. Ho, ho, ho!"

Kate knelt down and picked up a brightly wrapped package. Reading the tag, she passed it to Amelia. She repeated the process several times until the velvet tree skirt encircling the tree was empty and everyone in the room had several gifts to unwrap.

Grabbing a rectangular box from the pile next to her, Teagan checked the tag. The gift was from Amelia, and she tore off the reindeer-printed paper, eager to see what her future sister-in-law had given her.

She opened the gift box and pushed back the red tissue paper, gasping in delight and surprise when she saw a pair of redesigned Rileys nestled inside. The new jean designs weren't even in production yet, so Amelia must have made this pair by hand.

Teagan held the denim to her chest, tears springing to her eyes. She hadn't worn a pair of Rileys since she'd developed curves, and Amelia could not have given her a more perfect gift.

She waited until Amelia had finished opening one of her presents and caught her attention. She stared into her big brown eyes, trying to convey how much the gift meant to her.

"Thank you," she mouthed, and Amelia smiled.

Nick leaned down, placing his mouth near her ear. "I'm going to love seeing your ass in those jeans," he whispered.

She jerked away, glaring at him. She thought the jeans were fabulous, but she momentarily considered burning them just to spite him. She made a silent vow *never* to wear them in his presence.

In an effort to ignore Nick, she pulled another gift from the pile. Without checking the tag, she ripped off the shiny red paper. The cardboard box inside was taped shut, and she called out to her dad, asking for his pocketknife.

Once she had it in hand, she sliced open the box and cut through the bubble wrap inside. Pushing the protective material aside, she looked down at the gift.

She knew immediately it was from Nick. The sterling silver picture frame wasn't anything special, but the same could not be said for the picture in it, a black-and-white shot of Nick and Teagan.

It was a photo she'd never seen before, and it had been taken the day they'd gone sailing. Nick's arm was wrapped around her shoulders, and she leaned against him. While she looked into the camera with a huge smile on her face, he gazed down at her.

His expression in the photo sent chills over her. If she were looking at the picture without any knowledge of the people in it, she would have said the guy was in love with the girl.

*Crazy in love.*

But Teagan knew the people in the photo, and she knew their history. She knew there was only one person in the picture who had been crazy in love, and that person wasn't Nick.

She stared down at the photo, overwhelmed with emotion. She swallowed to push back the tears burning in the back of her throat and covered the image with the palm of her hand.

Nick leaned close to her, placing his hand on top of hers. He squeezed her fingers gently.

"Do you understand now?" he murmured.

THEY SAID A PICTURE WAS WORTH A THOUSAND WORDS, AND Nick hoped "they" were right, whoever the hell "they" were. He hoped the picture he'd given Teagan would tell her all the things he couldn't say.

*I love you. I loved you then, and I love you now. Please give me another chance. I'm miserable without you, and I'm afraid of what the rest of my life will be like if you're not with me.*

He held his breath, waiting for any indication the photo had impacted her like it had him when he'd first seen it. A few months ago, Letty had gone on an organization warpath and directed him to browse through the unopened boxes that were stored in the closet in his study.

Fearing her wrath if he refused, Nick had tackled the cardboard tower. He'd found the pictures in the second box he opened.

He had never even looked at the pictures when he'd received them in the mail shortly after their sailing trip. He'd shoved them in a drawer in his Boston condo, and Letty had packed them up when they'd moved to Nashville. When he'd finally flipped through them, he'd broken out in a cold sweat, shocked by what they had shown in black and white.

His feelings for Teagan were obvious in every picture—love, desire, admiration. Her feelings were obvious, too, especially in the photo of her looking at him when he hadn't been aware of her gaze.

That picture sat on his nightstand as a reminder that she had loved him. He prayed every night she still did, even if her love was hidden under layers of hate.

Teagan shook her head, just a small movement, but enough for Nick's hope to dissolve. He sighed. Maybe he should have given her jewelry instead.

"Hey, T, show us what you got," Cal called out, drawing the attention of everyone in the room.

Nick tensed, worried Teagan would give in to her older brother's request. He didn't want anyone else to see that photo. It showed too much, and it was for Teagan's eyes only.

When Teagan didn't respond to Cal's comment, Nick plucked the frame from the box. He waved it around too quickly for anyone to see the image within it.

"Picture frame," he said. "From me."

"You put a lot of thought into that," Cal quipped, obviously assuming the frame was filled with a stock image of strangers.

Nick returned the frame to the box before wadding up a piece of wrapping paper and lobbing it at Cal's head. The other man ducked like the paper could actually hurt him, knocking his dark head against Ava Grace's blond one.

"Oww!" Ava Grace exclaimed, her raspy voice slightly higher than usual. "You have a hard head, Cal."

"That's what all the ladies say," Cal replied, waggling his eyebrows.

Ava Grace rolled her eyes. "Do they also say your good looks don't make up for your lame sense of humor?"

The singer's quip made everyone laugh, everyone except for Teagan. She continued to stare down at the photo, her hand covering the image of the two of them.

Nick wished he knew what she was thinking, but before he could say anything, she turned the picture frame over and carefully tucked the bubble wrap around it before closing up the box. She placed it on the floor next to her and covered it with the jeans Amelia had given her.

He pushed down his disappointment. He had been stupid to think a picture would change things.

He directed his attention to his pile of presents, wondering if Teagan had bought anything for him. He wouldn't be surprised if she had given him a box of candy she'd laced with laxatives. She was both creative and diabolical, just two things he loved about her.

Finally, all the presents were unwrapped, and colorful remnants of ribbon and paper littered the floor. Nick had received a bounty of gifts, including a sweater from Kate, a book on San Francisco's history from Ava Grace, a bottle of fine Irish whiskey from James, and a handmade leather belt from Amelia.

His two best friends had picked gifts they knew he'd enjoy: Cal had given him a new golf driver, although Nick doubted it would make his game any better, and Quinn had surprised him with a digital camera and lessons from one of the top photographers in the city.

Teagan had given him nothing but a glare. And Cal noticed.

"Didn't you get anything for Priest, T?"

She glanced toward Nick, a glint in her eyes that made all the hair on his body stand on end. She smiled evilly, a tiny twist of her lips.

"Don't worry, Cal. I already gave Nick his present. At the Riley O'Brien holiday party."

"Really?" Cal asked, his dark eyebrows arched. "What did you give him?"

Teagan stood, tossing Nick a satisfied look over her shoulder. She bent down to pick up some of her presents, and he couldn't help but stare at her ass as her plaid skirt rose.

"Why don't you tell them what I gave you, Nick?" she suggested as she straightened.

He narrowed his eyes. He knew she didn't want her family to know about them, so she was just trying to put him on the spot—to make him sweat a little.

She walked toward the door, carrying a stack of goodies that did not include his gift. He pressed his tongue against his teeth so he could deliver a long sentence.

"She offered to help me look for a new house."

He had planned to tour houses with Letty, but he definitely liked the idea of touring them with Teagan better. He wanted to buy a place she liked, since he planned for them to live there together.

Teagan's head snapped around, and she stumbled. She stared at him, her dark blue eyes huge behind her black-rimmed glasses.

"Perfect gift," he added. "So thoughtful."

"It's always so helpful to have a second opinion," Kate noted, her blond bob swinging. "And Teagan is such a skillful negotiator. She always finds a way to get exactly what she wants."

Nick met Teagan's eyes, recalling her husky voice asking him to give her what she wanted. When her cheeks turned pink, he knew she remembered the same thing.

She licked her lips, and he wondered if she was thinking about the blow job she'd given him during their night together. He'd never forgotten the feel of her luscious lips sucking him deep as he slid his cock in and out of her hot mouth.

James cleared his throat, and Nick jerked his eyes away from Teagan, embarrassed he'd been thinking about her going down on him when her parents sat less than fifteen feet away. Thank God his black dress pants were roomy.

Gathering the rest of Teagan's gifts, he headed toward her. He tilted his head toward them.

"Car?"

"Guest room. I stayed over last night."

He waited for her to lead the way, since he didn't know which guest room she occupied. He followed her down the hall and into a large, airy bedroom filled with white cottage-style furniture. Stopping just inside the door, he watched as she made her way to a pair of high-backed chairs situated near the window.

"You can put everything right there," she directed, pointing toward the chairs. "And then you can leave."

The walls were a shade between lavender and baby blue, and they made her eyes look almost violet in contrast. He stared at her for a moment, taking in her gorgeous face. He wished she would smile at him the way she used to . . . the way she had in the picture.

Instead, she eyed him warily, as if he were a snake about to strike. Using his foot to push the door shut behind him, he ambled toward her. As he deposited the gifts on one of the floral-printed chairs, she tried to dash around him.

Thanks to football, he had faster reflexes than most people, and he caught her by the waistband of her skirt. He reeled her back to him like a fish caught on a hook.

She glowered over her shoulder. "You're going to rip my skirt."

He smiled, imagining how fucking awesome it would feel to tear that schoolgirl skirt from her body before spreading her legs and sinking into her tight pussy. His thoughts must have been a little too obvious on his face because her eyes widened.

Before she could put up much of a struggle, he wrapped his arms around her from behind and turned her to face him. Her hair was loose and wavy, and he threaded his fingers through the dark strands to hold her head immobile so he could look into her eyes.

"Did you like the picture?"

She tried to look away from him, but he clenched his hands in her hair and gently tilted her head back. She swallowed, her white throat rippling, before closing her eyes.

He waited for her to answer, but after several moments he realized she wasn't going to, not without some persuasion. He brushed his lips against hers, and she sighed, a breathy little sound that made his heart beat faster.

"Tell me," he demanded, nipping her bottom lip.

She gasped, and he darted his tongue into her mouth. Tilting her head, he delved more deeply into her sweetness. Her tongue twined around his, and he followed it eagerly before sucking it into his mouth.

Dropping his hands from her head, he palmed her ass and pulled her against his erection. She wrapped her arms around his neck and pressed her breasts against his chest.

It felt like it had been a lifetime since he had tasted her sweet, pink nipples, and suddenly that was all he could think about. He brought his fingers around to her stomach to slip them under her sweater, stroking her smooth skin until he reached the edge of her bra.

When he found her nipple under the stretchy lace, he rolled it between his thumb and forefinger. She moaned against his mouth, and he walked backward until his knees hit the empty chair.

Dropping down into it, he looked up into Teagan's face. Her lips were rosy and swollen, and her cheeks were flushed. Just as he reached for the hem of her sweater, a light knock sounded on the door. She jerked away from him, her eyes wide with dismay.

"Teagan," Amelia said softly through the door. "You have about two minutes before Quinn realizes Nick has been with you this whole time. *Alone*."

Teagan took a step toward the door, but he pulled her back. He wasn't ready to leave this room, and he didn't give a shit about who was on the other side of the door. She stared down at his hand before raising her eyes to his.

"Thank you for the picture."

*Touchdown, Priest!*

Teagan continued, "It's a good reminder of who I used to be and what I used to want." Without taking her eyes from his, she raised her voice to be heard through the door. "Amelia, you can come in. Nick and I were just reminiscing about the way things used to be. But we're done now."

## Chapter 26

IT WAS NICK'S FIRST DAY OF WORK THAT DIDN'T INVOLVE A FOOT-
ball and yard lines, and he was nervous. His success at Riley
O'Brien & Co. depended on his brain rather than his body, and
that scared the shit out of him.

Not to mention the fact that Teagan was going to be his
boss. Although Quinn made the final decisions for the charitable foundation, Teagan carried them out, and Nick would
report to her.

It might have made more sense to postpone his first day
until after the New Year, but he didn't want to wait even one
more day. Every day that passed without seeing Teagan was
just another day of his life wasted.

He let his gaze roam the reception area of the company's
global headquarters in downtown San Francisco. It was
deserted, probably because of the holidays.

He hadn't visited the offices in years, not since he'd played
for Denver, and the space had been redesigned since then. It
was an interesting mix of wood, metal, and glass—kind of
industrial meets rustic with a little contemporary thrown in.
And the color scheme was interesting, too, blues and greens
like the ocean, along with bright orange like the sunset.

One of the double doors in the corner opened, and Cal strode through it. When he reached Nick, the younger man gave him a fist bump before throwing his arm around Nick's shoulders.

Cal waved to the receptionist, a young brunette, and the woman blushed. Someone had a crush.

"Hey, Priest. Ready to start serving your time?"

Nick laughed at Cal's quip. He hoped his new job would be more pleasant than a life sentence at a maximum-security prison.

"W-w-w-where's Teagan?"

Quinn had told him that Teagan was supposed to handle his "on-boarding," a fancy way of saying "orientation." He was eager to see her, even though it had only been two days since Christmas.

Cal glanced at him, his light blue eyes speculative. Nick got a feeling the other man definitely had an idea there was something between his good friend and his little sister.

"Her assistant says she's tied up in a meeting," Cal answered, the tone of his voice suggesting he didn't believe it. "I'm going to show you around, and then I'm going to take you to her."

Nick nodded, and Cal slapped him on the back. He headed toward the elevator bank, gesturing for Nick to follow him.

"First I'm going to show you the most important room in the whole damn building: the break room," Cal said, stabbing the Up button.

Minutes later, they stood in the fourth-floor break room, a large space filled with café tables and leather-backed booths. It reminded him of a trendy coffee shop.

Cal opened the stainless steel refrigerator, removing a rectangular plastic container. He placed it on the counter before grabbing two forks and plates from the cabinets that ran along the wall next to the fridge.

"Coffee," he directed, pointing to the industrial-sized coffeemaker. "One sugar, one cream for me."

Nick quickly made the coffees and brought them to the booth where Cal sat. He slid into the booth, and Cal opened the container to reveal a huge piece of the dessert Ava Grace had made for Christmas dinner.

"I hid this so I could have it later," Cal said.

Ava Grace had called the dessert a *bûche de Noël*, pronouncing it "boosh duh No-el." It was a traditional Yule log with moist cake rolled into a log shape and covered with rich chocolate icing.

"You know bush is one of my favorite desserts," Cal added, his eyes glinting with humor and his lips turned up at the corners.

Nick shook his head, unable to keep from laughing. Cal could turn the most innocuous subject into X-rated material. It was a true gift.

Once Cal had halved the dessert, he placed the pieces on the plates, and the two of them dug in. It was pretty damn good, but Letty had spoiled him with her cooking, so he wasn't as enthusiastic as Cal, who moaned in gastronomical ecstasy. After a few more bites and several sips of coffee, their morning snack was gone, and Cal was ready to talk business.

"Your ad campaign has been a real success. Women fucking *love* you, Priest, and since they pretty much dictate what their husbands and boyfriends wear, our sales have really increased."

Nick smiled. He was happy Cal was pleased with the results of the campaign.

"Ava Grace has signed on to promote Amelia's new accessories, and she's also agreed to help with the new women's jeans."

Nick imagined Ava Grace's celebrity would have a big impact on Riley O'Brien's bottom line. She was tall, thin, and blond, and her unique raspy voice made most men think of sex. Women didn't get much hotter than Ava Grace. Except for Teagan, of course. She was exponentially hotter.

"Are you willing to do another campaign with us?"

Nick didn't need to think it over. He loved the O'Brien family, and he trusted Cal's business acumen.

"Yes."

Cal smiled and held out his fist for another bump before leaning back in the booth. "I'm excited," he said, his voice lacking any inflection.

He laughed. Unlike Quinn, whose emotions were much more visible, Cal was so laid-back it was hard to tell when he was happy and when he was upset. You had to pay close attention.

"Do you have any ideas?" Nick asked.

"I have lots of ideas," Cal answered, smirking a little.

*Such a smart-ass.*

"Ideas about the campaign?"

Cal nodded. "It's going to rock."

"No speaking for me," he reminded him.

"What about singing?"

Nick laughed, shaking his head. One of his speech thera-pists had recommended singing to help with his stutter, and it actually worked pretty well. Unfortunately, he couldn't carry a tune to save his life, and his efforts to sing sounded remark-ably like a wolf howling.

Cal shrugged. "I'll work around it."

Leaning to the side, Cal pulled his phone from the front pocket of his jeans. He checked the screen, his eyes narrowing.

"T just sent me a text. She says she's done with her meet-ing, and she wants to take the afternoon off, so I need to take you to her now or you can wait to talk to her until tomorrow."

"Now," he replied, sliding from the booth.

They made their way back to the first floor, where all the executive offices were located, and Cal headed toward the double doors. He swiped a key card in the reader, and the door made a popping noise.

"Usually there's a security guard posted outside these doors, but he's off for the holidays," Cal explained, pulling open the door. "You need a special keycard to get into the executive offices. We didn't want people wandering into areas where there might be sensitive information."

He nodded, following Cal down a long hallway featuring company memorabilia and a timeline of the company since its founding in the mid-1800s. Cal pointed toward the right as they walked by a closed door.

"Quinn's office." He continued down the hall and pointed to a door on the left. "My office."

Cal kept walking, his boots clicking on the polished con-crete floor, and Nick caught up to him. They reached the end of the hallway, stopping in front of another closed door with a plaque next to it that read "Teagan K. O'Brien."

Nick chuckled when he realized Teagan's initials were TKO, an acronym for "technical knockout" in boxing. He'd never noticed that before. Cal shot him a curious glance, and Nick pointed to the plaque.

"Technical knockout."

"She's worse than a black eye, that's for damn sure."

Cal knocked loudly on the door, and a moment later, Teagan opened it. She didn't look toward Nick but eyed her older brother.

"Thanks for showing Nick around, Cal. I was trapped on a conference call."

"We only made it as far as the break room."

She frowned, shaking her head. "Thanks for nothing," she muttered, turning to walk back to her desk.

Cal slapped Nick on the back before starting the trek back to his office. "If you're bored later, Priest, you can drop by my place," he tossed over his shoulder. "I have beer."

Nick entered Teagan's office, reaching for the doorknob to close the door.

"Leave it open," she directed.

Dropping his hand, he took a moment to look around. He'd wondered what her office was like, and now that he was here, he was a little disappointed because there was no sofa for non-work-related activities.

Her office was spacious, but other than that, it wasn't unique or interesting. In fact, the only interesting thing in the whole room, other than Teagan, was the collection of framed degrees hanging on the wall.

Teagan stood beside her large desk, which had two leather chairs situated in front of it. Floor-to-ceiling bookcases covered the left side of the room, overflowing with law and business books.

A long, frosted glass conference table took up the entire right side of the room. Several mesh-backed chairs were grouped around it, and two black phone speakers sat on top, along with several stacks of files.

Teagan cleared her throat, drawing his attention. He gave her a long look, taking note of every little detail. While Cal had been dressed casually in Rileys and a sweater, Teagan was garbed more professionally.

Her wavy, dark hair was twisted into a prim bun, and his fingers itched to pull it down. Her raspberry-colored shirt matched her lush lips, the high collar and square buttons tempting him to tear it open.

Her black skirt was just tight enough to show the shape of her hips, and it ended right at her knees with a small row of pleats. A pair of black leather boots with a tall, skinny heel completed her outfit.

Strangely, her business attire turned him on as much as the low-cut green dress she'd worn for her birthday dinner. His cock twitched, and he shoved his hands in his front pockets to make some extra room for it.

"Sit," she said, gesturing to one of the chairs in front of her desk.

Settling himself in the chair, he crossed his ankle over his knee as she took a seat behind her desk. She placed her elbows on the smooth surface and leaned forward to meet his gaze.

"I tried to get Quinn to change his mind about hiring you, but he refused."

He nodded, unsurprised she had approached her older brother. Likewise, he wasn't surprised Quinn had refused. Even if his best friend had suffered second thoughts, he wouldn't have gone back on his word.

"He must feel sorry for you. I can't think of any other reason why he would have offered you this job."

She was wrong. Quinn didn't feel sorry for him. He had offered him a job because he knew Nick would never let him down.

"You aren't qualified to handle a project like Grandma Vi's museum." She made a scoffing noise. "You've never even had a job that required you to do anything but catch a football."

She was right. He wasn't qualified to handle this project. But he was determined to make it a success nonetheless. He might not be as smart as she was, and he might not be able to speak without sounding like an idiot, but he wasn't going to fail. There was no way in hell he was going to humiliate himself in front of the woman he loved.

She sighed loudly, picking up a pen and rolling it between her slender fingers. "Nick, this museum is important to me. Grandma Vi was a really special woman, and I want to honor her."

"I know."

"I'm asking you again: don't take this job. Just walk away. Quinn will understand."

He stared into her eyes. He wasn't going to walk away from

the job. And he wasn't going to walk away from her, either. He'd already made that mistake once.

"No."

She threw the pen on top of the desk and pushed back her chair in a jerky movement before vaulting to her feet. Anger made her cheeks red and her eyes all squiny behind her glasses.

"You're such an *ass!*"

She pointed to the door before stalking over to the conference room table. He watched as she began to stack files while muttering beneath her breath.

*Guess the meeting's over.*


TEAGAN'S HANDS SHOOK AS SHE GATHERED THE FILES SCATtered across the conference table. She was one of those people who organized things when they were upset, and she'd reorganized her closet at least six times since Nick had come back into her life several months ago. She was a regular at The Container Store now, and her clothes were not only organized by season but also by garment type and color.

She leaned over the table to grab a fat file folder, pulling it closer with the tips of her fingers. She was beyond angry, but mostly she was angry with herself.

She might tell Nick to stay away from her, but her words rang hollow, since she forgot who she was and why she hated him the moment he touched her. She couldn't find the strength to resist him.

When he kissed her, she kissed him back. When he grabbed her butt, she rubbed against his erection. When he put his hands between her legs, she came.

She moaned, pressing the tips of her fingers against her forehead. *What am I going to do?*

A hollow clicking sound drew her attention, and she turned toward the noise. Nick leaned against the closed door, his arms crossed over his chest. As he stared at her, his green eyes reflected the bright sunshine filtering through the windows.

Even though she told herself not to ogle him, her eyes traveled up and down his long body. It was unfair, but he seemed to get hotter as the years passed. He was a man in his prime, and heaven help her, he was delicious.

Someone must have told him that Riley O'Brien & Co.'s dress code was casual, meaning that most employees wore Rileys and T-shirts to work. Dressing up meant a button-down shirt and Rileys, and that was exactly what Nick wore.

His long-sleeved shirt was a muted blue-and-orange-checked pattern, and it emphasized his broad shoulders and strong chest. Since his arms were crossed, the material stretched over his big biceps, and she had a fleeting memory of clutching those muscles as he rose above her to thrust inside her.

Unlike Quinn and Cal, who usually left their shirts untucked, Nick's shirt was tucked into his dark-washed Rileys, showing his toned abdomen. His brown leather belt cinched his lean waist, and his jeans cupped his package and skimmed his powerful thighs before falling to his brown leather shoes.

Dropping his arms, Nick pushed away from the door and walked toward her with a long-legged, masculine stride that looked just as good from the front as it did from the back. He was unhurried, but she didn't bother to move, knowing he'd catch her before she made it to the door. Plus, this was *her* office, and she wasn't going to be chased out of it.

He stopped in front of her, plucked the file folder from her hands, and tossed it on the table behind her. Then he touched the rim of her glasses, the corner of his mouth kicking up.

"Hot librarian."

His comment shocked her so much a snort-laugh escaped her. He smiled at the funny sound, the skin around his eyes crinkling.

Pressing his thumb against her bottom lip, he stroked lightly. She nervously licked the inside of her lip and accidentally caught the tip of his thumb. His eyes darkened, the verdant irises nearly obliterated by his expanded pupils. An ache settled between her legs, and she shifted on her high-heeled boots to squeeze her thighs together.

"You need to leave."

Nick crowded closer, and she backed up until the conference table hit her upper legs. She stumbled, and he grabbed her around the waist and placed her on the cold surface.

She stared up into his face, knowing where this was going. She needed to stop him, and she could only think of one thing that might give him pause: the truth. Although she didn't want to admit how much he had hurt her, maybe he would leave her alone if she told him.

"Nick, I can't do this with you." She looked down, squeezing her fingers around the edge of the table until her knuckles turned white. "You don't understand how much you hurt me."

He sucked in a breath as if she'd punched him in the stomach. After a long moment, he placed his palms against her face and gently tilted her head up. His eyes were solemn, his full lips compressed into a tight, straight line.

"If you care about me at all, you'll leave me alone," she added.

He made a rough noise in the back of his throat before letting his hands fall from her face. Slowly, he closed his eyes and dropped his head back. He swallowed audibly, his Adam's apple jumping in his tan throat.

He took one step back, and then a couple more. Relieved, she exhaled in a rush, glad she'd been honest with him. She scooted forward to slide off the table, and he brought his head forward and speared her with his green gaze.

"Give me another chance," he said slowly. "Please."

His words made her stomach tremble. At one time, she would have done anything to be with him, but he didn't deserve another chance. He had abandoned her once, and there was no reason to think he wouldn't do it again.

"No."

Her voice was firm, leaving no room for negotiation or compromise. She couldn't go through loving him and losing him again. She *wouldn't*.

"I . . ." He cleared his throat. "I won't hurt you again." He cleared his throat again, harder this time. "Give me another chance."

There was a part of her that wanted to trust him . . . a part of her that wanted to give him another chance. And that made her angry and scared.

"You don't deserve another chance," she said.

She needed the reminder. She needed to remind herself that this man had almost destroyed her once, and he would do it again if she let him.

He studied her for a long moment, his body still and his face blank. She shifted so she could wriggle off the table, but he placed his big hand in the middle of her chest and gently pushed her back.

"Don't, Nick . . ."

But her protest died in her throat as he moved between her knees. Using his lower body, he widened her legs until he was wedged between them. He flattened his hands on the table just inches from her hips, leaning over her until she had to brace herself on her elbows.

Once he had her where he wanted her, he reached between them to unbutton her blouse. She balanced on one elbow to slap at his hands, but he just swatted her away. His long fingers were fast and nimble, and he had her silky top open within seconds. He pushed it off her shoulders and down her arms, where it caught in the crook of her elbows.

He stared down at her breasts, and the heat in his eyes ignited a fire low in her pelvis. He stroked his fingers across the lace that edged the top of her bra before unhooking the front closure and pulling the material apart. Her breasts fell free, bouncing heavily.

Groaning softly, he cupped her breasts in his warm hands. The hardened tips of her nipples poked the center of his palms.

"*Fucking fantastic*," he murmured, his words barely audible.

He shaped her breasts, squeezing gently and occasionally brushing a thumb over her nipples. His fingers were callused from handling footballs, and she squirmed with pleasure, loving the way they rasped over her sensitive skin.

Rolling a hard peak between his thumb and forefinger, he lightly scraped his nail over the tip before squeezing gently. She bit her lip, trying to hold back a moan, and he abruptly pulled her to a sitting position.

She covered her breasts, embarrassed and ashamed she'd let things go so far. She hated the effect he had on her body almost as much as she hated the effect he had on her common sense.

She scooted forward to slide off the table, but he gently pushed her back again. Jerking one of the mesh chairs closer, he sat down in front of her and pulled her hands away from her chest.

The new position put his face almost even with her breasts, and he leaned forward until he was nose deep between them. He nuzzled against her, his stubble prickly and tickly, before licking circles down her cleavage.

He trailed his tongue across one of her breasts to pull a nipple into his mouth. He sucked deeply, and she felt it between her legs. More wetness flowed from her body, and she wondered if she was going to come just from his mouth on her nipples.

He bit down gently on the sensitive peak before swirling his tongue around it, back and forth, until her pulse pounded between her legs and in her ears. He pressed against her nipple with his tongue, and she quivered from the soft pressure.

Turning to her other nipple, he lavished it with the same attention. She clenched her fingers in his hair, holding his hot mouth against her when he sucked strongly. He gripped her knees as he nibbled the tip of her breast, sliding his callused hands up her thighs before tracing the edge of her panties.

She spread her legs, eager to feel his long fingers inside her, and he released her nipple with a soft pop. Wrapping his arm around her waist, he pulled her forward until her butt almost hung off the table.

He wrestled her skirt up to her waist before hooking his fingers in the top of her panties. She raised her hips, and he yanked the fragile lace down her thighs. It got stuck on the zipper of one of her boots, and he growled, his chest heaving.

He clenched his hand around the panties, and she expected him to tear them apart like he had in the linen closet, but he took a deep breath and carefully disentangled them from the zipper. Once they were loose, he pulled them over her boots and free from her sharp heels.

He looked down, his eyes focused on the space between her legs. When she'd lived in Boston, she had been bare except for a landing strip, but it had grown out since then. He petted the springy curls, smoothing them downward with tiny strokes. Clearing his throat, he met her eyes.

"Perfect," he said, his voice hoarse.

He traced her labia with the tips of his fingers before delving between them. He slowly eased two fingers inside her, and she squirmed from the delicious pressure.

He pushed deeper, and she gasped as arousal spilled from her body. He groaned, moving his hand to stroke her clit at the same time he thrust his fingers inside her. He flicked it lightly, and a jolt went through her.

She looked down, moaning when she saw the erotic vision of his strong hand working between her legs, glistening with her juice. She rocked her hips against his hand, faster and faster, and watched as he followed her rhythm. Suddenly, he withdrew his fingers, and she almost sobbed in disappointment. She had been so *close*.

He stood, kicking the chair away from him. It skidded across the floor on its rollers before crashing into her desk. Pulling her to her feet, he turned her until she leaned over the conference room table with her butt in the air. He pressed his knee between her thighs to widen them, and she heard the metallic rasp of his zipper behind her.

A moment later he reached under her and flattened his hand against her stomach. He pressed gently, pushing her toward him, and the broad head of his penis probed her body. She pulled in a breath as he nudged inside her. They'd never had sex in this position, and he felt different.

*Hotter, harder, thicker.*

She moaned as he pressed deep, filling her so completely she couldn't tell where she ended and he began. He shuddered behind her, and she could tell how excited he was from his labored breathing.

Moving his hands to her hips, he caressed them with long strokes of his fingers. After a long moment, he began a slow, steady rhythm, and she braced her hands against the table and pushed back against him so he could go as deep as possible. The feel of him inside her made her vision blur, and she cried out when he hit a deliciously sensitive spot. He froze, his fingers clenching on her hips.

"Please don't stop," she begged. "Please don't stop. I need more."

He groaned and began to thrust deeply inside her in a fast, hard rhythm. Sliding his hand from her hip, he found her clit and squeezed it between his fingers, rubbing gently as he surged into her.

Her orgasm crashed over her, unexpected, and she cried out, her internal muscles pulsing against his hardness, milking him strongly. The intensity of it made her vision go dark.

Nick groaned harshly, pressing his hand against her and rooting deeply with his penis. He shouted, jerking inside her as he came. She tightened her vaginal muscles to prolong his orgasm, and he let out a strangled moan.

She let her head drop forward, resting her forehead on the cool glass of the table. Her body still vibrated with the remnants of her orgasm, and every few seconds, she felt a small pulse from him.

Somehow, every time they had sex, it was even better than the last time. It had been like that the first time they'd been together. Each time, the sex had been hotter, the orgasms more powerful.

She sighed as he slowly withdrew from her body. Fluid dribbled down her inner thighs, and she froze, instinctively knowing what it was. She twisted around to face him, staring into his eyes. He looked shell-shocked, exactly the way she felt.

"Nick . . ." she gasped, her heartbeat thundering in her ears. "Please, please tell me you used a condom."

His eyes widened, and he shook his head. She pushed his chest, panicked and angry, and he stumbled backward.

*"Oh, my God!"*

Pregnancy didn't concern her. She had learned her lesson, and she'd gone on birth control pills after she had recovered from her miscarriage. But she knew Nick was beyond promiscuous, and she was worried he might have given her a horrible disease. She sucked in a deep breath, almost hyperventilating.

"Do you forget condoms a lot? When was the last time you were tested for STDs? How many women have you been with since you were tested? Am I going to need antibiotics? Or antivirals?"

Her voice had risen with each question until she had nearly shouted. Nick gripped her shoulders, hugging her to him.

"T, calm down."

"Calm down!" she shrieked, jerking away from him. "Calm down! We just had unprotected sex!"

Wrenching down her skirt, she cringed as semen trickled out of her. She fumbled with her shirt, frantic to cover her exposed breasts. Her trembling fingers couldn't manage the buttons so she tugged the fabric together in her fist.

Nick stepped in front of her and curved his hand around the back of her neck. He leaned down until his face was inches away from hers.

"I'm clean."

"How do you know?" she asked suspiciously.

"No sex." He cleared his throat. "No sex since I moved to Nashville."

She laughed in disbelief, jerking her neck sideways so he'd release her. He held tight, and she stopped struggling for fear she'd sever her spinal cord.

"That was more than two years ago. There's no way you could, *or would*, go that long without sex."

He lightly squeezed the back of her neck as he stared into her eyes. "Celibate." He squeezed her neck again. "For you."

## Chapter 27

OF ALL THE PLACES NICK HAD LIVED, HE HAD LIKED BOSTON THE most. The city's rich history had appealed to him, and he'd liked living close to water.

The weather had been okay for the most part, although the winters had definitely sucked. But he'd grown up in Upstate New York, so even Boston's frigid winters hadn't been enough to ruin things for him.

If not for Teagan, he probably would have been happy to stay in Boston. But she was in San Francisco, and he wanted to be with her. It sounded corny, but *she* was his home.

Because of the O'Brien family, he had visited Northern California too many times to count. He liked the Bay Area well enough, and San Francisco reminded him a little bit of Boston, and not just because of the water, either.

Like Boston, San Francisco had hundreds of neighborhoods, all of which had distinct personalities. He had spent hours online researching different neighborhoods, trying to decide where he should live. He wanted a house in a neighborhood that was good for families with young children.

He'd talked with Kate, and with her help, he had focused his search on four specific areas: Laurel Heights, where Quinn lived; Pacific Heights, which was adjacent to Laurel Heights;

Sea Cliff, which was a very expensive enclave with views of the ocean; and St. Francis Wood, where Teagan's parents lived.

San Francisco was one of the most expensive housing markets in the nation, but that wasn't a problem because he didn't have a budget. There were few homes that were out of his price range.

He'd been living in Riley O'Brien & Co.'s corporate penthouse since late December. Quinn had told him he could stay there until early March, which meant he only had four weeks until he had to either move into his own place or hole up in a hotel.

He had blocked off the entire weekend to house hunt, and he'd manipulated Teagan into coming along. He had dropped hints to both Quinn and Kate that Teagan had been too busy to help him find a new place, and that had done the trick.

Kate had recommended a realtor named Rayna Sullivan, a family friend. Rayna's husband, Sam, headed up Riley O'Brien & Co.'s real estate group, and the couple had known the O'Briens for decades.

Rayna had pulled together more than sixty listings for him to review. He had eliminated more than half of them right away, knowing instinctively Teagan wouldn't like them. He had a pretty good sense of her housing preferences, knowledge gleaned from her condo in Cambridge and her loft in downtown San Francisco.

They'd already visited six houses in Pacific Heights, and with each walk-through, the frown on Teagan's face had grown darker. He knew she wasn't happy to spend time with him, but he didn't think she had liked the houses much, either.

In some of his darkest moments, he wondered if it was ridiculous to choose a house based on the hope that he and Teagan would be together. But he couldn't give up on his dream of marrying her and having a family with her.

He wanted a beautiful, brainy wife and dark-haired, blue-eyed babies. He was surprised by how much he wanted them, especially since he had never expected to get married or have children.

His love for Teagan had changed him. *She* had changed him. He wanted more than an isolated, meaningless life, and he wanted to *be* more than a solitary, lonely man.

Footsteps sounded behind him, and he turned to face

Rayna. With her silvery-blond bob and blue eyes, she reminded him a lot of Kate.

"What do you think of the house, Nick?" Rayna asked. "Do you like it?"

Located in Pacific Heights, the house was a huge, two-story Italianate-Victorian situated high on a steep hill. It had been built in the early 1900s, and Nick really liked the exterior and the views. It also had a guesthouse, a rarity for San Francisco.

But the interior was a lot less impressive. Although the house was spacious, it needed updating. That wasn't necessarily a bad thing because it meant Teagan and Letty could redo it to their specifications. He would be happy with whatever they picked out.

"You'd probably have to gut the kitchen and the bathrooms," Rayna said. "But the sellers *are* motivated. They'd be willing to do a quick close."

Given his short time frame, he'd hoped he could find a move-in-ready home. He wasn't sure he wanted to take on a renovation, but if he decided to do it, Letty could definitely handle it.

"Are you ready to see the next one on our list?"

He nodded, and Rayna called out for Teagan. Seconds later, the love of his life appeared in the doorway, a scowl on her face. She crossed her arms over her chest, drawing his attention to her breasts.

She wore a soft pink sweater that made him think of cotton candy. It fell past her hips, and black leggings and black, low-heeled boots covered her legs.

The sweater had a large cowl neck, and he wondered if she'd chosen it specifically because it didn't show any skin. She had caught him eyeing her chest while they were in a meeting a few days ago, and since then, she'd worn tops that covered her from neck to navel.

Teagan didn't seem to realize he didn't need to see skin to get an erection. All it took was a whiff of her perfume or the sound of her laugh, and he was hard enough to pound nails. And when he actually got a glimpse of her skin, he lost his mind.

He still couldn't believe he'd stripped her out of her clothes and done her on the conference table. He might have fantasized about getting it on in her office, but he had never planned to actually do it. And he had never been so out of control that he forgot to use a condom. Not even once.

He understood why Teagan had freaked out about it, and he'd done his best to reassure her. He had offered to go with her to the gynecologist to be tested even though he had told the truth about his celibacy.

He knew it was almost impossible to believe he had gone without sex for more than two years, but he only wanted Teagan. Plus, he knew she would never give him another chance if he fucked other women the whole time he worked to win her back.

He had finally convinced Teagan that he was disease-free because she had calmed down enough to tell him she was clean, too, and also on the pill. When she told him about the birth control, he was overwhelmed with disappointment instead of relief.

Since then, he had become obsessed with the thought of making her pregnant. Maybe it was some kind of primal instinct left over from prehistoric days, but he got a thrill when he imagined her all round and awkward with his baby. He didn't know if other men felt the same way, but he couldn't be the only one who got turned on by it.

Rayna shifted next to him, pulling his attention from thoughts of procreation. They headed toward Teagan, and when he reached her, he leaned down and stole a quick kiss from her glossy mouth. She punched him in the upper arm, and Rayna laughed, obviously assuming Teagan was being playful. She assumed wrong.

"I didn't know you two were a couple," Rayna said, a big grin on her face.

"We're not," Teagan replied sharply.

He glanced toward Rayna, whose eyebrows had shot up at Teagan's bitchy tone. He gave the older woman his most charming smile.

"Give us a minute?" he asked, aware that Teagan had stiffened next to him.

Rayna nodded and left the room. He waited until he heard the front door open and close before facing Teagan. Wrapping an arm around her waist, he pulled her to him.

He bent down until his nose almost touched hers. "Got a problem?"

She pushed against his chest, but the action didn't have

much of an impact, since he outweighed her by more than one hundred pounds. She huffed out a breath in annoyance, her eyes flashing with tiny blue sparks.

"Yes, I have a problem," she snapped. "I don't want to be here. And you're wasting Rayna's time."

He frowned. Why would she think he was wasting Rayna's time? He was a serious buyer.

"Explain."

"You should be looking at the new condos downtown or smaller houses in Cow Hollow. They're more your style."

"My style?"

"The houses we've looked at aren't right for you. They're for families."

"And?"

"You don't have a family."

"Not yet."

"What?" she asked, clearly perplexed by his answer.

"I don't have a family *yet*."

Her mouth fell open, and he chuckled at the astonished look on her face. He wondered what she would say if he told her he wanted to have a family with her.

A FEW YEARS AGO, TEAGAN'S MOM HAD TOLD HER THAT MEN proved the evolutionary theory of domestication. Just as gray wolves had been domesticated by humans to create the modern dog, men had been domesticated by women to create the modern husband and father.

At the time, Teagan had found her mom's attitude both hilarious and sexist. But now she wondered if her mom had been right.

Nick had said he "didn't have a family yet," which implied that he would, in fact, have a family one day. Had he been domesticated like the gray wolf? And if so, how had it happened? She was sure there were plenty of female anthropologists who would love to study Nick's evolution, and by evolution, she really meant butt.

"When we lived in Boston, I asked if you wanted to get married and have kids, and the look on your face resembled Edvard Munch's painting *The Scream*."

Nick laughed, tightening his hard arm around her waist.

They were so close his belt buckle dug into her stomach, and she had to force herself not to lean against him.

"Good description."

"Now you're telling me you want a family?"

She waited for him to answer her question, and when he didn't, she poked his chest with her forefinger. The rest of her fingers must have wanted in on the action, too, because they flattened against his black sweater before roaming over his well-formed pecs.

"Yes."

Nick pressed his hand over hers, holding it against his chest and lightly caressing her fingers. He stared into her eyes, and even though she didn't understand what she saw in his gaze, it made her break out in goose bumps.

"I'm surprised," she admitted.

When she'd been pregnant with his baby, she had dreamed about marrying him and raising their child together. Her expectations had been more realistic. She had believed he would avoid her and be an uninvolved, absent father.

"Me, too," he replied emphatically.

She couldn't help but laugh at his response. It was so genuine—so Nick.

"You've never even had a long-term romantic relationship," she said, "that I know of."

"Yes, I have."

That was news to her. She couldn't recall any girlfriends, not even when he was in college. Maybe he'd had a high school sweetheart back in Syracuse.

"You have? With whom?"

"You."

His answer was so unexpected, so shocking, she was rendered speechless. Her astonishment must have been obvious on her face because he laughed softly. After a moment, her mouth cooperated with her brain.

"We did *not* have a long-term romantic relationship."

He cocked his head, his lips turned up in a small smile. "Are you sure?"

"Yes! We were . . ."

His smile grew, and a wicked glint entered his eyes. She swallowed, trying to ease the dryness in her throat.

"Friends," he said, drawing out the word. "Is that the noun you're looking for?" He brought her closer, and she found herself staring at his lips. "I prefer *lovers*."

Before she could reply, he dropped his head and slanted his mouth over hers. He pushed his tongue past her lips, licking deeply, and she sank into his kiss, savoring the pressure of his lips, the slide of his tongue.

Clenching her hand in his sweater, she pulled him closer and wrapped her other hand around his neck. He tasted like the hazelnut coffee he'd sipped in the car, and she twirled her tongue around his before sucking it into her mouth.

He groaned against her lips as he dropped his arm from her waist to scoop it under her butt. He pulled her up until the hard ridge of his erection pressed between her thighs, and she twined her leg around his to bring him even closer.

Without warning, he jerked away from her and spun her around in front of him. Less than a second later, Rayna peeked her head around the corner. The older woman gave them an appraising glance, her lips pressed together, and Teagan knew it was obvious what she and Nick had been doing.

"I'll just wait in the car," Rayna said, winking at Teagan before *click-clacking* back down the hall.

Teagan pressed her fingers against her lips, shocked by how quickly things had spiraled out of control. If Rayna had come in two minutes later, the older woman would have been treated to the sight of Nick's bare butt and Teagan's legs wrapped around his waist.

The incendiary kiss was more proof that she couldn't trust herself to be alone with Nick. That was why she had tried to get out of house hunting with him.

In fact, since they'd had sex in her office, she had gone out of her way to avoid him altogether. She had conducted all necessary work meetings with him in public places, and she had even managed to steer clear of him outside of work except for the night of Quinn and Amelia's New Year's Eve engagement party.

She had been vigilant and kept him in her sight all night long so he couldn't catch her unaware. When the clock had struck midnight, he was right next to her, but she hadn't been worried because she had assumed he wouldn't kiss her in front of her entire family.

She had been wrong. *So wrong.*

He had grabbed her butt in both hands, pulled her against him, and laid an open-mouthed, full-tongue kiss on her that turned her brain to mush. When it had ended, they'd been breathless, and half the room had stared at them. She had tried to laugh it off as a drunken impulse, and surprisingly, neither her parents nor her brothers had asked any questions about it.

Nick shifted behind her, brushing her hair to the side and placing his lips on the nape of her neck. He gave it a swipe with his tongue before sucking lightly.

"Do you like this house?" he asked so quietly she could barely hear him over the beat of her heart.

"It doesn't matter if I like it."

He trailed his lips from her nape to the ticklish place behind her earlobe. He gave the sensitive skin a tiny lick before placing his mouth against her ear.

"Yes, it does."

His deep voice rumbled through her body, and she shivered. Sliding his arm around her waist, he slipped his hand under the hem of her sweater. He rubbed circles on her stomach, his callused fingers creating pleasurable tingles up and down her spine.

"Do you like it?"

"Yes. It's nice."

Moving his hand from her stomach, he cupped her breast, stroking his thumb over her nipple. She bit her lip, trying to hold back a moan. He tweaked her nipple, and she gasped at the pleasure-pain.

"Enough to live here?"

"Yes."

He abruptly abandoned her nipple and grabbed her hand in his. He strode across the room, tugging her behind him, and pushed through a set of original French doors until he reached the kitchen.

He took a second to boost her onto the island before stepping back to stand in the middle of the room, his hands on his jeans-clad hips. His black sweater stretched across the dense muscles of his chest with the movement, and she had an abbreviated fantasy of delving under the soft material to stroke his pecs and fondle his flat brown nipples.

"I don't like this room," he announced.

She glanced around, a little bemused by how quickly they'd gone from kissing to kitchen design. Although the appliances were a little dated, the room looked okay to her.

"Why?"

"Can't see the backyard."

He was right. The kitchen was in the middle of the house, and its windows looked out on the neighbors. It also lacked backyard access; the door to the backyard was located in a guest room.

She wasn't surprised Nick had noticed such a small detail. He was one of the most observant people she knew. He had a nearly photographic memory, something she'd never realized before they'd started working together on the museum project.

He also had an amazing command of the written word, which she found odd, since he barely spoke. His vocabulary rivaled Bebe's, and his grammar, spelling, and punctuation were almost perfect. His reports were comprehensive, and his emails always started with salutations and ended with proper closings.

If not for the fact that Nick made her panties wet and her nipples hard, he was an ideal employee. His work was almost flawless, he never missed meetings or deadlines, and he was polite and respectful to everyone he worked with.

Although she had never doubted Nick's intelligence, she definitely had underestimated him. If he were anyone else on her team, she would have told him how pleased she was with his performance and how well he was doing.

But he wasn't just a member of her team. He was the man who tempted her at every turn—the man who'd torn her heart into a million tiny pieces.

"It's a problem," Nick added, and she pulled her attention back to him and the kitchen.

"Why is it a problem to not be able to see the backyard?"

He gave her a look that translated into *Are you an idiot?*

"I'm sorry." She shrugged a little. "I don't see why it's a problem. Why don't you tell me."

"Can't see the kids playing in the backyard."

His statement thoroughly confused her. "What kids?"

He rolled his lips inward, and she cocked her head. He was

looking at her with a strangely intent expression, and she wondered what he was thinking.

"What kids?" she repeated.

"My future children."

Those three words ripped open something inside her—something that had never healed completely. The pain was excruciating. It pierced all the way to her soul.

Nick had never even known about their baby. He hadn't cared enough about her to return her phone calls so she could tell him she was pregnant. He hadn't been there when she had miscarried. He hadn't been there when she'd cried herself to sleep night after night.

And now he was worried about being able to see his future children playing in the backyard.

*Bastard.*

She jumped off the island, tears blurring her eyes. Driven solely by the desire to get away from Nick, she darted out of the room, running as fast as she could down the hall toward the front door.

His footsteps pounded behind her, and she lunged toward the doorknob, flinging open the door. She ran down the steep steps, barely managing to stay upright, and dashed across the lawn to Rayna's Land Rover. The older woman opened the car door and jumped out to catch Teagan in her arms.

"Teagan! Honey, what's wrong?"

"Ray . . ." she sobbed.

Rayna turned sharply, pushing Teagan behind her. She glanced over Rayna's shoulder to see Nick standing a few steps away.

"What did you do to her?" Rayna shouted at Nick before shooting a quick glance toward Teagan. "Did he hurt you? Do I need to call 911?"

She stared at Rayna, too upset to answer. Her pulse pounded in her ears, and her shallow breaths had made her dizzy.

"Teagan! Do I need the call the police?"

She shook her head, but Rayna's attention was focused on Nick as he moved closer to them, and the older woman didn't see her answer.

"Stay back!" Rayna yelled.

He ignored Rayna, and with his eyes locked on Teagan, he

didn't notice the older woman's pointy-toed pump as it shot forward to nail him in the balls. Groaning, he dropped to his knees before falling to the ground and rolling into a fetal position.

Teagan stared at Nick, horrified by the wounded animal sounds that came out of him. Rayna turned to face Teagan, her blue eyes wide.

"I hope he deserved that."

# Chapter 28

THE COLD WIND WHIPPED ACROSS NICK'S FACE AS HE SPED down the double-black diamond trail on Lookout Mountain. The skiing conditions at Northstar California were perfect—sun, minimal wind, and fresh powder.

He and the O'Brien brothers had arrived at the Ritz-Carlton Lake Tahoe last night for Quinn's stag weekend. Quinn and Amelia's wedding was only two weeks away, and three more of Quinn's buddies would join them later tonight for three days of skiing, drinking, and eating. Cal would probably add sex to the itinerary, but Nick was going to stay zipped, and there was no question that Quinn would ever cheat on Amelia.

Through Nick's polarized sunglasses, he had a clear view of the steep trail ahead of him. Since it was insanely difficult and few skiers had the skill to navigate it, the trail was almost deserted. The pine trees were a greenish-black blur in his peripheral vision, and all too soon, he reached the bottom. He did a hockey stop, creating a spray of snow with his new Volkl skis, and turned to face the mountain.

Nick watched as Quinn and Cal ran the trail at a much slower speed. He was a better skier than either one of the O'Brien boys, and he wasn't being arrogant when he made that claim. He had no problem admitting that Cal was a much better golfer, and Quinn was just as nimble as Nick was on the football field.

Nick had learned to ski when he was in grade school. Upstate New York had plenty of resorts, and Simon had pushed him to excel at every sport under the sun. Nick even knew how to play lacrosse, maybe the lamest sport in existence except for kettlebell tossing.

He'd honed his ski skills while he had lived in Colorado, spending most winters and early springs bumming around the resorts high up in the Rocky Mountains. He'd loved his time on the slopes, whether he was in Aspen, Vail, or Purgatory.

Skiing was a solitary sport, something you could do alone, so it had been perfect for him. And there had been plenty of ski bunnies eager to shake their tails for him. He had a lot of memories of plowing through powder all day before plowing through pussy all night.

Quinn reached the end of the trail first, coming to a less-than-graceful stop. Seconds later, Cal arrived with a big spray of snow and an ear-splitting holler.

The younger O'Brien brother pulled off his helmet and shook his dark head. "Holy shit! That was fucking awesome! But I'm *never* going to do that again."

Nick laughed. He loved these guys, and it was nice to ski with friends rather than by himself.

"Want to go again?" Quinn asked.

Nick shook his head. He was cold, hungry, and thirsty, and he was ready to call it a day. They removed their skis and made the trek back to the hotel. After dropping off their equipment with the ski valet, they found seats in the hotel bar, which was nearly empty.

Nick leaned back against a leather club chair with a sigh, propping his snow boot-covered foot on his knee before studying the room. The Ritz-Carlton was one of the most luxurious resorts in the Lake Tahoe area, and he had decided to upgrade from a regular room to a suite so he'd have a fireplace and a balcony.

He would love to take Teagan to a place like this. He would love to lay her down in front of the fire and watch her creamy skin turn pink from the heat. He would love to lick a trail from her breasts to the sweet spot between her legs before pushing inside her and staying there all night.

His cock twitched, reminding him that he hadn't been inside Teagan's curvy body since they'd had sex in her office just after Christmas. He wasn't sure he would ever have the pleasure of being there again, especially after what had happened during the house walk-through.

The thought depressed him, and he forcefully pulled his thoughts away from Teagan and focused on the drink in his hand, a new bourbon whiskey called Trinity. One of Quinn's friends, Jonah Beck, owned the micro-distillery that produced it, and he would join them to celebrate Quinn's final days as a bachelor. Nick knew Quinn wished those days were already over, and Nick wished his own bachelor days were numbered, too.

He watched Quinn check his phone for the tenth time in so many minutes. His best friend seemed anxious, and he wondered why. Cal's hand shot out and grabbed his older brother's phone before shoving it between the cushions of his own leather chair.

"What the fuck, Cal?" Quinn snapped.

"Amelia is fine. Stop acting like a pussy."

Quinn narrowed his eyes before giving a self-deprecating laugh. Leaning forward, he grabbed his drink off the oak cocktail table and settled back in the chair with a sigh.

"I *am* acting like a pussy," he admitted before taking a swallow of his bourbon. "But there will come a day when you act like an even bigger pussy over a woman. And when that day comes, brother, I'm going to give you all kinds of shit."

Cal's face froze, and Nick studied his old friend. Cal and his girlfriend, Saika, had broken up a few months ago, and it didn't seem like the other man was over it. Nick knew what it felt like to have your guts ripped out by a woman, and a wave of sympathy washed over him. He wanted to tell Cal there were only two ways to get through it: distraction and denial.

"You're so whipped I'm surprised you even agreed to come up here this weekend," Cal shot back. "Especially since it means you're missing Valentine's Day."

"I didn't miss anything. We celebrated Valentine's Day last weekend," Quinn said, the smile on his face clearly conveying how enjoyable the celebration had been.

"What did you get Amelia for your first Valentine's Day together?" Cal asked.

"Pajamas."

"Pajamas?" Cal repeated. "Is that code for lingerie?"

Quinn laughed, shaking his head. "No. I really bought her pajamas. She has this one pair she wears all the time. They're so damn ugly. They're flannel, and they have eggs and bacon printed on them. I *hate* them. I hate them so much I want to burn them, so I bought her a new set with pink hearts on them. They're much cuter."

Nick stared at Quinn. The fool didn't have the good sense to be embarrassed that he'd just admitted to buying his future wife a pair of flannel pajamas with hearts on them for Valentine's Day instead of crotchless panties.

Cal was right: Quinn was whipped. Pathetically, appallingly whipped. There was no hope for mankind. It was over for all of them.

Cal glanced at Nick. "What about you, Priest?" he asked, his eyes speculative, and his lips quirked with amusement. "Are you missing Valentine's Day with anyone special?"

Nick threw back the rest of his bourbon so he could avoid Cal's question. If Teagan had given him one hint she wanted to spend Valentine's Day with him, he would have forgone the stag weekend without a moment's regret. But he had seen her only once since the house-hunting disaster. She had been traveling for work, and when she had been in the office, she'd been tied up with other projects.

When he had taken the job with Riley O'Brien & Co., he had looked forward to spending a lot of time with Teagan. He hadn't realized how busy she was and how much responsibility she juggled. Just as he'd always suspected, she kicked ass when it came to business. She was smart, dedicated, and a good supervisor.

Teagan had revamped the legal department when she'd returned from Boston. Apparently the company had used several outside firms to handle its legal work, and she'd brought most of the work back in-house and rebuilt the legal team. The move saved the company millions of dollars and also improved the quality of work.

Even though he had nothing to do with her accomplishments, he was proud of her success. She awed him, and he wished there were a way for him to let her know. But she avoided him, and after what had happened in the Pacific Heights house, he didn't want to do anything to set her off again.

He still had no idea what he'd done to make her run from him like he was a serial killer. The look on her face before she had dashed from the kitchen had been so anguished he'd felt as if someone had kicked him in the balls. And then Rayna *had*. The memory made him wince. The older woman had been painfully accurate with her pointy-toed shoe.

"What's wrong, Priest? You don't like the bourbon?" Quinn asked, assuming Nick's wince was related to his drink rather than memories of having his testicles abused. "I think it's really good."

"I like it."

"Good. I'd hate to think I invested in a company that produces paint thinner rather than quality liquor."

Nick was surprised to hear Quinn had invested in Beck's company. Quinn was an astute businessman, and he was very careful with his money. Although Nick had met Beck at Quinn and Amelia's New Year's Eve party, the conversation hadn't moved beyond basic introductions, and he was interested to know more about him.

"How long have you known Beck?" Nick asked.

"I met him in grad school. We were in the same MBA classes at Stanford."

"W-w-w-what's the story behind Trinity?"

"When we were at Stanford, Beck put together a business plan for a micro-distillery and asked me to look over it. It was solid, really solid—one of the best plans I've ever seen, in fact. So I provided the start-up capital for Beck. He brought in two college friends to help him, and here we are."

Abruptly, Cal shifted and pulled Quinn's phone from the seat cushion. He passed the phone to Quinn, who immediately popped open the screen. After a moment, he smiled and handed it back to his younger brother.

"Amelia says 'hello' and to 'behave like the men we should be rather than the boys we are.'"

All three of them laughed.

"W-w-w-what is Amelia doing w-w-w-while you're gone?"

"Ava Grace flew in a few days ago, and the two of them are going over to Teagan's for a 'girls' night.' Whatever the hell that means."

"They're probably going to watch *The Notebook* and drink wine," Cal said, his voice clearly conveying his disgust.

Nick choked back a laugh, looking down into his empty tumbler. Back when he and Teagan had been friends, he'd spent an evening with her watching *The Notebook* and drinking wine.

She had snuggled up to him, close enough for him to smell her fruity body lotion and hear her soft breathing. She'd fallen asleep against him halfway through the movie, her head nestled on his chest.

He remembered the night in detail because the movie had made him cry, and when Teagan had woken up and noticed his red-rimmed eyes, he'd lied and told her that he was allergic to her lotion. She'd never worn it again, which was a damn shame because it had smelled really good.

"Want another one, Priest?" Cal asked, gesturing toward Nick's empty glass.

Nick nodded, and Cal called over the waitress and ordered drinks for all of them. When she returned with the bourbon, she leaned toward Nick, putting her cleavage right in his face. She was young and pretty, and she had a nice rack, but it wasn't nearly as mouthwatering as Teagan's.

"She was friendly," Cal said, eyeing the waitress as she walked away, her ass swaying in an exaggerated motion. "And it's obvious she'd like to get a lot friendlier with you, Priest."

Nick shrugged, taking another sip of Trinity. The bourbon had a palate-pleasing vanilla undertone, and he wondered if Beck was looking for any new investors.

"Are you going to get *friendly* with her?" Cal asked.

Five years ago, Nick definitely would have gotten friendly with the waitress, and he probably would have asked her to invite a girlfriend. But he was a one-woman man now, and that one woman was Teagan.

Nick shook his head, and Cal's eyebrows rose. Quinn cocked his head, his expression speculative.

"Why not?" Quinn asked. "She's hot."

The O'Brien brothers studied him as if he had been invaded

by an alien being, and Nick abruptly decided to tell them why he wasn't fucking every hot waitress who smiled at him. He took a deep breath and got ready for the shit to hit the proverbial fan.

"Because your sister is the only person I w-w-w-want to get friendly w-w-w-with," he answered, meeting their eyes unflinchingly.

Neither Quinn nor Cal reacted to Nick's statement for several heartbeats. Finally, Cal punched his older brother in the upper arm.

"You lost. I want your sofa to be in my office no later than Monday at noon."

Nick looked back and forth between them, wondering what the hell they were talking about. Maybe they hadn't heard him.

Quinn groaned as he leaned his head against the leather cushion. "Priest, you *fucking* bastard," he muttered, looking up at the vaulted ceiling. "You just made me lose the bet I made with Cal."

Cal laughed evilly, rubbing his hands together. "I can't wait to roll around on your sofa. *With my shoes on.*"

Quinn growled, and Cal chortled loudly.

"W-w-w-what are you talking about?"

"When you kissed Teagan on New Year's Eve, I told Quinn you were interested in her, but he was insistent that you were drunk, and she was just convenient."

Nick snorted. Teagan was *anything* but convenient.

"So we made a bet," Cal continued. "The loser had to forfeit his most prized possession. If I lost, I had to give my Caddy to Quinn, and if he lost, he had to give his blue jean sofa to me."

Quinn raised his head, spearing Nick with his dark blue gaze. "I love that sofa like a mother loves her firstborn child."

Nick grimaced. Quinn wasn't exaggerating about his attachment to the sofa. Admittedly, it was one-of-a-kind. It was upholstered with hundreds of Riley jean pockets in different shades of denim, from light blue to deep indigo.

Of course, Cal wouldn't have been any happier if he'd lost his Caddy, which he had inherited from his Grandma Violet. He loved the powder-blue vehicle and drove it everywhere, even though it made an eighteen-wheeler seem fuel efficient in comparison. He'd even named it.

Cal took a sip of bourbon, his eyes steady on him over the rim of his glass. Nick met the younger man's gaze, relieved to see curiosity rather than fury.

"What's going on between you and Teagan exactly?"

"It's complicated."

Cal laughed dryly. "Since we're talking about Teagan, I would expect nothing less." He gestured to Nick with his glass. "Are you sleeping together?"

Surprisingly, Cal's voice was mild, almost uninterested. The tight muscles in Nick's neck and upper back relaxed.

"Yes."

"I thought so," Cal said, nodding.

"How long has this been going on?" Quinn asked. "Were you sleeping with her in Boston?"

Nick turned his attention to his best friend. Like Cal, Quinn seemed more curious than confrontational. They were taking the news of his relationship with Teagan much better than Nick had expected, and the relief he felt was overwhelming.

"Only one time."

"One time?" Cal repeated doubtfully.

Flushing, Nick looked down into his bourbon. "One night," he clarified.

"Was it a one-night stand?" Quinn asked.

Nick didn't know how to answer that question. Teagan had accused him of treating her like a one-night stand.

He met Quinn's gaze. "She thinks it w-w-w-was," he admitted.

Quinn frowned thoughtfully. "When she moved back home, she was so different. Sad, but angry, too. I thought it was because of Dad. What happened?"

"I fucked up," Nick answered simply, "but I w-w-w-want another chance."

"Priest, that was a long time ago." Cal sighed. "Maybe it's better to accept that things are over. Just move on."

Nick studied Cal. The other man's eyes were shadowed, and Nick knew Cal was thinking about Saika. Quinn had told him that Cal had been ready to propose when Saika's ex-husband had come back into the picture.

"Why are you so determined to get her back? Was the sex that good?" Quinn joked.

"Quinn! You're talking about our sister!" Cal slapped his

older brother on the back of the head like they were two of the Three Stooges—or maybe not, since that would make Nick the third Stooge.

"Sorry," Quinn grimaced. "I forgot for a second."

"It w-w-w-wasn't just sex," Nick said quietly. "I'm in love w-w-w-with her."

His words stunned the O'Brien brothers so much their mouths fell open and their eyes bugged out. Despite the seriousness of the conversation, he couldn't help but laugh at their expressions. He decided to really shock them.

"I w-w-w-want to marry her."

Cal sucked in a surprised breath as Quinn leaned forward in his club chair, his eyes fixed on Nick's face. "Are you serious, Priest?"

"Yeah."

"Holy shit!" Cal exclaimed, turning to look at Quinn. "Priest is going to be our brother-in-law. How fucking *great* is that?"

Cal held out his fist to Quinn, and his older brother bumped it with his fist. The O'Brien brothers returned their attention to Nick, and he eyed them suspiciously.

"I thought you w-w-w-would be angry. I thought you might b-b-b-beat the shit out of me."

Cal chuckled, his eyes sparkling with glee. "If you take on Teagan, you're in for a lifetime of trouble, Priest. You don't need us to add to it."

"Amen, brother," Quinn said emphatically.

Nick laughed. He would give anything—do anything—for a lifetime with Teagan.

"I'm ready for a lifetime of t-t-t-trouble," he assured them.

"How does Teagan feel about you?" Quinn asked, cocking his dark head. "Frankly, she doesn't seem to like you much. You know she tried to get out of working with you, right?"

"She loved me . . . back then."

Nick swallowed to ease the pressure in his throat. It always made him sick to remember that she had told him she was in love with him, and he had rejected her. He had been so stupid.

"And now?"

He didn't want to give voice to his deepest, darkest fear that Teagan no longer loved him. He was terrified he was never going to get her back. Terrified he would have to live the rest of his life without her.

"Now she avoids me. I've tried to apologize, to explain, b-b-b-but she refuses to listen."

"Yeah, you don't seem to be making much headway," Quinn noted.

Unfortunately, Quinn was right. In fact, Nick thought he might be losing ground with Teagan. Obviously, the house hunting had been a disaster, since it had ended with her in tears and him writhing on the ground in agony.

When he had decided to get Teagan back, he had known it would be difficult, but he hadn't had any idea just how difficult. Maybe he was arrogant or just plain stupid, but he had never imagined he would be in the exact same place now as he had been almost two years ago.

"I don't know w-w-w-what to do," Nick admitted.

"If your current plays aren't working, you need to throw out the old playbook and create a new one," Quinn said.

Nick considered Quinn's suggestion. Obviously Nick's efforts to talk to Teagan had failed, and having sex seemed to make things worse. Maybe he should try a new strategy.

"Any ideas?"

# Chapter 29

"ARE YOU SURE YOU DON'T HAVE A SINGLE PAIR OF SHOES THAT match your bridesmaid's dress?" Bebe asked skeptically.

Teagan shot her best friend a warning glance. "I already told you I didn't."

Bebe sighed and picked up a pair of shiny silver shoes with a kitten heel. She held them up for Teagan's inspection.

"What about these?"

"No. My dress is darker, more pewter. Ava Grace's maid of honor dress is closer to that color."

Bebe was in town for a huge biotech convention that would kick off Monday morning, and Teagan had suggested that Bebe fly in Friday night so they could enjoy the weekend together. The two of them were spending Saturday afternoon shopping for shoes in Union Square, and later tonight, Amelia and Ava Grace were going to drop by Teagan's loft for a girls' night.

"What's your dress like?"

"It's a Monique Lhuillier. It's strapless and floor-length. It's made out of chiffon, and the bodice is fashioned in a criss-cross pattern. The waist is tight, and the skirt is floaty."

"It sounds pretty."

"It's gorgeous. Amelia has good taste."

Bebe evaluated the shoes displayed on the table and picked

up a pair of strappy silver stilettos that were less shiny than the kitten heels. She twirled them by the heel, her eyebrows raised in a silent question.

"Maybe," Teagan said.

Bebe passed her the shoe, and Teagan inspected it. She didn't know if she'd be able to stand for hours in these shoes without taking painkillers. The straps would probably rub her poor feet raw.

She caught the eye of the sales associate roaming the floor and held up the shoe. The woman nodded and headed off to find Teagan's size, and Teagan put the shoe back on the table.

"What about these?" Bebe said from behind her.

Teagan turned, and when she saw the shoe Bebe held, she gasped in delight. The textured, metallic leather gleamed under the recessed lighting, drawing attention to the sharply pointed toe. The pleated vamp had little crystals scattered on it, and a skinny strap fastened around the ankle.

She grabbed the shoe from Bebe's hand to study it, caressing the one-inch platform and four-inch heels with her forefinger. It was *perfect*.

The sales associate had returned with the other shoes, and Teagan waved the metallic heel. Without a word, the woman passed Teagan the box she held and walked away.

"I hate places like this," Bebe said, rolling her eyes. "The women who work here are so snobby."

Teagan nodded. Most employees at really expensive boutiques were more haughty than helpful, and the woman assisting her today was ruder than usual.

"I really want to ask, 'Why are you so stuck up? Can *you* afford the shoes you sell?'"

Teagan laughed and transferred the box to her other hand so she could hug Bebe to her side. She leaned her cheek against her best friend's silky hair.

"I've missed you, Beebs."

"I've missed you, too, *kanya*."

Bebe had recently returned from a three-week trip to India. Because of the time difference, they hadn't been able to talk as frequently as they normally did. Teagan still wasn't clear on why Bebe had gone to India or what she'd done while she was there. She had been evasive when Teagan had asked her about it. As far as Teagan knew, Bebe's company had no offices in India, so she could only assume the trip had been personal.

With her arm around Bebe's shoulders, Teagan headed to one of the plush chaises scattered around the shop. The two of them took a seat, and Teagan put the box with the silver stilettos on the floor. She wanted to try on the metallic heels first, since she liked them so much better.

"How are things going at work?" Teagan asked.

"Good."

Although Teagan was happy Bebe had done so well at BioEdge, she secretly hoped that one day her best friend would take a job with a firm in the Bay Area. It would be so fabulous to see Bebe on a regular basis rather than every couple of months.

Over the past three years, Bebe had quickly ascended the corporate ladder at BioEdge to head up the company's investor relations group. She was a member of the executive team, and she regularly met with Wall Street analysts and large, institutional investors.

"What about you, *kanya*?"

"Things are okay. We're negotiating with some new suppliers for the materials for Amelia's accessories, and that's keeping us busy. Plus, we're working with the real estate department on a bunch of new deals. And I've been traveling quite a bit."

Bebe shifted on the chaise so she could see Teagan's face. After a moment, she sighed.

"You've been traveling so you can avoid Nick."

Riley O'Brien & Co.'s vendors, suppliers, and partners were scattered across the world, but thanks to phone, email, and FedEx, ninety-nine percent of Teagan's job could be done without any travel. Before she had been forced to work with Nick, she'd only traveled occasionally.

"I've said this before, and I'll say it again—if you had told Quinn about what happened with Nick, he never would have hired him. You could pick up the phone right now, call your brother, and tell him what Nick did, and Quinn would fire him."

"You're right."

"Then why haven't you told him?"

"I don't want to hurt my family. Quinn and Cal are so happy that Nick's in San Francisco and working for Riley

O'Brien. You should see them together. They're like the Three Musketeers. And my mom and dad act like the prodigal son has returned."

Bebe snorted. "So you're sacrificing yourself so your brothers can have a buddy to drink beer with, and your parents can have one more guest for Sunday dinner?"

Bebe's sarcastic tone made Teagan frown. She really didn't want to hurt her family, but part of her reluctance to talk to Quinn was pride. She didn't want anyone else to know how stupid she had been to sleep with Nick. Her lack of judgment embarrassed her.

And there was another reason she had decided to avoid Nick rather than get rid of him: he was really good at his job.

"How much longer do you think this particular avoidance tactic will work? I have a hard time juggling travel with my everyday workload. One day of travel puts me behind by two days. Do you know what I mean?"

Yes, Teagan definitely knew what Bebe meant. She was exhausted from being on the road, going to meetings during the day and catching up on the rest of her work at night in a hotel room. If she kept up this kind of travel schedule, she would end up sick.

"I didn't know what else to do," Teagan admitted. "If Nick and I aren't in the same city, I can't do anything stupid."

The sales associate returned with another box stamped with the words "Yves Saint Laurent" and passed it to Teagan. After asking if Teagan needed anything else, the snotty woman left.

Teagan handed off the box to Bebe so she could remove her shoes. By the time she'd finished, Bebe had the metallic heels ready for Teagan to try on. She slipped her feet into them and fastened the tiny buckles before standing and walking around the room.

"How do they feel?" Bebe asked. "They look gorgeous."

"Pretty good. As good as four-inch heels can feel."

Bebe laughed. "I've never worn a pair of shoes with more than a two-inch heel. I can't believe you can even walk in them."

The conversation gave Teagan a strong sense of déjà vu. Bebe had been with her when she'd purchased the nude patent leather stilettos she had worn the night of her birthday dinner with Nick. Her best friend had said almost the exact thing when she had seen the five-inch heels.

A wave of sadness swept over Teagan. She had been so happy that day—so excited to celebrate her birthday with Nick. More than anything, she had been full of hope.

She wished she could go back and relive that day . . . have a *Groundhog Day* do-over. In the new version, she would have canceled dinner with Nick and spent the evening with Bebe. Or maybe she would have been better off reliving that first day when Nick had shown up at her door. Instead of inviting him in and eating brownies, she would have ignored his knock.

Bebe called her name, and Teagan realized she was staring into space. Facing the mirror, she studied the shoes from the front and the side.

"I think they're perfect," Teagan announced.

Bebe exhaled loudly. "Thank God. Hurry up and pay for them. I'm starving. You need to feed me."

Teagan followed Bebe's directive, and ten minutes later, they sat in a cozy booth at a brasserie in Union Square. Bebe spent a few seconds reviewing the menu before snapping it closed. The gold rings on her fingers glimmered from the sunshine filtering through the windows, and Teagan wondered again what kind of significance they held.

When they had graduated from Harvard, the rings had been confined to Bebe's left hand. Now, every one of her fingers on both hands was covered in the wire-thin bands. If Teagan had to guess, she'd estimate Bebe wore more than a hundred rings. They were unique and pretty, just like the woman who wore them.

"So tell me what's been going on with Nick. When I left for India, you were still spending most of your time in the office instead of traveling, so something must have happened to make you even more desperate to avoid him."

"I went house hunting with him a couple of weeks ago."

"Why, for God's sake?"

"Because Nick sicced my mom on me. He told her that I hadn't made time to help him find a place to live, and my mom called me and lectured me for half an hour about how I couldn't offer to help someone and then not do it."

Bebe laughed. "Oh, he plays dirty. If I didn't hate him so much for what he did to you, I'd admire him for exploiting your weaknesses."

Teagan frowned. "He's conniving and manipulative."

"Now that's the kettle calling the pot black! Are you forgetting what you did to Quinn and Amelia?"

Bebe had warned Teagan that her plan to revamp the women's division behind Quinn's back would blow up in her face, and she'd been right. More important, Bebe was the one who had helped Teagan understand why she had been so fixated on the redesign and why she had been so angry with Quinn.

"Did you have sex with Nick in a closet while the real estate agent was in the other room?" Bebe joked.

When Teagan didn't answer, Bebe narrowed her eyes and leaned forward. "Oh, my God! Did you?"

"No. Not exactly."

"Then what exactly?"

Teagan recounted the entire house-hunting debacle, including the make-out session and Rayna's well-placed kick. She also shared Nick's revelation that he wanted a family and his claim that they'd been in a long-term romantic relationship.

"Did you ask him what happened to change his mind about wanting a family . . . wanting to get married and have children?"

"No. I was too shocked to say much of anything except to comment on his lack of relationships."

"You know what I think is interesting . . . the fact that Nick realizes the two of you had a long-term relationship. He must be smarter than you are because you *still* don't seem to realize it."

"He said we had a long-term *romantic* relationship, Bebe. I know we had a relationship. We were friends. But I definitely don't think the term 'romantic relationship' applies, since he was having sex with other women."

Bebe's eyebrows shot up, and Teagan realized her voice had risen to a volume where other people in the restaurant stared at them. She gave them a rueful smile before returning her attention to Bebe.

"I'm not sure I agree with you. You had romantic feelings for Nick long before you two had sex, and he had romantic feelings for you, too. Have you ever thought about it this way: you and Nick dated for ten months before having sex?"

She considered what Bebe had said before shaking her head in frustration. "It doesn't matter what it was or wasn't. It's in the past."

TEAGAN HAD JUST FIRED OFF AN EMAIL TO THE HEAD OF RILEY O'Brien's business development group when the guest receptionist called to let her know Bebe waited in the lobby. Since the biotech convention had started this morning and Bebe was supposed to be there, Teagan was immediately concerned. She rushed from her office to meet the other woman, and when she pushed through the double doors and saw the smile on her best friend's face, she let out a relieved breath.

"What are you doing here?" she exclaimed. "You're supposed to be at the biotech convention."

"I have some good news, and I wanted to tell you about it *tout de suite*."

"What is it?"

"Can we go to your office?"

Teagan nodded, and once the two of them were back in her office and seated at the conference table, she turned to Bebe. "Well?"

"I wanted to wait to tell you because I didn't want you to get excited for no reason, but I've been interviewing with a biotech company here in San Francisco. I met with the CFO this morning, and he offered me the job."

With a loud squeal, Teagan jumped out of her seat to hug her. She pulled back abruptly when she realized Bebe hadn't said she had accepted the job.

"Wait. Did you accept the job?"

Bebe laughed. "Yes."

Questions shot out of Teagan's mouth like bullets out of a machine gun. "What company? What are you going to be doing? Are you making more money? Where are the offices?"

Bebe laughed again before addressing her questions one at a time. When she finished, Teagan hugged the shorter woman again.

"I'm so happy for you. And for me! It's going to be so fabulous for us to live in the same city again. When are you going to start?"

"I'm not sure. My contract with BioEdge says I have to give them three months' notice, but I think they're going to be livid I'm leaving. They're probably going to have security escort me from my office the minute I tell them I've taken a job with GGB."

Just then, a hard knock sounded on the partially open door, and Cal's dark head peeked around it. He grinned when he caught sight of Teagan, and he pushed open the door and walked in. Bebe stood, stepping out from behind her.

When Cal saw Bebe, his smile disappeared as if it had never been there. He clenched his jaw, staring at the shorter woman with narrowed eyes.

"Bebe," he said curtly.

"Cal," Bebe returned in an equally curt tone.

Teagan sighed, suppressing the urge to roll her eyes. Cal and Bebe couldn't stand each other. It had been dislike at first sight when they'd met a little more than three years ago. Her brother's easygoing charm evaporated the minute he got within fifty feet of Bebe, and her best friend turned into an absolute bitch whenever Cal was around.

They eyed each other for a moment. Bebe crossed her arms over her chest, the movement making her rings shine in the midmorning sunlight that slanted through the windows. His eyes fell to her hands, and he frowned darkly before glancing toward Teagan.

"I need to talk to you, T."

"Can it wait? Bebe and I are in the middle of something."

"No, it can't wait," he snapped before telling Bebe in a rude tone, "You need to leave."

Dropping her arms to her sides, Bebe looked at Teagan. "Is it okay if I grab some coffee in the executive lounge?"

"Yes. I'll come get you when we're done."

Bebe headed toward the door, but instead of moving out of the way like a gentleman, Cal stayed where he was. Bebe was forced to skirt around him, and as she passed him, he turned slightly and looked down. Bebe looked up, and their eyes met for a long moment before she dropped her gaze.

Suddenly Teagan understood exactly why Bebe rubbed Cal the wrong way. He wanted to rub her the *right* away.

His gaze stayed on Bebe as she left the office, and Teagan watched her brother's eyes drop to Bebe's butt. Her best friend was slender and petite, but she wasn't shapeless. She had curves. All that kickboxing had given her a shapely behind, and right now it was emphasized by a pair of tailored gray trousers with big black buttons on the pockets.

Cal breathed deeply as Bebe closed the door, and Teagan chuckled under her breath. She was about to have some fun at his expense.

"I really wish you'd try to get along with Bebe." She sighed loudly. "It just breaks my heart that my brother and my best friend can't stand each other."

Cal jerked his head toward her, and she studied him. He was a little flushed, his light blue eyes kind of glazed.

"She's such a nice person. Why don't you like her?"

He rolled his shoulders. "She's too . . ." He paused, clearly trying to find something to say other than the truth. "Smart," he finally said.

Teagan pressed her lips together, trying not to snicker. "Mom would be appalled to hear she raised a son who can't appreciate a woman with a brain."

He frowned. "I can appreciate a woman with a brain. I appreciate you, don't I?"

He threw himself into one of the chairs in front of her desk, and Teagan sat down on the edge of it. She nudged him with the tip of her red snakeskin-print heel.

"So what's the problem?"

"I don't like her jewelry . . . all those rings she wears."

"Why not?" she asked, choking back her laughter.

"They're distracting."

"It must be hard for you to take your eyes off them." She gave him a sympathetic glance. "They draw attention to her fingers and everything she touches."

He nodded, his eyes unfocused. His face flushed darker, and he shifted in the chair. It didn't take a genius to know what he was thinking about, and she watched him with amusement for several moments. Abruptly, his gaze snapped to hers.

"What did you say?"

"Nothing," she answered, shaking her head.

He ran a hand over his short, dark hair. "Why is she here anyway?"

"There's a big biotech convention at the Moscone Center." She paused, getting ready to drop the bomb. "She got a job offer from GGB this morning. She's moving to San Francisco."

He sucked in a breath, and she smiled innocently. "I'm so excited. She's going to be working just a few blocks away, within touching distance. She's going to be around *all the time*."

His eyes widened. "*Damn*."

"What did you say?" she asked, even though she had heard his comment just fine.

"Nothing," he replied harshly before vaulting to his feet and striding out of her office without another word.

She convulsed into laughter and then laughed even harder when she realized that Cal had been so flustered by their conversation that he'd forgotten the reason he had dropped by her office in the first place. She was still laughing when Bebe returned to her office. The shorter woman smiled at Teagan's mirth, closing the door behind her.

"What's so funny?"

She shook her head. Bebe would figure it out soon enough. "I was just about to come and get you."

"I saw Cal walk by, so I assumed you were done." Bebe frowned. "I know he's your brother, but he's such a *jerk*. He's nothing like what you described when we were in school."

"I must have been blinded by sisterly love," Teagan said, pushing back a smile.

"Totally blinded." Bebe made a little moue. "I need to get back to the convention."

"Okay. Let me walk you out."

Bebe moved to grab her bag from one of the chairs grouped around the conference table, and just then, another knock sounded at the door. Teagan shot Bebe an apologetic glance, and her friend waved her hand, indicating she didn't mind the interruption.

"Come in," she called out.

The door opened, and Nick stepped into her office. He looked toward her desk, and when he realized she wasn't there, he scanned the room until he found her. Teagan gasped when she saw his face and rushed toward him.

"What happened to you?" she asked when she reached him, gently turning his face so she could see the damage.

His gorgeous face looked like someone had taken a baseball bat to it, and she could only imagine how much it hurt. He leaned down a little bit so she didn't have to stretch to reach him, and she stroked the horrible, purplish-black circle around his eye before tracing the terrible cut on his lip.

Cupping his bruised jaw, she looked into his green eyes, one of them swollen and bloodshot from the massive shiner. He rubbed his face against her hand and closed his eyes when she smoothed his hair with her other one.

"What happened?" she whispered.

"Double-black diamond. Cal's helmet. My face."

"Are you hurt anywhere else?"

He shook his head, dropping his hands to her waist to pull her closer. He opened his eyes, and they stared at each other.

"You need to be more careful. And you need to stay away from Cal when he's on skis."

He nodded, laughing softly. He looked over her head, and his lips quirked.

"Hi, Bebe," he said, dropping his hands from Teagan's waist and stepping away from her.

Teagan spun around. She had totally forgotten Bebe was in the room. She had forgotten everything but Nick.

"Hello, Nick. It's been a while."

"Yes," he agreed.

"And yet it feels like yesterday," Bebe continued.

Teagan looked back and forth between Nick and her best friend. His lips tilted in a small smile, and he nodded toward Bebe before meeting Teagan's eyes.

"I'll come back later."

Teagan watched as he left her office, his tight backside wrapped in a pair of faded Rileys and his broad shoulders covered in a light blue plaid shirt. Bebe cleared her throat, and Teagan jerked her eyes back to the other woman, flushing guiltily at the look Bebe gave her.

"I forgot just how hot Nick is," Bebe said. "Even with a

black eye and a split lip, he's hotter than 99.99 percent of the male population."

Teagan wished *she* could forget. But he was imprinted on her memory. Imprinted on her soul.

"I'm glad I was here to see that," Bebe added.

Teagan scowled. "Nick is not a 'that,'" she replied, insulted on his behalf. He was more than just a hot body.

*A lot more.*

Bebe laughed softly. "*Kanya,* for a smart woman, you sure are dumb sometimes. I was talking about how you reacted when you saw Nick's face."

Teagan grimaced. "It looks terrible. It shocked me."

"What's more shocking is the fact that you can't see Nick is totally, completely, *madly* in love with you. I have no doubt *you* are the reason why he changed his mind about getting married and having children."

"No. You're wrong."

"Yes," Bebe shot back. "And you're in love with him, too. You never stopped loving him, and you're never going to stop loving him."

Teagan stumbled over to her office chair and collapsed into it. Her heart thundered in her ears, and her chest was tight.

"That's not true. I hate him."

Bebe made a rude noise. "Stop lying to yourself, stop lying to me, and most of all, stop lying to Nick! You can't resist him because he's *it* for you."

Bebe rounded Teagan's desk and leaned down to stare into her eyes. "You can't keep denying your true feelings, Teagan. Deep down inside, you know I'm right. It's hard to forgive someone when he's hurt you so badly, but in Nick's case, it's worth it because you're not going to be happy without him."

Bebe rested her behind against the edge of the desk. "You need to stop running from Nick. You need to have a real conversation with him and tell him about the baby. You need to ask him why he never returned your phone calls and why he suddenly changed his mind and came after you. And when you've talked to him, *really talked to him*, you need to ask him what he wants so you can decide if you're going to give it to him."

# Chapter 30

"AMELIA, I KNOW QUINN GAVE YOU SOMETHING NEW TO WEAR today, but Ava Grace tells me you need something old, something borrowed, and something blue," Teagan said.

Quinn's bride-to-be turned from the mirror, her wedding dress making a *swooshing* noise with the movement. Her brown eyes were wide, and her rosy lips were opened in an O of dismay.

"I totally forgot about 'something old, something new, something borrowed, something blue,'" she said, her voice almost a wail. "I've never done this before."

Amelia was one of the most pragmatic, levelheaded people Teagan knew, but the bride was a wreck today. She was trembling and breathless, and since she didn't drink, there wasn't much anyone could do to calm her down.

Teagan reached for Amelia's hand, squeezing her fingers. "Don't worry, I've got your back," she said.

Dropping Amelia's hand, Teagan pulled two velvet jewelry cases from her leather bag and placed one of them on a nearby table. Opening the other box, she turned it so the redhead could see the earrings inside it.

"These were my Grandma Vi's, and when she died, she passed them down to me. My Grandpa Patrick gave them to her on their wedding day. If you want, they can be your 'something borrowed.' You can wear a little bit of O'Brien history when you walk down the aisle."

Amelia looked down and ran the tip of her finger over the drop-styled earrings. With a square diamond stacked on top of a circular diamond in a starburst platinum setting, they were one of Teagan's favorite pieces from Grandma Vi's collection.

When the future Mrs. O'Brien looked up, her eyes sparkled like Grandma Vi's diamond earrings. "Thank you," she said softly.

Teagan smiled and handed the case to Amelia. "Wait . . . there's more."

Turning to the table, Teagan grabbed the other jewelry box and faced Amelia. She raised the lid and handed it to her future sister-in-law, who gasped when she saw the bracelet displayed on the black velvet.

"This is my 'welcome to the family' gift to you. It's old *and* blue."

After an exhaustive search involving the Internet and local jewelers, Teagan had found a stunning vintage bracelet studded with diamonds and tanzanite, one of the rarest gemstones in the world. Tanzanite could be found only in one place: the foothills of Mount Kilimanjaro in Tanzania. The stones in the bracelet were a bluish-purple, and they were a perfect match for Amelia's bridal bouquet of lacecap hydrangeas.

"Oh, Teagan," Amelia breathed, looking down at the bracelet, "it's beautiful."

"It is, isn't it?" Teagan said, feeling very pleased with herself for finding the *perfect* gift for Amelia.

Amelia laughed and launched herself at Teagan, her arms outstretched in a big hug. The unexpectedness of the gesture caused Teagan to stumble backward on her tall heels and knock her hobo bag off the table. Fortunately, Ava Grace was there to steady her. Otherwise, both Teagan and Amelia would have tumbled to the floor in their wedding finery.

Teagan turned to pick up the fallen bag, but Ava Grace beat her to it. As the willowy singer scooped the bag from the floor, a leather jewelry case tumbled out. Teagan lunged for the case, but Ava Grace got to it first.

"What's this?" she asked, holding it up.

Ava Grace's question drew Amelia's attention, and the

shorter woman peeked around Teagan. She nudged Teagan's shoulder.

"I'm already wearing a fortune in diamonds, but I'm sure I can find room for more," she quipped.

When Teagan didn't reply, Amelia glanced at her alertly. Teagan's face heated, and she held out her hand for the jewelry case.

Ava Grace smiled mischievously. "Why are your cheeks so red, Ms. O'Brien?" she asked before glancing at Amelia. "Millie, I think there's something special in this jewelry case—something Teagan doesn't want us to see."

"I think you're right," Amelia said, tapping her manicured finger against her bottom lip. "We definitely need to take a look."

Ava Grace snatched the case out of Teagan's reach and lifted the top. Her eyes widened when she saw the contents, and she turned the case to show Amelia.

"Oh," the bride gasped, running her fingers over the bracelet and earrings. "I've never seen anything so gorgeous!"

Amelia looked up at Teagan, a little frown creasing the smooth skin between her brows. "Are these part of Grandma Vi's collection, too?"

Teagan shook her head.

"Are they yours?"

"Yes."

"Where did they come from?" Ava Grace asked, handing the case back to Teagan.

Teagan took a moment to smooth her fingers over the bracelet and earrings, which were a perfect match for the vintage necklace Nick had given her for her birthday. He must have commissioned the pieces months ago because it would have taken a jewelry designer several weeks to find the right gems and create the bracelet and earrings.

The hotel's concierge had delivered the jewelry case to her that morning. A handwritten note had accompanied it, and Teagan had recognized Nick's bold scrawl. *I'll never forget how beautiful you looked when you wore nothing but the necklace I gave you.*

After she had read his message, images of their night together in Boston flooded her mind. After hours of lovemaking,

Nick had pulled her on top of him, staring into her eyes as he trailed his long fingers over the diamond necklace. She had seen more than lust in his gaze, more than hunger.

She had ridden him slowly, letting the pleasure expand inside her until there was no room for anything else. Her orgasm had been so powerful it had bordered on pain, and when Nick climaxed, he'd called her name over and over in a hoarse, fragmented voice. In the deepest reaches of her heart, she believed that was the moment when they had made their baby.

The bracelet and earrings were the most recent (and most expensive) gift Teagan had received from Nick over the past two weeks. She didn't know what had happened, but since he had returned from Quinn's stag weekend, he'd changed the tone of his pursuit.

He had totally backed off, physically, at least. He no longer cornered her in dark hallways to kiss her senseless or bent her over conference tables to screw her senseless.

He gave her gifts instead, and all of them included a handwritten note. Some of the messages were sweet, some were X-rated, and all of them chafed at her poor heart until it was raw.

She had received a gorgeous bouquet of lavender roses with a note that said:

> *Do you remember the lavender roses I bought for you? I told you I bought them because you were sick, but I really bought them because I wanted you to be my Valentine.*

She had scoffed when she'd read the message, telling herself it was cheesy. But her heart had said it was more sweet than sappy.

The next day, she'd found a white wicker basket sitting on her desk, overflowing with candles, bubble bath, and body lotion in her favorite scent. She had thrown the note in the trash, but hours later, she'd dug through the wastebasket to find it.

It had read:

> *I want to see you in the bathtub, your face limned in the glow from these candles. I want to see your skin all pink*

*and slippery with bubbles clinging to it. I want to smooth
this lotion over your body until you moan my name.*

When she had finished reading the note, her panties had
been damp, and she had been unable to concentrate for the rest
of the day. The moment she had walked into her loft after work,
she'd filled the tub with water and poured in some of the bubble
bath Nick had given her. When it had overflowed with fragrant
suds, she had climbed in with her waterproof vibrator.

She'd tried to fantasize about Hugh Jackman, but she and
the *X-Men* star hadn't been able to get the job done. Finally,
she'd given in and imagined Nick in the tub with her, and she'd
enjoyed three orgasms before the water had turned cold.

A couple of days later, she had discovered a plastic container on her office chair filled with chocolate sugar cookies. The
note read:

*Letty came to San Francisco with me. She promises to
make your favorite cookies anytime you want if you'll
stop by the house so she can finally meet you.*

And two days ago, a big white envelope had been propped
against her computer monitor. Inside she had found several
brochures advertising tourist attractions around the Bay Area
with colorful Post-it Notes stuck on the covers. The messages
ranged from *This sounds fun* to *We sailed Boston Harbor, let's
sail the San Francisco Bay* to *Alcatraz probably has a cemetery we can explore.*

Nick wasn't stalking her anymore—he was *courting* her. It
was a subtle assault rather than the aggressive tactics he had
used in the past, and it destroyed her defenses faster than she
could build them.

"Teagan, where did the bracelet and earrings come from?"
Amelia repeated.

"Nick gave them to me," Teagan admitted, snapping the
case shut.

Amelia and Ava Grace stared at her, clearly stunned by her
answer. She slipped the jewelry case back into her bag.

"Why aren't you wearing them?" Ava Grace asked at the
same time Amelia asked, "Are you going to wear them today?"

"No," she said, answering Amelia's question.

"Why not?" they asked simultaneously, like they were Siamese twins who shared a brain.

Teagan held her bag in front of her body, feeling the outline of the jewelry case through the supple leather. Although she didn't want to answer their questions, she also didn't want to offend either one of them. She and Amelia had built a tentative friendship, and Ava Grace had extended her friendship to Teagan because of her relationship with Amelia.

After a lengthy hesitation, she answered, "Because he would see that as a sign that I'm giving him another chance."

Ava Grace laughed huskily. "If a man gave me jewelry like that, I'd give him anything he wanted."

"She's not as mercenary as she sounds," Amelia noted wryly.

"If you're not going to wear them, then why are you carrying them around with you?" Ava Grace asked.

"I didn't think they would be safe in my room," Teagan prevaricated.

Teagan didn't want to admit that she wanted to have the jewelry close by so she could ogle it whenever she got the urge, which was a lot. She was *so* tempted to wear the bracelet and earrings. They were so fabulous, and her bridesmaid dress would offer a perfect canvas to highlight them. But she was going to leave the jewelry in its leather case, and someday soon, she'd return it to Nick.

"And you think they'll be safer here?" Ava Grace asked doubtfully.

Teagan shrugged and tried to redirect the attention to the bride. "You need to hurry and put on the jewelry, Amelia. You don't want to be late to your own wedding."

Ava Grace nodded in agreement. "We don't want Quinn to think you're a runaway bride. All hell would break loose. That man would tie you up, throw you over his shoulder, and head for the hills."

Both Amelia and Teagan laughed at Ava Grace's comment because it was true. Quinn wouldn't let anything stop him from marrying Amelia—not even the woman herself.

Amelia and Quinn had chosen to marry and hold their wedding celebration at a newly renovated vineyard in Napa Valley. It featured a historic Spanish-style chapel, along with an indoor-outdoor reception area, gourmet restaurant, and boutique luxury hotel.

The entire wedding party was staying at the hotel, along with a large number of the wedding guests. Quinn and Amelia had booked the bridal suite for tonight and tomorrow night. The following morning, they would head back to San Francisco to hop a flight for their honeymoon. The location was a secret. Quinn wanted to surprise his bride, and he was the only one who knew where they were going.

Teagan helped Amelia fasten the bracelet around her slender wrist and watched as the other woman replaced the earrings she was wearing with Grandma Vi's diamonds. Amelia turned toward the full-length mirror to see how the old, borrowed, and blue jewelry looked with her wedding dress.

Amelia nervously smoothed her hand over the front of her dress, which was the color of heavy cream. With a sweetheart neckline, pleated bodice, and trumpet skirt covered with organza ruffles, it wasn't the kind of dress Teagan would have expected Amelia to choose, but it was perfect on her petite frame.

Amelia touched the necklace Quinn had given her, a delicate web of platinum studded with diamonds of varying sizes, before turning her head to study the earrings. Since her hair was piled on top of her head in a mass of red curls, they were very noticeable.

"Quinn is going to recognize the earrings," Teagan told Amelia. "He's going to be thrilled you're wearing them today. We all loved Grandma Vi, and let me assure you, she would have adored you."

Teagan and Ava Grace came up behind Amelia to flank her. The mirror was big enough to show all three of them, and Ava Grace laughed at their reflections.

"A blonde, a brunette, and a redhead walked into a chapel . . ." she quipped.

They convulsed into giggles, and when their laughter died down, Ava Grace picked up the long veil draped over the back of a chair. She placed it toward the back of Amelia's updo and fluffed it so it fell in filmy folds past the bride's waist.

"You're ready," Ava Grace said, her voice even huskier than usual.

Amelia sought Ava Grace's eyes in the mirror, and she smiled tremulously. "Now is not the day to start crying," she told her best friend.

Ava Grace's glossy lips tipped up in a small smile, her hazel eyes shining wetly. "I have no idea what you're talking about. You know I don't cry."

Teagan checked the clock on the wall. "It's time."

A light knock sounded on the heavy wooden door, and Teagan's mom poked her head around it. When she saw the three of them standing together, she smiled and made her way to Amelia's side. Grasping her future daughter-in-law's hands, she kissed her cheek.

"I'm so happy you picked Quinn, and I'm so lucky I get to be your mother-in-law." She grinned. "And I'm so excited you're going to be the mother of my future grandchildren. Hint, hint."

Everyone laughed at Kate's comment. She had made no secret of the fact that she was desperate for grandchildren.

"I wanted to let you know all the guests are seated, and the men are on standby," Kate said, heading toward the door. "We're ready when you are."

The door clicked behind her, and Amelia took a deep breath. She turned to face them.

"Let's go. I can't wait to see Quinn in a tux."

The three of them grabbed their bouquets and made their way into the chapel's vestibule. With the exception of the wedding coordinator, it was empty. Amelia's mother was dead, and she'd never known her father. She and Ava Grace were each other's family, and the tall blonde planned to walk Amelia down the aisle.

The wedding coordinator spoke into her headset, and the tempo of the music inside the chapel changed. The coordinator gestured to Teagan before opening the door.

She started the slow walk down the aisle, trying to keep her eyes on the officiant standing at the end of the rose-petal-strewn floor. She could feel Nick's gaze on her, and her hands shook around her bouquet. She gripped them tighter, focusing her attention on the ribbon-wrapped stems to prevent herself from looking at him. Every step she took brought her closer, and finally she gave in to the overwhelming need.

When she saw him in his stark black formalwear, she was

surprised she didn't trip and fall on her face. Nick in jeans and a T-shirt was enough to make most women drool. Nick in a tux could start an estrogen riot.

Teagan knew the male wedding party all wore Brioni tuxedos—the same ones the actor Daniel Craig wore as James Bond in the 007 movies. The wool-and-silk blend formalwear was outrageously expensive, but looking at Nick as he stood straight and tall next to her brothers, she almost thought the price was worth it. The black fabric hugged his broad shoulders and long legs, while his white tuxedo shirt emphasized his tan and his thick, shiny hair.

She met his green gaze, and he smiled slowly. Almost of their own free will, her lips tipped up at the corners to return it. His smile widened, his eyes heating. It was pretty obvious what he was thinking about, and a blush crawled up her cheeks as she took her place at the front of the chapel.

Over the past couple of weeks, Nick had dropped all pretense they were nothing more than family friends. He didn't seem to care that his interest in her was obvious to her brothers, her parents, and other Riley O'Brien employees. He waged an emotional war on her with every single look and every single word.

The string quartet shifted into Richard Wagner's "Bridal Chorus," signaling the bride's imminent arrival, and Teagan managed to pull her eyes from Nick to focus on the chapel's double doors. The guests stood, and Amelia and Ava Grace made their way down the aisle.

Teagan glanced toward Quinn but immediately looked away because she felt like a voyeur when she saw his face. His emotions were visible for everyone to see: need, adoration, pride, possession, and most of all, *love*.

That deep, soul-sucking O'Brien love.

Tears burned the backs of Teagan's eyes, and she blinked rapidly to push them back. She was happy for Quinn and Amelia. She really was.

But she was also jealous. She wanted what they had. She wanted someone to love her the way Quinn loved Amelia. She wanted someone to look at her the way Quinn looked at his future wife.

Amelia and Ava Grace reached Quinn's side, and when the

officiant asked, "Who gives this woman in marriage?" Ava Grace's voice rang out in the chapel. "I do."

Stepping aside, the tall blonde let Quinn take her place. He stared down into Amelia's face for a moment before wrapping his arm around her waist and pulling her to him. Dropping his head, he kissed her until the wedding guests roared with laughter.

Teagan laughed along with them, but her laughter died in her throat when her gaze collided with Nick's. His eyes were bright with hunger, and the expression on his face made it clear the courting phase of his strategy was over. He was moving on to the next one.

*Claiming.*

# Chapter 31

EACH LAYER OF QUINN AND AMELIA'S WEDDING CAKE WAS A different flavor, and Nick was greedy enough to wish he could have a piece of each one. He took another bite, moaning softly as the tartness of lemon and the sweetness of raspberries bombarded his taste buds.

"What kind do you have?" Cal asked around a mouthful of cake.

"Lemon and raspberry."

"Is it good? I have the devil's food cake with vanilla icing, and to quote Amelia, it's 'orgasmically delicious.'"

Nick chuckled. The cake was pretty good, but the only thing he would describe as orgasmically delicious was Teagan's curvy body.

"I think I'm going to try to sneak another piece," Cal said. "I heard there's coconut cake with lime buttercream. And I'm going to get a piece of the groom's cake, too. It's chocolate almond cake with mocha icing."

Cal sighed, and Nick glanced toward him. The other man's lips were tipped in a small smile, his gaze focused on Quinn and Amelia. The newlyweds were talking with a group of wedding guests, and Quinn's arm was curled tightly around Amelia's waist while she leaned against him.

"That's what I call 'Happily Ever After,'" Cal said, nodding his head toward his brother and his bride. "I would bet my life they're going to be like that fifty years from now."

Nick nodded in agreement. He was confident that no matter how many years passed, Quinn would still be holding Amelia close, and she'd still be leaning against him.

Taking another bite of cake, Nick tried to push down the envy that welled inside him. He was happy for his best friend and his new wife. At the same time, he wanted to be the one who held his bride close. He wanted to be the one who had fifty years of togetherness to look forward to.

Nick let his gaze wander the room. He could count on one hand the number of weddings he had attended. While he'd played football, a number of his teammates had married, and he had been invited to almost all the weddings. He only attended a couple, though, because he felt uncomfortable in social situations where he was expected to talk.

Without question, Quinn and Amelia's wedding was the nicest he had attended. The reception space was quite large, which was a good thing, since there were at least 450 wedding guests. Most of them were from the groom's side, since Amelia didn't have any family and only a few friends.

With its creamy stucco walls and dark wood plank floors, the room was similar to the Spanish-style chapel where the ceremony had been held. Wrought iron and crystal chandeliers hung from the unique, barrel-shaped vaulted ceiling, giving the room a sophisticated yet rustic feel.

It had a large dance floor, and the band was set up in the front of the room. Two sets of arched double doors opened to a huge patio area, which was strung with outdoor garden lights.

At least forty-five round tables were set up inside and outside. Light and dark gray table linens covered the tables, and large floral arrangements were situated in the middle of each. The flowers were the same ones Amelia and her bridesmaids had carried down the aisle.

Now that the meal was over and the cake had been cut, Nick assumed the dancing would begin. The seven-person band was ready to go, but it hadn't started playing yet. The string quartet that had played during the ceremony had provided music throughout dinner.

Nick heard the sound of Teagan's laughter, and his eyes instinctively sought her out. He smiled when he saw her chatting with Deda Aldridge, the head of Riley O'Brien & Co.'s business development group, and his partner.

Cal nudged Nick with his tuxedo-clad shoulder, and Nick brought his attention back to the younger O'Brien brother. Cal tilted his head toward Teagan, his eyebrows raised questioningly.

"How are things going with Teagan? Any progress with my stubborn but lovable little sister?"

Nick grinned at Cal's apt description. He loved everything about Teagan, but he wished she was just a little less stubborn, especially when it came to giving him another chance.

"Maybe," Nick answered. "She smiled at me."

That smile she had given him as she'd walked down the aisle had made his heart beat faster and his blood bubble inside his veins. He had been surprised she had even looked his way, and when her glossy lips had tilted up, he'd felt as if he'd been struck by lightning.

Cal gave him a look that combined pity and contempt. "You're pathetic."

Nick laughed. "Someday you might think a smile is p-p-p-progress."

"If that day ever comes, I give you permission to bludgeon me with the golf club I gave you for Christmas."

"I'll look f-f-f-forward to it."

"Has she said anything about the gifts?"

"No."

While they'd been drinking bourbon in the resort bar, the O'Brien brothers had suggested that he woo Teagan with gifts. He had liked the idea and had eventually decided on gifts that could do double duty as her favorite things and as reminders of their time in Boston—a time when he had been falling in love and had been too stupid to realize it.

Teagan hadn't mentioned his gifts, but he thought that was a good sign. He didn't want a thank-you, he just wanted her, and at least she hadn't rejected the gifts by dumping them on his desk.

He was even more encouraged by the way she had acted when she had seen the injuries to his face. It was the first time she had willingly put her hands on him (except for sex) since they had been in Boston, and her concern had been evident.

"What about doing something romantic?" Cal suggested. "Maybe a ride in a hot air balloon."

"You think that's romantic?" Nick asked, shooting Cal a doubtful glance.

"I don't know," Cal admitted. "I've never had to *be* romantic to get what I wanted from a woman."

Nick nodded. He knew exactly what Cal meant. Women threw themselves at him, and he'd never had to put any effort into getting laid. Before Teagan, Nick had never gone out of his way to do something special for any woman.

"Her birthday is in a few days," Cal reminded him. "Maybe you could do something special to celebrate it."

Suddenly, Nick's mind was filled with images of Teagan in her green dress the night he had taken her out for her birthday—the night when he had ruined everything. He wished he could go back and relive that night like the asshole main character in *Groundhog Day*.

If he were given a mulligan, he would make love to Teagan all night long and wake up in her bed. Maybe he'd take her slowly in the early morning light, or maybe he'd pull her into the shower and take her while warm water trickled over them.

Then he would treat her to brunch before texting Elijah and asking his agent to find him a place with the San Francisco 49ers or the Oakland Raiders so he could be with Teagan when she moved back home. And finally, he'd ask her what kind of engagement ring she wanted.

If he had done those things when he'd had the chance, they would have already celebrated their third wedding anniversary. They would probably have a kid, and given the fact that he couldn't keep his hands off her, they would likely have another baby on the way.

He could have had everything, and now he thought it was a big deal when she smiled at him. *Cal is right—I am pathetic.*

The band's guitarist strummed his instrument to get the guests' attention, interrupting Nick's melancholy musings. Once the room was silent, Ava Grace stepped up on the dais with her guitar and sat down on a stool in front of a stationary microphone. Crossing her legs, the beautiful blonde gave the crowd a big smile.

The guests began to murmur, and the air crackled with excitement. No one had known Ava Grace planned to perform, not even the newlyweds.

Ava Grace had won the national singing competition, *American Star*, nearly four years ago. Since then, she'd vaulted into stardom with several number one songs. She was a household name akin to Miranda Lambert and Carrie Underwood except she was even prettier and more talented.

"Hello, everyone," Ava Grace said, her unique raspy voice amplified by the mic. "Most of you know me as Ava Grace Landy, but you might not know me by my most important title, Amelia Winger's . . . oops, I guess she's Amelia O'Brien now, folks."

Ava Grace chuckled, and the guests laughed at her mistake. "My most important title is Amelia O'Brien's best friend," she continued. "Amelia and I grew up together. We're family."

Her voice softened. "Right after Amelia met Quinn, she told me he was too distracting—that she couldn't even be in the same city with him because she was afraid she'd rip off his clothes."

Nick laughed along with the rest of the wedding guests, glancing over to see how Quinn and Amelia were reacting to Ava Grace's speech. The bride's face was bright red, and the groom's face was split by a grin that stretched nearly ear to ear.

"Millie, you now have the legal right to rip off Quinn's clothes anytime you feel like it."

The guests roared with laughter, and Amelia hid her face against Quinn's shoulder. Ava Grace laughed. "Okay, that's enough embarrassment for one night. I wrote a song for you two, and I'd love it if you would dance your first dance as husband and wife while I sing. What do you say?"

The newlyweds nodded, and a couple of dark-suited men cleared the dance floor. Quinn and Amelia took their place in the middle of it, and Ava Grace winked at her best friend.

"This is called 'Empty Places,'" Ava Grace said before looking over her shoulder to count off the beat.

The band launched into a slow, sweet melody. Quinn twirled Amelia, and her fluffy dress belled out around her before he pulled her back into his arms.

Ava Grace began to sing, mesmerizing the guests with her

voice and lyrics. Nick took a deep breath, letting the music pour over him, and all too soon, the song was over. For several seconds, there was silence in the room, and he noticed several wedding guests wiping their eyes.

Ava Grace stood and waved to the crowd before stepping down from the dais. Quinn and Amelia met her, and the bride threw her arms around her best friend. The crowd broke into applause, and the band immediately launched into an upbeat song. Seconds later, enthusiastic dancers filled the dance floor.

Sometime during Ava Grace's song, Cal had disappeared from his place beside Nick. He had a pretty good idea where the other man had gone, and his suspicions were proved correct when he spotted him near the cake. While everyone else had been enthralled with the slow, romantic music, the best man had been stuffing his face.

Turning his attention from the glutton in the corner, Nick leaned against the wall. He spotted Kate and James on the dance floor, and he smiled when James dipped his wife over his arm.

Nick watched the guests dance through the first set of songs, and when the band took a break and the string quartet began playing again, he searched the room for Teagan. He had kept an eye on her all evening, debating whether he should approach her.

He didn't want to reverse the progress he'd made with her by putting her on the defensive, but at the same time, he wanted to dance with her. He wanted to feel her curvy body against his, look into her beautiful blue eyes, and smell her sweetness.

He saw her standing alone near the doors to the patio, and he let himself enjoy the sight of her in the strapless bridesmaid dress. Her shoulders and chest looked smooth and creamy against the silvery-gray material. The dress crisscrossed over her torso before cinching her waist and falling to the floor in smooth folds. A flat-chested woman would have looked pretty good in the dress, but Teagan, who had large, luscious breasts, looked liked every man's X-rated fantasy.

Teagan glanced his way, and he didn't bother to pretend he hadn't been staring at her. He didn't bother to hide his hunger for her, either. The corners of her mouth tilted up, drawing him like a magnet.

He headed her way, surprised and pleased when she stayed

where she was. He had expected her to rush out of the room. Maybe he *was* making headway.

Stopping in front of her, he shoved his hands in his pants pockets to keep from pulling her to him. She looked up to meet his eyes. Her glasses were absent, and he noticed the shimmery silver color on her eyelids and the length of her long lashes.

A dark curl had escaped from her fancy up-do, and it dangled over her forehead. He pushed it back, tucking it behind her ear, and traced the diamond stud fastened to her earlobe.

He'd hoped she would wear the earrings and bracelet he had given her, but he had doubted she would. He had planned to give the jewelry to her for Christmas, but he'd changed his mind in favor of the picture. The pieces had languished in a safe-deposit box in a downtown bank for months, and he'd decided to go ahead and give them to her as part of his new strategy.

He wasn't sure how long they stared at each other, maybe seconds, maybe minutes, but he finally managed to gather his thoughts. He cleared his throat so he could deliver a long sentence, and she tilted her head, waiting patiently for his words.

"You look beautiful," he said slowly, "I've never seen anyone or anything so beautiful."

Her eyes widened, and her cheeks turned pink. She licked her lips, leaving them shiny and wet, and blood rushed to his cock. Moving closer, he settled his hand on her waist, clenching his fingers in the smooth, filmy material of her dress.

"You look really handsome," she replied softly, smoothing the lapel of his tux with her fingers. "The most handsome man in the room."

Her words sent a tingle through him. He had always viewed his good looks as a consolation prize for what he really wanted—the ability to speak easily and clearly. But after hearing the admiration in Teagan's voice, he suddenly felt blessed by Mother Nature.

Cupping his hand around the back of her head, he slowly leaned down. He gave her plenty of time to pull away before placing his mouth on hers and gently stroking the seam of her lips with his tongue. Her lips fell open, giving him a taste of lemons and sugar, and he knew she had eaten the same cake he had enjoyed.

The chatter of conversation, the mellow tones of the string instruments, the ding of expensive crystal . . . it all faded away as she stroked her tongue against his. She slid her hands under his jacket to grip his waist and pressed against him until her breasts flattened over his chest and her stomach cradled his cock.

Teagan aggressively sucked his tongue into her mouth, and a sharp zing traveled down his spine to the tip of his erection. He gasped as it pulsed against his boxer briefs and jerked his mouth away from her to pull in a lungful of air.

He hastily stepped back to put some space between them, shocked that a simple kiss had brought him so close to disaster. He wasn't an etiquette expert, but he was pretty sure it was bad manners to come in his pants during his best friend's wedding and in full sight of 450 people.

Teagan glanced down, and he followed her gaze. He was hugely erect, and his tuxedo trousers did nothing to hide it. In fact, they seemed to emphasize his hard-on.

She raised her eyes to his, pressing her lips together, but he saw the hint of a smile on her mouth. A second later, her husky giggle reached his ears.

He scowled. "Not funny," he grated.

"You're right," she agreed solemnly before snickering.

Shrugging off his jacket, he draped it over his arm to hide the monster in his pants. When he brought his attention back to Teagan, bittersweet emotion washed over him. She was smiling at him, her dark blue eyes sparkling with happiness like they used to.

He missed that Teagan. The one who had chattered and laughed and teased. The one who had understood him like no one else.

*I miss the Teagan who loved me.*

The strum of a guitar drew their attention, and the band's lead singer announced that the bride and groom were ready to leave. Nick wove the fingers of his free hand through Teagan's and pulled her onto the patio, where they would give Quinn and Amelia a proper send-off.

The rest of the wedding guests joined them, and when the

wedding coordinators passed around baskets filled with rose petals, he and Teagan each grabbed a handful. ZZ Top's "Gimme All Your Lovin'" blared through the speakers on the patio, and Quinn and Amelia ran through the crowd hand in hand.

Nick tossed the rose petals with the other guests, showering the newlyweds. Once they were out of sight, he turned to Teagan, but she was gone. He blew out his breath in frustration. It was always one step forward and two steps back with her, and he wondered if he'd ever get ahead.

The first notes of David Grey's "This Year's Love" floated from the reception hall, and he slowly made his way back inside. Couples packed the dance floor, all of them swaying to the romantic music. Nick scanned the crowd for Teagan but couldn't find her.

Draping his jacket over the back of a nearby chair, he rubbed the back of his neck, squeezing the tight muscles with his fingers. He needed a drink.

"I love this song."

Teagan's voice came from behind him, and he dropped his hand before slowly turning to face her. She stood a couple of feet away, her hands clasped loosely in front of her.

"Would you dance with me?" she asked softly.

His heart thudded heavily, and he wondered if he had heard her correctly. Just in case his hearing worked fine, he held out his hand. He half expected her to walk away, but she slid her hand into his.

He followed her to the dance floor, and once they were there, she stepped into his arms. Wrapping his arm around her waist, he pulled her close, and she placed her hand on his shoulder before resting her head against his chest.

Somehow he managed to move his feet, and she followed his lead. The action jogged a long-forgotten memory of dancing with her at Cal's college graduation party. He had cut in on one of Cal's friends after watching the guy's hands wander to Teagan's ass one too many times.

He had been infuriated, but she had laughed it off. She had assured him that Cal's friend wasn't the first guy who had grabbed her butt, and *hopefully* he wouldn't be the last, either. He had laughed at her quip, but his mind had been filled with thoughts of palming her sweet cheeks.

Had he wanted Teagan even then? He truly didn't know. But he had no doubt he wanted her now.

Tightening his arm, he pressed her closer and closed his eyes to savor the feel of her curves against him. She sighed softly, the sound making the fine hair on his body stand on end. When her stomach brushed against his erect cock, he shuddered.

He knew he couldn't take much more of this. He couldn't take much more of wanting her and never having her. He needed her to fill all the empty places inside him.

"T," he rasped.

Looking up, she met his gaze. He swallowed deeply and pressed his tongue against his teeth, trying to get his mouth to work.

"Give me another chance. Come back to my room."

# Chapter 32

ALTHOUGH IT WAS RARE FOR THE BAY AREA TO GET ANY RAIN in April, or so Nick had been told, a random storm had kicked up in the Pacific Ocean. It had poured every single day for the past week, forcing the San Francisco Giants to play in crappy weather for their three-game home stand.

He took a swallow of his Fat Tire as he watched the Giants' young pitcher strike out the St. Louis Cardinals' best batter. Quinn had invited Nick to watch the game with him and Cal in the Riley O'Brien & Co. suite, but he had declined the invitation. He wasn't in the mood to socialize, not even with his best friends.

Over the past month, he and Teagan had fallen into a routine. She dropped by his house every night after work unless she had plans with Bebe, and they had sex on the floor, against the wall, in the shower. Anywhere and everywhere. She never said no, and she was willing to try anything.

The sex was hotter and more intense than he could ever have imagined, yet he had never been more miserable. He wanted more than sex. He wanted Teagan. He wanted her friendship, her dreams, and her future.

*I want her love.*

She ignored him at work, refused to stay the night with

him, and even worse, barely talked to him unless they were having sex. When she saw him at her brothers' or parents' homes, she avoided him, and she never accepted his invitations to hang out, whether it was a casual dinner or something planned in advance.

They weren't a couple. They weren't even friends with benefits. They were just two people who fucked each other whenever they had the urge.

His stomach growled, and he put the game on pause using the DVR remote. As he made his way to the kitchen, he took in the progress the contractors had made over the past three months.

He had bought the Italianate-Victorian mansion in Pacific Heights that he and Teagan had toured together. Vanessa had redesigned the entire ground floor so the kitchen looked out onto the backyard. It now had a large breakfast nook and a set of wide French doors leading to an outdoor living space.

Pulling open the door of the new stainless steel fridge, Nick grabbed the lemon icebox pie Letty had made earlier. Before Letty had told him about it, he had never heard of the dessert, which was apparently a favorite in the Deep South. It consisted of a pastry crust filled with a creamy lemon custard-like layer topped with whipped cream.

He thought about just grabbing a fork and eating directly from the pan, but Letty frowned on him doing that, so he placed it on the black granite island and turned to the cream-colored cabinets to grab a plate. Just as he opened the glass-fronted cabinet, he heard the doorbell.

He frowned, wondering if he should just ignore it. Letty had already gone home for the night, and Teagan had told him she had plans for the evening.

The doorbell pealed again, and he closed the cabinet door with a sigh. He walked slowly down the hall, hoping whoever was at his door would go away. When the doorbell pealed yet again, he picked up his speed, and when he saw Teagan's familiar outline through the stained glass, he hurried to unlock the door.

When he opened it, she was shaking out her fire-engine-red umbrella. She looked up with a big smile, and he noticed her glossy lips were the same color as her umbrella.

"Hi," she said.

He returned her smile, surprised to see her, since she had told him that she and Bebe were going out to dinner. He looked behind her, frowning a little when he saw her silver Porsche parked along the curb.

He had given her a garage door opener weeks ago and told her to park inside the garage, but she never did. He'd also given her a key to his house, but she never used it, either.

He held out his hand for her umbrella, and she passed it over. Opening the door wider, he waved Teagan inside. Her shiny trench coat matched her umbrella, and a pair of strappy black stilettos wrapped around her feet.

He shook his head in exasperation. Her legs looked awesome in those fuck-me heels, but it was too slick outside for her to be wearing shoes like that. She might hurt herself.

Teagan stood slightly to the side, waiting for him to lead the way deeper into the house, and he pushed down a wave of annoyance. She had spent hours here with him, and there was no reason for her to act like a guest. He wanted his home to be her home.

He dropped her umbrella in the aged bronze holder Letty had bought for the foyer before grasping her elbow and ushering her down the hallway and into the kitchen. She smiled when she saw the pie.

"You have such a sweet tooth," she teased, tucking a long strand of dark hair behind her ear.

Yes, he had a sweet tooth, and *she* was the sweetest thing he had ever tasted. Bending down, he dropped a quick kiss on her plump lips.

"No dinner?"

"Bebe had to cancel," she explained, frowning a little bit. "She's working on a big investor presentation."

Nodding, he turned toward the cabinets. He heard a rustle of fabric behind him, and he assumed she had removed her trench. He should have taken her coat at the door, and he made a mental note to show more gentlemanly manners in the future.

"Pie?" he asked as he opened the cabinet door and pulled out two aqua-colored plates.

"Actually, I was thinking you could have something else for dessert."

He looked over his shoulder and almost bobbled the dinnerware when he saw her. She had removed her trench, all right, but the only thing she wore underneath it was a sheer black bra with red ribbon around the edges and a pair of matching panties.

Pulling his eyes from her curvy body, he carefully put the plates back in the cabinet before turning to face her. She smiled slowly, her blue eyes glinting in the bright overhead lighting.

He ran his gaze over her, noting the black underwear made her skin look like freshly whipped cream. Her luscious breasts almost overflowed the bra cups, and he could see the shape of her nipples through the sheer fabric. The panties accentuated her round hips, and the dark hair of her pussy created a shadow between her legs.

Drawing in a deep breath, he tried to get himself under control, but it was too late. Blood rushed through his veins, heading straight for his cock. Her eyes dropped to his crotch, where his erection pressed against his zipper, and her smile widened.

She rounded the island to where he stood and hopped up on it. Her big breasts bounced with the movement, causing saliva to pool in his mouth. She tilted her head, a coquettish expression on her face.

"Oh, you really wanted pie, huh?" she asked with mock sympathy.

She dipped her finger into the whipped cream covering the pie, raising it to her mouth. He swore his eyes crossed as her pink tongue darted out to lick her finger. When she made another foray to the pie, she scooped a much larger blob from the top and held it in front of her.

"What about having your pie and eating me, too?" she suggested as she placed the whipped cream at the top her cleavage.

*Holy shit! She's going to kill me.*

He placed his hands on her smooth thighs, and she widened her legs so he could step between them. Leaning forward, he opened his mouth over her cleavage and licked the rich whipped cream from her warm skin.

He trailed his tongue along the edge of her bra before unhooking the clasp between her breasts. He pulled the cups away from the plump mounds, and she shrugged it off her shoulders.

Every time he saw her breasts, he marveled at how lush and perfect they were. Her skin was so pale he could see the light tracing of veins under it, yet her nipples were dark and rosy.

Right now, they were hard little buds, and he rolled one between his fingers. She gasped, leaning back slightly to brace her hands against the countertop. The action pushed out her breasts, and he stuck his fingers into the pie and smeared whipped cream and lemon custard over her nipple.

She shivered, and he watched as goose bumps broke out all over her arms and upper chest. He wrapped his mouth around her nipple, swirling his tongue through the sweet dessert to find her hard peak. He sucked strongly, and she slid her fingers through his hair and held him against her.

He bit down gently, and she moaned as she squeezed her thighs against him. The husky sound sent a spark up and down his spine, and he pulled back, closing his eyes to find some much-needed control. It was always a shock how easily she got him going.

"Is your sweet tooth already satisfied? I hope not."

He opened his eyes to find her lower lip stuck out in an exaggerated pout. Whipped cream and lemon custard covered her finger, and she dabbed them on the front of her panties.

His cock twitched excitedly at the thought of eating her sweet pussy, and he gripped her hips to move her farther back onto the island. Bending forward, he sucked the dessert off the scrap of fabric, and when all the cream and custard were gone, he pulled her panties to the side and slid his tongue inside her wet slit.

As the tanginess of her pussy flooded his mouth and mixed with the sweet and tart flavors of the pie, it felt like his cock doubled in size. Nothing, *nothing*, tasted better than her tender flesh, and he eagerly stroked his tongue over her clit while plunging two fingers inside her. Moaning, she gripped his wrist, and he looked up to meet her eyes.

"Please," she begged huskily, "I need you inside me."

He gently pulled her to a sitting position and worked her panties down her legs and over her sexy shoes. Reaching between them, she popped the button on his Rileys and unzipped his fly. She pushed his jeans and underwear down until his cock sprang free, and he sighed in relief.

Palming her ass, he pulled her to the edge of the island. She immediately wrapped her legs around him, and his cock brushed against her slick folds. She was drenched, and he couldn't wait one more moment to feel her around him. He slowly pushed inside her, and she dug her sharp heels into his ass.

"I don't want it slow, Nick," she said, her eyes a dark, smoky indigo. "I want you to fuck me fast and hard and deep. And even if I beg you to stop, I want you to keep going."

Her words sent a jolt through his whole body, and even though he tried to hold back, his cock jerked and a stream of semen shot out of him. He grunted from the fiery pleasure, and she tightened her legs around him to pull him deeper.

"*Oh*, I felt that." She laughed softly. "You must like it when I talk dirty."

He stared into her eyes, trying to catch his breath. She drove him crazy. She knew it, and she did everything she could to make him lose it.

Leaning into him, she licked the corner of his lips before darting her tongue into his mouth. She sucked his lower lip into her mouth, nipping it gently.

"Can you feel how wet I am?" she whispered against his lips. "It's because of you. I want you to fuck me with your big cock."

He shuddered and closed his mind to everything but the feel of her tight pussy. Clenching his fingers in the cheeks of her ass, he pulled out and plunged into her. He went so deep he bumped against her cervix, and she moaned.

"Yes," she gasped. "Just like that."

He thrust into her with deep, fast plunges, and to keep himself from shooting off, he slowly started to count backward from one hundred. She began to whimper when he reached sixty-five. By fifty, she was chanting his name, and she came apart at forty-five, her pussy clamping down on his cock so tightly his vision blurred.

He continued to pound into her, ignoring her pleas that she couldn't take any more. When he couldn't wait any longer, he rubbed her clit between his thumb and forefinger, a move that unfailingly sent her flying toward an orgasm.

She screamed his name, her voice raw and raspy, and the powerful squeezes of her pussy drove him over the edge. He buried his face in her neck and poured himself into her, trembling with the force of his orgasm.

She rubbed his back as they recovered, and after a few minutes, she pushed against his shoulders. Withdrawing from her snug body, he kept his face averted as he stepped away to fasten his pants. He had a pretty good idea of what would happen next, and he needed to prepare for it.

Out of the corner of his eye, he saw her slide off the island. She grimaced a little bit before laughing lightly.

"We made a *huge* mess, Nick."

She grabbed her panties and stepped into them before pulling on her bra and fastening it. Skirting around the island, she opened a cabinet under the sink and pulled out a bottle of kitchen cleaner. Moving the pie to another counter, she sprayed the cleaner on the granite and wiped it down with a handful of paper towels before tossing them in the trashcan.

"We should probably stop having sex on the island." She snickered. "It's fun but unsanitary."

She made her way to the kitchen table, and he tried not to stare at her ass, but it was nearly impossible. He loved its round shape, the way it flared from her hips.

Scooping her trench from one of the wooden chairs grouped around the table, she shrugged into it. "Thanks," she said brightly as she cinched the belt of her coat. "That was incredible." As she started for the hallway, she gave him a small wave. "See you tomorrow."

"Stop," he said harshly.

Halting abruptly, she spun to face him, her eyes wide. "What's wrong?"

He pressed his tongue against his teeth, wondering if he would be able to say what he needed to say. "This is."

She cocked her head. "What are you talking about?"

"I asked for another chance."

The color drained from her face, and he knew she understood exactly what he meant. That was the thing about him and Teagan. He didn't need to say much for her to get his point.

"And?" she asked, crossing her arms over her chest.

He cleared his throat and thought about what his life would be like if things continued like they were. Every time he was inside her, he lost a little bit of himself because she gave nothing back.

"This isn't another chance."

Her eyes narrowed, and she started to tap her foot. He had learned that was never a good sign, but even in the face of her anger, he wasn't going to stop.

"What do you call it?" she asked.

"Sex."

She nodded. "Yes."

"I n-n-n-need more than sex."

"Oh, really?" she asked sarcastically. "You seem happy enough when you're fucking me."

He winced. When she fought back, she went for blood.

"And I don't see you turning me down when I strip in your kitchen."

He laughed, but the sound was more bitter than amused. Even if someone held a gun to his head, he wouldn't be able to turn her down.

"I need more," he repeated, surprised because he was speaking clearly for once.

"What exactly do you *need*?" she asked rudely.

"Love."

Her eyes widened, and he took a deep breath, gathering the courage to tell her what he should have told her years ago. For some reason, his brain and his mouth seemed to be cooperating, so it was now or never.

"I love you."

She gasped and dropped her arms to her sides, her face etched with disbelief. As they faced each other, he finally realized how brave she'd been when she had told him she loved him, and how cowardly he'd been when he had rejected her.

"I loved you then, and I love you n-n-n-now." He swallowed thickly. "And I need you to love me back."

As he walked toward her, she backed away from him, her eyes huge in her pale face. He continued until she hit the wall and he was pressed against her, his arms on either side of her head and his hands flattened against the drywall. Bending down, he brushed his lips over hers.

"Please love me back," he implored, painfully aware he was begging for something he had once thrown away.

She pushed against his chest, trying to escape from the cage of his arms. "I don't want to love you." She shook her head vigorously, her dark hair spilling over her shoulder. "I can't."

Cupping his hand around the back of her neck, he rested his forehead against hers. He closed his eyes and pulled in a lungful of Teagan, his favorite smell in the whole world.

"T," he said hoarsely, "if you can't love me, I can't do this anymore."

"Then stop."

# Chapter 33

TEAGAN TOOK A DEEP BREATH AND REREAD THE EMAIL FROM Quinn.

> T,
>
> I'm transferring oversight of the museum project to Cal.
> Effective immediately, Priest and his team will report to
> our annoying brother.
> Thanks for your hard work.
>
> Q

She pushed away from her desk and hurried down the stained concrete hallway to Quinn's office. The door was open, and her older brother was talking into his headset. She hovered in the doorway, and when he noticed her, he waved her in.

"David, I want to discuss this further, but I need to run right now," Quinn said into the headset, his blue eyes intent on her face. "Send Jeff an email and get on my schedule for next week. Yeah. Thanks, chief."

As Quinn disconnected the call, he pulled off his headset.

Tossing it on the desk, he stood and crossed his office to close the door. When he turned back to her, the expression of loving concern on his face was one she had seen a million times.

No matter what she had done in the past, no matter what mistakes she'd made or the pain she had caused him, Quinn's love for her had never wavered. He was steadfast, and even more important, he knew how to forgive. For Quinn, love always triumphed over anger.

"How's it going, T?" he asked quietly.

"Why?"

He cocked his head. "I assume you're referring to the museum project."

She nodded. She knew Quinn didn't have a problem with her project management. He would have told her if he did, and he would have given her a chance to make it right.

"It's better for everyone if Cal takes over."

Quinn was right. It *was* better for everyone, especially her. But for some reason, the thought of not working with Nick anymore made panic well in her chest. She swallowed, trying to ease the constriction in her throat.

"Did Nick ask you to do this?"

Quinn stared at her for a long time before sighing loudly. He dropped down into one of the leather chairs in front of his desk and looked up at her.

"You didn't want to be in charge of the project in the first place," he reminded her.

"Answer my question, Quinn."

Looking away from her, he slouched in the chair and laced his fingers together against his flat stomach. "Sit down, Teagan," he ordered.

She walked around the desk and sat down in his big CEO chair. She raised her eyebrows, daring him to say anything.

He laughed softly. "You're such a brat, and yet somehow, I still love you."

"Stop stalling and answer my question."

"He gave me three choices. Assign him to another project. Transfer the museum project to another manager. Or he could resign."

Teagan's heart thudded heavily at the thought of Nick no

longer working for Riley O'Brien . . . of no longer seeing him every day. Even though she hated to admit it, seeing him was the highlight of her day.

Quinn held out his hands, palms up. "What was I supposed to do, T? You told me that he's a valuable asset to the company. That he's doing a great job on the museum project. So I asked Cal if he would take over the project, and he agreed." He eyed her across his desk. "I should have asked Cal to take over the minute I found out you and Priest were sleeping together."

Her cheeks heated with embarrassment, and she dropped her eyes. She had tried to keep her relationship with Nick private, if not secret, just in case her brothers were still in the dark.

"How long have you known?"

"He told me and Cal when we were in Tahoe."

She looked up, surprised that the three of them had actually talked about it. Neither Quinn nor Cal had given any indication they knew she and Nick were having sex.

"What did he tell you?"

Quinn propped his ankle on his knee, tapping his fingers against his leg. "Sorry. That violates confidentiality."

She blew out her breath in frustration. "You're not a doctor, a lawyer, or a priest," she snapped.

He laughed. "What do you want to know exactly?"

She wanted to know why Nick had treated her like a one-night stand the first time they had been together. She wanted to know why he had never returned her phone calls so she could tell him she was pregnant. She wanted to know why he had suddenly reappeared in her life after not seeing him for more than a year.

And most important, she wanted to know why she couldn't put the past behind her.

Dropping his foot to the ground, Quinn leaned forward to rest his elbows on his knees. He speared her with his dark blue gaze.

"T, he knows he messed up."

She laughed bitterly. "Messed up? Is that what he said?"

He shot her an alert glance. "Actually, he said he fucked up. Why don't you tell me what happened?"

His phone buzzed, and he leaned forward to pick it up. He spoke quietly into the receiver, telling his assistant to hold his calls before replacing the phone in its cradle and bringing his gaze back to her.

"Tell me what happened," Quinn ordered softly.

Tears prickled the backs of her eyes, and suddenly, she just couldn't hold in the pain any longer. Quinn was her older brother and Nick's best friend, and she knew she shouldn't share this kind of private information with him, but right then, she just needed someone to listen.

"He crawled out of my bed in the middle of the night like I was a slut he picked up in a bar. He was my best friend, and he just disappeared from my life. When I got the news about Daddy, I went to his condo. I was so scared, and I needed him."

She gulped back the tears that clogged her throat. "He looked at me like I was a stranger. He barely said five words to me, but I understood. He told me that being with me was a mistake. That I should forget it."

Quinn made a rough noise, his jaw clenched tightly, but she continued anyway. "I told him I didn't want to forget it. I told him that I loved him." She shook her head. "*God!* The look on his face was horrible."

"T," he began, his voice soothing.

"No!" she countered fiercely. "You asked, and you need to hear—"

"Sweetheart, I don't need to hear any more. It's okay."

"It's not okay!" She sucked in a deep breath. "I begged him, Quinn. I *begged* him. I told him it was okay if he didn't want to be with me. I told him that we could go back and just be friends again."

Tears trickled down her face, and she roughly wiped them away with her fingertips. "And he said no. *He said no.* I couldn't believe it, and when I asked why, he kicked me out of his condo."

"*What?*"

"Some woman was there. One of his gorgeous blondes. Nick just left me in his living room, and she escorted me to the door."

"*Motherfucker*," Quinn muttered.

She laughed sadly. "Oh, Quinn, that's not even the worst of it."

"How could it get much worse?" he asked, shaking his head.

She stared into his eyes. Bebe was the only one who knew about her pregnancy and subsequent miscarriage. But she needed him to understand why she was such a mess.

"Three weeks later I found out I was pregnant."

Quinn didn't respond immediately, and she wondered if he had heard her. He took a deep breath, and she noticed his fingers were clenched around the armrests of the chair so tightly his knuckles were white.

"I called and left messages telling him that I needed to talk to him. And I texted him, too. But he never responded."

He took several more breaths, his eyes narrowed. She could tell he was about to lose it.

"What happened?"

She swallowed noisily. She was afraid saying it out loud would make the pain worse.

"I was in the middle of one of my finals, and I started cramping. By the time Bebe got me to the ER, it was too late."

"Oh, no," he said softly, his eyes dark.

He stood and quickly rounded his desk. Pulling her to her feet, he wrapped his arms around her.

"Oh, sweetheart," he murmured, stroking her hair and rubbing her back. "I'm *so* sorry."

She started to cry again. "I lost Nick's baby. And he didn't even know. He wasn't there when I needed him."

"I'm here, T. *Always*."

She cried harder, huge gulping sobs. "I wanted the baby so much. More than I've ever wanted anything. I wanted Nick, too."

Quinn squeezed her tighter. "It's okay," he crooned over and over. "It's okay."

He comforted her for a long time, and when she calmed down, he gave her a gentle push into his chair. Balancing on the edge of his desk next to her, he met her eyes.

"Are you still in love with Priest?"

His question made her stomach tremble. She didn't want to admit her true feelings to anyone, not even herself.

"I don't want to be in love with him."

He narrowed his eyes, and after a long moment, he chuckled softly. "This is a situation where I can tell you're a lawyer. What you just said is the truth, but it's not the whole truth. You might not *want* to be in love with Priest, but you *are* in love with him."

When she didn't respond, he tilted his head questioningly. "Why don't you want to be in love with him? Do you think what he did is unforgivable?"

From Teagan's perspective, there were very few things in life that were unforgivable. But that didn't mean everyone had the capacity to forgive, and right now, she didn't know whether she could forgive Nick.

Intellectually she recognized he had made her no promises. She had known his track record with women, and a part of her hadn't been surprised by how he had treated her. But deep inside, she had hoped she was special. She had believed their friendship meant enough to him that he wouldn't treat her the way he treated other women.

"Priest told me and Cal that he's apologized. Many times, in fact."

"Are you on his side?" she asked with disbelief.

Quinn shook his head, his dark hair flopping over his forehead. "I'm on your side."

She eyed him with a fair amount of skepticism. Quinn loved Nick, too, and there was no way his loyalties weren't divided.

"This is a situation where I can tell you're a CEO because what you just said is the truth, but it's not the whole truth."

He laughed. "Touché." He crossed his arms over his chest. "Priest messed up. He hurt you. But he's trying to make amends. He said he's tried to explain, but you won't listen."

"There is no explanation!" She made a scoffing noise. "You just don't understand."

He raised his eyebrows. "Oh, really? I don't understand what it's like to be in love with someone who does something that rips out your guts?"

She flushed. Quinn definitely understood because Amelia had hurt him badly. And so had Teagan, for that matter.

"I'm sorry."

"What are you apologizing for?"

"For going behind your back. For almost ruining things with Amelia. For a lot of things."

He smiled and held up his left hand. A thick platinum wedding band glinted on his ring finger.

"I think it worked out okay," he said lightly with a cat-that-got-the-cream expression on his handsome face. "But if you're asking for my forgiveness, you already had it."

"Thank you." She patted his knee. "You're a good brother, Quinn."

His smile widened. "I'm a *great* brother."

She gave a soggy laugh at his response. He leaned back a little against the desk, crossing his feet at the ankles.

"I've been in your shoes, T, so you need to listen to me because I'm speaking from experience. You need to give Priest a chance to explain. And this is just my opinion, but you really need to tell him about the baby. Right now, he doesn't understand exactly how much he hurt you. You can't continue to keep it from him."

Bebe had told her the same thing, months ago. But Teagan hadn't been ready to take her advice. More important, she hadn't been ready to hear Nick's explanation, and she hadn't been ready to share her pain about the baby, not even with its father.

He placed his hand on her shoulder. "I probably shouldn't violate best-friend confidentiality, but I think you need to know Priest is in love with you."

"Did he tell you that?"

"Yes. When we were in Tahoe."

"He only told me a few days ago."

"*Oh*," Quinn said, grimacing.

"What does that mean?"

"That's about the same time he came to talk to me about his job. I'm guessing your response left something to be desired."

"I told him the truth."

"A version of the truth, but not the whole truth, right?" He cocked his head. "I think there's more going on here. What is it?"

Glancing down, she picked at her manicure. She used to favor deep, dark red, but over the past couple of months, her taste had changed, and right now, a shimmery light pink covered her nails. If she were honest with herself, she would admit the color change reflected her emotions. *She* was lighter, and it was because of Nick.

"Teagan, I love you. I want you to be happy, and you haven't been for a long time. It's like you've had a perpetual case of PMS."

Since he was sitting on the desk next to her, she punched him in the stomach. He grunted and laughed at the same time.

"Actually, you seemed happier when Amelia and I got back from Italy."

Quinn's surprise honeymoon trip for Amelia had been a tour of Italy. According to the bride, it had been two weeks of fabulous food and fashion with a little bit of history thrown in. According to the groom, it had been two weeks of great sex. .

"And Priest was happy, too," Quinn added. "Happier than I've ever seen him. But it didn't last long."

She didn't want to hear about how happy or unhappy Nick was. Pushing back from Quinn's desk, she stood. The new position put her eye level with him, and he clasped her hand.

"What's stopping you from being happy?" Quinn searched her eyes. "Talk to me."

"I'm afraid," she admitted, her voice barely audible.

"Of what?"

"Of letting myself love him like I used to. It almost destroyed me." She swallowed thickly. "I think the people in our family love too hard. You saw what happened to Grandpa Patrick when Grandma Vi died. And Mom could barely keep it together when Dad was sick."

Quinn sighed softly. "Yeah."

"And you . . ."

"What about me?"

"Quinn, your love for Amelia is . . . I don't even know how to describe it. It's scary to think about what you would be like if something happened to her. I don't want to love like that. It's too much of a risk."

Her big brother stood and wrapped her in his arms. Squeezing her tight, he kissed the top of her head.

"It's not a choice, T. It's the way we're wired. And I hate to break it to you, but it's too late. You already love Priest *like that*. You never stopped." He cleared his throat. "You have a chance to be happy with him. Take the risk. It's worth it."

IT WAS STILL LIGHT OUTSIDE WHEN TEAGAN WALKED UP THE stairs to Nick's front door. Her heart was racing, and she couldn't catch her breath. She rang the doorbell, and while she waited, she practiced some of the breathing exercises Bebe used for her kickboxing.

She saw a flash of blond hair through the stained glass, and her knees trembled at the thought of seeing Nick. Since Quinn had transferred the museum project to Cal last week, she hadn't seen more than a glimpse of him.

The door swung open, and Teagan felt as if she had been catapulted back in time. The tall blonde from Boston stood on the other side of the threshold, and she was even more gorgeous than she had been four years ago.

*Vanessa.*

Teagan stepped backward, tripping over the edge of the doormat. Vanessa's hand shot out and grabbed her forearm, saving her from a fall.

"Whoa! Careful, Teagan."

Teagan was shocked that Vanessa not only recognized her after all these years but also remembered her name. She shook her arm to dislodge the younger woman's hand, and Vanessa laughed and put her hand on her chest.

"You probably don't remember me. I'm Vanessa." She tilted her head. "Are you okay? You're really pale."

Teagan shook her head, and Vanessa frowned before placing her arm around Teagan's shoulders and ushering her into the foyer.

"Let's go into the kitchen so we can get you some water," Vanessa said, shutting the door with her hip and steering Teagan down the hall. "I'm having some serious déjà vu. You were sick the last time I saw you."

Teagan jerked away from her. "*Who are you?*"

"I just told you. I'm Vanessa."

"Why are you here? I thought you lived in Boston."

"No, I've lived here for a few years now. I was so happy when Nick moved here and asked my mom to come with him."

Teagan stared at Vanessa. "Your mom?"

Vanessa nodded before her eyes widened in understanding. "Oh! You really don't know who I am." She laughed lightly. "I'm Vanessa Andrews. I'm Letty's oldest daughter."

*Vanessa is Letty's daughter?*

"I guess my mom doesn't talk about me as much as I thought," Vanessa joked. "And I'm sure Nick doesn't."

Teagan had always assumed Vanessa was one of Nick's lovers, which had made the whole scene at his condo even more horrible and humiliating. But she obviously had misread the situation, and knowing Nick hadn't been so insensitive as to have one of his lovers throw her out of his condo helped diminish some of the hurt.

"Let's go into the kitchen," Vanessa repeated, beckoning Teagan with a wave of her hand. "My mom made some strawberry lemonade, and it's really good."

She walked down the hallway, and Teagan trailed after her. "I was just doing a final review of the downstairs renovation work. I wanted to make sure the contractors took care of my punch list."

"What?"

Vanessa looked over her shoulder. "Oh, sorry. A punch list is a to-do list."

Teagan laughed somewhat hysterically. "Vanessa, you and I need to work on our communication skills. Why are you reviewing the renovations?"

"Because I did the design for the house. I'm an architect."

"*You're* the architect? Nick never mentioned that."

"Big surprise," the blonde quipped. "He rarely speaks."

They reached the kitchen, and Vanessa opened the stainless steel fridge and pulled out a glass pitcher full of strawberry lemonade. Grabbing a couple of glasses from the cabinet, she filled them with the pink liquid and passed a glass to Teagan before taking a sip of her own.

"My mom told me that you and Nick were back together."

Teagan took a big gulp of the lemonade. It was delicious, the perfect blend of sweet and tart. No wonder Nick had brought Letty with him to San Francisco.

"I'm glad you guys were able to work things out."

Teagan frowned, trying to process Vanessa's chatter. Apparently the other woman was under the impression Nick and Teagan had been a couple in Boston and had reunited.

"He was really messed up when you broke up with him," Vanessa continued.

"*What?*"

Vanessa leaned against the counter. "After you left Boston and moved back here, Nick was a hot mess. He would leave the brownstone in the early morning and run for hours . . . like Forrest Gump. And when he got home, he didn't eat. He drank.

*A lot.* My mom was so worried. You know she thinks of Nick as another son. But he wouldn't tell her what happened, just that things were over . . . that you had moved on."

Teagan shook her head in confusion. Nick was the one who had pushed her out of his life.

A buzzing noise echoed in the room, and Vanessa pulled her phone from the pocket of her slim-fitting black trousers. She looked at the screen before placing it on the granite island and returning her attention to Teagan.

"Honestly, I've never seen a guy so devastated by a breakup. It was *ugly.* But I don't really blame you. I know it must be hard to be with someone like Nick."

*Someone like Nick. Smart, funny, kindhearted, and gorgeous. Yeah, it's a real hardship.*

"What do you mean?" Teagan asked.

"Well, I don't want to sound cruel, but it *is* hard to talk to him. His stutter is pretty bad. I didn't notice it for a long time because he hides it so well. But the more he talks, the more noticeable it is."

Spots danced in Teagan's vision, and a roaring noise filled her ears. Vanessa had dropped a bomb on her, and she was deaf and blind in the aftermath.

"What are you talking about?"

Vanessa grimaced. "Being in a relationship with someone who stutters has to be really difficult. How do you connect without speaking? And how do you argue? You can't talk things out with someone who barely speaks."

Teagan's heart pounded heavily. She had never noticed that Nick stuttered. *Never.*

However, Vanessa made it sound like he not only stuttered, but stuttered a lot. Either Teagan was the most unobservant person on the planet, or he had purposely hidden it from her for *years.*

Vanessa took another sip of her lemonade. "My mom told me that you and Nick have figured out a way around his stutter, though. You have your own way of communicating." She smiled. "Nick says you're like the iPhone. You have predictive word capabilities."

Suddenly, Teagan realized the connection she had with Nick was even more special than she had thought. She had never noticed Nick's stutter because she didn't *hear* it. They had their own way of communicating because she listened to Nick with her whole body and not just her ears.

She could finish his sentences because she understood him emotionally, intellectually, and physically. He could say one word, and she instinctively knew what he meant . . . or at least she did when she wasn't so emotionally raw that she ran away from him.

A slideshow of the past two years flashed through her mind, and Teagan suddenly realized Nick *had* been trying to explain, but he hadn't been able to get the words out. And the knowledge of his stuttering put the horrible scene in his Boston condo in a new context.

"What do you think of the renovation?" Vanessa asked, abruptly changing the subject. "Nick was so determined to have a kitchen that looked out on the backyard. I told him it would be a huge pain in the ass, but he was insistent. He wanted your home office to look out on the backyard, too, so you'd be able to keep an eye on your future kids, but I couldn't make that work. He was pretty annoyed because he wanted your office to be downstairs near his."

*"What?"*

Vanessa frowned. "I thought he told you. I couldn't fit your home office and the family room on the first floor, so your office is upstairs. I hope that's okay."

All the blood rushed from Teagan's head, and she almost dropped her glass of lemonade. Yes, Nick had asked for another chance with her. Yes, he'd told her he loved her. And yes, he'd told her that he wanted a wife and kids. But she hadn't realized what that meant, maybe because she was blind, maybe because she had been afraid to hope . . . to let herself want something that seemed so unattainable.

When Teagan's vision had cleared and her breathing had calmed, she carefully placed the glass on the island. Gripping the edge of granite to anchor herself, she met Vanessa's curious gaze.

"Where's Nick? He and I have some things to discuss."

# Chapter 34

AS NICK STARED DOWN AT THE GLASS DOORKNOB LEADING from the mudroom to the kitchen, he wondered if any of the house's previous residents had felt the same unpleasant mix of hope and dread that swirled in his stomach. He had seen Teagan's car parked on the street when he had driven into the driveway, so he knew she was in the house waiting for him.

He had no idea why she was here, especially since it was nearly midnight. He had met the guys at a sports bar to watch the Giants game, and it had gone into extra innings. Quinn had tried to talk with him about Teagan, but Nick had shut him down.

What was there to say? Teagan had made it clear she didn't want to be with him. She didn't even acknowledge his existence. When she saw him at work, she looked through him as if they were strangers passing on the street.

Even though he reported to Cal now, and even though he really liked working on the museum project, he was thinking about resigning. He didn't need the money, so there was no reason to continue to torture himself. The only thing stopping him was the knowledge he'd be letting down Quinn and the rest of the O'Brien family.

Taking a deep breath, he turned the knob and entered the

kitchen. The newly renovated space was empty, but he could see a faint glow coming from the adjacent family room. He slowly headed that direction, and when he looked in, he was surprised to find Teagan wrapped in a cashmere throw and curled up on the brown leather sofa, totally conked out.

Moving closer, he noticed a pair of red high-heeled sandals on the floor next to her. A bottle of Trinity, an empty glass, and her black-framed eyeglasses sat on the end table near her head.

He frowned, wondering what the hell was going on. As far as he knew, Teagan didn't drink bourbon. She drank girly drinks like pomegranate martinis and mango margaritas.

As he sat down on the edge of the sofa, he ran his gaze over her face. A little frown was notched between her brows, and her lower lip was stuck out in a pout. He wondered if her dreams were unpleasant.

Wrapping his fingers around her shoulder, he shook her gently. Her lids opened slowly, and he stared into her sleepy blue eyes. He could tell the moment she came fully awake because her eyes widened and her pupils dilated.

He scooted back to give her room to sit up, quickly averting his eyes when the neckline of her navy blue dress fell open to show her lacy beige bra and delectable cleavage. The last thing he needed right now was a hard-on.

"I'm sorry. I didn't mean to fall asleep. What time is it?"

"Midnight."

He stood, and she swung her legs to the floor. The new position put her face level with his crotch, and his unruly cock twitched. It didn't care if she loved him or not. It wanted her.

*Badly.*

Plucking her glasses from the end table, she situated them on her nose before looking up at him. She pressed her lips together, and he tensed, instinctively knowing he wasn't going to like what she had to say.

"I know it's late, but I think we need to talk."

He shrugged. An ugly conversation wasn't any prettier at noon than it was at midnight.

Teagan gestured to the leather chair situated near the sofa. "I think you should sit down."

*Oh, shit.*

Grabbing the bottle of Trinity, he poured a hefty measure

into her glass before sitting down. He threw it back in one swallow, and her lips quirked.

"It's good to know I'm not the only one in the room who needs liquid courage."

Her comment made him wonder if he should just start drinking straight from the bottle. She took a deep breath, and he met her eyes.

"So here's how I'd like this conversation to go. I'm going to talk for a little bit. Then I'm going to ask you some questions, and then you can talk. I don't want you to interrupt me, and when you're talking, I won't interrupt you. Does that sound okay?"

He frowned but nodded. She tapped her lips with her fingers, a clear sign of her nervousness. A couple of tense minutes passed before she finally spoke.

"I told you that I don't want to love you, and that's the truth."

Her words sliced into him, and he looked down into his glass, wondering how much he was going to have to drink to dull the pain inside him. He wasn't sure he had enough liquor in the house.

"I don't want to love you, but I do," she continued.

He jerked his head up, certain he had imagined her words. She met his gaze head on.

"I love you. I have loved you for *years*. I fell in love with you even when I was sure there was no hope of you ever loving me back."

Leaning forward, he opened his mouth to dispute her words because he *did* love her. She held up her hand, and he fell back against the cushions, stunned by her words.

*She still loves me.*

"Before you knocked on my door, we were friends. But you became my *best* friend. And when I realized I was in love with you, I decided that I wanted you badly enough to risk our friendship." She swallowed. "If I could go back and have a *Groundhog Day* do-over, I'm not sure I'd risk it again."

She dropped her head, picking at the belt on her dress. "That night . . . it wasn't just sex. The intensity of my feelings scared me, and I knew that if you felt even half of what I felt, you were scared, too, and needed time to adjust. I understood."

As she looked up, her eyes filled with tears. "When I came

to your condo, I wasn't looking for my lover. I was looking for my best friend. Quinn had just told me about Daddy's cancer, and I needed the reassurance and the comfort that best friends are supposed to provide."

She sniffed before continuing. "The moment I saw your face, I knew you regretted having sex with me. But I was so sure you cared enough about me as a friend that you wouldn't cut me out of your life completely. But you did. And when I called you and texted you and told you that I needed to talk to you, I thought you would have the decency to honor our friendship. But you didn't."

She speared him with her dark blue gaze. "I need to know why. Why couldn't you be there for me? Why didn't you return my calls or texts? And why did you suddenly change your mind and decide that you wanted to be with me? *I need to know.* You said you could explain, and I haven't given you the chance to do it before now. But I'm going to sit here, and I'm going to listen."

She took a deep breath. "One more thing . . . Vanessa was checking the renovations when I got here, and she brought something to my attention, something I've *never* noticed before. She told me you stutter, quite severely, in fact. I don't know if you've gone out of your way to hide it from me or not, but you don't need to. And if it's difficult for you to get the words out so you can explain, give me a sign, and I'll wait until you can."

She gestured to him. "Your turn to talk."

Nick stared at the woman who had turned his life upside down and his soul inside out. He slowly rose from the chair, took two steps to reach Teagan, and pulled her to her feet. Wrapping one arm around her waist, he cupped the back of her head with the other and covered her mouth with his. He kissed her until she was limp against him and he was hard against her.

Pulling back, he rested his forehead against hers. He waited for a few moments for his mouth to catch up with his brain, and when it did, he started talking.

"I love you. *I love you.* I'm sorry for hurting you . . . for being an idiot and w-w-w-wasting so much time."

She pressed her hands against his chest. "You need to sit down in the chair. I'm going to sit on the sofa. And you are going to spill your guts like I just spilled mine. And then maybe you can kiss me."

Taking a step back, he dropped heavily into the chair. She curled up on the sofa, the sage-colored throw over her legs, and raised her eyebrows.

Sweat broke out over his body. He didn't know if he could explain, not just because of his stuttering but because his feelings were so difficult to put into words.

"T, I didn't w-w-w-want to ruin our friendship." He wiped his damp palms on his thighs. "I tried n-n-not to. Your friendship was more important than sex. But the more time I spent with you, the more I w-w-wanted you."

He stood up, pacing back and forth in front of the sofa. Sometimes his mouth worked better if his body was in motion.

"I tried to stay away from you, but I couldn't." He pointed at her. "I didn't w-w-w-want to want you. But you're . . ." He paused, trying to think of a word that would describe how special she was.

"Incredible," he finally said.

Darting a glance toward her, he noticed her cheeks were tinted pink. She still didn't have any idea how tempting she was or how hard he had tried to resist her.

"I dreamed about you. Your lips, your ass, your fantastic rack."

Her eyes widened, and a wave of red washed over her face.

"I thought about you all the time, even w-w-w-when I fucked other women." She gasped, shaking her head, and he nodded. "Yes, I know I'm an asshole."

She put her hand over her mouth, muffling her laughter, and he smiled ruefully before sobering. "The night of your birthday, I felt things w-w-w-with you I had never felt before. It scared me to d-d-d-death."

He ran his hand over his hair, trying to figure out the best way to explain how confused he had been. "I had a meltdown. I thought I had ruined everything by sleeping with you. You n-n-n-need to understand that I had never been in love before. I never thought I could have a relationship because of my stuttering."

She pressed her lips together, and he could tell she was

holding in her questions, trying to honor her promise not to interrupt him. "My stuttering ruined my relationship with my d-d-d-dad."

He looked away from her. He hated to admit his own father thought he was stupid and worthless except for football.

"He thinks m-m-m-my stuttering is a reflection of my intelligence."

He had never talked this much in his whole life, and he could feel his mouth and his brain start to disconnect. He pressed his tongue against his teeth, hoping to squeeze out another couple of sentences.

"If I'm upset, I can't t-t-t-talk. That's w-w-w-what happened at my condo."

His mouth locked up, and he knew he had said all he could. The familiar panic built in his chest, and he glanced at Teagan, half expecting her to get up and leave. She tilted her head, and after a moment, she pushed aside the cashmere throw and stood. She walked over to the iPod docking station, scrolled through the songs, and hit Play.

"You have good taste in music," she said, looking over her shoulder at him.

He might have good taste in music, but he had *great* taste in women. Obviously Teagan had noticed his stuttering had gotten worse, and she was giving him time to get his mouth and his brain to cooperate.

The sexy sounds of Norah Jones's "Turn Me On" poured from the speakers. She turned toward him, holding out her hand.

"Dance with me?" she asked softly.

Taking her hand, he wrapped her in his arms. She felt so good against him, her warm curves shaping to his harder form. She laid her head on his chest, and he nuzzled his face in her sweet-smelling hair.

Like always, a tingle of desire ran through him, but mostly he just felt an overwhelming sense of peace. When he was with Teagan, everything was right in his world. He prayed he would have a chance to dance with her like this at their wedding, at their children's weddings, and hundreds of other special occasions.

They danced through Norah Jones and Ava Grace's hit

song "Lost & Found." Holding Teagan had calmed him, and he was relaxed enough to talk again.

"I'm sorry for not being there w-w-w-when you needed me," he said as they swayed together to the music. "I didn't know about your d-d-d-dad. After you left my condo, I caught a flight to Denver. I holed up in a cabin for three w-w-w-weeks with my phone t-t-t-turned off."

She jerked back to look into his face. "You didn't get my messages for three weeks?"

He shook his head. "As soon as I got them, I flew b-b-b-back to Boston. I knew you would be devastated about your dad, and I drove straight to your condo from the airport."

She gazed up at him, her face etched with disbelief.  "You came to my condo? When?"

He ignored her question because he thought it was more important to explain his decision not to see her. "By then, I had figured out how I felt about you. I knew I loved you. I w-w-w-was sitting in your stairwell trying to find the balls to go see you, and I ran into Marshall."

His words backed up again, and he cleared his throat. That didn't work, so he hummed a little, and the muscles relaxed.

"T, this is really hard for m-m-m-me to talk about. Marshall said some things . . ." he trailed off, struggling to find the words.

Stepping away from her, he took several deep breaths and paced around the room. She took a seat on the sofa, watching him with wide eyes.

"He told me I w-w-w-wasn't good enough for you. He t-t-t-told me you wanted a husband and kids. I thought you w-w-w-would be better off with someone else. So I left."

Dropping down into the chair, he placed his elbows on his knees before resting his head on his hands. He had made so many mistakes, and he wondered if he had made *too* many for Teagan to forgive him.

"It almost killed me to w-w-w-walk away from you," he admitted.

They sat silently until he could talk again. "I'm sorry," he squeezed out. "I'm sorry for b-b-b-being a coward . . . for being stupid."

"What happened to change your mind?" she asked.

"You know about m-m-m-my car accident? The one I had in Nashville?"

"I heard about it, but I purposely didn't listen to any of the news reports or read any of the stories." She swallowed noisily. "I wanted to be there with you, but I thought you didn't want me."

He had wanted her. He *still* wanted her. More than anything.

"I almost d-d-d-died in that car accident."

All the color drained from her face, and he rushed to fill the silence. "I almost died, but God gave me a second chance," he continued. "And I w-w-w-wanted that second chance to be w-w-w-with you."

"You told me you didn't believe in God," she said, her voice barely audible.

"I didn't believe in love or m-m-m-marriage, either," he said, staring into her eyes. "But I do now."

Looking down, she hugged herself. Her body language made anxiety shoot through him. Something was wrong.

"Did I explain enough?"

She didn't respond, and panic welled in his chest again. Somehow he had to make her understand. He had to make her forgive him.

"I'm sorry," he repeated, not knowing what else to say.

Teagan raised her head, and the look on her face made his stomach clench. This was going to be bad, he could feel it.

"I need to tell you something," she said.

She looked up at the ceiling and exhaled loudly before abruptly lurching to her feet and pacing around the room. He eyed her with trepidation, concerned because he had never seen her so freaked out.

"*God!*" she exclaimed harshly. "I don't even know how to say this!"

He rose and quickly made his way across the room to where she stood. Stopping in front of her, he slid his hands into her hair and tilted her face to his.

"Just tell me, T."

"I left you all those messages because I was pregnant."

*What?*

She searched his eyes, and his heart started to pound in a

hard rhythm. Adrenaline pumped through his body, making it impossible for him to speak.

"I was pregnant. And I hated you because I thought you had ignored my messages. I hated you because I never got a chance to tell you about the baby."

*Teagan had been pregnant. Their amazing night together had created a baby. Their baby. His and Teagan's.*

He dropped his hands, his breath coming in shallow pants and his ears roaring from the blood racing through his body. Words were trapped in his throat.

*What had happened to their baby?*

He was desperate to know the answer, but he couldn't get his mouth to work to ask the question. Squeezing his eyes shut, he began to recite the Gettysburg Address. He mouthed the words over and over, trying to focus on shaping the letters and sounds.

"Nick?"

He held up a hand, and finally he felt a click inside him. Opening his eyes, he met her gaze.

"What happened?" he rasped.

He saw her mouth move, and words buzzed through his head. *Cramps. ER.*

*Too late. Too late. Too late.*

*Lost.*

"I hated you for abandoning me."

He stared into her eyes, which glistened wetly. She blinked, and tears began to roll down her cheeks.

"I miscarried a few days after Marshall stopped by my condo. If you hadn't run into him, if you had ignored him, you would have been with me. I *needed* you."

With wobbly knees, he stumbled to the sofa and collapsed onto the cushions. The backs of his eyes burned with tears, and he leaned forward, dropping his face into his hands.

Painful waves of emotion drowned him. Sorrow, regret, shame, guilt.

They buffeted him, sucking him down into a dark abyss. Because of his fear, his stupidity, Teagan had been forced to deal with the shock of an unplanned pregnancy and the anguish of a miscarriage alone.

His heart ached when he thought about how scared she must have been when she'd found out she was pregnant and the emotional and physical pain she must have experienced when she'd lost the baby. He should have been with her. He should have been there to soothe her fears and ease her pain.

Before Teagan had told him about her pregnancy, he had wondered if she could forgive him. He hadn't known the full extent of what he'd done to her, but now he knew. He understood why Teagan didn't want to love him, why she hadn't wanted to hear his explanations.

His actions were unforgivable.

USING HER FINGERTIPS, TEAGAN WIPED THE TEARS AWAY FROM her eyes. She took several deep breaths, trying to gain some control over herself. She was relieved to finally have answers, but she also was stunned by everything Nick had disclosed.

His meltdown. The trip to Colorado. The conversation with Marshall. The car accident.

He *hadn't* ignored her messages. He *had* come back. He *had* loved her.

That knowledge made the pain she had carried around for years evaporate like raindrops on a hot sidewalk. At the same time, she still didn't understand why he had walked away from her and what they could have had together.

"Nick, why did you believe what Marshall said?"

She studied him closely, taking in the way his broad shoulders drooped forward over his knees and his big hands cupped his face. Obviously, the news of her pregnancy and miscarriage had stunned him.

He didn't acknowledge her question for a long time, but finally he looked up and met her gaze. His eyes were shiny and wet.

"I didn't believe I could be enough for you. I thought my stuttering made it impossible to be a good husband and father."

She digested his answer. At one time, she would have scoffed at his explanation because it was hard to imagine he had *any* insecurities. On the surface, he had everything. Looks, money, fame, and amazing athletic talent.

She had always viewed him as supremely confident, a textbook alpha male. But now that she knew about his stuttering and his belief that it ruined relationships, his behavior made a lot more sense.

She wanted to hunt down Nick's father and beat him to a pulp for making his son feel less of a person because of his speech impediment. And then she wanted to find Marshall and slap his face for the role he had played in keeping her and Nick apart.

For years, she had wanted Nick to know how much pain he had caused her by not being there for her. She had wanted him to feel guilty. She had wanted to hurt him like he had hurt her.

But now she thought Nick had suffered enough. He had wanted to be with her, but he had walked away because he had believed it was the best thing for her.

He had been wrong, though. *He* was the best thing for her. He always had been, and he always would be.

She slowly walked over to Nick and dropped down to her knees in front of him. Placing her hands on his jeans-clad thighs, she stared into his eyes.

"Nick," she said, tears clogging her voice, "you would have been enough. Until I got pregnant, you were all I wanted. And then I wanted you *and* our baby. I wanted us to be a family."

He dropped his head back into his hands. He said something, but she couldn't discern the words. She moved closer so she could hear him.

"What?"

He raised his head. "I wanted you, too. And I would have wanted our baby."

They sat there silently for a long, long time with her kneeling at his feet. Finally, he cleared his throat roughly, and she held her breath, waiting to hear what he was going to say.

"Do you still want those things, T?"

She looked into his eyes, which were shadowed with regret. She could feel the self-loathing roll off him in waves, and she knew he expected her to reject him. Even so, he wanted her badly enough to risk it. Just as she had wanted him badly enough to risk their friendship so many years ago.

"Yes, I still want those things."

She placed a hand on his chest and pushed him back until he fell against the cushions. Leaning over him, she popped open the button on his Rileys and reached for the tab of his zipper.

As she began to pull it down, she said, "And you know I always find a way to get exactly what I want."

Rising in front of him, she hiked up her dress just enough to shimmy out of her panties and straddle his lap. She gazed into his gorgeous face, the face she planned to see every day for the rest of her life. His expression was full of surprise, hope, and most of all, *love*. She leaned forward until their lips almost touched.

"Are you going to give me what I want, Nick?"

Her question was an echo of what she had asked him on their first night together. His eyes glowed with the memory, and he smiled slowly as he settled his big hands on her hips. She had no doubt this night would end very differently.

"Always."

## Epilogue

Five Years Later

TEAGAN SIGHED LOUDLY AS SHE FELL BACK AGAINST THE leather sofa. Nick draped a cream-colored blanket over her and passed her the TV remote before dropping a quick kiss on her lips. He pointed to her legs, and she pulled them up as far as her belly would allow so he could drop down next to her.

Once he was settled, he pulled her swollen feet over his lap. Just like always, he tweaked her big toe before beginning to massage her arch.

"*Oooh*," she moaned. "Foot massages are *so* much better than sex."

Nick slanted an amused glance toward her. "That's not what you said a few months ago."

She laughed, pressing her toes into his hard stomach. "They're only better than sex when I'm nine months pregnant and look like an ugly elephant."

He chuckled. "Not an ugly elephant. A pretty elephant."

"*Jerk*," she growled. "It's your fault I'm like this."

"I know," he said solemnly, but his eyes glinted with a wicked light. "But I didn't ask Letty to make the lemon icebox pie. *You* did."

*Oh, yeah, I did.*

Nick switched his attention to her lower leg, and she shifted to give him better access. Apparently, the baby didn't like the new position because he kicked her hard in the ribs.

"Oomph," she exclaimed loudly, rubbing her big belly.

Nick's hands froze on her leg, his eyes shooting to her face. "Contraction?"

"No. Just a big kick. Your son might end up playing professional football as a kicker."

She was due in two weeks, so the baby could come anytime. She and Nick were a lot less nervous with this pregnancy than they had been with her second one.

Since she had miscarried her first pregnancy, they both had been apprehensive at the beginning of the second one. Their anxiety had grown exponentially after her first prenatal appointment when the doctor had told them they were having twins, but their girls had been delivered healthy at thirty-seven weeks.

As a new parent, she had wondered how they would handle identical twins without losing their minds, but Nick had told her not to worry. He'd said the babies were a special blessing because of her earlier miscarriage and all the heartache they had suffered.

Studying her gorgeous husband, she took in his thick blond hair and bright green eyes. The girls looked just like their daddy, and she wondered if the new baby was going to take after her or Nick. She knew one thing for sure: their son was going to be spoiled rotten by his father, just like his big sisters.

The girls were named after Grandma Violet and Nick's mother, Audrey. Their names hadn't required much discussion, but she and Nick were having a hard time deciding what to call the new baby.

"What about Dexter? Dexter Priest. We could call him Dex."

Pursing his lips, he said the name a few times. They had to be cognizant of his stutter when they named the kids since he needed to be able to yell their names without hesitation.

For her part, she still didn't hear Nick's stutter. She heard *him*, in her head and in her heart.

"Maybe," he said finally. "I still prefer Patrick."

During the research and planning for Grandma Vi's museum, Nick had come to know Grandpa Patrick posthumously. He was fascinated with him, especially the time the O'Brien ancestor had spent in Europe during World War II.

"Patrick Priest. I still don't like the alliteration."

Nick frowned, and she quickly changed the subject. He *really* wanted to name the baby Patrick, and she was way too close to giving in, especially since his warm hands were stroking higher on her leg.

"How's the planning for the new exhibit going?" she asked.

The Violet O'Brien Gold Rush History Museum had opened three years ago. Since then, it had been recognized as one of the best history museums in the nation, and it had welcomed millions of visitors from near and far.

Ava Grace had come up with the idea for the new exhibit, which would feature popular music and songs from the Gold Rush Era. Nick was working with a music historian to determine the pieces of the exhibit.

"Good. Might showcase some old instruments."

"Oh, that would be so cool." She wiggled her toes against his stomach. "I still think Bebe had a good idea for an exhibit."

"Diseases common in mining towns in the mid-nineteenth century?" Nick laughed. "Not an exhibit I'd pay to see."

She frowned, offended on Bebe's behalf. As he shifted his ministrations to her other foot, he tilted his head toward the remote.

"Thought you wanted to watch *Groundhog Day.*"

Her favorite movie had grown on Nick, and he no longer made rude comments throughout it. And she no longer had to bribe him with kisses to get him to agree to watch it with her, either.

Teagan rubbed her finger over the Play button. She glanced over at him, catching his gaze.

"Do you remember when I had the flu back in Boston and you took care of me? We watched *Groundhog Day*, and I asked if there were any days you wanted to relive."

"Yeah."

"You said there weren't any. Not even the good ones."

He nodded. "I remember."

"Is that still true?"

Nick stared at her for a moment before smiling slowly. "T, every day I spend with you is one I want to relive." He lightly squeezed her foot. "They're all good."

Turn the page for a sneak peek at
the next Riley O'Brien & Co. novel,

# *Hanging by a Thread*

Coming soon from Berkley Sensation!

CHASTE. UNTOUCHED. MAIDEN. PURE. INNOCENT. THE WORDS
that described virgin might sound pretty, but the truth was downright ugly, at least in Bebe Banerjee's opinion. She was convinced
her virginity was the reason her heart raced, her breath seized,
and her palms sweated whenever she was near Cal O'Brien.

Bebe surreptitiously studied Cal, trying to ignore the wave
of lust that surged over her. If she had some experience between
the sheets, she was sure she'd be able to handle the way he
made her feel.

If she had gotten naked with a few guys, maybe she
wouldn't obsess about his glacier-blue eyes and his thick, dark
hair. Maybe she wouldn't notice the way his jeans clung to his
tight behind and long legs. Maybe she wouldn't fantasize
about his lips, his smile, his big hands . . . .

Bebe desperately wished she could just avoid him, but his
little sister, Teagan, was her best friend. If she wanted to spend
time with Teagan, she had to put up with Cal. She said no to a
lot of Teagan's invitations to hang out because of him, and she
had to be very careful not to offend her best friend.

That was why the object of her X-rated fantasies stood next
to her in a club-level suite at PacBell Park. The San Francisco
Giants were in the playoffs, battling against the Atlanta Braves

to win the National League pennant, and Teagan had invited her to attend the game in the Riley O'Brien & Co. suite.

Founded by Teagan's great-great grandfather, Riley O'Brien & Co. was the nation's oldest designer and manufacturer of blue jeans. Americans had worn Rileys for nearly two centuries. In fact, Bebe was wearing a pair right now.

Beside her, Cal shifted slightly and took a pull on his Shiner Bock. He was close enough to touch, and she clenched her hands into fists just in case her fingers suddenly decided to act out her secret fantasies. He didn't even look her way, and he probably wouldn't unless he felt the need to toss an insult at her.

"How was Antigua?" Cal asked, directing the question to his sister and her new husband, Nick Priest.

"It was the most amazing place I've ever been," Teagan said, her blue eyes shining and her glossy lips turned up in a smile.

Teagan and Nick had just returned from their three-week honeymoon to the Caribbean island. Both of them were glowing from their tans and their newlywed status.

"We were lucky we had our own private beach because Nick is an exhibitionist," Teagan added with a lustful gleam in her eyes.

Nick was a former professional football player, and he had been voted as one of the "Sexiest Men Alive" by *People*. With his blond hair and bright green eyes, he was gorgeous, no doubt about it. But in Bebe's opinion, he wasn't nearly as gorgeous as Cal.

*No one is as gorgeous as Cal.*

Nick leaned down and whispered something into Teagan's ear, something that was obviously naughty because her face turned the color of cherries. When he straightened to his full six five and saw her red cheeks, he chuckled.

"You're so bad," Teagan muttered, lightly slapping Nick's chest. In response, he grabbed her hand, hauled her up against him, and kissed her . . . with tongue.

Cal made a gagging noise. "Jesus Christ," he groaned, "do you have to do that in front of me?"

Teagan pulled away from Nick. "*Please,*" she shot back, her voice full of disgust. "Do know how many times I had to listen to my high school friends talk about you and your big—"

Much to Bebe's disappointment, Cal covered his sister's mouth with his hand and cut off the rest of Teagan's sentence. She tried to pull his fingers away, and finally she got free by elbowing him in the stomach.

Laughing, Cal stumbled sideways into Bebe, almost knocking her over. He grabbed her forearm to steady her, his hand hot against her skin, and she gasped. Even the slightest touch from him made her pulse pound, and she tugged her arm to get away from him.

Instead of releasing her, his fingers tightened. She looked up . . . way up. He was almost as tall as Nick, and he loomed over her by more than a foot. He was a little leaner than Teagan's husband but still solid muscle. His faded Giants T-shirt showed off his broad shoulders, impressive biceps, and ropey forearms. He'd paired the shirt with ancient Rileys that fit him like a glove and well-worn boots.

"Sorry about that, Cookie," Cal said.

"I told you not to call me that," she snapped, trying to jerk her arm free.

She *hated* it when he called her Cookie, and he knew it. Of course, that was why he did it.

He had come up with the nickname right after he'd found out she had a medical degree in addition to her MBA and law degree. He'd claimed it was a better moniker than Bebe, since she was such a smart cookie, but she knew it wasn't a compliment.

"I thought you liked nicknames." He smiled angelically and widened his eyes to look innocent. "You call Teagan *kanya* all the time."

*Kanya* was Bebe's nickname for her best friend. It meant "girl" in Hindi, the native language of her Indian ancestors. She had been born and raised in the United States, but using Hindi words was one way she stayed connected to her heritage.

"Teagan and I are *friends*," she pointed out.

He got her message loud and clear because his eyes got all squinty. "I can be friendly."

Yes, he could be friendly. In fact, he was friendly to *everyone* but her. He never had anything nice to say to her, and she returned the sentiment.

She wasn't sure who had struck first, probably her, but now they launched verbal missiles at each other with frequency and precision. He went out of his way to be rude and antagonistic, and she did the same.

Bebe knew the real reason she acted like such a bitch around Cal. She liked him, and she didn't want him to suspect how she really felt. She didn't want to be the pathetic geeky girl with a crush on the hot guy.

Before Cal, she had never been attracted to any man. She'd never even experienced a high school crush because she had entered the ninth grade when she was twelve and had graduated when she was fifteen. She had immediately headed off to college, and she'd obtained two bachelor's degrees in three years.

By the time she had been able to vote, she had been in her first year of medical school. She'd become accustomed to being viewed as a study partner rather than a sex partner.

She wasn't oblivious, though, and over the years, she had noticed good-looking men. But she had never felt that zing of sexual attraction until she had met Cal four years ago. She hated the way he made her feel: gauche, nervous, and over-stimulated. When he was near, sounds were louder, colors were brighter, and smells were stronger.

Right now, she could smell him, a panty-soaking aroma of warm male and expensive cologne. It was so delicious she could barely concentrate on the conversation swirling around her.

"Even though Antigua was amazing, I'm glad to be home," Teagan said. "I missed everyone. Mom and Dad. Quinn and Amelia. Bebe. Letty."

"You didn't miss me?" Cal asked, feigning hurt feelings.

Bebe knew Teagan had intentionally excluded Cal, trying to annoy him. The O'Brien siblings teased each other mercilessly. Their relationship was so different from the one Bebe had with her older brothers.

She rarely talked with Pritam and Ranjit, and when she did, they definitely didn't tease her. They didn't even call her Bebe. They insisted on referring to her by her full name, Bindu, which she hated.

"No. I missed Kim more than I missed you," Teagan replied,

referring to the woman who did her nails at the swanky spa she frequented.

Teagan's snarky response made laughter well in Bebe's throat. Before she could choke them back, giggles escaped her. Cal stiffened next to her, and she mentally prepared for their next verbal battle.

*Ready. Aim. Fire.*

CAL TRIED TO IGNORE BEBE'S SOFT LAUGHTER, BUT THE MUSIcal sound washed over him, and his cock twitched. He shifted away from her, annoyed with his unruly body.

Bebe didn't bother to hide the fact that she couldn't stand him. She was pretty much the only woman who *didn't* like him, and he didn't know what he'd done to make her hate him.

He had told himself a million times he didn't care, but he was lying. It bothered him . . . *a lot*. It bothered him so much that he acted like an asshole anytime he got within fifty feet of her.

Cal slanted a sideways glance toward Bebe, who was staring at her feet. Her shiny hair, the same color as his favorite dark roast coffee, was in its usual bun. He had never seen it any other way, and he'd spent more than a few minutes thinking about what it would look like around her shoulders. He had imagined holding it in his hands while she knelt in front of him.

A few wispy tendrils clung to the nape of her neck, and he wondered if they were as soft and silky as they looked. Everything about her looked soft and silky, from her smooth, golden skin to her full, pink lips.

He felt Teagan's gaze on him, and he pulled his attention from Bebe's lips. His little sister was way too observant, and he had a feeling she knew exactly why he was rude to her best friend.

"Nick and I have decided to throw a Halloween party to show off the house," Teagan announced.

After Priest had retired from the NFL at the end of last season, he'd taken a job with Riley O'Brien & Co. and moved to the Bay Area. He'd bought a historic mansion in Pacific Heights, and the two-story Italianate-Victorian had been under renovation for months.

Cal was surprised Priest had agreed to host a party, since he tended to avoid situations where he was expected to talk. He went to great lengths to hide his severe stutter, and most people didn't even know he had a speech impediment.

Teagan leaned against Priest, and he pulled her closer, squeezing her waist. Suddenly, Cal realized why they were throwing a party: his new brother-in-law would do anything Teagan asked.

"Costumes will be mandatory," Teagan added. "I think Nick should be a Greek god."

Priest groaned dramatically, and Cal chuckled, imagining the other man in a white bedsheet. "Which one?"

"Zeus," Teagan answered promptly. "The king of the gods."

Cal took a swig of his Shiner Bock, and as he lowered his arm, his hand accidently brushed against Bebe. She jerked away from his touch, and irritation rushed through him. She acted like he was a fucking leper, and it pissed him off.

*What the hell is her problem?*

"I bet I can guess what you're going to be," he said, pointing his beer toward her.

Since she was looking down, she didn't realize he was talking to her. He tapped her on the shoulder with the neck of the bottle, and she jerked her head up.

Her eyes were the same color as the gold that his Grandma Violet's ancestor had found during the California Gold Rush, luminous and ringed with long, dark eyelashes. She blinked slowly and licked her lips, leaving them shiny and wet.

He gritted his teeth as his cock thickened behind his fly. What was it about her that made him so hot?

"Did you hear me?" he asked, his voice nearly a growl.

She shook her head, and he repeated what he'd said. She frowned.

"Oh, really?" she snarked. "What am I going to be?"

He bared his teeth in a semblance of a smile. "Since you're so smart, I figured you'd go as a dictionary." He snapped his fingers. "Or maybe an encyclopedia since you think you know everything."

Priest gave a muffled laugh, and Cal met his eyes. The other man raised his dark blond eyebrows, and Cal flushed. He just couldn't seem to stop himself from acting like a jerk.

"That's a good idea." Bebe smiled brightly, but there was

an edge of anger behind it. "I have a suggestion for your costume, too. Since you're such a jackass, why don't you go as a donkey?"

It took him a second to process the insult because he was fascinated by the emotions swirling in Bebe's eyes. When he realized what she'd said, he couldn't help but laugh. He *was* a jackass when he was around her.

Teagan snorted. "Come on, Nick," she said, grabbing her husband's hand. "I'm tired of hearing my best friend and my brother hurl insults at each other. And I'm thirsty."

His sister stalked off, dragging Priest behind her. Bebe shifted to face him, and he took another swallow of beer, studying her as he did so.

She was so petite the top of her head was even with his chest. She was even shorter than Quinn's wife, Amelia, who was a couple of inches over five feet.

He doubted Bebe weighed more than a hundred pounds soaking wet, but she was slender rather than skinny. In fact, her breasts looked like a nice handful under her orange Giants T-shirt. He wouldn't mind finding out if they would fill *his* hands.

She tucked a loose strand of dark hair behind her ear, and the movement drew his attention to her small hands. Thin gold rings covered every finger, wrapping around the slender digits like delicate metal vines.

She probably had a hundred rings on her fingers, and the sight of them glimmering in the sunlight mesmerized him. They made him think about what her hands would look like on his body, wrapped around his cock, stroking him to orgasm.

He let his gaze wander lower, lingering on her narrow waist and the subtle curve of her hips. She wore a pair of Rileys, and satisfaction trickled through him. He loved seeing his last name stamped on a nice ass, and he'd stared at Bebe's enough to know hers was more than nice.

The sound of Teagan's laughter filtered to him, and Cal pulled his gaze from Bebe. He searched for his sister and found her across the room with her new husband. Priest was perched on the back of one of the leather club chairs, and Teagan stood between his legs. His hands clasped her hips, and a huge smile lit up her face.

Bebe looked over her shoulder, her gaze landing on the

newlyweds. After a moment, she brought her attention back to Cal.

"I was worried that I'd never see her again," he admitted.

When Teagan had come back from Boston, she'd seemed like a completely different person. The funny, loving sister he had grown up with had turned into a sarcastic, angry woman. Cal hadn't known, but Teagan had suffered from a broken heart. Now that she and Priest had worked things out, the sister he had adored was making a comeback.

Bebe tilted her head, her eyes intent on his face. She obviously understood exactly what he meant because she smiled slowly—a real smile—and his heart kicked in his chest.

"I was, too," she replied softly. "And I'm really glad she's back. I missed her."

Cal nodded. He had missed her, too.

They stared at each other, and he realized it was the first time he and Bebe had managed to have a conversation that didn't involve sly digs and over-the-top insults. He didn't want her to walk away, so he tossed out the first thing that came into his head.

"How's the new job going?" he asked.

"Great. It was a smart move for me."

Earlier this year, Bebe had taken a position at Generation Global Biotechnology, GGB for short. Its headquarters were located in downtown San Francisco, just a few blocks from Riley O'Brien & Co.'s high-rise.

When Bebe had lived in Boston, he'd only seen her a few times a year. He had always looked forward to her visits but had dreaded them, too. Each time, he'd hoped she would miraculously like him, and when it became obvious she didn't, he would provoke her just so she wouldn't ignore him.

Now that Bebe lived in San Francisco, he saw her all the time. Teagan invited her to most of the O'Brien family gatherings, and Bebe dropped by Riley Plaza to see his sister at least twice a week.

He knew he should stay away from Bebe, but he always sought her out, whether they were at a barbeque, a baseball game, or Sunday brunch. And he always found a reason to stop by his sister's office when Bebe visited. He picked and poked and prodded until her golden eyes narrowed in anger and her sharp tongue slashed into him.

Deep inside, he knew the real reason why he fucked with Bebe. He did it because he couldn't do what he really wanted to do: fuck her.

# Discover Romance

**berkleyjoveauthors.com**

See what's coming up next from your favorite romance authors and explore all the latest Berkley, Jove, and Sensation selections.

**See what's new**

~

**Find author appearances**

~

**Win fantastic prizes**

~

**Get reading recommendations**

~

**Chat with authors and other fans**

~

**Read interviews with authors you love**